Warriors from the past, present, and future
fight to save us all.

Arden, home to a culture that has existed for thousands of years and which spans dozens of worlds. Regardless, their sophistication cannot prevent calamity at the hands of an unstoppable nemesis. Known only as the Horde, this enemy has proven relentless. They have not only stripped the outer colonies bare but now threaten the existence of the entire Ardenese way of life.

Realizing there is nothing they can do to prevent the inevitable march toward extinction, the Ardenese governing body comes to a drastic decision. They gather together at their capital city, Rhomane, and place their remaining genetic heritage in a vast underground ark, in the care of an advanced AI construct called the Architect.

Its mission? To use Rhomane's dwindling reserves and safeguard their race by reaching out across time and space toward those who might be in a position to help reseed a devastated world at some time in the future.

Soldiers from varying eras and vastly different backgrounds are snatched away from Earth at the moment of their passing and transported to the far side of the galaxy. Thinking they have been granted a reprieve, their relief turns to horror when they discover they face a stark ultimatum:

Fight or die.

Despite overwhelming odds, this group of misfits manages to turn the tide against a relentless foe, only to discover the true cost of victory might exact a price they are unwilling to pay.

If you like your science fiction to include fast-paced, gritty, realistic action and dark humor in the face of overwhelming odds, then The IX is definitely an adventure for you.

The author deftly weaves the horrors of the Horde stealing human life-essences, with the beauty of his prose and imagery. I was right there, on Arden, while reading. Action-packed through every chapter, the story unfolds as former enemies are forced to learn how to trust each other, to trust the visions and experiences of those who walk the spirit-world, and to share information. I highly recommend this book to fans of SF, horror, and fantasy.
— Ann Stolinsky, *Amazing Stories*
    AmazingStoriesMag.com

Weston's mix of history, metaphysics and real science ventures into territory not often explored in science fiction. What happened to the IX Legion of ancient Rome? Find out here, where Past, Present and Future are masterfully blended in an epic novel that takes classic elements to new heights. Weston has a true gift for superb storytelling and memorable characters. This one is not to be missed.
— Joe Bonadonna, author of *Mad Shadows: The Weird Tales of Dorgo the Dowser, Three Against The Stars*

A PERSEID PRESS BOOK

THE IX

ANDREW P. WESTON

Perseid Press
P. O. Box 584
Centerville, MA 02632

The IX
Copyright © Andrew P. Weston

First Perseid Press Edition, 2015
First Perseid Pres Kindle Edition, 2015
First Perseid Press ePub Edition, 2015
First Perseid Press Hardcover Edition 2016

The Perseid Press
P.O. Box 584
Centerville, MA 02632

A Perseid Press Original

Cover art: Roy Mauritsen
Map image: Andrew P. Weston, Roy Mauritsen
Cover image © Perseid Press 2015
Cover design: Roy Mauritsen
Book design: Sarah Hulcy

Trade Paperback edition: ISBN 13: 978-0-9864140-0-8, ISBN 10: 09864140-0-X
Kindle Digital edition: ISBN 13: 978-0-9864140-1-5, ISBN 10: 09864140-1-8
ePub Digital edition: ISBN 13: 978-0-9864140-2-2, ISBN 10: 09864140-2-6
Hardcover edition ISBN 13: 978-0-9864140-8-4, ISBN 10: 09864140-8-5

Library of Congress Control Number: 2015931683

Published in the United States of America

10 9 8 7 6 5 4 3 2 1

DEDICATION

"I only regret that I have but one life to give for my country."
— Captain Nathan Hale
(June 6, 1755 - September 22, 1776)

Dedicated to our veterans who faced the ultimate choice.

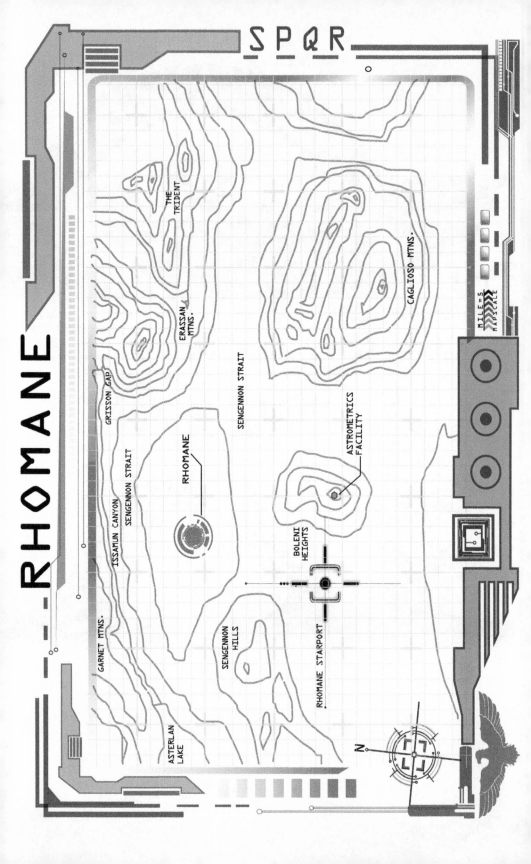

Table of Contents

ACKNOWLEDGEMENT

To the team at Perseid Press, who embraced a simple idea,
and turned it into something awesome.

Prologue

For as far as his eye could see, the endless tide of rabid hunger continued to advance. They came pouring into the valley from all sides, and the entire basin was soon filled with seething, shrieking monstrosities of every conceivable shape and form. Not one of them stood under two decans in height.

Nearing their goal, the leading entities of the Horde howled with malice and leaped forward. Dashing their bodies against the augmented might of the battlements seemed pointless to Sariff, for the attackers achieved nothing but to spend their vitality in a blaze of explosive fury. Yet the utter futility resulting from their lack of imagination did nothing to lessen their frenzy. In spite of their comrades' fate, wave after wave of them continued throwing themselves to their deaths in wanton abandon. So great did the overwhelming press of shadow and flame become that the repeated detonations of each attacker's self immolation grew into one prolonged cacophony of light and heat. Despite its density, the entire breadth of the wall thrummed under the weight of the assault.

And still they come. Sariff blanched in the face of the onslaught, witnessed here on Arden for the first time. As First Magister of Rhomane City, he seized the opportunity to study the enemy closely, for his would be the deciding vote in a decision that would seal the fate of their people.

He shook his head in disbelief, for he could see no respite from the relentless storm threatening to engulf them. *Thirty planets overrun in the space of just fifteen months. More than fifty billion souls lost. A history and a culture spanning more than twelve thousand years brought to this. It's a bitter pill to swallow. And we risk it all on an idea . . .*

What choice do we have?

Everywhere he looked, Sariff saw only the inevitability of death. Unless, by some miracle, Calen's gamble paid off. That thought reminded him. *I'd better get a move on.*

So mesmerized was he by the display of savagery below, he almost collided with the duty commander, Sol Beren. Sariff hadn't heard the soldier's silent approach, but that was understandable. The veteran warrior was a skilled tracker, renowned for keeping his men on their toes by his sudden, wraithlike appearances at different stations along the wall. Everyone marveled how he could be seen taking the lead at one post only to be spotted minutes later on the other side of the city entirely, without having used the transport pads.

His face a mask of determination, Beren studied the conflict before him. A cold and empty gaze reflected the bitter frustrations of a man who had seen too many men die worthless deaths. Sariff wished there was something he could say to ease the commander's burden. Instead, all he could ask was: "Will it hold?"

"Oh, it'll hold all right." Beren brushed the smooth texture of the defenses with his fingertips. "For now at any rate. It's pure lydium, the densest known material in existence. A marvel of technological adaptation." He glanced down again and almost to himself whispered, "It has to hold . . . ."

Sariff caught the hint of helpless acceptance in Beren's voice. *He thinks we're doomed.* Closing his ears to the baying howls of myriad atrocities, Sariff nodded stiffly, entered the portal and was instantly snatched from the reverberating terror of battle. Materializing moments later to deafening silence, he stepped down from the teleport dais and hastened into the sanctuary's hushed interior.

Despite the emergency, no guards were posted. In their encounters thus far, the Horde appeared unable to use the matter transporters. Whether it was due to their biophysical properties or simple lack of understanding wasn't known. Regardless, it was looked on as a blessing. And as this location had been positioned within a tear in the very fabric of reality, it was felt additional security was unnecessary, especially as the soldiers were needed at the wall.

That fact did little to stifle Sariff's growing unease.

Automated sensors tracked his progress toward the Archive-Architect, a self aware AI construct of stunning complexity and one of their greatest achievements. If all went well, it would also serve as their last bastion of hope against total extinction.

If all goes well.

Snorting at that unlikely outcome, Sariff paused before a concealed entrance and allowed himself to be scanned. Within moments an archway appeared, etched within a glowing framework of light. As it solidified, hidden doors glided back into invisible recesses on either side. A sentinel appeared in midair before Sariff. Looking much like a tiny, concentrated ball of plasma it thrummed with power, and the crisp, cheery voice of the Architect rang from it. "Welcome, First Magister Sariff. Chancellor Calen awaits you within. You will find him completing the final calculations required to activate the Ark."

Of course I will, he never leaves anything to chance. Aloud Sariff replied, "Thank you, Architect. Is he alone?"

"Yes, First Magister. The rest of the Senatum await you both within the council chambers."

"I see. Please advise them we will be there shortly. One way or another, this issue must be decided today."

"Certainly." The glowing sprite winked away, leaving Sariff alone to ponder the unenviable choice he faced.

But what will I decide? Shaking off the doubt still threatening to cloud his judgment, Sariff crossed into the inner sanctum. As the doors closed behind him, he swore he could hear faint cries from the conflict over a league above, filtering down through the intervening layers of rock. Suppressing a shiver, he quickened his pace, almost running the rest of the way along the arterial corridor.

Calen looked up from his work as Sariff burst into the control room. A look of mild amusement creased the scientist's face. "In a hurry, Sariff?"

Ignoring the jibe, Sariff cast one last glance over his shoulder and threw himself into the nearest available chair. "I just want this matter resolved." Using the back of his sleeve, he wiped the perspiration from his brow.

Adopting a more serious mien, Calen stood and made his way around to the other side of the console. Sitting back across the desk, he crossed his arms. "Well, that decision now lies with you, old friend. Remember, the Senatum is tied. Your vote will decide whether we fight to the last man or —"

"Or put trust in your schemes," Sariff cut in.

Looking past his friend, Sariff had to admit the Ark was an impressive concept. He and Calen sat at the top of a borehole that cut straight down for over two leagues through the planet's substrata. Within that shaft, millions upon millions of genetic samples had been placed in storage. Preserved for a future time when they could be automatically released into a safe and sterile environment to reseed a ravaged world. The only part that stuck in his craw was the fact that none of the Ardenese would be there to actually see it. Their culture would be embryonic; they would have to crawl their way back to the stars all over again. Furthermore, they'd have to rely on outside help for the plan to stand any chance of success.

Struggling to quell his doubts, Sariff asked, "Are you sure this strategy of yours will work?"

"I'm positive. It's our only real option." Activating one of the groundside monitors, the scientist brought the full horror of the siege to bear. "Look at them, Sariff. Just look at them. When we unearthed their hibernation grounds, waking them from slumber, how could we know what we'd unleash on the galaxy?"

They watched silently as the devastating crush continued. Nightmare apparitions in a million different guises continued to expend themselves against the wall without thought or remorse. So driven were they by their urge to feed on life force that they appeared lost to any other consideration.

Calen nodded toward the screen. "Three of the outer colonies fell before we even realized the extent of the danger. A further five when they sent rescue ships. Then ten more when they responded to calls for assistance. We never contemplated the possibility we would ever meet a force sufficient to overwhelm us. Why would we, considering all we have achieved? Our science. Our might. Yet one by one our settlements fell. And each life lost provided our enemies the puissance they needed to overwhelm us.

"Stripping everything of life, the Horde allowed the survivors to flee. In our arrogance, little did we realize the danger. Hiding away among our refugees, the Horde gradually worked its way here, to the richest feeding ground of our civilization. And now, of the eight billion souls once filling Arden with life, only eighty thousand remain, trapped within this city's confining walls."

Turning to face his friend, Calen concluded, "If we continue to fight, there will be nothing left. They have followed us here, to home world, and here they must stay. In denying them the opportunity to spread, we consolidate our only real hope for the future."

Sariff's face was pale. "So it's only a matter of time before they breach our defenses and consume us all?"

"As dense as it is, I fear the lydium simply won't hold. Oh, it may take millennia, but one day those fiends will find a way to negate the electron instability, and when they do . . ." As an afterthought, Calen added, "Of course, without access to supplies or transport, we'll all be dead long before that. So, we've got to make sure we employ an alternate, more radical option, yes?"

"The gateway and the Ark?"

"The gateway and the Ark. I know many will view it as a defeat, Sariff, but my strategy will preserve the seeds of our culture intact . . . And even bless it."

Sariff sat forward. "Remind me again how it will work?"

"Come and see." Calen invited the magister across to a larger console and activated a wall screen. An overview of the entire facility bloomed into view, reminding Sariff just how immense the structure was. Constructed from the same fermionic matter as the walls, the Archive existed within a fabricated tear in space-time. Termed *rip-space*, there was only one way in and one way out. Manipulating the controls, Calen zoomed in on a vast chamber occupying almost the entire bottom floor.

Enlarging the interior of that vault, Calen said, "Following my successful adaptation of the rip-space theorem, I wondered what might happen if I phased the targeting nodes through the DNA buffer of the Ark, and meshed them with the harmonics of the shield. After all, if we're going to make this grand gesture to deny the Horde, we still need to be able to attract the right *caliber* of assistance. Look what the test runs revealed."

He let the simulation run.

Sariff watched as the drama played out. Each time the artificial singularity coalesced, it tore a void through the fabric of subspace, and the telltale corona of a stable wormhole appeared. Even though he wasn't a scientist, Sariff had witnessed the spectacle often enough to understand what he was looking at. He recognized what Calen was alluding to, for he could plainly see something that shouldn't be there within the swirling vortex. Every time a link was established, an additional skein of energy materialized, lining the inner fabric of the quantum tunnel itself.

"What's that?" he gasped, intrigued by the sight of the unexpected phenomenon.

"*That*," Calen replied, "is what might save us." Amplifying the area of the event horizon, he continued, "As you noticed, each time we activate the portal, we manage to generate a stable tunnel. It leads to the same place. However, that sub matrix you're seeing within the bore, the one shimmering through all the colors of the rainbow, *that's* something else entirely."

"What do you mean? Does it go somewhere else?"

"Not some*where* else, Sariff. Some*when*."

"What?"

"It's an unexpected chronological or time-related component, which I think has been added by what I call the *death factor*."

"Death factor?" Sariff was confused by a term he'd never heard before.

"Yes, my friend. Remember, to activate this gateway we need to energize the matrix with life force. Ours to be exact. Now, as I say, some look on this as a defeat. But in sacrificing ourselves to the Ark, I've become certain that we not only deny the Horde our essence, but ultimately guarantee our eventual salvation. And these tests confirm it."

"How?"

"Well, from what I've been able to determine, the sum of our surrendered soul energies will cause a subtle variation in the equation every time a conduit is established. While it won't affect the geophysical focus, it will influence the temporal manifestation site. In effect, we'll be looking at a bridge that will flick across time, in its search for . . . a corresponding frequency—a mortality signature if you like—to lock-on to."

Comprehension dawned. "But . . . but that means the candidates it selects won't be missed! Nobody will come looking for them."

"Precisely! The flux will allow the Architect to choose those poor unfortunates who are about to die, and bring them here."

"But Calen! That can't be ethical? To snatch someone from the jaws of death, just so they can give their lives here in a hopeless venture on our behalf? It . . . it . . . ."

"They're dead anyway, Sariff. At least *here* they might have a fighting chance."

Both men stared at each other for a while, daunted by the scope of the undertaking before them, and the fact it might actually work. Eventually, Sariff expressed a question he'd forgotten to ask. "So where does the gateway lead?"

Calen had anticipated the request. Flicking a switch, he brought a holographic image of the galaxy to life in the air about them. As it rotated in majestic grandeur, Sariff could see two points within it had been highlighted, respectively, by glowing blue and green discs. Both were connected by an effervescent thread which obviously represented the wormhole.

Sariff knew the position of Arden and all her colonies intimately. Pointing to the green light, he said, "That's home world, obviously. And the other?"

Walking slowly across to the very edge of one of the galactic spiral arms, Calen used a remote control to enlarge that area of space. A small solar system appeared, centered upon an unimpressive yellow star. The image shimmered again, elaborating the third planet out from the sun in greater detail.

Looking at it, Sariff couldn't help but voice his thoughts. "It's certainly a beautiful little world, Calen, but are you sure the Architect has chosen correctly? I mean . . . look at it. They've only recently ventured into deep space. How could they possibly hold the key to our salvation?"

"That, I don't know, my friend. I merely asked the Architect to guarantee, beyond any doubt, that it would select the best possible candidate to ensure our race's survival. It came up with this. Don't be fooled by first impressions. Remember, the gateway is temporal. Who knows what surprises this civilization may possess in their future that might turn the tide in our favor?"

"So what do they call it?"

"I've been listening in to their radio and microwave chatter for a while now. Evidently, the citizens of this planet like to call it 'Earth.'"

"Earth?"

"Yes, and she really is our greatest hope for the future."

They were interrupted by the arrival of a sentinel. "Magister, Chancellor," it chimed merrily, "the Senatum awaits your presence."

"We're coming, Architect," Sariff replied. "Tell them we'll be there in a few minutes and they shall have their answer."

"Very well, good day!" The construct disappeared, leaving the two men to deliberate in private.

Sariff couldn't tear his eyes away from the image of the tiny blue-white globe. *It's so small and inconspicuous to carry the hopes of our future. And yet . . . .*

"So, you've made up your mind," Calen stated flatly.

Turning to his companion, Sariff straightened his back, adjusted his robe, and took a deep breath. "Yes, my friend. Let's go and get this started."

Chapter One

The Eagle

(November 12 AD 120)

Despite the atrocious weather, Marcus Brutus, Prime Centurion of the First Cohort of the Ninth Legion of Rome, was dozing in his saddle. The steady gait of his mount had lulled him into a state of happy reverie, and he was currently reliving the successes enjoyed by the battalion in Gaul only two short years ago.

At that time, the Senate had been committing more and more of its resources to the expansion into Britannia. However, efforts were being hampered by repeated guerilla raids against Roman supplies as they passed along the Rhone, especially within the Jura region, between the areas of Lugdunum and Divodurum. A special unit comprised of the second, third, and fifth centurae, together with elements of the mounted squadron, had been dispatched under Marcus's command to remove the problem. And remove it he had. Devising a cunning strategy, it had taken Marcus a mere nine months to eradicate the raiding parties and restore operations. Not only did his actions earn him the distinction of being hailed in Rome before the Senate, but his leadership potential was recognized in the highest of places. Caesar Hadrian himself had ordered the bestowal of one of their greatest honors, the golden torc. Thereafter, Marcus's promotion to Triari—Captain of the Legion—was sealed.

A grin creased his lips, but it wasn't the memory of his elevation. It was his recollection of something else entirely.

Repeatedly covering so many leagues up and down the length of a large and difficult country had been problematic enough. But a mild spring followed by a glorious summer had facilitated the execution of his mission no end. The crowning glory of a golden autumn had only sealed the fate of the insurgents all the quicker.

Yes, he thought, as evidence of his pleasure spread across his whole countenance, *I wouldn't have minded serving there for another ten years, or so. Once the rabble had been controlled and peace restored, I found that land most idyllic. Somewhere I could retire to and—*

"Happy about something, my captain?"

The intruding voice yanked Marcus from his quiet place back to the bitter misery of reality. "I'm sorry. What?" Focusing his gaze, Marcus looked into the amused face of General Quintus Petillius Cerialis, commander of the Ninth Legion.

"I asked you what you were happy about, and if you'd be willing to share the joy?"

Hearing the jest, several heads turned, eager for any respite from the soul-sapping drudgery of the cold now soaking its way into their bones.

Snapping to attention, Marcus suddenly comprehended who had dropped back to speak with him. Bringing his mount, Starblaze, to a halt, he replied, "My apologies, Sir. I was worlds away. Gaul, to be exact. Reminiscing over better times . . ." he glanced up into the endless, drenching mist, " . . . and more appealing weather."

"Even Erebus has better weather than this cesspit," someone grumbled from within the column. Laughter broke out around them at the reference, for the third layer of Hades was a place well known to soldiers for its perpetually gloomy environs.

"Yes, it does seem that way, doesn't it?" Quintus's voice was loud, attempting to raise the spirits of those within earshot. "But it makes you appreciate why the savages hereabouts are so fierce, eh? I mean, could *you* imagine having to live in these conditions all year round? It'd be enough to permanently foul anyone's temper."

Marcus chuckled to himself as the general's infectious humor spread among the men, for they all knew their commander had made a valid point. Having served this far north for nearly four months now, everyone had come to realize Caledonia only had one true element to its nature. And it was called *gray*.

From its miserable skies and oppressive cloud-shrouded mountains. Through its dark, impenetrable forests and ink-stained lochs. Across the cruelly open, windswept hills and glens, this hell on earth had forgotten the simple joy of color.

The brief summer they'd experienced had attempted to add a thin green veneer of life to the landscape. Yet it did little to hide the frigidity of stark granite hiding just beneath the surface. All too soon their temporary respite from the cold had bled away, lost to the consuming mists of what passed for autumn here. Wreathing the gray in silver veils, the crawling fogs hid a speedy transition toward the true nature of this godforsaken land. Eternal winter. Its icy grip crept ever closer with the passing of each day. For now, whenever the rains did manage to stop for long enough and the haze thinned, you could see the carbon mountains, tinged blue-white under the onset of snow. Savage weather for a savage people. It was not a place for civilized man to be.

And yet, here they were, extending the peace of the Empire to heathens who were not in the slightest bit interested, nor thankful for what Rome could offer them.

Trudging along in the gloom, Marcus sensed when the sun began to set. A chill that had nothing to do with the clouds or falling temperature set in, leeching any inclination toward merriment from the air. The men felt it too, and he noticed with sadness that their humor evaporated along with the receding daylight. Huddling into their cloaks, they became more subdued. Cautious. Heads began turning from side to side, as shadows were checked and rechecked. Some of the more experienced soldiers along the center file loosened their swords in their sheaths and brought their shields to bear. As if responding to a subliminal command, everyone drew closer together and adopted a grim-faced alertness that reduced them all to silence.

Marcus acknowledged them. They may have been uneasy, but his men were professional. Nevertheless, that did little to ease his apprehension. *We've left it too long to make proper camp. I know the general's trying to make up for lost time, but marching through the night is becoming far too risky. Especially here.*

Despite his reservations, Marcus could appreciate why Quintus was anxious to press ahead. They had marched from Fort Dalginos just six days previously, with fresh orders to establish a foothold in the mountains. Once in place, they had been directed to construct a serviceable fort and hold position until reinforcements could be sent from Eboracum. Following normal protocol, subjugation of the highland rabble would begin soon after.

They quickly discovered it was impossible to maintain the usual pace set by legions of twenty-five miles per day. Not only did foul weather, swamps, and lack of suitable roads slow their progress, but the actual mechanics involved in moving five thousand men—along with their livestock and equipment—had become a logistical nightmare.

As if that were not frustrating enough, no sooner had they left the lowlands behind than the skirmishes began. Using the bog-riddled glens and tight-knit forests to their advantage, the raiders had approached under the cover of the mists to begin picking away at the army's nerves and defenses. Already the detachment had lost four of their most heavily laden wagons to the marshes, and the same number again to the howling ghouls who would attack, only to vanish seconds later among the swirling vapor. Too many times his men would turn to find a cart afire, or a companion with an arrow in his throat. Sadly, because the column was so long, there was nothing they could do except be wary, and maintain a constant state of alert.

The general had dictated a slower pace to compensate, but still the shrieking banshees attacked. One by one, soldiers disappeared . . . along with morale.

Marcus could empathize. They were used to the terrifying confrontation of man against man. The focus of steel on steel. Not this cowardly tactic of hit and run. As Caledonia also appeared riddled with hidden fens and quicksand, it was making them feel as if the very land itself were conspiring to send them all to Hades.

That thought made him shiver. As if on cue, a stiff wind began blowing from the north, causing some of the men to grumble.

At least I can do something about that. Twisting in his saddle, Marcus called, "Flavius! To me."

The sound of approaching hooves lifted out of the gloom. Within moments, Flavius Velerianus, Decurio of the cavalry squadron, appeared. Reining in before his Triari, he asked, "Marcus?"

"Flavius, I want your reserves to light torches and ride back and forth along the line. Extend the rangers, too. I want to know what's out there in plenty of time. Assign . . . ."

The clouds abruptly rolled back allowing the dying rays of the setting sun to burst forth in burnt umber splendor. A sea of faces turned to the unexpected sight, and relief flooded the ether. The baleful disc dipped behind the mountains, stray beams catching the legion's standard square on. Adorned as it was in a coat of glittering dew, the eagle blazed with golden glory. A beacon of radiant hope in a darkened world.

"For Rome," someone called.

"The General," shouted another.

"To our Captain," another added, nearer to Marcus.

"For the Ninth!" Marcus roared, drawing his sword and holding it high.

"The Ninth!" responded the crowd, eagerly pumping their own weapons into the air. The sound of their cry was picked up by those farther along the line, and echoing reverberations were soon ringing their way across the valley.

"Now there's a sight for sore eyes," Flavius muttered. "Talk about timing."

"The gods must be with us after all," Marcus replied, "and about bloody time, too!"

"Pity they don't fight for us more often, eh?" Fighting to tear his gaze from the ruddy disc as it dared to sink behind the intervening peaks, Flavius shook his head. "Anyway, you were saying something regarding my mounted patrols?"

"Ah . . . yes. Look, make sure you assign archers to the roving pickets as well. The rabble is out there, and if they didn't know we were here before, they do now. At the slightest sign of trouble, I want a signal in the air and the area under scrutiny lit up like a whorehouse celebrating Fortuna Virilis. Understood?"

"Understood." Nodding toward the general, Flavius added, "Just get him to act more prudently, will you? Those mountains mark the borders of the Iceni berserker tribes, and we can't be more than a day's march away from them. From what Cornelius told me back at Zeta Fort, that lot eat human flesh. They don't feel the cold—there's a surprise—and nothing short of decapitation will stop them. If we stumble into the fringes of their territory, they'll give us the nastiest buggering we've ever had the misfortune to suffer."

Marcus grinned at the image his friend's statement conjured in his mind. But it was a valid concern. Clasping Flavius by the shoulder, he said, "I'll do my best. So far, he hasn't shown an inclination to listen. But I will make another attempt. You have my word."

Turning his horse to leave, Flavius maneuvered closer. "Might I make a suggestion?" His eyes flicked toward the head of the column. Marcus followed his gaze and caught sight of the former Triari of the Ninth, Drusus Vergilius Cicero. Promoted to Praefectus, the veteran officer now served as second-in-command of the entire legion. Leaning in, Flavius whispered, "Although he's been tightlipped about the general's latest decisions, I know for a fact our new colonel is itching to have things done in a . . . more *orderly* fashion. Why don't you ensure your paths cross tonight at dinner, so you can have a timely chat with him? I have a feeling a combined approach by our most seasoned officers might sway the general's mind."

Flavius trotted off to issue his orders, leaving Marcus to mull over how to broach the issue. *Yes. I'll speak with him dur-*

ing our evening stop. Better this is done sooner. Drusus can twist the old man's arm in ways I wouldn't dare.

As the vanguard crested the hill the sky darkened to indigo, and through the expanding gap in the clouds, the full moon began its climb into the sky. Casting a critical glance at the heavens, Marcus thought, *Why couldn't the break have occurred just a few hours earlier? It would have raised everyone's spirits, as well as warmed us up. Still, at least we can see where we're going now.*

The order was abruptly passed for the column to halt. Intrigued, Marcus trotted ahead to see what the problem was. Topping the crest, he found Quintus deep in conversation with Drusus and several scouts. A number of the sentries were gesticulating wildly, and all of them had a haunted look in their eyes. Moving up, he caught a pair of the outriders glancing nervously down into a glen. "What's happened? Why are we halting where we'll be exposed?"

"Because of *that*, Sir," the soldier replied, pointing to a swirling dome of mist coalescing across the center of the basin, not half a mile in front of them. "That and the fact that most of our pathfinders are missing."

Marcus's blood ran cold. In the moonlight, a narrow river could be seen running directly across their path. It looked as if a huge axe had cleft the earth in two, leaving behind an oily scar. A steep-sided ravine ran the entire length of the watercourse, effectively blocking their way. A narrow defile had been formed—most probably the effect of years of attrition from bad weather—which appeared to allow a meager point of access to the mountains. On either side of that chokepoint, stunted oaks hunched like gnarled sentinels in the shadows. To Marcus's eye, they seemed to highlight the only viable route across for miles in both directions. The Legion was heading straight for them.

Above the trees, a concentrated bank of fog congealed, apparently out of nowhere. Rotating slowly, as if stirred by a giant unseen hand, the miasma swelled and thickened before tendrils of vapor undulated lazily to the ground. Once there, the mist distended in all directions.

Voices cried out.

"That can't be normal."

"Omen!"

"It's Charon, come to drag us into the Styx."

"Keep that nonsense down," Marcus commanded. "The next one I hear spouting crap like that will lose a day's pay. Do you he–"

A piercing howl resonated through the air.

All chatter throughout the ranks abruptly ceased.

Another ululating shriek split the night.

Marcus closed his eyes and sat forward in his saddle; frowning, listening.

"Wolves?" gasped the infantryman nearest him.

"No, soldier, I think this is an animal of an entirely different sort."

"Marcus!" snapped the the general. "Your thoughts, please."

"That's easy, Sir," Marcus replied, spurring his horse forward. "Form up and protect the eagle."

Chapter Two

The Guidon

(August 20 1860)

Eyes streaming, Lexington "Lex" Fox, First Lieutenant of One Platoon, Fifth Company, Second Mounted Rifles Cavalry Unit, leaned into his saddle and spurred his horse to greater efforts. He was already exhausted from the long ride they'd endured, and the combination of harsh sunlight and bitter north winds radiating down off the Rocky Mountains only exacerbated his misery. This journey was turning into a one-way ticket to hell, and he felt as if he were stuck in the first-class compartment of the ultimate train wreck.

Beside him, their 'package', Princess Inuck-Shen — known affectionately among the men as Small Robes — rode in silence, seemingly immune to the strident conditions now reducing her escort to shivering, saddle-sore wrecks.

Can you blame her for not speaking? Lex cast a side-long glance toward her. *She's just sixteen years old and has the weight of two worlds on her young shoulders . . . and the enmity of factions from within her own people, it would seem.*

Thinking back to what had led them here, Lex was deeply concerned as to whether any of them would come out of this alive.

As the eldest daughter of Blooded Chin, chief of the Blackfoot, Small Robes had been presented as a gift to unite the Cree nations by marriage. Her husband-to-be, Chief Snow Blizzard, was a warrior of fearsome reputation. It was his clan, currently encamped at the foot of the Bitter-root Mountains, west of Kalispell, Montana, that held sway throughout the entire region. Without Cree influence, the splintered, volatile tribes of the center plains would not come to the table with those willing to seek resolution. The peace treaty proposed by presidential candidate Abraham Lincoln would fail, and the long and bitter conflict with the native populations would grind on. Something congress was keen to avoid, especially as a number of the northern and southern states had been divided in recent years as to the policies they should pursue to establish a stronger presence within those municipalities currently overrun with native American Indians.

Only a week ago, the Second Cavalry regiment had dis-patched their long-range reconnaissance experts, the Fifth, to Blood Mountain; the heart of Blackfoot territory. Their mission was to escort the princess and her chaperone to their new home, nearly four hundred miles away. A bold and risky undertaking, but one made less hazardous by the scouts who had been sent ahead to gain the cooperation of successive, subordinate tribes.

All went well until the company crossed the Rockies and entered the Great Wilderness. Once there, all signs of help — and life, it seemed — had been swallowed whole.

At first, their company commander, Captain James Houston, had forged ahead, thinking the emissaries had simply missed the rendezvous points amid the densely packed forests of the northern ranges. But as the days wore on and the pace gradually slowed, tensions increased.

Three days previously, they had arrived at what should have been a major resupply settlement on the northern shore of Flat Head Lake. There they had hoped to replenish their dwindling provisions before starting the final push into the heart of the Cree's domain.

The post was deserted.

Small Robe's uncle, Stained-With-Blood, was the Blackfoot's greatest warrior. He was also, fortunately, her chaperone and an accomplished tracker. It hadn't taken him long to determine that a large number of people had recently died at that location, and that a concerted effort had been made to conceal evidence of the massacre.

Looking back, Lex could appreciate the subterfuge.

Had the company been traveling alone, they would have no doubt turned back, returned the princess to her father, and reported the mission a failure. The peace talks would have been jeopardized, and further efforts to secure a lasting peace would have failed. In the meantime, the Plains War would have endured, the American nation would continue to fragment, and no one would have been any the wiser . . . . *If* they had turned back.

But they hadn't been alone. As one well used to living in harmony with the land, Stained-With-Blood had spotted the telltale signs that revealed the true culprits behind the massacre. It was, unbelievably, the Cree themselves. When the veteran warrior informed Captain Houston of his discovery, the commander was furious and unleashed a fusillade of bullets into the sky in sheer frustration.

Lex shook his head in disgust at the memory. *What a stupid thing to do. Even a rookie wouldn't have made a mistake like that, especially that deep inside enemy territory. What the hell Houston thought he was doing, we'll probably never know.*

It was a poignant thought. Lex shuddered at his recollection of what happened next. As the report of gunfire echoed away into the distance, the surrounding hills trembled to the thunder of hooves and bristling activity. Spears and feathers, thousands upon thousands of them, suddenly sprouted up in response to the sound, bursting to life as if summoned from the depths of hell.

It was a surreal yet horrifying experience. Stained-With-Blood calmly gazed toward the massed ranks before listing the extent of the double-cross. "We are betrayed. Lakota, Sioux, and Apache reveal their true faces. Peace was never Snow Blizzard's goal. We must flee."

And flee they had.

Bolting first toward the northern pass, the company hoped to make it back through the Rockies and into territory dominated by Blackfoot and Cheyenne. But they'd only been in the saddle for a day before it became evident the way was barred. Their flight had been anticipated. Not only was the trail blocked, but the surrounding countryside was now saturated with warriors loyal to Snow Blizzard and his war party. The only apparent route open to the Fifth led back in the direction of Kalispell Fort.

Declining Stained-With-Blood's offer of help, the captain chose to lead, driving them along at such a relentless pace that soon people were almost dropping from the saddle.

Despite the panic, lady luck seemed to be watching over them. Houston managed to navigate the endless canyons and ridges hindering their getaway at such breakneck speed that the group always remained one step ahead of their enemies.

Their first night spent weaving the trails of Green Heart Forest proved pivotal. Although a dozen outriders disappeared among the confusing maze of trees and rocks, the cover provided by the densely packed pines gave them the break they sorely needed. After resting up for a few hours at an unknown, isolated creek, they redistributed supplies and armaments and resumed their drive toward safety at a more sensible pace.

Finally winning free only yesterday, the company now faced the open, windswept expanse of the Flat Head Plains. Safety lay on the other side, for once across the north fork of the Flat Head River, they would be home and dry.

Lex shielded his eyes as he took in his surroundings. Sweeping grassland stretched away toward infinity in every direction. Not that he would ever stand a chance of seeing it clearly, for the open savanna was one vast ocean of braying muscle. Shaggy beasts, their shoulders more than six feet high, numbering in the tens of thousands, grazed the endless expanse, complaining loudly and scattering in panic as the van cut through them. The Fifth's pennant flew crisply in the breeze. Despite its brave statement, the motley crew of desperados made a sorry sight.

At least there shouldn't be any chance of the Cree nipping unexpectedly at our heels now. If we don't see them first, the buffalo certainly will.

Lex glanced at the seething wall of brawn closest to him. It amazed him that the two and a half thousand pound juggernauts didn't just turn and trample the intruders flat in anger. They were certainly capable of it: he'd once seen what a stampeding herd could do. He was thankful for the living barrier their enemies would have to navigate before standing a chance of getting close enough to launch an attack. *Surely they realize that would be a mistake? Even though they must outnumber us more than ten to one, most are only armed with spear or bow. Now we're out in the open, our Spencer carbines will take them down so fast they'd be crazy to even think about facing us head on.*

Lex reached down to pat the butt of his rifle. The .52 seven shot repeater was the latest innovation to leave the Sharp factories. As those chosen for this special mission, the Fifth were among the first to be equipped with them.

Our luck can't hold out forever. I've got a feeling we'll all be very grateful for these little beauties before long.

Without warning, Stained-With-Blood motioned for everyone to slow down and stop. For a reason unknown to Lex, the tribesman was staring intently at a hillock only a mile or so in front of them.

Captain Houston looked particularly vexed at having to halt their mad dash, but nevertheless signaled for the unit to reduce speed to a canter while he discovered what troubled the warrior.

Lex stood in his stirrups to look ahead. A small area of grass, like an island, stood apart from the rest of the prairie. Turning in his saddle, he scanned the plain from horizon to horizon. Everywhere he looked, buffalo rambled idly about. Snorting and grunting, with calves occasionally bleating as they ran to catch up with their mothers. Lex couldn't discern what would worry the brave so much.

His gaze eventually returned to the small island of grassland. Then it hit him.

The buffalo on that hill aren't moving like the others, and the rest of the herd is giving them a wider berth. While they're not exactly spooked, something's up.

Lex turned to find Small Robes studying him. Her eyes held a knowing look, and the beginnings of a smile creased the corners of her lips. He was about to ask her if she'd noticed the strange behavior of the animals when all heads were drawn to the sound of a sharp outburst of anger. Although he was too far away to hear properly, Lex could plainly see that the exchange between Captain Houston and Stained-With-Blood had become heated. And one sided. The commander shouted and gestured wildly, while the Indian ambassador sat impassively on his mustang, glaring back and occasionally shaking his head. The wind began to pick up. Knifing at them from every quarter, it added an ominous overtone to the standoff.

Stained-With-Blood wheeled away and galloped toward Lex and the princess. Reining in sharply in front of them, he addressed his niece in Standard English so everyone could understand. "This white-eye is a fool! Our brethren know how to hunt and run with these beasts. Does he not realize they could approach in numbers, undetected?" Placing his hand upon the young woman's shoulder, his face became a picture of calm. "Child, come with me. I will not allow him to lead you into danger."

"They're up ahead, aren't they?" Lex said "On the hillock, disguised as animals." *And directly in our path . . . How did they . . . ?*

"Not everyone is as ready to stumble into darkness as first appears." Stained-With-Blood's eyes narrowed and respect colored his tone. "Perhaps all is not as lost as I thought."

Houston rode up with an entourage and cut in on the conversation. "Very well, I know of a blocked valley only an hour's ride from the river. If we regroup there, we can send out scouts to assess the best way forward past the ford."

Stained-With-Blood's countenance turned hard. "Forgive me if I don't put much confidence in your scouts. So far, they only appear skilled in leading us into traps. Perhaps I may be of assistance in finding a . . . clearer path?"

The two men stared each other down. Houston's gazed flitted for support to his officers. He cleared his throat and said, "If you don't mind my saying, Sir, that won't be necessary. We checked these plains thoroughly in the weeks leading up to the treaty. We know the lay of the land. It would be a great help, especially now, if you'd remain close to the princess. Just knowing she's in safe hands would be a great weight off my shoulders and allow me to get us all out of here without . . ." he glanced anxiously about, " . . . too much bloodshed."

Stained-With-Blood looked to his charge. Small Robes jutted her chin toward Lex. Letting out a deep sigh of frustration, her uncle maneuvered his horse around next to the princess and muttered, "As you wish." Pointing toward the Lieutenant, he told Houston, "But *he* will come with us. He is not as blind to the signs about him as others are."

Lex was shocked to be singled out, but secretly pleased. No one else among the company appeared to have made the connection to the hillock yet.

A calculating look entered the captain's eyes. He ruminated before coming to a decision. Straightening, he began issuing orders. Raising his voice to make himself heard above the stiffening gusts, he said, "Lieutenant Smith, take second platoon and divide it into two sections. Use Sergeant Wainwright's detail to engage the renegades. Go with them. You are to keep your distance, use your rifles to maximum effect, and keep heading toward Kalispell. Draw them off for as long as you can. If it looks like you might get overrun, make for the fort until sunset, then turn and head for Skull Canyon. In the meantime, I want Corporal Mitchell's section to run ahead and lay a false trail adjacent to the river and away from our rendezvous. As with the rest of your squad, once night falls they are to beat it out of there and join up with the rest. Is that clearly understood?"

Smith didn't bother answering. Raising two fingers to the brim of his hat, he trotted away. Lex didn't know if his subordinate had failed to reply because of the strengthening wind or not, but he had caught the way both men considered each other, as if trying to exchange hidden thoughts. *Handy, Wilson Smith being the company commander's cousin and all. I doubt Houston would let me take such liberties. Still, I suppose blood is thicker than water.*

"Fox?"

Lex snapped out of his musing. "Sir?"

"Take your entire platoon, and the princess, and head directly to the ravine. Protect the guidon. We've never lost it. If we don't join you by dawn, do what you can to get to Kalispell. The fort was expecting us yesterday. While they might wait a day, I doubt they'll put off sending out patrols for much longer. One way or another, we'll get this settled tonight."

"Yes Sir." Lex paused. "Are you not coming with us?"

"No, I think I'll join Corporal Mitchell on our little ruse. Make sure things don't get messed up again." With that, the captain dismissed Lex as if he'd ceased to exist, and turned to issue further instructions to those closest to him.

Lex shrugged. Using the horn of his saddle to pull himself up, he scanned the milling throng, quickly locating the Fifth's bannerman, Quincy Shelby. Whistling, Lex attempted to draw the private's attention. The strengthening gale thwarted his efforts and Lex had to close the distance until he could catch the soldier's eye. Motioning for Shelby to fall-in on him, he watched as the reversed, red-on-white/white-on-red colors of the guidon drew closer. Whipping about like a torn rag in a storm, the pennant looked so fragile Lex thought it might get ripped away from them at any minute.

Where on earth is this wind coming from?

Lex scanned the plains, surprised to discover a strange cluster of clouds forming only half a mile from their location. As he watched, the mass thickened and darkened. It started rotating, and a distinctive swirling vortex distended toward the ground.

You don't get tornados this far north. The weather's all wrong . . . .

He looked about again.

What the hell is going on?

Lex jumped as someone tapped him on the shoulder. He whirled to find Surgeon Major Samuel J. Clark, and his second, Surgeon Captain William Anders huddling close. "Can I help you, Sirs?"

The eldest and most distinguished of the two officers — a portly man with long silver-grey hair and a matching goatee beard and mustache — replied, "You certainly can, young man. It would appear Mr. Houston wants us to ride along with your party. Look after the princess, and all that . . ." He paused to tip his hat toward her before continuing, " . . . and to be quite honest, I've never been all that good in a shoot-out. My specialty is sorting out the mess you guys cause."

"No problem with me, Sir. As far as I'm concerned, the more the merrier. It might put the Cree off attacking us in the first place. Do you mind acceding to my orders if it comes to a fight?"

"Son," the older gentleman replied, "I'm a doctor first and foremost. I leave the shouting and the shooting up to capable young men like yourself. If you're half as competent as this here Indian fella says, I'll not only do as you say, hell, I'll happily dance a jig at your birthday party. You just tell us what you need, and we'll do our best not to get in the way. Sound like a deal?"

Lex grinned. The thought of the major's offer was uncannily appealing. "I may hold you to that, Sir. Just be ready to move at a moment's notice. If what Stained-With-Blood said is true, we need to be leaving . . . now!"

Lex's gaze was drawn back to the strange bank of clouds. A tingle, which had nothing to do with their current predicament, skittered along his spine.

In fact, we should already be gone.

Without warning, the long grass about them erupted with howling and death.

Chapter Three

By Strength and Guile

(May 4 2052)

"Gold Command, emergency hatchway has been breached and preliminary seal established. We now have access to pylon three. Repeat, pylon three is secured. Beginning final appraisal."

"Roger that, Sunray," a muted, metallic voice acknowledged. "You are *go* for tactical ingress, on your mark."

Lieutenant Alan "Mac" McDonald, officer commanding SBS Four Troop, UK Special Forces Anti-Terrorist Wing, remained a shadow in the dark. His night optics brought the scene around him to life in lurid, silver-green detail. As he began his final assessment, he could clearly see the seven other members of his team bobbing about in the swell beneath the Husker-Trent oil and gas platform. Each of them was silent, alert, and professional. Highly trained killers. But skill and training weren't the only things on their side tonight. Thanks to their reactive micro-com network and chameleon armor, they were also invisible from prying eyes, eavesdropping, and covert surveillance. Scanning their arcs, each specialist waited patiently for their leader to complete his evaluation and give his final affirmation.

From their briefing of only two hours ago, Mac knew this gravity-base derrick, situated nearly a hundred miles out into the North Sea, was the very latest in platform design. A floating, self-sustained city in one of the harshest environments known to man, she was also the apple of the Corroco Corporation's eye. And the Corroco Oil and Technologies Corporation were not happy at being the latest targets of White Dawn, a group of eco-terrorists who had kept a number of security agencies around the world busy over the past thirteen months.

No one knew who the leaders of this faction were, or indeed how they were funded. The only facts available tended to support the theory that White Dawn operatives were highly trained, incredibly motivated, and skilled in a wide variety of scientific disciplines. Their goal appeared to focus on public embarrassment, rather than financial gain. More worryingly, if cornered and unable to achieve their objectives, they weren't above making the ultimate gesture for their cause. Suicide.

The group was also thorough when it came to researching possible targets, and this evening's venture was no exception. Husker-Trent was fitted with the very latest in AI camera-motion detector recognition technology. If unidentified persons approached, they could either be blown out of the water by .50 caliber rail-mounted cannons, or the rig would go into safe mode. Security bulkheads would lower to seal off the strategic centers of operations, emergency valves would cut off oil and gas pressure, and automated distress signals would be sent via com-sat and wireless. Additionally, the platform was constructed in such a manner that the drilling module was entirely separate from the run off vents, and the combined work-cum-habitat ring. The only way on or off was via the central helipad, accessed by any one of three retractable gantries. These safety features should have made it almost impossible for anyone to breach her security measures. The fact that White Dawn had done so this easily smacked either of exceptional planning and execution, or an inside job. Gold Command were hedging their bets and treading cautiously.

Mac zoomed in on a number of the defensive systems as he made his assessment. The thermal and electronic heads-up display emblazoned across the left side of his visor showed they were primed, tracking, and ready to deploy.

Difficult to get past, but not impossible. Not for my team . . . especially with what's at stake.

He glanced at his radiological detector. The glowing red patches confirmed the presence of the real reason why Special Forces had become involved so quickly.

When it was realized Husker-Trent had been taken by an unknown number of assailants, contact between the derrick and the outside world was suspended. Negotiators and law enforcement agencies were put on alert and, as a precaution, the Special Forces Directorate notified. Standard procedure, especially where oilrigs were involved. However, when an opening dialogue was offered by trained mediators, they were resolutely ignored. Each subsequent attempt at communication was met by a similar wall of silence. No ensuing ransom demands or political statements were made, neither was a release of hostages offered. The prime minister was extremely worried.

When a high altitude fly-by was ordered, the drone quickly picked up the telltale signs of suspicious activity and the unmistakable signatures of a scattered number of nuclear devices. Odd; especially when White Dawn purported to be ecologically sympathetic. Needless to say, the discovery of such ordnance guaranteed a swift response. One with an aggressive focus.

As the lead team on the duty roster, Four Troop were deployed to gather intelligence, ascertain the reason for the attack, secure all radiological materials, and bring the standoff to an end. *And we'll do that all right!* Mac thought as he completed his assessment, *by strength and guile.*

Smiling over his reference to the SBS motto, Mac gave a thumbs-up to his team and depressed his throat mike. "Gold Command, this is Sunray, do you copy?"

"Go ahead, Sunray."

"Traffic lights are at green. Repeat, traffic lights are at green. Waiting for final authentication."

"That's a go, Team Four. Use of lethal force authorized. Gold Command authentication—Alpha, six, six, six, omega."

"Alpha, six, six, six, omega, confirmed. From Sunray, we are now going dark. See you when this is all over."

"Roger that, Team Four. See you on the other side. Good hunting."

The radio went dead. Turning to face his section, Mac motioned for radio silence. Each team member moved to adjust their equipment to ensure they were cut off from all forms of outside communication. Once done, they switched to covert internals before checking back in again.

Facing his second-in-command, Mac said, "Mark, take Bravo Squad and tag the location of each radiological device. Let me know if they'll be suitable for tactical removal or deactivation. Secondary protocol, ascertain strength and deployment of the enemy."

Throughout the entire process, Mac didn't have to raise his voice. The covert set enhanced his vocals until the whispers rang loud and clear in his teammate's ear.

Sergeant Mark Stevens, a nine year veteran of special operations, raised his left index finger and tapped the side of his head twice. "Roger that. I am *Bravo-one*. Primary objective, locate and tag radiological devices. Secondary, ascertain strength and deployment of the enemy." Addressing his squad members, he added, "Bravo confirm?"

Specialists Sean Masters, Richard "Fonzy" Cunningham, and Andy Webb both replied in the affirmative, going through their call-signs and orders in turn to confirm they fully understood their operating procedures.

Twisting, Mac continued with his own squad. "Alpha, we will be concentrating on the hostages. Preliminary sat-recon shows almost the entire complement of ninety-seven rig personnel are gathered together within the dining and kitchen areas. At least half a dozen managers have been relocated to the operations and radio rooms. Verification of their well-being is our priority. Secondary objective is intelligence, namely: rescue and casualty viability. I am *Alpha-one*. Alpha confirm?"

Specialists Stu Duggan, Sam Pell, and Den"Jumper" Collins sounded off in turn.

Once they had done so, Mac addressed them all again. "During the first stage, we will not engage the enemy unless forced to do so. And then, only in order to save life. If we *do* go hot before phase two, take them down. No quarter . . . understood?"

Seven thumbs rose into the air.

Moving his own hand in a circular motion twice, Mac clenched his fist and opened his fingers wide. Each of them moved to their designated points for insertion through the lining of the gravity-base pylon.

Forming an outward facing fan about the hatchway, each specialist paired off. They made sure to cover the movement of their teammate as they gained access. Having entered, the respective partner likewise kept on the watch for his buddy.

Mac was quietly complimentary of his men. Moving covertly was a time-consuming process. However, they were so well rehearsed that the maneuver was over in less than two minutes. Fast going, considering the change in conditions.

As last man in, Mac remained in the water the longest. When they had started to breach, the area was relatively calm, exhibiting a mild chop that had them bobbing up and down through six- or seven-foot swells. Nothing unusual. However, in the time that had elapsed since then, the sea had begun to heave alarmingly, as if agitated by a leviathan stirring in the depths. Mac was also sure he could hear the distant roll of thunder.

That's odd. How did it move in so quickly? It wasn't on satellite.

Adjusting his optics to get a better look, Mac let out a gasp. A solid wall of cloud and rain was moving toward them. Darker than the surrounding star-filled night, it was still a few miles out. Even so, he could see it seethed with a powering menace that gave him goosebumps. Mac couldn't shake the impression that the approaching tempest was a missile, with the rig as the bullseye on its target.

"Alpha-one? What is it, Boss?" Being the first in, Mark was higher up inside the platform's structure and had totally missed the change in weather.

Mac paused to check he was seeing things right.

A seething maelstrom of midnight black punctuated by bursts of lurid brightness charged toward them. Where it touched the sea, the water churned and frothed as if being distressed by a thousand propellers. Even at this distance, Mac was sure he could see the entire storm front rotating, both above and below the surface.

"Oh, for Christ's sake!"

"Alpha-one? What is it?" Mark repeated.

"Trouble," Mac replied. "I think we'd better crack on, gentlemen. Our evening might get complicated . . . real soon."

Chapter Four

The Lost Legion

Spinning his horse about in a frenzied dance, the general tried to rally his troops. "Form up! Form up on me," he bellowed. The legionnaires closest to him rushed to obey. Slashing and stabbing their way forward, they attempted to counter the heaving mass of attackers swarming them from all sides.

Despite the mayhem, Quintus was well defended. Seeing this, Marcus chose to ignore the call. Instead, he fought his way back along the line to see how the rest of the column fared. Their professionalism made his heart sing. Although the swirling mists added to the confusion, having a tangible enemy in front of them had galvanized the men. They now had something to focus on. Barbarians to kill. Despite the hit-and-run tactics, his soldiers were at last able to vent their frustrations. *And they're doing it well.*

Marcus flinched as an unseen arrow sped past his ear, taking yet another rider from his saddle. *They're targeting the mounted officers. These savages aren't stupid. If they can remove the advantage of our cavalry, they'll have us.*

Catching Flavius's eye, Marcus waved his sword in the air and made a chopping motion toward the ravine. He knew they stood a better chance of surviving the ambush if they controlled the chokepoint across the river. The trees would also give any remaining archers an opportunity to increase their elevation and keep the approaches clear. *Hopefully, they'll get a better view through this damned fog. Why will it not disperse?*

He watched as Flavius cast his gaze toward the chasm. Grasping Marcus's intent immediately, he barked orders. In moments, more than thirty warhorses were battering their way through the intervening press of bodies. As they moved, Flavius organized them into a tight phalanx that Marcus noted with satisfaction decimated everyone in its path. He was also pleased to see Flavius commandeer every mounted sagittaria he passed. *A wise decision. Their arrows will keep more of the enemy at bay while they consolidate a defensible position amid the rocks.*

A grinning, wide-eyed fiend materialized out of the haze. Running forward, his blood-painted face and bare upper torso only served to make his visage more terrifying. Ghostly trails of vapor clung to his body, making him appear wraithlike in the moonlight. Marcus recognized the black and blue plaid of an Iceni.

Realizing he'd been spotted, the berserker warrior's face split into a mask of hatred. Raising his bone club and long knife high, the maniac shrieked and launched himself at the centurion.

Digging his heels into Starblaze's flanks, Marcus spurred his horse forward and yanked hard on the reins. Trained for battle, Starblaze reared as commanded, and lashed out. The sickening *crunch* of crushed bone followed, and the clansman dropped like a stone. Wheeling about, Marcus looked toward Flavius's company once more. They had momentarily faltered as a huge knot of rebels impeded their progress. However, the pause was only temporary, the sheer advantage of weight and ferocity allowing Flavius and his men to move slowly forward again. Within the space of a few heartbeats, everyone who had stood between them and their avenue of escape was dead.

More mounted archers raced to add their strength to the charge. A break began to form, revealing a clear path through the sea of milling fighters.

We must seize this chance.

Marcus espied a signifier close by, safely protected within a shielded squad of men. Stomping and slashing his way across to him, he barked, "You there! Sound the advance . .. ." Pointing toward the gnarled oak trees at the crossing, he confirmed, ". . . that way. Proceed by descending cohorts. Signal the Tenth. They are to begin at double time. Once they have passed this position, the rest of you are to march in extending box formation. Hold until then. Is that clear?"

"Yes, Sir."

"And don't worry, once we've secured the ravine, I'll make sure you get cavalry support."

As the soldier issued instructions by horn, Marcus shouted across to the two closest groups of defenders, about forty men in all. "Extend a square around the signifier. Form turtle if you have to defend against arrows. This is our secondary rally point. Work slowly back toward the crossing so the rest can catch up."

Once the officers had confirmed his instructions, Marcus sought out the general. He was surprised to discover Quintus had become separated from the main column by a mass of baying clansmen, each as desperate as the others to tear him apart. It only took Marcus a moment to realize why. *The eagle!*

The rebel tribes knew the significance of an eagle. To the legion, it stood for everything. Their honor, their reputation, their very reason for existence. Capturing it would be a great prize for the savages, even if they couldn't defeat the army itself.

Not today, Marcus swore.

Both the general and the standard were protected by the entire first cohort. Despite their strength, they were dwarfed by an overwhelming press of plaid-wearing berserkers. All manner of tartans, in blue, green, red, and black swarmed the shield wall, revealing the appalling number of tribes involved. So hard-pressed were his comrades that no one in the main party had realized an avenue of escape had opened up behind them.

Spurring Starblaze forward, Marcus flanked the fighting. Drawing half a dozen riders to his side, he increased his pace and peeled in toward the square. Falling on the mob from behind, they cut an easy path through the unsuspecting attackers until they were within earshot of the general.

"Quintus. General! Fall back. Fall back, see?"

Drusus saw them first. Circling about, the colonel looked in the direction indicated by Marcus and started in surprise when he beheld the road that had been cut through the throng. He immediately turned to confer with the general.

A trumpet blast sounded. As one, the first cohort adjusted position to fall-in on the eagle and its officers. Once in place, they maneuvered again, adopting an open formation that allowed them to run while maintaining tactical readiness. The clansmen quickly recognized what was happening. Halting their attack, several warriors raised strange-looking horns to their lips.

Ah-ooooooooo. Ah-ooooooooo.

The battle paused for a heartbeat, then resumed in earnest.

What now? Marcus dropped in alongside Quintus, Drusus, and Aemilus Nerva, the Ninth's aquilifer, and shouted, "Keep your eyes peeled. Flavius has secured the crossing. The rest of the legion is moving up to regroup. If we make a stand there, we can at least consolidate our position before deciding what to do next."

"Agreed," Quintus replied. "Thank the gods they chose to hit us here. The choke point will slow them down a little, and allow us to build some form of fortified defense. It'll give us a chance to catch our breath too, if nothing else." He shifted his balance in the saddle, and looked about in the confusing gloom. "Who knows? This damnable fog may even work in our favor. How much thicker can it get?"

Marcus could appreciate what the general was alluding to. In the heat of fighting, their eyes had adjusted to the conditions about them. The darkness. The murk. The coagulating haze that now clung to them like spider's silk. It wasn't until they all took a moment to step back that they appreciated just how bad visibility had become. And how vulnerable it made them feel.

Ah-ooooooooooooooooooooooh.

A longer blast sent icicles trickling down Marcus's spine.

"What the hell was that?" Drusus muttered.

"Better pick up the pace, Sirs," Marcus hissed. "Get yourselves and the eagle to safety. Use the cavalry we have here to assist you. I'll bring the rest of the cohort in myself."

The horses started nickering. An odd rumbling sensation made the ground tremble. Marcus didn't know if these events were connected in some way or not, but the rotating miasma about them had thickened again.

The general glanced at his second, then at his aquilifer. Inclining his head, he acceded. "Very well. We'll move the command post to a point between the stunted oaks we saw earlier and make our stand there." Raising his voice, he commanded, "The Triari will fall back with the first cohort. All other mounted officers are with me. Protect Aemilus and the standard. Let's go."

As they turned to leave, Quintus glanced back over his shoulder. "Marcus, please make sure you bring the men home."

"I will, Sir. Nothing will stop me, I prom–"

An arrow lifted the general out of his saddle. Spinning through the air, Quintus hit the ground hard before flopping over onto his back. As he came to rest, already dead, the astonished group could see a clumsily fashioned shaft protruding from his eye socket, waggling as if it were mocking their impotence.

"Move!"Marcus roared.

The mounted party leapt forward and disappeared into the fog.

Marcus cast about, incensed that his commanding officer had been slaughtered in such a cowardly way. The reverberations were louder now, more intense. Flickering sparks of light, like miniature streaks of lightning had begun to flare along the vapor trails. The wind had picked up too, and was starting to bite with a vengeance. Marcus found the experience strangely mesmerizing. Fighting off the urge to stare, he caught sight of the eagle bearer's brother, Sextus Nerva, among the men.

An idea came to him.

"Sextus. Take the general's horse and get Quintus back behind our new forward line." Waving several other legionnaires over, he commanded, "Help him lift the body over the saddle. Quickly."

The ground visibly shook, small stones dancing along the floor in defiance of gravity. Perplexed, it took Marcus a moment to realize another sound had intruded, lifting above the ethereal resonance surrounding them. *Is that keening I hear?* An alien rider flashed past. Uttering a strange, high pitched wail as he rode, the plaid apparition vanished in a blaze of sparks and metal. Men fell to the ground, bleeding or dying.

"Riders!" someone shouted.

Where did they come from?

The stiffening breeze opened a path through the enveloping fog. Marcus's blood ran cold. By the light of the full moon, he could see the hillside and mountains on either side of the river. Thousands of horsemen, all Iceni, now ringed their position. Some were already descending toward the units who had made it to the erroneous safety of the defile. Those squadrons of enemy cavalry already on this side of the glen were charging to intercept the command party.

This isn't a spur of the moment attack. Look how many of them there are. And when did they start mounting their warriors? He snorted at the irony of his question. *As if knowing the answer will help us now.*

Marcus held his breath as a number of the colonel's riders peeled off to engage the attacking vanguard. Despite the sound of battle about him, the clash of steel rang out as the two sides met. Several riders from both sides were unhorsed, and the melee quickly dissolved into a confused free-for-all. It was soon over. Letting out a huge sigh of relief, Marcus noted that most of his compatriots regained their saddles. But not all. Nearly a half dozen of his brave comrades now lay dead upon the floor, their remains already being desecrated by the berserkers. He watched, horrified, as a mob of barbarians lowered their heads to their victims. They remained there, ignoring the conflict around them, tearing and slavering at the flesh until forced to relinquish their feast by sheer weight of opposing numbers.

They are cannibals then? That changes things. "Quicken the pace," he screamed. "We're almost within range of our archers, so we'll have support soon. Keep going. Show no mercy. If you go down injured, you're dead. Don't let them take you. Use your teeth, stab with fingers, gouge with nails. Make them bleed."

It was a rousing speech, but Marcus needn't have bothered. This was the first cohort. The cream of the legion. Before the night was over, the Iceni would fear them.

The minutes dragged by; time devolved into one, long, grueling marathon of butchery. Every blow was met by a counter strike. Each attack by a riposte. Shouting and cursing, chopping and hacking, they fought on and on. Sweat bled into their eyes, exhaustion robbed them of the strength to simply lift their arms to wipe it away. In the end, it was often the first to make a mistake that died, their cries snatched away on the wings of the gale.

Just when it felt like they would be overwhelmed by fatigue, it was over. One moment they were surrounded by a howling, baying mob of painted maniacs, and the next? A chorus of melodic yodels rang out about them, and the savages turned and ran. Within seconds, the night had claimed them. All that remained were the dead and the dying, and the shimmering vapors that cloaked the ravine and lower mountainside in a languid death shroud.

Marcus couldn't believe how sore he was. Groaning, he massaged his neck in an attempt to soothe away the pain. His arms were covered in a patchwork of cuts and grazes where weapons had gotten a little too close on too many occasions. Resting his hands on his thighs, he winced with pain. *Ah! I'd forgotten about that.*

At one point during the battle, he'd been pulled from his mount by some kind of fishhook-style device the savages had employed to unhorse their opponents. Starblaze herself had come to his rescue. Crushing the tartan-clad killer beneath her hooves, she stomped their assailant unconscious until Marcus ended it with a knife to the heart.

*The wound's still open and raw. I've got to get Cornelius
to take a look at it. Those filthy bastards poison their weapons.
It'll fester if I don't get it treated.*

Swaying, Marcus almost toppled from his saddle as a gust
of wind caused Starblaze to shy. He nearly went down again
when someone punched him in the arm and offered him a cup
of water. "Thirsty, Colonel?" Drusus shouted above the gale.

Turning to face him, Marcus could see his friend's countenance had become a wilderness of grime and ugly bruises.
One of his teeth was missing, giving him a lopsided grin. Stifling a snigger, Marcus was nevertheless confused. "What did
you say?"

"I asked you if you were thirsty . . . *Colonel*. You're my
acting second now. You'll find me a great deal more approach-
able than our former commander." He glanced about him as
the tail end of the legion limped in. "Not that it will do us much
good now with half an army left, and an indefensible position
to hold."

"Why? How bad is it?"

Drusus ran bloodied fingers through his hair, exposing a
nasty cut on his scalp. "From reports so far, most of the first
three cohorts, and some of the fourth, are intact. Fortunately, our
most experienced soldiers were at the head of the column, and
were able to take advantage of this position. We have Flavius
to thank for that. His equitata gained the high ground without
much in the way of opposition. He also saved half a cohort of
sagittaria and used them to great effect, keeping the approaches
clear . . ." His voice trailed off.

"But?" Marcus knew the worst was to come.

"We've heard nothing from the trailing cohorts."

"Nothing? But the lip of the valley is only half a mile
from here. The eighth cohort was already over it before the
fighting started. I was with the fifth myself as the battle got

underway. It was their aquilifer who sounded the advance to arms. How could so many . . . just . . . ?" He gazed out into the all-enveloping fog. It moved about them like a living entity, swirling and sparkling sedately in defiance of the windstorm now hammering down on them. Every time he moved Marcus noted how the tendrils of vapor would follow, as if attracted in some arcane way to his essence. His skin seemed to be shining too, in imitation of the mist itself.

The temperature abruptly dropped and the wind died to almost nothing. Marcus was appalled. "What *is* this stuff? It seems to be concentrated about this location as if, as if . . ."

"It's what's keeping us alive, Marcus," Drusus countered. "You can't have failed to see we are surrounded. The Iceni knew we were coming, and waited for us with a superior force. Cavalry too, if you can believe it. If they hadn't already been lurking in the mountains on this side of the river, I'd have said we had a fighting chance. Once we constructed a few fortifications, dug a few ditches, their cavalry wouldn't have mattered. But there's no time now. They're not here to take prisoners . . ." he waved his fingers in the air, " . . . only this *stuff* is keeping them back. I for one am very glad it's here, for I fear without it we'd already be dead."

"Ware the plain!"

The sudden warning from one the sentries caused everyone to come alert.

As if Mercury were keen to taunt them with his bag of tricks, the mists began to peel back a little. From out of the moonlit gloom, a stream of soldiers could be seen making their painful way toward salvation. Some jogged, more stumbled. Yet others struggled to carry injured comrades.

The same voice announced, "It's our brothers from the fifth and sixth cohorts."

"Over here," someone yelled.

"This way," called another.

Shapes materialized within the haze behind the fleeing men. The moon's luminescence added a terrifying perspective to their size.

"Run! You are pursued," yelled the lookout.

The intervening curtain closed momentarily, muting the cries of pain and anguish that suddenly rang from out of the darkness. A number of heads turned toward Drusus and Marcus, looking for direction. Demanding an answer. Drusus stared coldly back.

Further shrieks of agony stabbed the night. They were joined by howls of delight from the inhumane savages gleefully inflicting their tortures on exhausted and helpless men.

Drusus trotted along the line. Using the unexpected calm to his advantage, he raised his voice and addressed the Ninth. "They're testing our mettle. They know we are loath to leave our wounded in the field. Our brothers, brave, to the mercies of animals with the scruples of pigs. But if we are foolish enough to underestimate them again, it will be to our cost. We are already reduced. Anyone going to their aid will die a meaningless death. I will not lose more men in such a way tonight. We will live. We will survive. And we will make them rue the day they ever thought to cross the Ninth Legion of Rome."

Coming to a standstill directly in front of the massed ranks, he raised his sword and yelled, "We are the Ninth!"

"The Ninth," everyone responded, surging to their feet.

"The glorious Ninth," he repeated, punching his hand aloft once more.

"The Ninth," resounded the reply.

"The Ni–"

Choc!

Those nearest Drusus caught their breaths as the new commander rocked forward in his seat. He tried to regain his composure, but started jerking in his saddle as if he were a puppet being tormented by a sadistic fiend. Even in the filtered moonlight, Marcus could see Drusus had turned a sickening white, as if suffering extreme shock. At that same moment, the hairs on Marcus's arms stood on end. "Drusus?"

Drusus stared back. His lips moved but he was unable to catch his breath. He glanced to one side, mesmerized by the ubiquitous mist that had closed about them to form a glittering, opaque wall. Eyes glazing, Drusus attempted to scrutinize his surroundings. Fascinated, he struggled to focus on the stones and small rocks littering the ravine that were lifting up from the floor in front of them. He finally seemed to remember where he was. His gaze intensified. Latching on to Marcus, he hunched forward and hissed, "Marcus. Look after them for me, will you?"

As he spilled to the floor in a heap, everyone saw the war axe buried in the commander's spine. Drusus Vergilius Cicero twitched once, then lay still.

Howls erupted all about them.

"I will, brother," Marcus whispered. *That's the second promise I've made tonight.*

Rage coursed through his veins. His heart burning with fury, Marcus ignored the extraordinary events unfolding all around them and wheeled Starblaze about. "Sentries!" he roared, "light up the foreground. Archers! Kill every pale-faced, wide-eyed, naked bastard you see. Flavius! Take your equitata and scour the field clean of scum. Cohorts! Form up and prepare to fight. This night we–"

Thunk!

Marcus experienced the oddest of sensations. He felt both hot and cold at the same time. Lightheaded, but unbelievably weary. Invincible, and yet as fragile as an insect in the beak of a nightjar. For some reason, the world appeared lopsided and out of phase with reality. His perspective tilted and the ground rushed up to meet him. Impervious to the shock of landing, Marcus was more astonished by the spectacle of the arrow protruding from his chest than anything else.

His skin tingled. Sounds began to echo and recede. The world went white. Spinning, he felt himself being lifted from the floor . . . and then the ice cold grip of death closed in on him.

Chapter Five

Last Stand

Sword in hand, his scarf bound tightly across his face, Lex hunched as low as he dared across the neck of his horse and clung on for dear life.

It was always dangerous, riding in such a manner. Not only couldn't you see where you were going, but you wouldn't have time to maneuver away from hidden dangers if they suddenly manifested. And that was at the best of times. On occasions like this, when visibility was seriously reduced by inclement weather, or with enemies lurking at every turn, it was near suicidal.

Lex trusted his gelding, Samson, implicitly. The two had ridden together for three years now, and had formed a close bond. He'd always proved a sure-footed mount, and today was no exception. Samson had trampled at least a half dozen rebel

45

warriors who had lain in wait in the long grass, leaving Lex only a handful to deal with directly.

Lex hadn't trusted everything to blind luck. *Thank God I don't have a stick up my ass, like the captain. Letting Stained-With-Blood lead the way is the best decision I've made in a long time. How the hell he can spot the safest route in conditions like this, I'll never know. I bet Houston's already dead. There were hundreds of—whoa!*

Something moved in the wildly dancing sward below him. Lunging upward at the last moment, the assassin attempted to skewer Lex with a spear. Reacting instinctively, he slashed down with his blade. A shock ran along his arm, and Samson shuddered slightly as whoever it was got bowled over. "Good boy!" Lex crooned.

Soothing Samson's neck, Lex strained to make sense of the confusing blur whipping by on both sides. He quickly gave up, concentrating instead on Stained-With-Blood's back. As one born to such savage delights, the Native American forded the wilderness with consummate ease, and Lex couldn't help but feel a twinge of envy.

Riding bareback, Stained-With-Blood looked completely at home. Tomahawk in hand, long flowing locks streaming behind him in the gale, the brave was a vision of the very land itself come to life. Power, vitality, unity. The stinging hail and driving wind didn't bother him one bit. Unlike the rest of them.

Crouched as he was, like a hunchbacked invalid across his horse, Lex felt like an old man and jokingly admitted, *I hate him!*

The feeling was only reinforced by the sight of Quincy Shelby. The private had tried desperately to keep the colors flying during the first few miles of their flight. But in the end, the battering both he and the pennant had taken from the elements had forced Quincy to demount the guidon and stash it within his saddlebag.

Not that Lex minded. Even though he had the use of both hands, Quincy was only just managing to hang on. *And that isn't surprising— considering.*

Glancing behind them, Lex realized that the Cree coalition weren't the only ones pursuing them. The tornado-like formation that had appeared over the open plain seemed to be grinding straight for them. The billowing clouds had darkened and solidified into a churning vortex of power that filled the air with grit and small stones. All across the savanna, the long grasses were being whipped and thrashed about so mercilessly Lex thought they would surely be torn from the earth.

This weather can't be natural. The sooner we make it to Skull Canyon, the better. We'll find some degree of shelter, and with properly placed rifles can start picking a few of them off— If we don't get ripped off our horses first.

Risking a peek toward Small Robes, his awe only increased. Despite her delicately small frame, she epitomized her uncle and sat high in the saddle, challenging the elements to bow before her. She looked glorious, and Lex couldn't help but think what a fool Snow Blizzard was for spurning the proposed alliance.

His heart skipped a beat as an anguished howl caught his attention. Craning around to his left, Lex saw another riderless horse keeping pace with the pack. *Is that Chip's gelding? Chip Walton? Damn! He was our newest recruit.*

Flapping reins and empty stirrups taunted him. Lex could feel the itch of impending death worming its way ever deeper between his shoulder blades. He dare not stop to scratch, not even for a second, lest an arrow take him or his fate leap up out of the ground to claim his life. *He was only nineteen, and engaged to be married.*

Hunching further down, he ground his teeth in mounting frustration.

From somewhere behind, several gunshots rang out in quick succession. The empty satisfaction of knowing Chip's assailant was probably dead did nothing to stop the bile rising in his throat. *Bastards! We've got to get out of here. Soon.*

The sound of gravel underfoot indicated they must be near a watercourse or an outcrop of some kind. Lex strained to look ahead again. Without warning, Stained-With-Blood leaned heavily over on one side of his mustang. Swinging savagely, the blade of his tomahawk bit home. Rising once more, it left a scarlet spray in the air. Flashing past, Lex only had an instant to recognize another skin-covered body spiraling to the floor, this one with a gaping wound across its face.

How on earth are they managing to get so far ahead of us? he thought, concerned he was missing something important. *Have they been here all along?*

He was about to call ahead to ask Stained-With-Blood's advice, when the brave waved furiously toward their right flank. Changing direction, he charged off, shouting, "This way, quickly. Follow me."

Lex gave the signal to follow, and the platoon wheeled in pursuit.

The wind dropped as they descended a stony track. The trail widened and the gradient became steeper, getting rockier with every step. Hanging back, Lex encouraged the stragglers to make haste and counted them off as they rode in. Peering back out toward the plain, he realized the depression would be totally hidden from view.

Is this the entrance to the hidden canyon Captain Houston referred to? Already? We might just make it after—

Lex gasped as he caught sight of the storm. It was only now, while he wasn't running, that he was able to look at it properly. And *feel* it!

A huge, anvil-shaped cloud formation spread out for miles in every direction. Turning from gray at the edges to midnight-blue at the center, it seethed as if some inner conflict were threatening to tear it apart. Unseen reverberations made Lex's teeth and nasal cavity throb. He was reminded of the feeling he had once experienced as a boy, when his parents had taken him to see the Philharmonic Society of New York. He had been sitting in the front row and as the orchestra had prepared, the combined resonance produced by over a hundred tuning instruments had given Lex a headache. He was experiencing that exact same sensation now, but on a much grander scale. And the pit from which these vibrations issued was vast. It bit into the ground with a savagery that blotted out the horizon and made him gawp in wide-eyed horror. And it was altering course, to correspond with the new direction they were taking.

That can't be right.

"Have you ever seen anything like this before?" Stained-With-Blood asked.

The warrior had approached silently. Startled, Lex was nevertheless unable to tear his eyes from the monstrosity growling toward them.

"No. Never. You?"

"In all my seasons under the care of our creator, Napioa, I have never witnessed the likes of this. But—"

"But?"

The old Indian narrowed his eyes as he considered the tales of his ancient people. " . . . But we have stories. We are reluctant to speak of them outside of our tribes, for such law does not concern the white man. What you are about to hear has never before been spoken of, to one such as yourself.

"Legends from the birth of time, when Chaos still contended with his brother, Balance, for dominion of the earth, tell us of the unleashing of the storm wind. Napioa, our father, found two skin sacks on his journeys one day, containing summer and winter. He was determined to gain possession of those bags, for then he could bless our people with two perfect seasons of equal months. However, Chaos interfered, and the sacks proved to be most elusive, so Napioa sent a little animal to retrieve the skins for him. The creature was successful in capturing the summer bag, and made haste to return it to his creator. However, the guardian of the sacks, at the behest of Chaos, chased after the thief and decapitated it. In the turmoil that followed, the bag burst apart, opening a doorway to the celestial powers— and through it, the storm wind was unleashed."

The older man eyed the tempest in front of them before concluding, "I fear we may be looking at such a doorway now, for never do the cycles of nature act like this."

Lex shivered. "Not wanting to appear rude, Stained-With-Blood, but how dependable are these legends?"

"Our ancient law comes from histories handed down from chief to son. From shaman to apprentice. We are not prone to the exaggerations of your race, and pride ourselves on truth." Turning to look the young officer in the eye, he smiled, and admitted, "But of course, we are only human. And sometimes we lack the words to properly describe the events experienced by our forefathers."

Gawking at the leviathan before them, Lex could appreciate how such fables could be born, for the maelstrom had an ethereal quality to it that made it appear like a herald of doom from another world.

The last riders began their descent into the canyon, and Lex made haste to follow.

"How many of your company have survived, young soldier?" Stained-With-Blood asked.

"If I counted right? At least forty-four." Cocking a thumb toward the towering clouds, Lex added, "But I did get a little distracted. I'll find out soon enough once I get the princess safe and the men deployed."

The horses shied as the dirt in several places around their feet exploded into the air. Muffled echoes of gunshots flittered away on the gale.

"They've found us," Lex spat.

"They never lost us," Stained-With-Blood countered. "Quickly, we must make ready. It would appear my Lakota, Sioux, and Apache brothers have not only been poisoned against reconciliation, but corrupt the purity of our fighting methods too. Your thunder sticks will make them invincible."

As they galloped down the track, Lex shouted, "We'll see about that. I'm more concerned as to where they got them. Peace was very much on Senator Lincoln's agenda. If someone is supplying our enemies with rifles, it makes me wonder just how long this deception was in the planning."

"Or how deep it goes?" the warrior added, looking thoughtful.

Catching up with the main party, Lex began issuing orders.

"Private Dermot? Sound for battle. They realize we're here, so we might as well let them know we're prepared. Sergeant Rixton! Take your section and head back out to the beginning of the defile. Although it's low ground, position your men as best you can along the edge of the cut. Pick off as many as you can at long range. Some of them have guns now, so make use of the extra range afforded by our Spencer carbines. I want those savages to think twice about trying to rush us."

Scanning the gorge, Lex picked out several points where the rocks allowed access back up onto the plain. Turning to the native warrior, he asked, "Stained-With-Blood, would you mind helping Corporal Williams pick the best locations to protect our position from up there? You know the way Snow Blizzard thinks. How would *he* try and take us? Put us in the right spots to counter that. Okay?"

The brave nodded and ushered the corporal's section away.

Turning to the remaining soldiers, Lex beckoned to the medical officers and addressed the princess. "Small Robes? May I ask that you follow my instructions to the letter?" The young woman eyed him solemnly for a moment, then smiled. Lex took that as a yes. Pressing ahead, he said, "I want you to stay close to Major Clark and Captain Anders. Both men are trained healers as well as soldiers, so they'll be able to keep you safer than anyone else." Surgeon Major Clark looked uncomfortable about that statement, but had the good manners not to disagree.

Scanning the bottom of the defile, Lex noticed the strengthening wind was already lifting dust from the canyon floor into the air, reducing visibility and making it harder to pick out individual people. *Good. That should make us much more difficult to hit.*

He espied a cluster of rocks at the base of the cliff, masked beneath a slight overhang. Pointing at it, he said, "If you lead the horses over there and stay apart from the fighters, I'm hoping you'll avoid the worst of what's coming."

As the small group moved off, Lex was distracted by noise and movement from the team making their way back onto the ridgeline. He heard someone shout, "Stay your hand!"

Stained-With-Blood?

"Hold your fire, it's us!" Corporal Williams cried.

Blinking furiously to clear his eyes, Lex examined the crest. It was crowned by a multitude of silhouettes, but they were hard to distinguish among the flying debris and stinging grit. His heart jumped into his mouth as he saw his soldiers pointing their weapons upward. Then he recognized one profile in particular. "Captain Houston? Is that you, Sir?"

The men about him paused, their confusion evident.

"Yes, Lieutenant, it is. Ask your men to lower their weapons, please."

"Sir? How come you got here so quickly? We only just arrived ourselves."

"The weapons, Lieutenant? We don't want to make this any harder than it is." Houston's voice trembled from a subtle undercurrent. For some reason, Lex found the captain's manner worrying. So did the men. Although they had initially started to relax, most now had their rifles trained back on their comrades from second platoon.

Houston was joined by more people. Manifesting from out of the haze behind him, they came to stand silently at his side. Thunderclouds had now formed overhead, directly behind and above them, making it appear to the poor unfortunates trapped in the canyon that a crowd of grim reapers had just materialized, intent on an orgy of imminent death.

"Snow Blizzard!" Stained-With-Blood snapped, "your treachery is boundless. You are allied with this— this scum?" The veteran warrior's countenance had turned as hard as flint.

Lex couldn't believe what he was hearing. "Stained-With-Blood? What are you talking about?"

Turning his back on the gathering crowd, Stained-With-Blood addressed the bewildered lieutenant. "This explains everything, young warrior. Why your company was betrayed by an outburst from someone who should have known better. How we miraculously managed to avoid capture by those who know these lands with the intimacy of a people born to it. And most of all, it reveals why we were led here. These traitors are allied. And have been all along." Turning to face the tribal leader and the army officer once more, he bellowed, "Do you dare deny it?"

Captain Houston glanced at Snow Blizzard, shrugged, and tightened his shawl about his shoulders. Leaning into the wind, he called, "No, I don't deny it. But we are no traitors. You are naïve if you think yours are the only proposals on the table. Our nation is confused. Divided. Not everyone feels our best interests are being served by congress. We'll soon be taking things in a different direction. Especially in the south, where we have growing support to form a new government. Five states are with us. If we are successful here today, that'll grow to seven. Lincoln will be ruined, and we'll be free to take our country forward in a way more conducive—" he flicked a look at Snow Blizzard once again, " . . . to a mutual and beneficial understanding with our Native American friends, here."

Lex was stunned. "Are you saying this whole thing was staged? Planned to fail from the very beginning?"

Laughing coldly, Houston stepped forward a few paces. "But of course. You may be a career officer, Fox, but you don't have the connections my family has. Why do you think the fifth was chosen to undertake this mission? My brother, Samuel, will be delighted at the outcome, despite the hiccup along the way."

A veil dropped from Lex's mind. *Governor Sam Houston! My God, how high up does this conspiracy go? I've got to warn someone.*

As if sensing the first lieutenant's thoughts, Houston cupped his hands to his mouth and called through the storm. "Lieutenant Smith? Wilson, you and your new buddies can come out now." Next to him, Snow Blizzard put his fingers to his lips and made a shrill whistling noise.

Within moments, further shapes materialized out of the gloom. Soldiers and braves. All were carrying rifles.

Lex shook from head to toe. For some reason, a thrill that had nothing to do with his worsening situation had taken hold of him and was refusing to let go. "Are you crazy? Do you realize the division this will cause?"

"Oh yes. We're counting on it." The menace in Houston's voice was clear. Leveling his rifle toward Lex, he sneered, "Now lower your weapons."

Lex knew it would be suicide to do so. He felt lightheaded. The blood pounded so hard in his ears he thought he might pass out. A hot flush came over him, and yet,, he couldn't stop shivering. The thought of what he must do dominated his mind. Glancing around his platoon, he could see they were looking to him to take the lead. They appeared to resonate where they stood, becoming somehow spectral, like luminescent wraiths come to haunt him. Each of them waited intently for him to give the next order.

Can I do this to them?

The answer was painfully obvious. *If I don't, they're dead anyway.*

He tightened his grip on his pistol. Noting that his palms were sweating, he took a deep breath, threw himself to the floor, and yelled, "Fire!"

Despite the rage of the storm, the roar of the gunfire was louder, dominating his world and deafening him to anything else. He tucked and rolled, bounced off a ledge and came to rest on the floor. Dirt sprayed about him. Each particle hung hypnotically in the air and commenced dancing around him in concentric spirals.

The sting of steel on flesh punched Lex sideways. Grimacing in pain, he attempted to rise, only to feel another. Snapping into him from behind, it caught him in the shoulder and knocked the wind from his lungs. Bowled across the ground, he landed heavily on his back. His head became a lead weight. Struggling to breathe, Lex watched, mesmerized, as everyone seemed to slow down, moving as if they were wading through water.

Surgeon Major Clark tried desperately to hold on to Small Robes. In turn, she fought to break his grip, frantic to get to her uncle. Horses ran every-which-way in panic. Soldiers came and went. Crouching for a moment to pick a new target, they would fire and disappear off, back into the blinding turbulence spinning about them.

Rebel Indians lined the lip of the canyon. Struggling to stay upright, they shot at random into the milling crowd below. In seconds, they were joined by the traitors from the second company. People from both sides fell.

The eye of the storm appeared directly above them. Lex could feel the unadulterated power of its potential coalescing in the air. A lull in battle manifested, and all heads turned to look upward. Lex spotted the captain. Raising his gun, he fought to steady his shaking hand and took aim.

Houston saw him. Dropping to one knee, he raised his rifle and fired at the same moment Lex squeezed the trigger.

Unbearable pain filled Lex's world, and he was lifted into chaos.

Chapter Six

Take No Prisoners

Mac paused behind a wire mesh screen and surveyed the scene. A single corridor nearly fifty yards long stretched away before him. The only source of illumination came from a series of flashing red security strobes, evenly spaced along the center of the ceiling. Because of the lockdown, they only served to increase the claustrophobic atmosphere and created a stark contrast between areas of clarity and shadow. Although the passage was lined with doors on either side, Mac's interest lay in those situated exactly halfway along. The ones with a double set of paired sentries outside to be exact, as they marked the entrance to the dining room and recreation center. His head-mounted active-cam recorded everything he saw, and relayed it onto the HUDs of his squad, waiting patiently in the darkness at the back of the switch room.

Sam Pell was busy preparing the fiber optic web that would give them a thermal and holographic image of what was taking place inside the mess hall. While he set up, Mac continued to watch the intruders. Doing so always revealed little indicators or patterns of behavior that could be exploited to help achieve their own mission objectives. And as professional as these terrorists were, they were only human. They were expecting an aggressive response from the government, but they didn't know what form it would take, or when. The structure shuddered. Unexpectedly foul weather was testing the integrity of the rig's state of the art stabilizing system, and from the strength of the vibrations thrumming through the walls, it felt as if they were being stretched to maximum. Mac could see their targets becoming increasingly anxious the longer things played out. *Perhaps this flash storm will work in our favor after all?*

Two of the guards were part of a roving patrol from the deck above, the operations level. They had just arrived via an open metal stairwell positioned on the far side of the passage, directly opposite the common room doors. This was their second visit in ten minutes. Although Mac was sure the constant checks might be part of the terrorists' adopted security procedure, he could see the men were using the opportunity to encourage each other.

Yup! Repeated glances up and down the corridor. Needless fiddling with their night vision optics. Incessant chatter, face to face, instead of radio checks. They've managed to lock this place down tight, but they don't like waiting for something to happen.

He smiled. *Don't worry, chaps. We'll be helping you out there shortly.*

Mac knew that at least half a dozen managers had been frogmarched to the higher level after the rig was taken. *Most likely to ensure any unexpected hitches can be addressed quickly, should our friends encounter anything—unusual. Right, let's get this show on the road.*

Speaking quietly into his microphone, Mac addressed his Tec specialist. "Sam? How long before you're ready?"

"About a minute, Boss. The system is integrated and running through its final diagnostic. We should have an update of what's going on inside the mess hall soon."

"Roger that." Changing his focus, Mac called his second-in-command, Mark Stevens. *He should have managed to work his way through the upper modules of the platform by now.* Using call signs, he said, "Bravo-one, this is Alpha-one, do you copy?"

"Bravo-one. Go ahead."

"Mark, do you have a sit-rep?"

"Yes, Sir. We have just completed our preliminary sweep of the primary ring. The weather would appear to be playing to our advantage. It's atrocious, with swells broaching the heliport pad. I can confirm there are no bogeys outside. Repeat, no bogeys are stationed outside. They have initiated whatever protocols they deemed necessary to their plans, and have retreated indoors."

"Good to hear." Mac then spoke to bravo squad's own technical expert, Richard "Fonzy" Cunningham. "Fonzy. I know it's early, but I need your preliminary assessment from what you've seen so far."

"Boss, I have confirmed nuclear ordnance at the following locations: One has been placed on the high pressure separation manifold. Another is in the reinjection unit. Both are straightforward gun-assembly devices, employing a sophisticated microwave web. Scans show further bombs have been positioned in the battery room, and dining hall."

"Copy that. Are these things small enough to be moved?"

"That's a yes. Once I've determined the extent of the network linking each unit together, I can formulate a solution. A simple interruption of the relay should suffice if we have to go hot. We can disarm them later. If you can get Sam to isolate the frequency of the emitter at your location, I'll start working on a looped patch."

"Excellent work, Fonzy."

Mac resumed his conversation with the bravo squad leader. "Mark. What's the strength and deployment of the hostiles?"

"Sir, we can confirm at least fifteen, repeat fifteen targets on the upper ring. Three are tucked up nice and cozy with the managers in the operations office. We have a two-man team in the entrance portico to the drill module, and a further pair within the vent chamber itself. Both sets are sheltering from the storm. Other roving patrols have been moved inside the habitat ring. If you haven't seen them already, you will shortly. Be advised, we also have static sentries guarding the devices themselves. These guys are strategically deployed and armed with AK-48-GMR assault rifles. Confirm?"

"From Alpha-one, confirmed," Mac replied. "I have eyes on four, repeat four hostiles. Two appear to be a roving patrol, possibly one of the teams you've already mentioned from the command ring. The other pair is positioned outside the main entrance to my primary target. They are likewise armed with AK-48s, and look to be a little more relaxed, with weapons slung over their shoulders. Thermals will be operating shortly—"

"Boss?" Sam interjected. "Enhanced imaging is online. Relaying to your HUD now."

"Everyone wait!" Mac paused to digest the implications of what was now appearing on his screen.

The interior of the large, forty yard square dining and recreation center had been rearranged. Mac could see that all of the furniture had been pushed to one side in an untidy heap, and the vacated space was now filled with people. All were blind-folded, bound and gagged, and had been positioned in such a way as to surround a large device in the middle of the room. Ten armed sentries were stationed around them. All had their weapons trained on the hostages.

No wonder their guys outside the door are much more re-laxed. Hang on . . .?

Mac adjusted the controls to his HUD and broadcast the scene to the rest of his unit. "Fonzy? You said the bombs already spotted are portable, confirm?"

"Yes, Sir. They're much smaller than what I'm looking at now. The other ones are capable of being carried by two men. *That* is something entirely different."

Mac felt a chill worming its way along his spine. He didn't know if he was spooked by this latest development or not, but he got the distinct impression *something* had changed for the worse.

Then another fact caught his attention.

The kitchens are cold! The terrorists have been here for hours now, and yet no refreshments have been served? Depressing his headset, he asked, "Sam? Can you adjust the resolution so we can zoom in on the hostages themselves? Incorporate bio-filters. I want a chemical and thermal analysis of their condition."

"Will do, Boss."

Mark Stevens cut back in. "Alpha-one, this is Bravo-one. New developments?"

Mac trusted his instincts. He always had. His ability to notice obscure details and make connections had saved his life, and the lives of those he worked with, on many occasions in the years he had worked within Special Forces. And his *something's not quite right* bump was irritating him right now. Mac signaled with his hand for Sam to hurry up with his assessment, and replied, "Mark, I've got a feeling we're going to have problems. Tell me, what conditions are you facing topside?"

"Crazy, Boss. In the time we've been speaking, wind speed and wave height have increased again. Hailstones the size of golf balls are coming in horizontally, putting a few holes through windows and many of the lighter structures. If it wasn't for our armor, I'm sure we'd have been drilled by now. The storm itself appears concentrated solely about the rig, and the eye is almost over us. We can't see more than a hundred yards past the outer gantry. More serious structural damage is now taking place along the vent manifold and drill mod–

"Watch out! Take cover."

Mac caught his breath. "Report!"

"Sorry, Sir," Mark replied after a short delay, "we're gonna have to get out of this shit-storm. Part of the support boom stabilizing the vent just tore loose and narrowly missed taking Sean's ugly head clean off. While I'm sure we'd all agree it would be a vast improvement, I don't want to be the one explaining to his wife why we let a bit of weather get her man killed."

"Agreed," Mac replied. "Get your asses inside. Make your approach via the control center. I want to know what's going on with the managers, and final confirmation regarding the ordnance our friends have planted in the battery cabin. Understood?"

"Roger that, Alpha-one. Bravo is on the move."

No sooner had the conversation ended than Mac's presence was demanded at the rear of the switch room. "Boss, come and see this!" Sam muttered.

The optic web's principal display held much more detail than could be presented on their HUDs, and Sam was clearly worried by what the sensitive instruments were now recording.

Mac shuffled back. "What is it?"

"These colors represent different chemicals," Sam replied, indicating a bar chart on one side of the screen. "What we've got here are excessive amounts of nitrogen, sodium, potassium, various sulfides, bitirubin, and a whole host of other bacteria."

Mac looked confused, so Sam got straight to the point. "Basically, those guys are sitting in their own shit and piss. And from the analysis, many have been like that for hours."

"Seriously?"

"Seriously. It looks like the hostages aren't being allowed to move. Not even to go to the bathroom. That's a little strange, especially when you *then* take the temperature into consideration." Sam tapped a set of figures along the bottom of the display.

Mac was surprised. "What? Fifty-four degrees! Is that in Celsius or Fahrenheit?"

"That's the current reading in Celsius. *This* is what it is in Fahrenheit. And just so you know, yes, the air conditioning unit is working fine. Whatever that device in there is, it's radiating a lot of heat."

The entire structure groaned about him, and Mac sat back on his heels to think things through. *No cooking. No refreshments. Herded like cattle into one location where they're literally forced to stew in their own juices.*

Another piece of the jigsaw fell into place. *Hey! This is no hostage situation. It's an execution—*

. . . But why go to all this trouble? I must be missing something.

As if agreeing with his assessment, a hollow *boom* resonated throughout the rig.

We can't let this continue. Addressing the entire team, he said, "Four troop, this is Alpha-one. Standby. Standby." After pausing for a few seconds to allow them to prepare for the message, he continued, "Four troop, we are going hot. Repeat, we are going hot. Safety of the hostages is now paramount. Mark, do you copy?"

"Copy that, Sir. Operating procedures?"

"You are to divide into pairs and take out all bogies on the way in. If possible, remove the sentries in the drill module and vent chamber first. I want anyone who can raise the alarm or be in a position to give covering fire, dead. Confirm?"

"Confirmed."

"Once completed, slot the babysitters guarding the nuclear ordnance as well. Work your way to the control center. That will put you directly above alpha squad. We will prepare to breach the recreation room in the meantime. I will update you further once we form up. Understood?"

"Understood. Bravo-one out."

Turning to his own squad, Mac continued, "Guys? Set up for rapid deployment. Stu, you're with me. We will secure the main door and stairwell. Sam, prepare an entry charge here. I want you within the switch room itself. Stay with the scope and update me regarding any changes inside that room. Jumper, once the sentries are out of the way, take your explosive to the opposite end of the hall. I want a breach point adjacent to the kitchen. When bravo squad joins us, we'll get a final sit-rep from Sam and go in as a team. Hard and fast. No prisoners. We'll sort out the bombs afterward. Do you all know what to do?"

Everyone checked off.

"Right. Let's get this done. Stu, we're up."

Like two well-oiled machines, both men ran through their preparations as if born to them. Communications, weapons, ammunition and armor.

Moving to the edge of the meshing, Mac waited for another squeal to grate through the rig before slipping the catch. Sure enough, the sentries looked every-which-way in alarm, but they hadn't been alerted to the team's presence. Using the flickering lights as cover, Mac eased through the doorway and took up position against the far wall. Stu came next. Following the same procedure, he was soon invisible on the opposite side of the corridor. Jumper waited behind the door, his detonation-charge held at the ready.

The chameleon armor was a marvel of technological achievement. It worked by bending light from the environment around it, so that it mimicked its surroundings. It was powerful enough to mask the wearer from sight during daylight, especially if they moved slowly. Under current conditions, Mac knew they'd be impossible to spot.

Both men edged forward until they were within several yards of their targets. Once in position, Mac took a final look around to make sure the coast was clear. Bringing his gun to the shoulder, he calmly said, "Stu, are you ready for my mark?"

"Yes, yes."

Mac lowered his head to the scope and waited.

The structure throbbed under the assault of another gigantic wave. The sound of grinding metal quivered throughout the platform. As it did so, Mac quietly counted down, "Three, two, one. Mark!"

Phhut. Phhut! Phhut. Phhut!

Silenced weapons spat death into the night. Four men fell to the floor, the sound of their collapse masked by the storm-induced stresses.

Mac twisted toward the switch room and gave a thumbs-up. Jumper Collins immediately scampered out into the gloom, carrying a strange, rubber-like hose over his shoulder. While Mac and Stu provided cover, Jumper worked his way past them and went further along the passage. Selecting a suitable point along the wall, he pressed the hoop against the surprisingly warm steel to form a ring of explosive cord.

They waited.

The thrumming bounding along the hallways became more pronounced. To Mac's eyes, the walls appeared to flex, as if being subjected to enormous pressure. Plasma discharges erupted from the floors and ceilings, and wormed their way along the metal surfaces for yards at a time before fizzling out. Both Stu and Jumper looked about, earnestly checking their defensive arcs again and again as if expecting an attack at any moment.

Mac still felt he was missing the last piece of the jigsaw. *I don't like this. What have those bastards done?* Scanning back down the corridor, he said, "Sam, are you there? What are you seeing?"

Static filled his earpiece.

"Sam?" he repeated.

"I sai—weird! The—uild up of energy. I've never seen anyth—like it befo—Do you copy? Please respo—Sir?"

That's Sam all right, but we're getting interference. I'd better go and see what the hell is happening. Signaling for his teammates to wait, Mac scurried back toward their rally point. The closer he got to the meshed cage, the more concentrated the electrical emissions became, and he was forced to slow his approach.

Mark's voice suddenly broke through on the radio. " . . . peat, Alpha-one, do you copy? Boss? Are you receiv—yet?"

"Yes, I am now," Mac replied. Startled, he dropped to one knee and continued, "Mark, are you getting any weird phenomena up there? Unusual stuff, like ball lightning or ghosted images?"

"Too right we are. It must be this damned storm. There's an obvi—ectrical element to it. We've been tryin—for a few minutes now. Do you wa—update?"

"Go ahead. Where are you now?"

"On the outer rin—Standing posts have been eliminate—Weathe—appalling and making—Now, we're about to take down the sent—guarding the nuc—in tandem. I thought you might like—Okay?"

"You're breaking up," Mac replied. Exasperated by the hitch, he nevertheless managed to keep his temper. "Am I hearing right? Stationary sentries are dead, and you're just about to hit the boys guarding the bombs? Yes?"

"That's a ye—yes. Wait, out!" Mark left the line open as his squad carried out the hit. "Bravo squad, on—mark. Thre—one—fire!"

Time seemed to drag by as Mac waited for confirmation of the kills, turning the seconds into an eternity of suspense. Out of the blue, Sam stuck his head out of the switch room door and hissed, "Sir, you'd better get in here now!"

Mac noticed his specialist had removed the microphone patch from his throat. "Why have you taken your com-strip off, Sam?"

"The interference. It's beginning to attract a static charge that will cause a nasty shock." Sam pointed at the display. "And here's why."

Conditions within the mess hall had changed. Instead of the subdued atmosphere of frightened men and determined killers, it was evident panic had taken hold. Forked lightning crackled down from the ceiling and through open wall vents. Like harbingers of death, coruscating fingers of plasma stabbed about the interior, searing flesh and incinerating bones alike. It was Dante's Inferno come to life, and bodies were flying everywhere.

"But I can't hear anything." Mac was not only shocked, but confused as well. "Why is that?"

Sam tapped the screen. "Look here. The event is confined within some kind of localized barrier."

A rippling vortex had encompassed the people inside. Penetrating the frame of the rig as if it didn't exist, it was now expanding with each passing moment. As Mac watched, a halo of power bloomed outward from the center of the nuclear device. It was followed by further concentric waves of corresponding energy.

"Oh for fucks sake! What now?"

Without warning, the platform shook violently, and the entire corridor began to buck and bend as if the rig had been seized in the grip of an earthquake. Despite the shriek of twisting metal, Mac could hear the sound of running feet pounding along the gantry above them. So did his men. As one, they dropped into firing positions.

"Hold your fire," a voice screamed. "Alpha squad, hold your fire."

Mark? "Mark? Is that you?" Mac called.

His second-in-command came bounding into view. Leaping down the steps four at a time, Mark yelled, "Boss! The bombs are rigged to the bio-signs of the terrorists. We took them down, and it initiated a countdown sequence. We gotta get out of here. Now!"

A physical shock coursed through Mac as the final penny dropped. *I knew something wasn't right.* "How long have we got?"

"Unknown. But from the way those things are winding up, Fonzy thinks a few minutes at the most."

Mac knew immediately what they had to do. "Mark, haul your ass back upstairs and see if you can prime the lifeboats. One member of bravo squad is to captain each craft. Alpha squad will see what we can do down here."

The tone of his voice made it clear the subject wasn't open to debate.

Mark nodded and thundered back up the stairs.

Mac called his team together. "Boys, we don't have long. On my count, we will enter, and then kill every bastard scumbag we see. We're going to do our level best to get as many hostages as possible away from this place before it blows. We stay, we die. At least we might have a chance out there in the storm. Understood?"

Three heads nodded.

"Stu? You and I will go right. I'm high, you're low. Sam? Jumper? You go left. Sam is high. Jumper low. Flash-bangs go first."

Each specialist readied his weapon and withdrew a small anti-personnel grenade. Designed to incapacitate, the flash-bang contained a magnesium-sonic core which would blind and stun any individual within its range. As the prisoners were bound and gagged, they would be spared the full effects. However, the terrorists would be further distracted for a few seconds. And a few seconds were all his men needed.

They fanned out around the door.

As focused as he was, Mac was momentarily distracted by a strange warping effect that was distorting the composition of the walls. In some places, the lining turned transparent. In others, flecks of light, like ethereal sprites, wove sedately in and out of the metal in a multitude of different colors.

Shit! Keep it together, man! Taking a deep breath, he yelled, "Now!"

Heavy boots smashed the doors inward. Two men broke left, the others right. Mac felt a tingling sensation as he crossed the threshold. Grenades detonated, adding their confusion to the unfolding drama. Men were shouting, screaming, dying. Writhing and burning within a nightmare crucible from hell.

Mac couldn't afford to feel sorry. Without waiting for the glare of the flash-bangs to subside, he started shooting. Keeping to his designated arc, he watched an already injured terrorist disappear amid a spray of scarlet mist.

A body flew through the air in front of him, and Stu Duggan was knocked to the floor. Mac tucked and rolled, and another assailant turned his gun on him. Coming to his feet, Mac fired again. Tracking the bullets up his target's torso and into his face, he kept his finger depressed until the man fell and stopped moving.

Prolonged bursts blistered the air. As Mac looked for someone else to kill, an unexpected glare overwhelmed his visor's capacity to shield him.

What the—?

A high pitched drone bit into his ears, forcing him to his knees. He writhed on the floor, screaming louder and louder. A pressure wave sent him reeling. For the briefest moment, Mac felt the frigid breath of death wash over him, and then he was flying, upward and into the light.

Chapter Seven

Coming to Terms

Echoes resounded within echoes. Muffled sensations intruded on the fringes of discernment. A morass of confusing thoughts and ideas fluttered sedately in the ether like snowflakes before settling around him. The all-consuming waves of pain gradually receded, and after an eternity of solitude, one defining impression remained.

I'm dreaming.

Marcus reached for that hope and clung on. A sense of awareness slowly returned.

So why am I not waking?

Then he remembered.

My chest! Hands flew to his breastbone. He probed and prodded for any sign of the arrow that had taken him from his

saddle, but his efforts only left him more perplexed. *Nothing?
I . . . Oh, no! I'm dead and on my way into Hades.*

He lifted his head and tried to get a sense of where he was,
but an all-encompassing void surrounded him, confusing his
perceptions.

*But if so, where in the underworld am I? This doesn't fit
any of the descriptions.*

His vision rippled, and a strange tingling sensation washed
over him. Marcus became conscious of the fact that he could
now feel the air entering and exiting his lungs. He was surprised
to see a point of light appear in the distance. It grew larger by
the second. Marcus attempted to sit up, only to discover his
muscles couldn't obey. Struggling to avoid rising panic, he
willed himself to patience and tried to formulate a plan of action. *Okay. If I'm dead or dreaming, there's nothing I can do
at this point. It's beyond my control. Perhaps I'm merely expected to observe?*

He contented himself to watch, and found himself feeling
much more confident.

The brightness continued to swell. Marcus realized it was
approaching him, and he was sure he could hear a faint shuffling sound, as if someone were walking along a corridor. The
image slowly clarified into that of a man carrying a lantern.
Marcus fixated on him, the first object of clarity he'd laid eyes
on for what seemed like an age.

Marcus could see that the man was dressed like a member
of the senate.

But what would a member of our government be doing here?

The visitor came closer, seemingly unconcerned by the
strangeness of the surroundings. As he did so, certain details
Marcus had initially missed became manifest. The man's gait
was almost regal, as if he were someone used to wielding power.
His clothes, although similar to that of a senator, were subtly

different. Instead of the usual white toga dictated by law, this new arrival wore a textured robe of opulence. The fabric appeared similar to mother of pearl, and shimmered through all manner of pastel shades in the lantern's light.

As mesmerizing as this was, Marcus gasped aloud when he caught sight of the stranger's features. *He's not . . . he's . . . How can anyone be that tall?*

The man extended his hand, palm forward, in salute. The gesture conveyed a sense of camaraderie and open friendship. A kindly face smiled in welcome. The wisdom of ages was reflected in his countenance and aquamarine eyes which, along with an abnormally high forehead, gave the stranger the appearance of someone who had spent decades amassing knowledge.

But who is he? I've never seen anyone like him before.

As if replying to Marcus's thoughts, the visitor inclined his head. "Greetings, Marcus Galerius Brutus. I am but an ambassador to those who desperately need your help. You may call me Gul Sariff, or simply Sariff. First Magister of Rhomane and representative of the Grand Senatum."

"I don't know you, Sir," Marcus countered, "nor am I aware of anyone like you. You refer to Rome as if familiar with it, yet you mispronounce certain words."

A chair appeared beside Marcus. Taking a seat, Sariff replied, "That's because we've never met, Marcus. Nor have I been to the city you know of as Rome. In fact, I've never visited your world, although I am amazed by the many similarities between our two cultures."

"My world?" Marcus was confused by the inference. "What do you mean? Who are you and where are you from? What *is* this place? And where are my men?"

"Please, Marcus, do not vex yourself. You have many questions and I assure you, I am here to answer them all. But first, I must help you understand the changes now taking place among the people you arrived with, yourself included."

Sariff waved his hand in the air, and Marcus discovered he could move. Seizing the opportunity to do something of his own volition, Marcus sat up and kicked his legs over the side of the bed. Leaning forward, he attempted to grasp the mysterious messenger by the shoulders, demanding, "How did you manage–?"

He froze in shock as his hand passed right through Sariff. "What are you, Sir? A demon? A trickster sent by Mercury to torment me?"

The light of the lantern flared and as its radiance faded, Sariff reached out to clasp Marcus's right wrist in formal greeting. Marcus jumped as he felt the strong and reassuring grip of his new acquaintance.

"Forgive me, Marcus," Sariff sighed. "I did not mean to alarm you."

Releasing his grasp, Sariff made himself more comfortable. "As you have correctly surmised, you are dreaming. I am a mere representation of someone who once lived here long ago. I have been sent to welcome you to your new home. Think of me as a portrait come to life. An animated sculpture if you will, dispatched to help you understand what has happened. Let me assure you, both you and a great many others are safe. They are likewise being instructed in things that are essential for your continued wellbeing. The experience of this waking dream allows me to assist you more speedily than would otherwise be possible."

Marcus digested the implications of Sariff's words in silence. He glanced about. *How dire this place is. If only I could see my home, one last time.*

The air shimmered once more, and Marcus was amazed to find himself in the kitchen of his house back in Rome. Neither his wife, Sophia, nor any of the family's slaves were anywhere in sight. Regardless, the fire roared warmly in the hearth, and the smell of baking bread made his mouth water. He moved, and the stool scraped loudly across the floor.

This can't be real. He rubbed one of his fingers along a knot of wood in the tabletop, and clearly perceived the difference in texture. Narrowing his eyes, he stared at Sariff. "You did that. Somehow you know what I'm thinking and . . . and want me to be happy. Relaxed."

Sariff's face broke into a broad grin. "Excellent! You are most perceptive for one from your era." He became serious. "But please, allow me to introduce a companion. Time is precious, and as leader of a great host, I need *you* to understand what's at stake. Like me, my friend is only a representative of someone we call the Architect. Do not be alarmed by his appearance, for together we will help you understand what you need to know."

Sariff gestured to one side, as if ushering in another guest. "Marcus, please meet a sentinel. You will find his insights most revealing . . .

" . . . Sentinel?"

A ball of light appeared in the air between them, thrumming with power. Before Marcus could say a word, a cheery voice rang out. "Greetings, Marcus Galerius Brutus. I am a custodian of the Architect. It is a pleasure to meet you."

Marcus lurched backward, knocking his stool over. "It speaks!"

"Of course I do," replied the construct, gravitating toward him. "Like Sariff, I am but an instrument through which our two cultures can communicate in fellowship and understanding. I apologize if my appearance shocks you, but I find it suits my function rather well. Now, as Sariff has inferred, time is pressing. May we begin?"

Marcus was lost for words. Looking between the image of a man long dead and a wraith come to life, he clamped his jaws firmly shut and refused to give in to the madness he felt sure was trying to devour him. Nodding mutely, he thought, *why not?*

"Excellent," replied the sentinel. "Now, although you will find this difficult to comprehend at first, you are, in fact, within the fortified city of Rhomane on the world of Arden. You were transferred . . ."

*

A jumbled maelstrom of conflicting images and energies stormed about Lex. So overwhelmingly powerful were those sensations, he didn't know which way was up or down. Neither could he comprehend where the hell he was, nor what was happening to him. The only thing he felt sure about was that he was falling from an obscene height, and plummeting to certain death.

His mind tumbled with him, the thoughts cartwheeling over and over. *He shot me! The bastard actually shot me. One of his own men. In cold blood. And he'd sided with the enemy, too. Rebelled against the government. I can't believe he shot me.*

Unadulterated fear skittered along his spine as the terrifying drop continued. His skin burned like ice and it felt as though his stomach were endeavoring to burst free from his throat. He clamped his teeth shut in an attempt to keep the bile from rising, but that only increased the pressure in his chest.

Am I actually breathing?

Without knowing how, Lex sensed something change around him. It was almost as if someone had strummed an immense chord, and an incredibly deep tone was now throbbing through the ether. An overwhelming desire to relax infused his psyche.

I might as well. I've been falling for so long now, there's no way I'll survive when I hit the ground. Oh well, here goes nothing.

Willing himself to obey the compulsion, Lex went limp. Almost immediately, the relentless spiraling began to lose its rabid ferocity. A sound like babbling water gushing over rocks rushed toward him. He thrilled to a cool surge of vitality that washed across his skin.

His perspective sharpened, and the added clarity allowed Lex to gain a degree of control over his equilibrium. Although the plunge still dominated his world, he became detached from it, as if he were a spectator in a circus watching himself perform. He was sure that any moment his nose-diving doppelganger would somersault like a trapeze artiste, and land lightly on his feet to thunderous applause.

As if responding to his thoughts, the medium through which he was traveling thickened. Something pressed into him on all sides, and Lex felt his ears pop. His world spun and he found himself sitting on a log in front of a roaring campfire in the dead of night. So abrupt was the change that Lex tottered forward, almost tipping into the flames.

"Whoa, young man!" a friendly voice cried. Strong hands gripped his arm, pulling him away from danger. "I just made that. Pity to waste it, eh?"

Eh? I'm holding a cup of coffee. Where the hell did that come from? Lex jumped up and only just saved the scalding liquid from spilling down his pants.

"Thank you. That would have hurt a—" The words choked off in his throat. His jaw dropped open. The mug clunked to the floor.

"Here, let me get you another one," his companion offered. "It's a cold night, and I think you'll be needing something to warm you up after the shock."

Lex couldn't help but stare at the person next to him. Although he was dressed like a cavalry general, he obviously wasn't. Some of the minor details in the insignia and cut of the uniform he was wearing were off. Additionally, he was just too darn tall.

Ignoring him, the officer retrieved Lex's cup and busied himself pouring some more coffee. Then he stood up. *Jesus! He's towering over me, and I'm six feet tall. So what does that make him?* Lex looked closer. *And look at his eyes. No one I've ever seen has eyes that color. Come to that, his face is . . . is . . . ?*

"What's up, son?" The mystery soldier grinned and slapped Lex heartily on the arm. "Cat got your tongue? Never seen a stranger like me before?"

"Er, I apologize . . . Sir? But you're not from around these parts, are you?"

Lex turned to study the sky. He recognized many of the familiar constellations, and the half moon cast sufficient light for him to distinguish the open plains about them. *But exactly where these parts are, I couldn't tell you. Something about them is . . . I don't know. Strange?*

"My name is Beren. Sol Beren," replied the imposing figure in front of him, "and in answer to your question, Lex . . . Yes, I am a *Sir*. By your references, a general. Although not one you'd find in any of your armies."

"So who do you serve, General? And how did we wind up in this place?"

"Ah, the answer to that is quite complex. But it's why I'm here." Extending a huge hand back toward two logs positioned side by side, Beren said, "Come. Let's sit down and talk. I know you'll have a huge list of questions, and my associates and I will be happy to answer them in a way that will help you come to terms with what's happening."

As they made their way to their seats, Lex asked, "Before I . . . before all . . . *this*, I was with some friends. We were in an ambush. Do you know if any of them survived?"

"Oh, you mean your commander and the native people of that prairie you were snatched from? Yes, many of them are quite safe."

Lex almost dropped his mug again. "What? Do you mean Captain Houston is here?"

"Of course. As are your fellow officers. What were their names again? Smith? Yes, that's it, Wilson Smith. Samuel J. Clark, too. A charming surgeon with a most cordial manner. Oh, and quite a number of those indigenous folk. Their chieftains are quite remarkable. Do you know, they've remained calm during the entire relocation process? My colleagues are quite impressed."

Chieftains? Does he mean Snow Blizzard and his cronies?

"I see," Lex mumbled. Slumping down, he vented a huge sigh of frustration. Then he cursed himself for forgetting the obvious. "And what about the young woman we were escorting? And her uncle? Please tell me they made it?"

"Lex! Relax. The process involved in bringing you here was quite complex. Let me assure you, almost your entire platoon survived the transition without incident. The young native girl and her protector included."

"Thank God!" *At least I didn't screw that aspect up.* He gazed into the flames. *I wonder what other surprises I'm going to get tonight.*

A ball of lightning appeared above the fire.

Lex managed to retain a firm grip on his coffee cup until it spoke.

*

Mac soared. Blinding white light engulfed him, burning him as it purified his soul. Transformed, he was lifted ever higher into the heavens.

So this is what it feels like to die. Strange, I thought it'd be over before I knew it. Still, this isn't so bad.

The light dimmed. As his sight returned, he dared to peek between eyelids that had been squeezed firmly shut. A frantic, kaleidoscopic rush of conflicting impressions rushed past. They were followed by a deafening roar that threatened to swamp him. He screamed, only to discover no sound issued from his lungs.

I must be riding the leading edge of the shockwave.

Mac thought back to a previous time in his career when he'd been caught in a car bomb blast. On that occasion, he had been swatted away from the source of the explosion as if he were an insect in a gale. As the initial surprise receded, he had found himself sailing serenely through the air, as if swimming in a water-like medium. The trauma of the incident had turned everything into a torpid, slow-motion drama, and Mac remembered how weird it was to see every detail of the incident unfold around him so lethargically.

But this was different.

This experience was like being trapped in a wind tunnel, bowled along by a hurricane that was straining to overtake him. It overpowered his ability to think straight. Yet he hadn't managed to qualify for Special Forces without being resilient.

Straining against the gale, Mac twisted and turned as hard as he could in an attempt to check on the welfare of the men under his command. *Nothing! I can't see a damned thing.*

An overwhelming compression blossomed behind him. Mac felt as though he'd been impaled on a thousand red-hot needles. His skin bubbled and blistered. The burning sensation sank into the pit of his stomach, and he doubled up into a fetal position. Just when he thought he might burst, his senses shattered. Before he knew it, he found himself in open free fall.

What . . . What the hell?

Surprised by both the transformation and the abrupt cessation of pain, he tumbled out of control. Over and over he went, cart wheeling at an ever faster rate as his speed of descent increased. A thrill surged through him. Familiarity gained from thousands of hours in the air filled him with sudden confidence. *This, I know how to do!*

Reining in his panic, Mac adjusted his position, managing to slow the spin sufficiently for him to lean into the dive. Seconds later, he was on the hill and accelerating to terminal velocity. *Yeeeeeeehaaa!*

The sheer exhilaration of the experience temporarily wiped his dilemma from his mind. Arching his body to achieve the perfect stable position, he did his best to take stock. *Where on earth am I?*

Using his hands and feet, Mac began a very slow spiral and surveyed his surroundings. Blue sky, as clear as a lens, and cotton-candy clouds stretched off in every direction. Although he appeared to be bathed in glorious sunshine, he couldn't actually pinpoint the sun anywhere above him. When he looked down, Mac was also unable to see any sign of land. And that was a paradox. *If I can't see land, that means I'm so high I shouldn't be able to breathe. I'd be on the edge of space. And I'd be freezing to death. But I'm not.*

Then he noticed he wasn't wearing a parachute.

He accepted the situation stoically. *Okay! Actually, this helps. There's no way it can be real. I was on an oil rig and a nuclear bomb had just gone off in my face.*

He glanced around the endless vista. *So. I'm either dead or dying, and on my way to goodness knows where, or I some-*

how survived and am in a hospital. Whether in a coma, on
drugs, or a combination of the two, I don't know. But this *isn't*
real. So what—

"An excellent deduction, Alan," a voice out of nowhere
announced. "Or would you prefer Mac?"

A shadow flashed past and before he knew it, Mac was
buddies with an unknown, fellow skydiver. Someone, he noted,
who also wasn't wearing any equipment. Nor, if he was seeing
things right, did he appear to be entirely human.

Mac suppressed a snort. *Looks like I'm suffering from*
severe head injuries, too. Where am I getting this stuff from?

"Oh, you're not suffering from hallucinations, if that's
what you're worried about," his mystery companion said as
he maneuvered closer, "but, as you have correctly surmised,
neither are your current surroundings authentic. They are, in
fact, a fabrication. Think of them as a lucid dream-like reality,
through which we can communicate safely."

"Okaaay," Mac replied. "Say I buy what you're selling.
Who are you? What is this place and why am I here?"

"A man who likes to get straight to the point," the stranger
countered, with a smile. "Very well, this may save a lot of time
in the long run. My name is Psi Calen. Just call me Calen. Like
you, I'm not really here. I am part of a very sophisticated AI
program left behind by the residents of the planet you now find
yourself marooned on. And yes, before you ask, you really are
on an entirely different world than Earth. A fact that will be
proven to you very shortly.

"My image belongs to one of the leading scientists of the
people who once populated this place. Through him, we hope
to explain why it was so necessary to bring you here against
your will."

"Seriously?"

"Seriously, my good friend. Here, let me demonstrate."

Calen waved his hand, and they both began to rapidly decelerate. Coming to a halt in midair, the avatar pointed to one side. "Observe. Thankfully, you come from a time period sufficiently advanced for you to grasp many of the concepts you are about to see."

The air rippled in front of them, and Mac found himself peering down on a vast chamber. Although the lighting within it was subdued, illumination was provided by a large number of very complex-looking monitors lining the walls and arranged in ranks through the center of the room. A cushioned therapy platform was positioned in front of each console, and a multitude of patients lay sleeping on the beds beneath them.

Every person wore a simple coronet made of what looked like silver metal. The bands themselves shone brightly from within. Above them, strange glowing balls zipped to and fro, buzzing and thrumming with power and hidden purpose. Calen pointed to one of the slumbering occupants. "Do you know him?"

Mac peered closer before letting out a whistle of surprise. "That's me!"

"Yes. You will be pleased to know all members of your particular team survived the transition through the gateway to Arden. They, along with a number of other people from the drilling installation, are currently undergoing treatment and induction."

The radiance encompassing several of the nearby positions brightened momentarily, allowing Mac to recognize Mark Stevens, Sean Masters, and Sam Pell. Looking further along the ward, he could see the series of medical stations curving away into the distance. *There must be thousands of people!* Mac was stunned. "So, why have you gone to all this trouble to get us here?"

"Because we need your help," Calen replied solemnly. "May I introduce the colleague I spoke of earlier?"

"I guess so. Are you going to wake me up for that?"

"Not just yet, my friend." Calen's kindly face creased in regret. "Forgive me, but the neural cocoon we have placed about you allows us to download information directly into your mind at a much faster rate than would normally be possible."

Mac couldn't help but laugh as he thought of one of his favorite sci-fi trilogy classics from the turn of the twenty-first century. He had always loved the series, as it depicted the struggle of a group of human survivors who fought an ongoing guerilla war against their machine overlords.

Calen looked thoughtful as he assessed the contents of Mac's mind. Then he broke into a broad grin. "A reasonable analogy. While our techniques are not as succinct as those employed within your work of fiction, you will nevertheless find our methods quite remarkable."

"I'm sure I will," Mac replied, still not quite believing he was really here. "When do we start?"

"Now would be as good a time as any. We are still treating some of the radiation burns you sustained when the nuclear device initiated, so we can use the time wisely."

Gesturing calmly, Calen removed the scene of the chamber. Mac discovered himself seated behind a desk within a familiar briefing room back at Special Forces Headquarters, London. An inviting pot of Earl Grey tea awaited his attention, next to a bone china cup and saucer.

How thoughtful!

Helping himself, he noted Calen now stood in front of the incident board at the head of the room. Calen caught his eye, inclined his head, and said, "Mac, please let me introduce a sentinel."

A concentrated ball of plasma appeared in the air, midway between the two men. A cheery voice rang out, "Welcome to Arden, Lieutenant Alan McDonald. It is a pleasure to meet you.

As you have a basic grasp of current events, I will begin by summarizing the history of Arden. Through it, you will appreciate what led to our predicament, and why it was felt necessary for us to reach out over eighty thousand light years for help."

"Eighty thousand light years?" Mac was astonished by the scope of the task involved.

"Yes. Although we occupy the same galaxy, we are as far apart as you can get."

A rippling curtain of energy fluttered down from the ceiling. As soon as it touched the floor, a holographic image of the Milky Way bloomed to life. Two glowing points of light within it were joined by a sparkling ribbon of diffused colors.

The sentinel continued, "The blue area represents your home world, Earth. The green one, Arden. That glittering thread is the medium through which you were brought here. Now listen carefully, I am about to alter your state of consciousness into one more conducive to accelerated learning. Are you ready to begin?"

Mac gulped down his tea. After replacing the cup on the saucer, he nodded. "Please. Go ahead." *Take the red pill! Take the red pill!*

The room spun, and everything went dark. A brilliant point of light appeared directly overhead. No sooner had he seen it than Mac was sucked into a maelstrom of scintillating horizons.

Chapter Eight

Salt in the Wound

Commander Saul Cameron scrutinized the latest findings with growing concern. To say what he saw troubled him was an understatement. Ruminating for a moment, he widened the holo-field of his projector and incorporated the results of similar reports from the previous six years. For the next five minutes, his eyes flicked from side to side as he compared the multitude of charts and graphs.

"Mohammed. Are these estimates accurate?" he mumbled, without shifting his gaze from the confusing mass of facts and figures before him.

"I'm afraid they are, Sir," Mohammed Amine replied. "If degradation continues at its current rate, we'll be unable to sustain viable crop rotation within three years. Four at the most. Livestock will last longer than that, but without a varied diet, quality will suffer."

"Sentinel!" Saul snapped. "Does the Architect have any suggestions as to how we can reverse, or at least delay the . . . the slow death that's being projected here?"

"I'm sorry, Commander," the custodian replied cheerily, "but I have been unable to extrapolate that information. The calculations required are as infinite as they are complex. Remember, since the siege began, Rhomane's choice of bio-templates has been severely limited. We have to utilize what we have very carefully to maintain the delicate balance of nutrients, minerals and trace elements. Add to that the harsh reality we face of a gradually diminishing herd stock and you can appreciate the factors that need considering before we even think of suggesting an official resolution."

Sighing heavily, Saul flopped back in his seat and massaged the bridge of his nose between thumb and forefinger. His voice was heavy with resignation. "I don't suppose Calen is available? I could do with his gut instincts right now."

"Calen's avatar is still engaged with our fresh candidates," the sentinel responded, "however, I will convey your request via main-stem."

Saul bit down his frustration. He knew it was no use arguing with the Architect. His request was logged in the AI's nervous system now, and would remain there until the Archive felt inclined to free the stored sum of Arden's former scientific champion from what it felt were more pressing matters.

"Very well," he muttered, "just leave us a précis of what we've been delivered this time, and I'll give our imminent starvation greater thought tomorrow. Hopefully by then you'll have something more constructive to add."

"Very well, Commander. Downloading data to your console . . . now."

Having completed its task, the construct disappeared, leaving the two men alone to stare at each other in bemused silence. Neither wanted to be the first to acknowledge this latest development, which was sure to be viewed as another nail in their collective coffin lid.

Leaning slowly forward, Saul placed two great hands on the desktop. Made of native orach wood, its color and texture reminded him of a compelling blend of both mahogany and oak. Tough, resilient, and full of character.

Exactly the qualities I need to display now, more than ever.

Swiveling in his chair, he reached down, tugged open the bottom drawer, and removed two, elaborately designed, quartz tumblers. Saul placed them on the table before him. As he chewed things over, he twirled them between his fingers, absentmindedly watching as the sun refracted along the keen edges of the glass.

His mind made up, Saul dipped again, a squat block of a decanter clutched tightly in his grasp. The rich amber liquid within it also caught the light, and flickered through subtle hues of topaz, gold, and ochre. Holding the fiery beverage before him, he raised an eyebrow toward his companion. "Join me?"

"Make it a double," Mohammed replied. "I think I'm going to need it after *that* news."

Pouring two generous measures, Saul handed one to his friend and tapped glasses. A satisfactory *clink* echoed around the room as the heavy crystal kissed. "To absent friends," he murmured.

"Absent friends."

Taking a gulp, Saul savored the satin smooth burn of the potent spirit now working its way toward his stomach. It put him in a reflective mood. "How long have we known each other, Mohammed?"

"Altogether? Ten years, why?"

Saul swirled his drink around as he reminisced over former times. "Ten years. Such a short space of time when you think about it. But we've been through so much together, haven't we? The Tyrian Colony uprising of 2339, where you were first assigned to my command. The Breach of Pintus 12 the following year. Operation Trident, which ended the war in 2342. Then, just when you thought you'd seen the last of me, I go and get chosen as commander of the Pegasus Dwarf Galaxy expedition. The very latest design in deep space starships to play with. New experimental Light-Drive engines to test over the long haul. And they gave me a choice as to who I'd like as my executive officer. I remember thinking, what fool would love to throw a safe and secure life in civvy street away, to come and accompany me on a one-way mission to another world in a different galaxy? Who would be crazy enough to want to join one thousand five hundred other souls, encased in four hundred million tons of metal, hurtling through the void in excess of the speed of light in suspended animation? Of course, I immediately thought of you—"

"Why, thank you!" Mohammed saluted him with his tumbler.

"And so, we all went to sleep in 2345, expecting to wake up thirty years later in orbit around our new home. And where do we end up?"

"A lot, lot further away," Mohammed murmured, staring off into space, "in time, anyway." His gaze hardened. "But do you know what really gets me about all this, Sir? It's the fact I didn't have a choice. Yes, I know we volunteered for a one-way trip. And yes, I understand we would have all died, ten months out, as we accelerated into the meteor storm that led to our transference here. It's just so damned frustrating not having any . . . any . . . ."

" . . . control over your own destiny?" Saul offered, knowing exactly how his friend was feeling. "Because I know for a fact some of the crew would have chosen oblivion and release, rather than the endless nightmare of existing here for the last two years."

"Amen to that!" Mohammed raised his glass again, this time for a refill.

As he poured, Saul continued, "But what really sticks in my craw is the fact that we've been through all that. Cheated fate on numerous occasions. Skipped certain death by being selected to come here. Faced countless assaults from the Horde. And now we face defeat from starvation, just because some genius in the past didn't think to leave a wide enough source reservoir for the replicators to get their base samples from. I tell you, Mohammed. I feel as if someone's taking a huge dump on us from a great height."

"I don't think it was Calen's, or anybody's fault, come to that," Mohammed said quietly. "What the Ardenese did was a stroke of brilliance. Who'd have thought their survival would come down to a simple war of attrition *after* they'd entered the Ark? The livestock and grains they left should have been sufficient for survivors to be able to guarantee suitable replenishment. But things don't always go as planned, eh?"

"Until now, perhaps?" Easing back his top drawer with one hand, Saul removed an oilcloth-covered item. Placing it on the desk between them, he leaned forward and flicked back the folds, one at a time, until its contents were finally revealed. An old Webley .445 break-top revolver from the early twentieth century. World War One vintage. "Who would have thought such an antiquated weapon might hold the key to our salvation?"

Setting his glass down, Saul lifted the gun, flipped a catch and watched as the drum and barrel fell forward. His gaze came to rest on the remaining bullets. *Just three.*

Sighing, he flicked his wrist, and the housing snapped back together with a satisfying *clunk!* Saul caressed his thumb up and down the side of the revolver and listened to the satisfying click of the chamber as it echoed around the stillness of the room. *But one's enough.*

"You look as if you've made your mind up about something," Mohammed stated.

"I have, my friend." He replaced the gun on the tabletop. "It's all down to this outdated little relic here, which reminded us all so poignantly that progress isn't always to our advantage. You can't blame the Architect, or course. It naturally selected the first candidates from temporal references as close to the Ardenese level of development as possible, thinking that technological sophistication would be the key to salvation. But as they, and successive waves discovered, it was a false hope. Energy-based weapons only fed the Horde, strengthening them as it stirred their savagery to new heights." Saul nodded at the little piece of history in front of him. "It was blind luck that Simon brought this through with him on the seventh intake. An heirloom, passed on from father to son for hundreds of years. Cherished and kept in pristine condition. And just as well, for who could have guessed that centuries later, on a world far, far away from home, a descendent would resort to using it in panic, only to witness its devastating results just before he died?" *And it was blind luck too, that I happened to be there to witness his sacrifice, or we'd still all be stumbling around like fools in the dark.*

"So that's why you asked the Architect to focus on a regressive timeframe?" The realization set Mohammed's eyes alight. "And it also explains the unusual hiatus we've enjoyed over these past few months."

"Precisely! If we're going to survive, we've got to take the fight to them. Before, that would have been impossible. The

Horde would have eaten us alive. But now? This last intake might be just what we need to turn the tide, even if they aren't what we expected."

Mohammed leaned forward. "How goes the induction?"

"Interesting would be the word I'd use." A wry smile graced Saul's face in a rare moment of humor. "It would appear we have candidates from a very wide spectrum . . ." Bringing a more detailed précis up on the screen, Saul skimmed the basics, " . . . ranging from the first through to the twenty-first century. Quite a mix, especially when you realize it's been spiced up by the inclusion of a whole bunch of natural antagonists."

"What? Combatants from *both* sides have been included?"

"Oh yes. As I say, it'll make things quite volatile until they've had a chance to calm down."

"Do you envisage any serious problems? You know I hate handling disciplinary matters."

"That's why I campaigned to have you elected as my second-in-command, old friend. You don't like it, which makes you exactly the right candidate for the job." Saul sat back again and retrieved his drink. "But to answer your question. No, I don't see you having too much difficulty. Their mutual antipathy aside, I think an early introduction to our friends outside will help refocus all that aggression in the right direction. Don't you?"

Mohammed didn't look convinced.

Saul had an idea. "Look, it indicates here, the respective leaders of each faction should be through the first phase soon. Why don't you see if Doctor Solram is free? Ayria is the longest lasting survivor of any of us. She, more than anyone, can emphasize what's at stake. Then, while you're giving them the grand tour, make sure they witness how close we are to the edge. Waning crops. Dwindling livestock. The new skills everyone has to learn. All that devastation on the other side of the wall. Once they see the benefits of mutual cooperation far outweigh their former petty disputes, we'll have them onside soon enough."

"And if not?"

"Well, I'll leave the mechanics up to you, but make it clear to each and every single one of them that we can't afford to have loose cannons in our society. *Their* actions will directly govern *our* choice."

"Choice?"

"Yes. Leave no one in any doubt that how they act will help us decide which side of the wall they get to live on."

"Ouch! That'll rub salt in the wound."

"I do hope so, Mohammed. I really do hope so."

*

Stained-With-Blood sat cross-legged on the floor of his sparsely furnished room. Staring wide-eyed off into space, he saw nothing of his surroundings. Neither did he give conscious thought to the sharpening stone he was repeatedly grazing along the razor-keen edge of his tomahawk, Heaven's-Claw. Instead, he was consumed by the vision quest now spreading its tendrils through his mind.

Reciting an ancient mantra as he soared, Stained-With-Blood let the intuitive rhythms generated by his actions guide him to the spirits.

The air wavered, and before he could fully appreciate what had happened, Stained-With-Blood found himself atop a wide, barren plateau. An old warrior squatted on the ground near the precipice, staring out at the plains below and the setting sun in the distance. To one side, a huge roaring fire saluted the darkening sky with its light and warmth. Walking toward the elder,

Stained-With-Blood struggled to recognize the stranger's identity. The flickering glow added fluidity to the brave's features, which caused them to ripple as the shadows increased.

As he drew closer, recognition caused Stained-With-Blood to halt mid-stride. *Napioa! The Old Man himself is here.* As quietly as possible, Stained-With-Blood moved to sit next to the Father Creator. Whatever happened now, he knew he must remain silent and still in order for the vision to unfold.

Napioa let the dying rays of the setting sun stream across the landscape, forming contrasts of magnificent hue. He took no notice, for his eyes were focused beyond the veil between life and death. A wind sprang into existence, its fetid breath hot and stale. It lashed at the aged warrior without letup, continuing its rampage until the world had fallen dark and the moon was high in the sky. Yet nothing could ruin the Creator's composure. To Stained-With-Blood, the Old Man looked to be waiting for a sign.

A star fell from heaven. Landing lightly in the fire, it sizzled and crackled for over an hour before cooling sufficiently to form a pool of glowing metal. Deciding the time was right, Napioa rose from his position and scooped the molten blob from within the crucible. Using his bare hands, he compressed the mass together and fashioned an intricate blade from the remains.

The knife pulsed with an argent gleam, reflecting the moon's rays about the mountaintop. Brandishing the dagger toward the stars, he sliced the restraining band around the crown of his head. Raven-black hair flowed free, streaming into the breeze behind him. His mane grew longer and longer, and soon, whirlpools of midnight iridescence swept across the hilltop with obsidian tornados.

Turning his back to the gale, Napioa slashed through the swirling strands, cutting them free from his body. Condensing into a single, spinning vortex, they rocketed skyward before plunging back into the embers. Sparks flared. Like miniature fireflies, they danced around Napioa's head, singing.

The Creator took his newly fashioned weapon and drew the blade across his palm. Holding his hand before him, he squeezed his fist tightly, so that scarlet vitality pooled into a natural bowl-shaped depression in the rock at his feet. Stained-With-Blood noticed a thin gully leading away from the hollow and toward the cliff.

As the ruby-red ichor flowed toward the edge, it ran into a wall of invisible resistance. After surging and boiling for a moment, it reared upward. A birch sapling sprouted from the depths of the turbulent liquid. Growing quickly, it pushed down thick roots and matured into a majestic specimen of impressive height.

The rock along the lip of the chasm cracked. The tree shuddered and began to tip forward. As it fell, it abruptly budded, before exploding into the air. Stained-With-Blood watched, transfixed, as the seeds were caught up by glowing cinders from the fire and carried away into the starlit sky.

A further blast rang out. Sooty ash like leprous snowflakes descended across the valley. An unknown amount of time passed and the moon wheeled through the sky. Whines and whistles echoed up from the plains below. Drawn by the scent of fresh blood, others came to investigate.

Glowing eyes appeared. Crawling out of the gloom, coyotes slunk forward with their tails between their legs. Tricky beasts, deceptive and sly, each wearing the mark of Lakota, Sioux, and Apache. Reaching Napioa, they cast sidelong glances toward Stained-With-Blood before curling up at the Creator's feet. They seemed ill at ease in the presence of a dream-walker. Some raised their heads, bared their fangs, and growled.

The Old Man reacted instantly. Cuffing them with the back of his hand, he glowered at each beast until they huddled on the floor, yowling in submission to his will.

Fish fell from the heavens. Salmon, trout, and pike. Each branded with the familiar sigil of enemies. Raising his hand, Napioa seared them instantly, and the succulent smell of roasted flesh stung the back of Stained-With-Blood's nostrils.

The coyotes fell to, eating with gusto. With an expectant look on his face, the Creator stared at the alpha. Yipping once, the huge male left his feasting and nudged through the pack. Selecting the choicest fish, he lifted it tenderly within his jaws and skulked toward Stained-With-Blood. Dropping a fat salmon at the warrior's feet, he nudged the morsel toward the brave with his nose and sat back, tail wagging, waiting.

"Do you understand?" Napioa said, his voice deep and resonant. Holding Stained-With-Blood's gaze, he swept a hand toward the east and bellowed, "Behold!"

The fresh clean sun of a new day crested a ridge of unfamiliar mountains in the distance. Behind it, shining in glory, another star flared. Its brilliance intensified, growing to form an orange-red titan that dwarfed the yellow pretender before it. Everyone atop the plateau was bathed in solace, warmth and unity.

Napioa's eyes blazed white, and Stained-With-Blood reeled away. The world dimmed, and the Cree warrior felt himself flowing backward along an invisible tunnel as the brightness folded in on itself.

Napioa's words echoed in his mind. *Do you understand?*

Sensation returned. Stained-With-Blood could feel the cool hard floor once more, hear the sound of stone on metal, and see the subtle glow of artificial light through his eyelids. He sighed deeply, and released a breath that had strained to be expressed for what seemed like hours.

Before he did anything else, he reviewed the events he had just witnessed. Reflecting both on the vision and his knowledge of the first nations, Stained-With-Blood couldn't prevent the bitterness from overwhelming him. *We are a united people. Cree, all tribes created from the same blood. How could we have turned against ourselves in such a manner? Never before have the clans betrayed their own flesh in support of another's.*

Do you understand? A voice whispered from the shadows, making him jump.

"I understand all right!" he grumbled, "but I don't have to like it."

Surging to his feet, he approached the only door within his room and knocked once. A sentinel appeared in the air.

"Good afternoon," it said, "how may I help you?"

Stained-With-Blood had discovered it helped him to think of these apparitions as messengers to the gods. "I need to speak with the other leaders of my people. Soon. We must fill the hole that has eaten its way into our souls."

"I see," replied the sprite, flaring warmly in response. "That is gratifying to hear, especially under the circumstances. Please remain here while we facilitate such a meeting."

It blinked out of existence, leaving Stained-With-Blood to answer to an empty room. *Where else would I wait?*

Resigning himself to another delay, he returned to sit on his bed and meditate on his experience. One part of the dream quest still troubled him, for it had been cryptic in its flavor.

Why am I to look to a distant star that turns into a sun? Isn't that a bit obvious?

Chapter Nine

We Are the Ninth

The domed Hall of Remembrance was vast. Despite its size, the chamber had been cunningly designed to amplify sound. Doctor Ayria Solram's steps rang out clearly as she walked toward a huge cenotaph-like structure that had been constructed in the exact center of the room, opposite a set of massive windows. Clicking off into the furthest reaches of the auditorium, her footfalls echoed twice about the room before fading.

Over fifty pairs of eyes followed her closely. That wasn't surprising. At forty years of age, Ayria cut an imposing figure. Standing well over six feet tall, she matched the stature of most of the men now staring at her in wide-eyed admiration. Ayria wore her waist length, midnight blue hair in a no-nonsense braid which didn't hide the fact that her mane was glorious. Curling over her shoulder and across her torso like a well-fed python, it captured attention whenever she moved.

Her smooth, softly tanned skin and dark eyes were in stark contrast to the sterile white lab coat she wore. Nevertheless, the overall effect was striking.

Indicating the monument with a sweep of her arms, she said, "Now, this should be of particular interest to you. This is called the Reverence."

All faces turned to study the twenty-foot high monolith. Fashioned from a richly veined slab of rock, it appeared to be seamless, and resonated gently from all four sides with a softly pulsing, blue phosphorescence. The top of the structure was formed into a trapezoid, upon which rested a glowing sphere.

Aryia pointed to it. "The light you see is not just a power source. It's also an indicator, intimately linked to the life energies of every living soul currently residing on Arden. Your esoteric signatures were added shortly after you arrived here, and as you can see, the device is glowing with a gentle aquamarine radiance."

Gesturing around the outer edge of the hall, she drew the crowd's attention to a number of astonishing bas-reliefs which had been cut directly into the fabric of the wall. Stretching from floor to ceiling, each was of a similar size and gave the impression that the open leaves of a gigantic tome had been superimposed onto the rock.

A small dais had been erected before each frieze, upon which an artifact or plaque had been positioned, highlighted by a softly humming radiance.

"Are those the names of refugees I can see on the pages?" Marcus Brutus asked, astonished by the sheer volume of people who had been taken from their homes.

"I'm afraid not," Ayria replied. "While it is true that the Architect has relocated literally thousands of us over the years, the lists you see here represent our dear brothers and sisters who have fallen to the Horde."

A palpable shock ran through the entire group.

"Are you serious?" spluttered James Houston. "But there are . . . thousands. How many names are up there, lady?"

"Just Ayria, please. Or Doctor. In answer to your question, the sacrifice of over twenty-one thousand souls has been recorded here. When someone dies, the Reverence registers the missing life force and turns red for an entire day. It also burns their name into a corresponding page."

"Holy God!" Houston turned to stare at a young cavalry officer standing next to him. Addressing him, Houston whispered, "We've got to stick together, Wilson. Just you and me. Watch each other's backs."

Some of the other men standing close by glared at the pair in disdain.

"If I may ask a question, Ayria?" Marcus interjected. "How is it that I, a humble soldier of Rome, can read and understand this writing? I recognize it as a form I have never witnessed before, yet I find myself comprehending its meaning almost instantly."

"That's due to nanotechnology," Ayria replied. Walking toward him, she tapped the side of her own head. "Remember, the avatars explained something of the process we use here. Because a great many people are being brought together from across time, the Ardenese had to make sure we understood each other clearly. Even a single language can change radically during the course of many centuries, so they thought it best we were educated in theirs. They were a very advanced people, socially as well technologically. And because they had employed the use of artificial intelligence as a means to educate themselves for a number of decades prior to their fall, they realized the best way to help us was to adapt those tiny little machines for our use. They're inside our brains right now, teaching us and allowing us to learn new things at a greatly accelerated rate."

Marcus frowned.

"Have I confused you?"

"No, my lady, not at all. I look bewildered because I can grasp the sense of what you're saying . . ." He turned to look about him in wonder, " . . . and yet, this is all so very strange to me."

Marcus glanced toward his compatriots and shrugged. Like him, Flavius and their fellow legionnaires were still finding the adjustments difficult to cope with. They were warriors, and unaccustomed to such godlike contrivances.

An awkward silence ensued.

Seizing the moment, Mac stepped forward. "I take it each engraving represents an actual influx of candidates?"

A sea of faces turned to look at him. Until now, Mac and his men had kept themselves apart, content to stand quietly to one side with a group of stoic Native Americans. However, Mac had noticed how each of the lists was arranged. Pointing to the wall, he continued, "There are nine open books along the circumference. One is blank, so that must indicate us, as no one is dead yet. Therefore, the other eight obviously refer to those who have come and gone before us, yes?"

"Very astute. Lieutenant Alan McDonald, isn't it?"

"I'm famous!" Mac replied, surprise evident on his face. Cocking a thumb toward his team, he added, "But the guys will tell you I'm quite informal. *They* call me all sorts of things, most of which I can't repeat." He smiled. "*You* can call me Mac."

"Mac," Ayria replied, inclining her head toward him, "and in case you were wondering, yes, I have read your file. Your whole team's in fact." Her eyes narrowed. "We'll be putting *your* particular skill set to very good use in the coming days, believe me." Sighing, she appeared lost in thought for a moment, before continuing, "But as you have correctly surmised, each frieze does in fact contain a list of those who have perished, respective to their date of arrival and—"

"So we are the ninth?" Marcus cut in, eyes wide with delight.

Everyone stared until the point registered. Although new, the leaders of each faction present had been made aware of all the other parties who had joined them on their very special journey. It was already common knowledge that by far the largest of the groups to arrive during the most recent gathering were the surviving officers and men of the Ninth Legion. A smattering of laughter and light applause rippled through the crowd, although it was noted the Caledonian contingent didn't appreciate the irony.

Grinning broadly, Ayria acknowledged Marcus's point. "Yes, well spotted. You are indeed the ninth and final choice of the Architect to be brought to us. A rather appropriate moment, don't you think?"

Mac stepped forward. Addressing Marcus and his men, he adopted a reverential air. "You were the subject of legend in my time, you know. Even though thousands of years had passed since you disappeared, they had books and films made in your honor."

"Films?" Marcus looked distracted as he tried to employ the nanobots within his brain to translate the concept.

"Think of them as a visualization of a play," Mac explained. "Your legion was one of the finest ever formed. And history records you as marching into the mists of Scot . . . er, Caledonia, and simply disappearing. An entire army of five thousand men." Mac gestured toward the chieftains of the highland tribes, standing in a sullen group at the back. Focusing on one shaven-headed man in particular, dressed in the distinctive blue and black plaid of the northern Iceni tribes, he continued,

"And *your* people were attributed with the distinction of the massacre. No easy feat by anyone's standards."

Cathal MacNoimhin's entire stature swelled with pride. His eyes flashed and he snapped, "And we would have had them too, if it wasn't for that fey storm. They think us wild and stupid. Animals, incapable of rational thought. They were wrong."

Legionnaires and savages eyed each other, posturing, flexing their fingers and chests before Marcus admitted, "Oh, you can fight all right. I'll give you that. Caught us with our pants down, too. Dirty way to fight. But effective."

"Victory is victory," hissed a brutish hulk standing next to Cathal. Covered in tattoos and wearing the purple and green tartan of Clan Underwood, he cut an imposing figure, even among the outlandish gathering of his kindred.

"Peace, Kohrk," grumbled Cathal, "they cannot doubt our quality or methods. It is the living who write history. Not the dead."

"I don't think there's any doubt you can both fight," Mac continued, diffusing an awkward situation, "both your peoples were . . . *are* experts in your own particular style of warfare. And history does indeed give testimony to the legacy of your efforts. It's amazing to think that your battle continues to be the subject of debate so many centuries after the event. They've even devoted university study articles to 'Whatever happened to the Ninth and their eagle?' Those films were the least of it." He chuckled in appreciation. "At least we all know now, eh?"

Marcus was swayed by a sudden thought. "Where *is* our eagle? It was safely among our lines the last time I saw it, with Sextus Nerva, our aquilifer. Did he make it through?"

"He's here," Mohammed Amine answered, stepping forward from among the throng. Nodding curtly, he added, "Please excuse me. I am second-in-command of the city's defenses, and our strength and deployment comes under my office. Your eagle made it, too. It's safely tucked away in the vault. With your permission, we would like to use it as the sigil for your particular intake."

"Because we're the ninth group?" Marcus asked.

"Mostly." Mohammed paused to consider everyone present. "But as Doctor Solram just mentioned, you are also the last help we will ever receive. We're hoping your standard will represent a fitting symbol of your efforts here on Arden, as you may be our best hope yet."

That statement caught them cold. When no one replied, Mohammed used the silence to his advantage. "As you might imagine, powering a machine capable of spanning a galaxy is taxing enough. For that device to also be able to pierce time is another thing all together. You will all now be aware of the fact that you were snatched prior to your certain deaths, and not only relocated geographically, but also temporally. Even the most sophisticated of the candidates to be brought through previously were jumped hundreds of years into their future. For those of you from Caledonia, we're looking at a five thousand year window. Understand, such a procedure places a huge drain on our resources, for the Architect must not only maintain a constant supply of energy for the Ark itself, but also for the city's defenses, and the everyday functioning of its infrastructure."

"Wasn't that part of the Architect's original strategy?" Mac asked.

"Yes. But the Ardenese didn't expect the Horde to be able to withstand the best the AI could find. The gateway was designed to constantly probe the energy lattices between our worlds, and to home in on the mortality signatures of those showing the most outstanding potential for their needs. Then, once every two to three years, it would activate and pull the most suitable potentials through en masse, usually from three closely related, but alternate time-frames. The Architect hoped the lull between intakes would reduce the amount of concentrated life-force within the city to a bare minimum, thereby reducing the Horde's frenzy. But it didn't. They kept coming. The city wall, along with some of the more important strategic posts within it, is comprised of the densest material we've ever encountered. The Ardenese called it lydium. It's so incredibly compact that nothing should be able to penetrate its structure . . ."

"But it's weakening."

"I'm afraid so. As the respective leaders of your people, you'll all be given the specifics in our first major briefing to-gether, tomorrow morning. In a nutshell, the Horde appears willing to sacrifice every last one of its members in the frenzy to get through. They've lost millions against the shield wall and don't seem to care. We've even seen them storm it and climb over themselves in an effort to reach the ramparts before their biometric thresholds disrupt. It's a crazy strategy, but in the end, it's one that might work. Even a few of those monsters could screw us."

"Why do you think they do it?' Mac was sure the other man was keeping something back. "I've only read a brief report on this enemy, the Horde, but from what I can tell, if they got in, they'd drain us all until we were dead, yes?"

"That's correct. They gain strength and vitality from a wide variety of energy sources. The human body's chemical and electrical processes are like a snack to them. While it's not directly fatal per se, their feeding shuts down the brain and its ability to pass the everyday signals that keep our autonomous systems going. Obviously, without them, we die very quickly."

"And what then?"

"I'm sorry?"

Mac moved through the crowd to position himself in front of the ninth bas-relief. Gesturing to it, he repeated, "And if the Horde *do* manage to breach the city and kill us all, causing the Reverence to inscribe our names here, on this stone, what then? We'll all be dead and they'll have no source of vitality, will they? Will they be trapped here?"

Mohammed appeared uncomfortable with the question. Taking a deep breath, he glanced toward Ayria, admitting, "We're not exactly sure . . ."

Dissatisfied grumbling rumbled through the assembled men.

Signaling for patience, Mac cut them dead. "Let the man speak!"

Miraculously, everyone complied.

Mohammed struggled to find the right words. "What I'm trying to say is, I and a growing number of our strategists think the Ardenese were wrong in their original assessment of the enemy. Because of their single-minded savagery, the Horde was able to overrun thirty planets in twenty-seven star systems in a relatively short period of time. They were relentless, displaying the basest of instincts in their exigency to consume everything in their path. We're beginning to suspect that urgency hid some form of hive-mind mentality that is not only very astute, but cunning, too."

The room remained silent, hanging on every word.

"Define *cunning*, and what that has to do with us?" Mac urged, correctly guessing the question on everyone's lips.

"The record shows that to reach Arden, some of the Horde hid away on fleeing ships. Many of those vessels had been stationed on the outer colonies and were in flight for over two weeks. Some didn't return for months, remaining on standby in deep space until called to assist in the ensuing siege. In each case, it wasn't until they landed on Arden that the enemy finally revealed themselves."

"So they can choose to stop feeding?"

"Yes."

"Voluntarily?"

"It looks that way. They muted their bodies into a condition very similar to hibernation. That's how they were originally discovered. Suspended in some kind of neural-net that allowed them to exist in an undetectable dream-like state."

Mac was intrigued by that information, and turned away, deep in thought.

"So what happens if they kill us all?" Houston chipped in. "You think they'll go back to sleep like a pack of bears waiting for someone else to stroll by?"

"If we lose, we won't be the last food source they could gain access to." So quiet was Mohammed's reply that the men standing at the rear barely heard him.

"What do you mean?"

"Don't forget, the Ark's inside. It contains the remaining essences of the Ardenese people. Men, women, children. Flora. Fauna. All of it. Although it's protected within an artificially created tear in the space-time continuum, it's still there. And the Horde might be able to sense it."

"Oh, that's just great!" Exasperated, Houston threw his hands into the air. "We're trapped in the only diner on the prairie. Talk about out of the frying pan and into the fire. It's just not—"

"You're overlooking something else, too."

Everyone's attention snapped back to Mac. He had the distinct look of someone who had just swallowed something disagreeable. Pointing to the artifacts about them, he explained, "If the Horde is as switched on as you suspect, what makes you think they aren't after the Tec? They are beings of pure energy, after all. Do they have enough to operate the gateway? A portal to a juicy new world they could manipulate time and time again—no pun intended—to guarantee a never-ending feast of unimaginable proportions."

Mohammed and Ayria were clearly shocked. It was plain no one had thought of this strategy before.

"Is that possible, Mohammed?" Ayria gasped. "Could we have overlooked something *this* obvious?"

Mohammed's jaw flapped open.

Mac wasn't finished. "Come to that, doesn't the Architect have a failsafe fitted to prevent such a calamity? A self-destruct button? Or isn't that an option while the Ardenese still exist in retro-vitrio? I'll be damned if I'll just lie down and die while a bunch of monsters are set free to ravage my world."

"It's something I'll make sure we look into immediately," Mohammed mumbled, "thank you for your . . . insight, Lieutenant." Glancing at the doctor, he shrugged and added, "Its prime function *is* to protect their species at all costs. God! How did we miss it?"

"So what about us?" Mac said. "You mentioned earlier we might represent the best hope you've ever had. Why? Aren't *you* from a more advanced era?"

"Ayria would be the best one to answer that," Mohammed replied. "You won't know it yet, but she's one of the longest surviving refugees."

Stepping to one side, Mohammed allowed Ayria to take center stage again.

"I'm from the year 3314," she began. "I was one of over four thousand souls brought here from the Vega Collective, a deep space project studying the viability of Reality-Fold technology. In my time, Earth had been filled to overflowing. The Moon, Mars, and Titan were thriving, self-sustaining, independent municipalities, and mankind had spread throughout our part of the galaxy. Although we'd developed faster-than-light drive centuries before, it wasn't until we took to the stars that we realized how truly vast space is. Even FTL travel was considered too slow, so we were looking at ways to journey a lot further, much more quickly. Our star-orb, the *Discovery*, was a self-contained mini-world leading the charge in Reality-Fold design. Unfortunately, we pushed things too far, too quickly. Lucky for us, our flight path took us into the quantum thread employed by the gateway. We were snatched away as the ship exploded, and brought here.

"On materialization, we arrived with a great deal of salvageable kit. However, our technology proved to be our undoing. It was energy-based, of course. And as the group to arrive before us also discovered to their cost . . . we only made the Horde stronger."

Mac frowned. "Hang on a second. So, you weren't among the first ones here?"

"No. *They* were from over millennia into my future, 4450AD to be exact, and had been here for three years by the time we were taken. We thought everything would be all right, especially when we saw their weaponry. But then they told us how many of them had survived the original translation. Five thousand."

"And how many did you find?"

"Just two hundred."

"Two hundred? Jesus!"

"None of them are left now. And of my own group, only one other is still alive."

"So how long have you been here?"

"Eighteen years. It seems those with the highest likelihood of survival are doctors, scientists, or engineers. Obviously, we tend to be kept away from the fighting."

A murmur passed through the crowd.

Mohammed took up the story. "I came through with Commander Cameron on the seventh jump. We're from the year 2345, and like everyone before us, our weapons were ineffective. The only good point in all this was the fact that several of our technicians were able to reverse-engineer the *Discovery's* engines and adapt its null-point energy. Basically, Ayria's people used it to generate the void through which two points in space can be linked at the sub-quantum level. It's a very similar principle the Ardenese used to operate the gateway. Most of the drive survived the temporal shift, so we adapted it to form an ancillary shield about the city. It taxes our resources severely, but it's effective, especially as it basically does what the Horde can do. Drain energy. When it's activated, if any of those monsters attempt to breach the null-field, it disrupts their biometrics to the point of exhaustion. Needless to say, they avoid it like the plague."

"Why don't you just use the shield instead?" Lex asked. "I admit, I don't understand the principles you're talking about, even with these nanorobot things in my head. But common-sense tells me, if the enemy is repelled by the mere presence of this special field, wouldn't it be safer to use it all the time?"

"It certainly would. But, as I mentioned, it consumes a great deal of power. If we used the shield continually, it would burn out the drive in less than a week. Our reserves would follow about a fortnight after that, even with solar backups. The gate wouldn't be able to operate, the Ark would malfunction. We'd be at their mercy. That's why we only use it where the wall's integrity has been threatened. It gives the fermionic matter time to drain the excess charge away."

"I still don't see how that relates to us." Mac said. "We don't have anything near your level of technology. Not that it seems to matter, judging from what you said."

"This is where it gets interesting." Mohammed appeared brighter at last. "We've had a bit of a breakthrough. Although we didn't know it at the time, one of our compatriots from the eighth intake brought a family heirloom through the gate with him. It stayed among his belongings for years, until a few months ago, in fact, when he was forced to use it as a last resort. It . . . unbelievably, it worked. And we're not exactly sure why." He walked toward the Reverence. "Regardless, it's given us more than eight weeks of rest from a foe that has never shown the slightest inkling of stopping. Of course, your arrival here has stirred them up again. They must have sensed you, and the equipment you've brought."

"What is it about us exactly?" Mac insisted. "We at least deserve to know *why* we were specifically targeted."

"And you will be told, believe me," Mohammed replied, looking genuinely apologetic, "but Commander Cameron has insisted the tactical briefing wait for tomorrow when all the team leaders are gathered together. Yourselves included. In the meantime, he has authorized me to emphasize why your previous petty disputes and conflicts will now be a thing of the past."

Mohammed paused to scan each face before depressing a large orb protruding from the side of the monument. The huge panoramic windows behind the Reverence glided silently into the walls on either side. The room was immediately assailed by the echoes of a nerve-jarring howl of myriad throats roaring in unbridled lust.

Gesturing toward the bay, Mohammed concluded, "Gentlemen, although we are over two miles from the city wall, come and get your first glimpse of your true enemy."

Appalled, they crowded forward.

Chapter Ten

Possibilities

Saul Cameron's gaze roved over the faces of the men and women crowded into the confines of the senior officers' mess. Despite the significance of what they were hearing, many of them looked numb, especially those from among the less technologically advanced groups of the latest arrivals. Saul had adjusted the minutes of the briefing to take into account their lack of understanding. Nevertheless, things had dragged on.

He glanced at his watch. Damn. The session's gone over more than I'd anticipated. Still, it's served its purpose. With one or two minor amendments, the proposals should be agreeable to everyone and will help them all blend into the larger family.

Mohammed wound up his discourse regarding the city's defensive capability. Grabbing the opportunity, Saul skimmed through the list in front of him for the final time. *And I know exactly which changes are needed.*

Making one or two adjustments as he went through, Saul couldn't help but feel smug. The alterations conveyed a sense of symmetry that looked rather elegant. *Oh yes. I think I've earned myself a shot of the good stuff when this chore has finally ended.*

"Commander?" Mohammed invited Saul to the chair once more.

"Thank you." Saul got to his feet and waved the report in the air. "And now to the part you've all been waiting for, not least because it's the final item."

A smattering of impromptu cheering and applause circulated the room. As he waited good-naturedly for the joking to die down, Saul stooped to remove something from within his briefcase. Placing it on the table before him, he paused to judge everyone's mood. He wanted them alert and focused for this last item, and he was glad to see he'd captured their attention, despite their obvious fatigue.

Judging the time was right, he began. "As you know, up until now we've been forced to tolerate a relentless assault that has not only worn us down, but one that has steadily chipped away at our resolve as the years have gone by. Quite by chance, an incident recently occurred which changed all that, and we were granted our first ever respite. Today, I will publicly reveal for the first time *why* we were given this miraculous break, and what we intend to do with it. Anyone interested?"

He moved to uncover the mystery item.

Everyone craned forward.

His revelation was met with stunned incredulity. Those who had served in Rhomane for years seemed puzzled. An expression closely echoed by almost everyone else in the room. But not all.

Saul snorted as he caught a look of recognition on several faces. One in particular stood out from the rest. *I might have guessed. Ayria said he was sharp.*

"Is that an old Webley .445 break-top revolver?"

"It certainly is . . . Lieutenant McDonald, isn't it? Or should I say Mac?"

"Mac's fine. Where the hell did you get that? They were antiquated even during my day, in 2052."

Saul smiled. "Antiquated? They were relics by my time, but fortunately for us, this one works just fine."

"The marvels of solid design, eh? It's nice to see something of the old British Empire living on. Pip, pip, and all that. But if I might ask, what's it doing here?"

Saul lifted the gun into the air and addressed the entire room. "This is indeed a British manufactured Webley pistol from the early twentieth century. World War One vintage to be exact. It was an heirloom belonging to one of our colleagues who, fortunately for us, was from a proud line of soldiers stretching back through umpteen generations to the late nineteenth century. I say fortunately for us, because the family was very particular when it came to their heritage. It seems anything they passed on, be it a weapon, a token, diaries or keepsakes, were all kept in pristine condition. And this was no exception. Simon inherited it from his father and had it in his possession when he was brought to Arden eight years ago. Obviously, he didn't know what a treasure he had at the time, and stashed it away among his belongings after he settled in here. And there it remained, forgotten, until a couple of months ago.

"There's a cave network about ten miles north of Rhomane. We call it the Rainbow Cathedral. It's full of rough, fist-sized diamonds that the Ardenese use in their gel packs, to regulate the city's AI systems. We go there from time to time to get replacements for upkeep, maintenance and so forth. We have to keep such trips to a bare minimum so as not to attract the attention of our friends out there. When we do go, we employ a six-man team. Two extractors and four armed watchers in a skimmer craft kitted out with a mobile null-field generator. As we're still not fully conversant in meshing the different technologies, the portable units aren't too reliable. Thus the need for secrecy.

"Anyway, I was part of the last crew. We were on the way back when the shield emitter frizzed out. As we were only two miles from the city at the time, we thought we'd make a run for it. Needless to say, the sudden exposure of the skimmer's power unit drew the attention of a small group of scavenging Horde. We lost Pete, Michelle, and Dmitri during their first wave. Then Vigor on the second, along with the rest of the weapons. I took over the driving while there was still a little charge left. Simon began rummaging around in his pack. At the time, I wondered what the hell he was doing."

Saul held the revolver up even higher. "Turns out he was digging for this. He was always cleaning it. Said it was a waste of time having such a gift if you didn't look after it properly. Lucky for us he felt that way. When the ghouls swarmed us for the final time, he started firing. The noise was deafening. I remember thinking, you idiot! Why are you wasting your time with that piece of junk? Then the monsters hit us. We crashed. I felt the awful sense of dislocation associated with being drained. All of a sudden, I was bewildered by the silence . . ."

Saul's narrative trailed off as he relived the horror of the attack. His eyes came back into focus and his voice took on a softer edge. "He gave his life to save mine. It was blind luck I was there to witness what happened; otherwise we'd have never known. We'd all be doomed. I've no doubt about that now."

"What *did* happen?" someone called out from among the crowd.

Saul depressed a stud and broke the weapon in two. He briefly fiddled with the revolving chamber and removed a tiny object from inside. Grasping it tightly, he held it aloft for them to get a clearer view. "Basically, he screwed them! Simon only managed to let off a few of these rounds before he went down from the shock of their attack. But because the Horde are mostly comprised of energy, the bullets passed right through his attackers, and then disrupted those behind as well. Four exploded instantly as their matrixes were shredded. Several more dissipated as they ran. Apparently, these insignificant bits of metal mess up their ability to maintain a cohesive field."

Rolling the .445 projectile between his thumb and forefinger, Saul said, "It's the first time I've ever seen them panic. Not even the null-field scares them as much. Whatever it is about these godsends, they are capable of doing what our advanced technology can't." Addressing the ninth group in particular, he added, "That's why we sought the Architect's help to bring *you* through. We didn't need any more useless Tec. We needed cold steel."

"You need iron," Cathal MacNoimhin bellowed. "And we have plenty of that to—"

"I'm sorry," Ayria Solram cut in, "why iron in particular?"

The Caledonians looked to each other as if the doctor had lost her mind. "Iron. Is it not obvious, woman?" Cathal repeated. "Blood metal. The bane of furies and devils. How can you not know this?"

The rest of the clansmen murmured assent.

"The painted warrior speaks truth," said Jishnu Kuruk—also known as Victorious Bear—chieftain of the Apache tribe formerly allied with Snow Blizzard. "We of the first peoples also have our stories of the fey metal that demons fear to touch."

The assembly began to buzz.

Saul motioned for order. Once it was restored, he tossed the bullet in his hand toward his second-in-command. "Mohammed? I want you and Ayria to get onto this immediately. Full spectral, chemical, and whatever else you can think of, analysis. Find out why iron has this affect on the Horde. Involve the Archive. We need to know what oxides, magnetite, and hematite deposits this planet has, and where they are."

He turned to the clansmen and tribesmen. "I'd be grateful if you could spare one or two of your own people? We need to understand everything you know. Your knowledge, legends, stories. Anything you feel might be helpful regarding the mythos of this particular element. There's a connection here somewhere. Possibilities we need to exploit."

The mood was becoming more jubilant by the second.

Yet Saul was puzzled. I wonder? Is that why the Architect brought these particular people to us? Did it know? If so, how? I've got to think about this more deeply. Shaking his head to clear his thoughts, Saul returned his attention to the briefing, and the new amendments in particular.

"Okay everyone, listen in. Our latest breakthrough aside, we still need to protect the city. It looks as if the Horde has had long enough to lick its wounds. The arrival of the ninth has stirred them up again, and any day now they'll be throwing themselves at the wall with fresh abandon." Opening the report, Saul presented the proposals. "In anticipation of that, a new strategy has been devised as follows:

"John Edwards? Sebbi Farah?"

A man and a woman raised their hands at separate ends of the table. Acknowledging them, Saul continued, "You both represent the factions taken from the Husker-Trent oil platform. Put your animosities aside. We desperately need the skills and expertise your teams can bring to the table in the everyday running of a city this size. In fact, your assistance will be invaluable, because you'll free up over a hundred other people who are trained fighters. Please liaise with our quartermaster, Jagpal. He will assign your staff appropriately. Jagpal?"

A gentleman of Indian origin identified himself, and signaled for the opposing leaders to come find him once the meeting had ended.

Saul pressed on. "By far the largest contingent of new arrivals are the soldiers and officers of the Ninth Legion. Colonel Marcus Brutus? I'd like you and your men to speak with Sub-Commander Shannon De Lacey over there." Saul pointed out an athletic-looking woman with piercing eyes and hawk-like features. "City defenses are in her charge. Arrange with her the best deployment of your men. Emphasize the skills and expertise you can offer, and ensure an appropriate watch schedule is devised so the enlarged teams can stay fresh and alert. Something, I'm sure, which won't take long."

Marcus nodded and began threading his way through the crowd.

Saul resumed. "Captain James Houston? Your arrival means we can now start to take the offensive. As most of your horses and equipment survived the transition unscathed, I'd like you to organize your platoons to form flying pickets. Your skills lie in long range patrol and reconnaissance. While we can't promise you'll ride as far as you used to, we can ensure your experience provides us with the intelligence we've sorely missed since the last of the flyers were zapped. Please, report to Commander De Lacey as well."

Houston beamed with pride. Surging to his feet, he swaggered through the press, slapping his gloves on his thigh with every step.

"Flyers?" interrupted Mac. "Manned or unmanned?"

"Unmanned drones. Eyes in the sky, to be exact. The sentinels now operate within the city confines as a safety precaution.

They're a coherent mass of pure energy, you see. The further from the Rhomane they travel, the more power is required to maintain their matrix. In the past, they could roam at will because of the abundance of booster-stations scattered across the planet. Obviously, the advent of the Horde ended that. However, we were able to facilitate the use of over a hundred flyers which had been stashed in a hangar within the city's own commercial grav-port. Sadly, attrition has taken its toll. One by one, they were either destroyed or drained. Municipal archives show a massive stockpile of them out at the spaceport, twelve clicks south of here. The trouble is getting there. We can't risk a land run, as there's a sea of monsters between us and it. There used to be a direct link via underground shuttle and surface transporter platforms, but we disabled them and filled in the tunnel for good measure."

"Transporter? You mean matter teleportation? We were only just beginning to lay the foundations for that."

"Yes. Back on Earth in my day, we'd solved the conundrum of signal degradation which had bugged scientists for over a hundred years. They were in common use in all military, commercial, and private luxury facilities. But as good as they were, they didn't employ anything like the sophistication of those we have here. The Ardenese were . . . *are* incredible when it comes to technical marvels. And that's a pity. If we could only get our hands on some of the kit holed up in the port, it would make life so much easier, especially as we know how to adapt quite a lot of it."

"Are the Horde capable of using the pads, then? I thought they were mostly energy?"

"We're not sure," Saul acknowledged. "Although they've never been known to risk the quantum flux, it doesn't mean they can't. We've seen them use sneaky tactics before, so we're not going to take a chance with them again. But . . ." He glanced toward the clan leaders, the native chiefs, and back to Mac and his team. " . . . Actually, this is where you and the other specialist squads are going to help us. Come with me, I want to run something past you all in person." Saul called to his sub-commander. "Shannon? Take over, would you? The rest of the deployments are listed in the outline."

Saul led the smaller contingent into an ancillary room. Once they were seated, he activated a small box positioned at one end of a long oval table. A barely discernible whine thrummed into existence, which rose in pitch until it was indistinguishable. A tingling sensation crawled across his skin.

"Just a precaution," Saul explained. "This is for your ears only. And those of Vice-Commander Mohammed Amine. Unlike everybody else, you and your people will be reporting directly to him, or me. Is that understood?"

Nobody replied. Some inclined their heads, while others raised an eyebrow or two in surprise. Most just sat still and waited patiently for Saul to explain the situation. At that moment, Saul knew he'd made the right choice.

Look at them. They've been torn further than any of us, and yet you wouldn't know it by the way they act. He thought back to the earlier assignments. The legionnaire took his appointment in his stride, too. Cool, calm, efficient. I could use him in the future. Unlike that cavalry officer with a king-sized ego. Thank goodness not all his men are like him . . .

. . . Right, let's see how they take the news.

Aloud, he said, "If you're up for it, I have some *off the grid* tasks for you. Think of them as missions that will employ the very specialized skills you all posses. Guerilla warfare and living in harmony with your environment. Moving silently. Escape and evasion. We've never been in a position where we can put the Horde on the defensive, but I think we are now."

Speaking to the highland and native contingents in particular, Saul stressed, "I don't think you need to worry about the lack of sophistication of your weapons. If they're made of steel or plain old iron, those fiends will sense it and avoid you. But if they don't, a single shaft will travel—what? Over a hundred yards?"

"Easily," Victorious Bear answered. "Why?"

"I was just thinking how many spooks the arrowhead would be able to penetrate before falling to the earth. Especially if you cast it into a massed charge. Remember what I told you about Simon before he died? He was standing in the back of a skimmer and shooting downward. Every single entity a bullet passed through was instantly destroyed. Those that were grazed or in very close proximity seemed to . . . I don't know . . . unravel. It was as if the very presence of concentrated iron acted as anathema to their existence. Look, it will require experimentation, but I want to discover just how much of the stuff needs to be in the mix to cause a rupture of their biometric fields. If your warriors are willing to play, the next week or so should be rather fun."

The Caledonians came to a decision almost instantly. Ullas Ferguson, Searc Calhoun, Red Buchan, and Kohrk Underwood each looked to Cathal MacNoimhin and nodded once, assuring the participation of their respective clans.

Cathal's eyes and nostrils flared with pride. "It would seem you have the support of my tribe, Commander Cameron. We are keen to test our mettle against these devils."

The highlanders then stared toward the Native Americans who, in turn, appeared to be studying each other closely. After some minutes, they came to an unspoken agreement. Amazingly, it was Stained-With-Blood who stepped forward.

Indicating each respective chief in turn, he said, "I speak on behalf of Snow Blizzard, White Bear, Diving Hawk, and

Victorious Bear. For Cree, Lakota, Sioux, Apache, and my own family, the Blackfoot. Whatever our differences in the past, the People would be honored to strike a blow against Chaos and his dread spirits. In this we are united."

Bowing formally, Stained-With-Blood drew his dagger and scored the tip across his opposite palm. Allowing everyone to view the cut, he declared, "We Cree so avow." Then he clenched his fist and held it to his heart.

"Thank you," Saul murmured. "You must forgive me. I am unaware of your customs, so I don't know if there's anything you require from me to accept your pledge?"

Neither faction responded.

Apparently not, he thought wryly.

Turning to Mac and his team, Saul found it difficult to hide his excitement. "Gentlemen, I have something quite radical for you. I'd like you to take a look at this."

Activating a projector, Saul brought up a 3D image of a complex structure spread over a vast area. He allowed the representation to rotate slowly through the air before fixing it into position above the tabletop in front of them. Once it had steadied, he said. "This is the spaceport I mentioned earlier. While certain aspects appear similar in many ways to the aerodromes of your time, there are some major differences. The first being the absence of runways. The Ardenese employed the use of retractable anti-gravity scallops along the edges of their craft. They would use them to shuttle out to the launch area before gaining altitude. Once in flight, they would fire up the Aqua-Cell engines and boost themselves into orbit for FTL initiation."

The picture rippled and the perspective changed. Now everyone had a clear view of a massive edifice of shining glass and metal. "This is the main terminal," Saul said as he continued to manipulate the controls. "To the right, you can see the shuttle dome that links the facility to seven other major cities within a thousand mile radius: Cumale, Floranz, Locus, Genoas, Napal, Elan, and of course Rhomane."

"Are you joking?" Mark Stevens gasped. "They sound . . ."

"Yes, they sound familiar, don't they? Too similar for it to be a coincidence. It made us chuckle when we found out."

Mark was stunned. "Did the Ardenese ever admit to visiting Earth in their past?"

"Not that we know of. But as you might appreciate, we've only uncovered a fraction of their history. Even their space faring epoch stretches back thousands of years. So, we're still—"

"Er, the mission?" Mac interjected. "I'd appreciate it if we cut the chitchat until after we know what we're doing."

"Ah yes, sorry!" Saul adjusted the settings once more. "I tend to get a bit carried away when I consider the amazing comparisons that keep popping up between our two cultures."

He began a slow aerial circuit of the facility. "To the right, behind the terminus, we have the pens and hangars where each craft was refueled and prepared for travel. That area was once awash with rippling energies. Obviously, it was one of the first places to become depleted when the Horde first emerged from their ships. The original liners are still there, even now, like a beached flotilla of Marie Celestes. Very spooky. However, we don't need to concern ourselves with them just yet."

Tweaking the scene once again, Saul made a gradual approach toward the far side of the facility. "Now *this* is what I'd like you to pay particular attention to. The eastern zone facilitated maintenance, emergency services and stores." One building glowed red. "And according to the inventory, *that* warehouse contains over a thousand flyers, still in their crates. To avoid damage, such items were always packed inert. All the Ardenese had to do was add good old aqua-pura, and the fully integrated AI/diagnostic systems would initialize and power them up ready for final program download. If we could get our hands on them, it would make life a lot easier."

"In what way?" Mac probed.

"Let's just say, they weren't designed only to hover in the air and look pretty. Depending on the encryption package, they could be tasked to observe, map, gain intelligence, repair, or even defend strategic locations. Now you're here, I'm hoping to extend the possibilities."

"And how many were you hoping we'd appropriate for you?"

"First, we'd like you to complete a test run. Remember, I mentioned earlier that we had a problem converting the null-shield applications to our portable units. That's entirely down to the differences within the hardwired security software. Think of it as two different sides not speaking the same language. They just don't communicate as freely as we want them to. However, we noticed your tactical armor is equipped with a most intriguing form of stealth technology. Primitive by current standards, and yet perfect for our needs."

"Because it'll do as it's told if you start tinkering with it?" Mac caught Saul's meaning instantly.

"Exactly." Saul beamed. "It should be much easier for our guys to adapt its frequency to one that will mesh with the existing generators. If it works, I'm told there's a high probability we can reduce the size of the cells down to something you'd be able to carry individually. Just imagine it. Being able to do what you do best, without having to worry about Horde ghouls materializing out of thin air trying suck you dry."

As an afterthought, he added, "Mind you, even if they did, I don't see them trying it on for too long, especially with the firepower you have at your disposal. If they turned tail and fled when Simon popped off a few rounds at them, how are they gonna react when they meet you?"

"Let's hope they don't start getting brave then," Mac grumbled. "Don't forget, we only have the ammunition that was brought through with us. Even with the U.S. Cavalry and our nuclear-happy friends out there, all those bullets will soon disappear without proper fire discipline."

Saul didn't appear too upset by the statement. Instead, he ushered everyone closer and said, "You let me worry about that. We're not without our . . . resources."

Without explaining his statement further, Saul expanded the holographic projection to present a topographical overview of the surrounding region. Satisfied he had the correct resolution, he addressed them all once more. "Right, you're the experts in this kind of situation. Let's talk tactics . . ."

Chapter Eleven

A Testing Time

(Sengennon Strait-7 miles northwest of Rhomane)

Lex wasn't happy to be under the command of a traitor.

But what can I do? Everyone's circumstances have changed drastically over the past week, and now it's a case of 'better the devil you know.'

Tearing his gaze away from Houston's back, Lex scanned the countryside about him. He was reminded of a recent journey through rolling hills and sweeping plains full of hidden dangers. Except this wasn't Montana. And the savanna here was lifeless, devoid of the buffalo, birds, and myriad other critters that brought the prairie to life about you. Even the strange purple-green hue of the grass had been stripped back to bare bones in a way that was unsettling.

And it won't be Red Indian braves jumping out on us if we do find anything.

He reached up to adjust his chromatically active eyepieces. Provided only three days ago when the patrol started, Lex soon discovered that Samson's gait made them slide down his nose.

Strange things, pity we didn't have them in my day. Although it's a little odd, looking at everything through a dark tint, you soon get used to it.

He glanced over the top of the rims and squinted. *Mind you, it's a question of having to. The Ardenese must have had exceptional eyesight.*

The sun was incredibly intense, especially at midday, when it cast a harsh blue-white tinge through the air that glared back off every bright surface. Even the horses had to wear specially designed blinders to protect their eyes.

They're obviously forcing us into a 'put them through hell together' scenario in the hope it will make us gel into a team again.

Lex snorted. *As if we have any choice.*

He watched as the highlanders loped easily along beside them. Glistening with sweat, they appeared to revel in the challenge of keeping up with the rest of the patrol. From time to time, they would range out onto a hillock to survey the land ahead or behind. Adjusting the magnification on their sunglasses, they would then look for telltale signs of Horde activity, and communicate with each other by whistles and hand signs. *They're a fierce bunch, and tough. I think we'll be very glad to have them at our back in a fight.*

Peeking toward his captain out of the corner of his eye, Lex couldn't prevent himself adding, *and they might even protect us from cowardly snakes-in-the-grass like him when things turn nasty.*

The rumble of approaching hooves resonated through the air. Wilson Smith's platoon was returning from their latest sweep, and the second lieutenant was making no effort to remain quiet. Horses came into view. Shouldering their way through a patch of head-high grass, they broke free and made a beeline for the main body of the patrol.

"What news?" Houston snapped.

Wilson shook his head and cast his eyes downward in resignation. "We cleared the ridge leading onto the Thunder Plain, but we didn't see a soul. I even managed to make out the hills rising toward the Rainbow Cathedral, but nothing's moving there, either. If the Horde is about, and these glasses work like they said they would, the monsters must be hiding."

"They're there, all right," Red Buchan grumbled, "I can feel it in my bones. In the air. Can't you? Fey creatures have our scent, and the bitter tang of dark metal holds them in thrall. They dread its presence and keep their distance, but not for long. Their hunger is rising. Soon, it will outweigh their fear."

Rumblings of agreement echoed through the tartan-clad warriors who had heard the statement.

"Well, I don't give a damn about their hunger." Houston's tone was condescending and unfriendly. "Let them come. They'll find our Spencer carbines picking them off before they get within a hundred yards of us."

Wheeling his horse about, he faced Lex. "Lieutenant. Take your detachment and made a wider sweep. If there's still nothing, swing toward the Issamun Canyon. Sub-Commander De Lacey tells me that since they started their diamond runs, there's always a concentration of brutes in that area. Let's see if we can flush them out, eh?"

While you're safely back here. Aloud, Lex replied, "Yes, Sir. Do you want me to lead them to you, or engage them myself?"

Houston tried to look thoughtful. And failed. "Test them first. If our bullets are as effective as we hope, send a scout to advise us. Then we can prepare a little trap for you to lead them into." His face lit up as he had an idea. "The dry riverbed we ran across this morning should do nicely. It'll conceal us from line of sight and hopefully they'll be so intent on eating you, they won't realize we're there until it's too late."

The riverbed? That's another eight miles in the wrong direction, away from the city. "Certainly, Sir, I'll prepare my men now. Which clan would you like to come with us?"

"Oh, I'll keep the highlanders here, Lieutenant Fox. Let them rest up a bit. We wouldn't want any unfortunate accidents to occur because people got exhausted now, would we?"

Turning away to hide his disgust, Lex started issuing orders.

Within minutes, First Platoon was ready to deploy. As they formed up in file, Lex called to his officers. "Sergeant Rixton? Corporal Williams? A word, please."

Taking them to one side, he continued, "Keep things tight out there. I don't care what the captain says. I trust the highlanders' instincts. They're more attuned to the land than the rest of us . . . even if we are on some new weird and godforsaken world a lifetime away from home. When we go out, we're going to form our own sub-patrol. Rixton, you'll lead the first ranging. Take your section and divide them into squads. Arrange them in compass point formation about the column, a hundred yards out. Any sign of trouble, hightail it back and we'll take on the Horde together. No heroics. Williams? Ensure your men are rested. You'll swap positions every half hour. Understood?"

"Sir!" Both men replied.

Lex had turned away when a voice made him jump.

"And what about my fighters, laddie?"

"Jesus!" Lex gasped. "Red. I didn't hear you sneak up. What the hell are you talking about?"

"I'm asking you, where you would like my . . . or should I say Searc's clan to go? They're more rested than we are and have volunteered for a wee stroll."

Lex was confused. "I'm sorry, Red. I thought the captain just ordered your men to stay with the main patrol?"

"Ah, forget what that blithering idiot said, boy. We highlanders don't take our orders from him. In his wisdom, Commander Cameron gave us free rein as to how to acclimatize our own people. We chose to come on this expedition so the men could get a little exercise. And Searc has decided his Vacomagi need to stretch their legs. If by a strange coincidence they happen to jog off in the same direction as you, well there isn't much his grand ass-wipe can do about it, is there?"

Lex couldn't prevent a huge grin from lighting up his face. Leaning down in his saddle, he whispered, "Then by all means, do thank Searc Calhoun and his clan on my behalf." Jerking his chin toward the north, he added, "Please ask him to *stretch his legs* in that direction. We should meet up within the hour."

Red returned the smile and sloped away. Lex muttered, "Thank God for Commander Cameron."

Red heard the comment. Over his shoulder he called, "Don't thank God, laddie. Thank Caledonia. Cameron's a highland name. The man has the salt of the earth running through his veins. Of course he'd be disposed to making wise decisions."

*

(Boleni Heights-6 miles southwest of Rhomane)

The hairs on the back of Mac's neck prickled. He couldn't honestly say if it was due to the effects of the obscure puissance pulsing through his stealth armor, or the presence of the nightmare apparitions in front of him.

Roughly humanoid in shape, Mac judged them to exceed ten feet in height. It was hard to tell because they had no defined parameters. Comprised of a confusing blend of shadow and *nothing*, the actual proximity of each specimen was revealed by their constant expressions of hunger and passion. Each time they rumbled or howled, an angry skein of shimmering blue-black and orange-red energy skittered through what passed for their bodies, defining their matrixes and exposing a horrific array of horns, talons, and teeth.

If they remained quiet, the only way you could spot them with the naked eye was by the distortion wave their presence generated in the ether. It looked to Mac as if he were viewing cryptic objects through a prism.

He flipped through the settings on his HUD, and broadcast the results simultaneously over his covert radio. "Now trying infrared. Ultraviolet. Sonics. Aha! Gotcha, you bugger." *No wonder these monsters were able to take people by surprise. They barely register.* "Four Troop, listen up. The Horde's biometric frequencies absorb most forms of energy. No surprise there. However, their mere presence creates a deformation of the atmosphere. Switch to sonic motion diffusers. It seems to define their silhouettes much more precisely. You'll see what I mean.

"Sam? Liaise with the command vehicle and patch your screen through to their console. Make sure they and our Native American friends don't miss this."

He waited while his team carried out his instructions.

Moments later, several gasps alerted Mac to the fact that the others were now viewing what had appalled him. "Yes, ladies and gentlemen," he said, "say hello to our enemy."

"Jesus, Mac," Mark Stevens exclaimed, "have we walked in on a photo shoot for Demons Illustrated, or what? They look like the monster from that sci-fi classic from the 1950s . . . I can't recall the name of it at the moment, something about the id, but . . ."

"I appreciate the sentiment, Mark. But can you wait one moment, please?" Mac diverted his attention to the support skitter. "Penny? Is this typical of what we can expect?"

Penny Frasier, a xenobiologist from the year 3060 and a specialist on the Horde for the past thirteen years, replied, "Yes, Lieutenant. These are what we call grunts, or spooks. They usually come in at around ten feet high, and as you can see, they have the bulk to match. Although abstruse in nature, they have a direct influence on the physical plane and are as strong as they look. We see before us a compressed nucleus of vitriolic rage, exceeded only by their hunger. Notice how the energy vortex they generate converges around their extremities, like an aura? When they roar, it enhances the vibrancy of that nimbus, and tends to concentrate it around their eyes and jaws."

"And they feed by draining the life-force from living things, or the resonance of specific power frequencies?"

"That's right."

"So why the talons and fangs?"

"Good point," she acknowledged. "We're pretty sure it's to elicit a fight or flight response in bio-based prey. And to settle issues among themselves, of course. Now and again, we do see violent outbursts between individuals that result in physical confrontation."

"So they're not merely for show?" Mac was intrigued by an apparent discrepancy. "They do actually serve a purpose?"

"Oh yes, they're a nasty bit of work all right. I've seen too many shredded carcasses to doubt that. But the surge of adrenalin their appearance causes in others creates an energy spike along the synapses. Remember, nerve fibers conduct chemical and electrical impulses. If the Horde can create a boost in those transmissions as they feed, they'll derive a lot more nourishment than they would from a passive host."

"I see." Mac felt numbed by the fact that anything so large and horrific would need any further help instilling terror in its victims. "And from what the briefing report implied, there's also another type we need to be aware of. A . . . what did you call them . . . Horde Master, correct?"

"That's right. Or Controller, or Boss. We don't appear to have any here among this pack, but you'd know it if there were. They emit a purple corona, and are over twelve feet high. Oh, they have halos, too. Or perhaps I should more accurately say, coronets of flames dancing around their heads. As hard as it is to believe, they make this lot look like puppies."

"You're kidding?"

"I'm afraid not. We think they serve some form of command function within the hive. As Saul mentioned, the longer the conflict goes on, the more we suspect there's a hierarchy and intelligence to the Horde that we never expected. We just wish we could find some way to communicate with them to find out what they want."

"Or who they answer to."

"Pardon?"

"The Masters. If they have a pecking order, there must be someone *they* answer to, like a queen perhaps. Has anyone ever considered that?"

"No. We haven't." Penny was plainly aghast at the implications. "If there *is* such an entity, we've never seen it. My God. It . . . it—"

"We can worry about that later, at the debriefing. Tell me. Are White Bear and Diving Hawk seeing this?"

"Yes. They're here . . ." she paused to confer with the others aboard her craft, " . . . and they say they can see the demons well enough to recognize their presence."

"Excellent. Then we're just about ready to go. Our new stealth capability is obviously working. The Horde doesn't even suspect we're here. Tell me, how well do these monsters hear? They obviously can't listen like we do, but how sensitive is their capacity to recognize sound, or the vibrations we create by movement?"

"To be honest, that's another thing we're in the dark about." Penny sounded impressed by Mac's lateral thinking. "They're usually so busy vocalizing their hunger that we've never given it much thought."

"So, everyone's been tiptoeing around in their proximity as a matter of habit? Hmm." Mac organized his thoughts. *Time consuming and exhausting. Especially if it causes their prey to remain in a high state of anxiety. All those juicy energies congealed into one handy snack.*

He came to a decision. "Right, heads up, everyone. We'll be going live in just one moment. Penny? Please ask White Bear and Diving Hawk to ready their braves. They're your last line of defense if things go wrong.

"Sam? You stay in the command vehicle. Let our Indian friends do all the work. They've got to test their capabilities and see for themselves how effective they can be in a fight. However, if it looks like they're losing control, introduce the Horde to the Remington. Wide choke. It'll be nice to see what they make of a shotgun.

"Guys? Safeties off. Don't make any attempt to be stealthy. We need to establish standard operating procedures while we're around these brutes, so let's test how far we can go without raising a shit-storm for anybody else . . .

" . . . Teams confirm?"

Affirmations rolled in.

"Good. Then let's get this show on the road."

A sudden impulse, hard to resist, caused Mac to address the professor one last time. "Penny? I think we'll be making one of your wishes come true in just a few seconds time."

"Wish? Which one's that, Lieutenant?"

"One way or another, we'll soon be communicating exactly how we feel to the Horde." Mac grinned and patted the Heckler-Koch G40 carbine slung around his neck. "I think they'll get the message."

*

(Thunder Plain-10 miles north of Rhomane)

A shrill whistle from behind caused Lex to rein in sharply. Whirling around, he scanned the savanna and was able to make out a couple of the warriors from Clan Calhoun, running hell-for-leather away from the lip of the Issamun Canyon. The rim was only about two hundred yards off, but seeing the fleeing pair made the distance between them seem like an ocean divide.

As one, the Caledonians interrupted their flight to turn and make a stand. One dropped into a fighting crouch, sword drawn, while the other released several arrows in quick succession at an unknown target still within the draw of the ravine.

Several riders from Three Squadron were galloping toward them in support. Over the sound of hooves and shouting, Lex thought he could hear the noise of muted explosions.

Thank goodness I extended the outer pickets when we entered the grasslands. I knew the extra space would come in handy.

Lex looped around a second time, reassessing the position of the other Vacomagi in relation to his own troops.

Good. This can work in our favor. "Sergeant Rixton? Take One Section and form a line about half a mile northwest of here. We're heading toward the dry riverbed as ordered. The captain should be ready and waiting for us as planned. When Corporal Williams comes in, I'll lead Two Section through your position and form another column, four hundred yards beyond you. We will maintain order, and leapfrog steadily toward the RV. The signal to move each time will be a three-blast bugle call. It'll also let Houston know we're coming. Understood?"

"Yes, Sir," Rixton snapped.

Lex turned to Searc Calhoun. The clan leader stood close by, studying the unfolding drama. "Searc, will your men want to ride double or will you make your own way out of here?"

The sound of urgent whistling followed by several shots interrupted the conversation.

Searc didn't bother looking away. Grinning like a madman, he calmly waited for the reports to fade before answering. "Och, me and the lads will run along for a while to see what happens. They've just signaled the fact a whole hornets' nest has been stirred up. If things get too troublesome we can always jump on board for a turn or two. Catch our breath and rest our legs while you put some distance between us and certain death."

Lex couldn't help but smile. "Okay, you crazy kilt-wearing maniac. But if things get too hairy, I'll have my men lasso you and drag you along."

Searc's reply was drowned out by further shots and the sound of Sergeant Rixton's section riding out. His gesture, however, made it clear what he thought of Lex's idea.

Chuckling, Lex trotted over to his bugle-boy, Bobby Fisher. "Bobby, sound the fall-back. I want Corporal Williams and his men to muster around me. The highlanders will follow them. Once the fighting begins, stay behind us and away from the beasts. We have to tease them, slowly but surely, toward the ambush. The success of our mission depends on you staying alive and able to signal to everyone what's going on. Okay?"

"Yes, Sir," the boy replied, struggling to hide his fright behind a look of stolid determination.

At seventeen years of age, Bobby had only served in the Army for six months, and Lex couldn't help but feel sorry for the young man. And his family. *It doesn't seem fair. He's too young and inexperienced to die, but to all intent and purpose he's already dead. To the folks back home, anyhow. And instead of being able to hang up his hat and rest, he's being forced to face an enemy that shouldn't exist.* Lex spat in disgust. *If there is a God, he's surely abandoned us. Ah well, at least I can watch over him.*

Corporal Williams and his outriders came charging through his position. As he passed, Williams shouted, "There must be over fifty of them, Sir. Looks like we discovered a whole nest in a cave," he cocked a thumb over his shoulder at the following Vacomagi, "and those idiots think it's fun!"

Sure enough, as the Caledonians ran past hot on the heels of the cavalry officers, every single one of them was whooping in delight.

Incredible! It's— Lex caught his breath. The long grass near the edge of the gorge was swaying and bending madly, as if being trampled by a great weight. The horizon started to shimmer. Lex fumbled with the control on the side of his sunglasses in an attempt to define what was causing it.

A rippling, ululating cry squeezed through the ether. As it did so, angry flashes of blue and red lightning skittered through the air in the same proximity. A terrible enmity congealed along the ridgeline. Lex's blood ran cold.

They're here!

The screams united, rising into a terrifying roar. Then the monsters charged.

And they're not running away.

Lex drew his saber. "Corporal Williams. Draw carbines and divide your section into squads. Retreating lines. Keep pace with Searc's men. Wait until they are a safe distance away on each occasion before firing a volley into the spooks. One round only. And if the highlanders begin to lag, drag them."

Lex's comments drew a peppering of colorful metaphors from those Vacomagi close enough to hear. Ignoring them, he cantered over to the nearest soldiers and joined their file. Standing in his stirrups, he raised his sword and cried, "Wait for it . . . wait . . ."

The seconds stretched into eternity. The bellowing got louder, rising in volume until it threatened to overwhelm them.

Eventually, Lex deemed the time was right. Dropping his arm, he yelled, "Fire!"

And the nightmare began.

*

(Sengennon Strait-2 miles southwest of Rhomane)

Ignoring the reverberations rolling through the air, Sam spoke quietly and calmly into the com-link. "Bravo team leader. Be advised, you have half-a-dozen sneaky bastards trying to circle around behind you. They're staying out of bow range and seem content to wait for us to close on them."

"Where and away?" Mark asked, squeezing off a short burst toward a target that suddenly presented itself.

"Do you see that large outcropping of boulders two hundred yards away, back toward the city, the ones at the base of the Boleni Mountain?"

"Yes, yes."

"Well, six or seven of our friends just scuttled down the hillside and into the depression behind those rocks. I think they're planning a Kamikaze run as we go past. The trail's only twenty to thirty feet wide. Good spot for an ambush."

"I thought these buggers couldn't think? Thanks for the heads up, Sam."

Mark signaled for the remaining members of his section to adjust their positions to compensate, and then called to Mac. "Alpha-one, this is Bravo-one, did you copy that?"

"Affirmative," Mac replied, "I'm drawing in the rest of alpha team to support. Mark, which tribe members are closest to your position? I want—"

Mac dropped to his knees at a signal from Dancing Snake—one of Diving Hawk's sons—and an arrow thrummed over his head. A concussion only ten yards behind him caused Mac to roll away. Coming to his feet, he saw a shallow indentation in the dirt where the spook had lain in wait for him.

Clever. They're adapting to our new strategy. Flashing a thumbs-up to the young warrior, Mac warned, "Heads up, guys. They're lying inert on the ground, waiting for us to literally walk into them. Adjust optics to rotating wavebands. One second phase. Buddy up, back-to-back, with the nearest tribesman to you."

Mac paused while his team repeated the instructions out loud for the benefit of the Native Americans. As he waited for everyone to get on the same page, Mac was forced to take out a number of ogres trying to swarm him from several different directions at once. *Oh yes, they're adapting all right.* When the shockwaves subsided, Mac found himself partnered with Running Deer.

Good. This lad's on the ball, my back will be safe. Seeing the young warrior reminded Mac of what he'd been about to say. "Bravo-one. Are you listening?"

"Bravo-one here. Go ahead."

"Mark, which braves are closest to you?"

"I've got a bunch of White Bear's guys nearby. Why?"

"I want you to task them with clearing that ambush. Assign one of our boys to go with them so they have backup. Just in case."

"Will do."

As his second began relaying orders, Mac adjusted his com-set to a broader waveband. "Bravo-four, this is Alpha-one, are you listening, Andy?"

Andy Webb, the sniper specialist, was positioned on top of Rhomane's south wall to provide long-range tactical cover for the mission. "I'm here. Go ahead, Boss."

"How far until we're in your kill zone?"

There was a delay while Andy checked his instruments. "I'm lighting you up now. Can you see?"

Mac glanced down at a ruby dot dancing across his chest. "Yes, I can confirm red-wash. Clear and steady."

"I'd say another half mile, and then you'll be at optimum distance."

"Roger that. Once we've cleared a choke point a few hundred yards from my position, we'll be coming in hot. This exercise has served its purpose, there's no need for us to be out here any longer. What's activity like at the wall?"

"Busy. We've got about a thousand Horde gremlins at both the north and south entrances. The patrols have attracted their attention, so they're working themselves up into a bit of a frenzy. Marcus has an entire cohort at each gate. I'm here now with Flavius and a contingent of archers. So far, the arrows have prevented the grunts from completing their usual swarming tactic . . . talking of which . . ."

"Yes, Andy?"

"Wait one. I just need to check something again."

There was a momentary lapse before Andy resumed speaking. "Boss, as I scoped around your location, I noticed something odd near the astrometrics facility on top of Boleni Mount."

"Define *odd*?"

"I've checked it on laser scan, D-light, and Sonics. I have what appears to be an area of concentrated distortion about two hundred yards from the summit. It's incredibly powerful, and is positioned so as to have a clear view of Boleni Heights itself, and the Sengennon Strait. What got me is the fact it appeared minutes after you revealed yourselves, and it has hardly moved since then."

Mac was stunned. *It can't be.* "Have they set up a command post?"

"That's what I was thinking. They've been reacting very differently to the mindless berserkers we were expecting."

They're watching us. Assessing our strategies. "Andy? We're on the way. Report this to Commander Cameron immediately."

Mac got on the internal channel. "Four Troop. Stand-by, stand-by. This is an end exercise. Repeat, endex. We are leaving now. Fall back to the skimmers and check weapons. We are going hot.

"Sam? Get our native friends back on board immediately. Have Penny pick Mark and his team up, too. Use their firepower to take out that ambush and get the hell out of here. I'll follow in the spare skimmer."

Everyone rushed to obey. The change in mood must have caused an abrupt surge of anxiety to saturate the air, for the Horde erupted. A sudden chorus of snarls and shrieks burst forth, rising in volume until the earth shook.

The clamor abruptly cut off as the brutes gathered into smaller groups to charge.

A hovercraft pulled alongside Mac's position. Climbing in, he ignored the building menace and stared back up the hillside.

Damn, I can't see them from here. What the hell are they up to now?

*

(Rhomane city wall-South Gate)

Employing a slow, deliberate, figure-of-eight motion, Andy scanned the vista before him. It was important he didn't rush.

Staying relaxed allowed him to be alert for any out-of-the-ordinary markers that might betray the presence of a lurker.

Doing his best to ignore the advancing dust cloud that marked the presence of the returning team, Andy adjusted his focus and glanced at the visual countdown on his HUD.

There's the final marker.

An abrupt manifestation four hundred yards in front of the skimmers caught his attention. Closing his weak eye, Andy cut off the holographic display and brought his head to the scope. The scene leapt into crystal clear clarity.

They were buried? How long have they been lying there?

Depressing the rangefinder button, Andy slowed his breathing as he waited for the firing resolution to be confirmed. The ANS-1X .338 magnum sniper rifle was one of the most sophisticated long-range weapons in existence, and Andy's skill in using it was second to none. Moments later, he was ready.

Safety off, he took one last, deep breath. His world became crosshairs in a prism. Holding his exhalation partway through, he gently squeezed the trigger. Once. Twice. Three times. *Clack! Clack! Clack!*

Seven hundred yards away, three miniature shockwaves resonated into the air, right in front of the hovercraft.

Mac was on the radio in seconds. "Bravo-four? Trouble?"

"Not any more, Boss. Be advised. You are half a mile out."

"Is everything ready?"

"Yes, yes. Flavius has archers standing by and I'm about to activate one of the .50 millimeter robot guns we brought from the rig. As soon as you hear and see me clearing your path, accelerate toward the wall. You have about twenty seconds. Shannon is about to drop the fermionic resonance so you can ride right through."

"Please ensure she does. I'd hate to drive straight into the densest material known to exist at ninety miles an hour."

Snorting, Andy shuffled to one side and brought the cannon online. Nodding toward the buttress where Flavius and Shannon De Lacey were waiting, he shouted, "Ten seconds. Make sure the far side of the gate is clear."

Both officers waved in reply.

Andy activated the battlement Tannoy system. "Ladies and gentlemen. If you would please be so kind as to give it everything you've got, in . . . three, two, one. Fire!"

The bottom of the wall disappeared amid a cacophony of light and sound. Terrifying roars of pain and outrage resonated throughout the terrible explosions that ripped a huge swath through the seething ranks of Horde below.

The returning skimmers juddered through the holocaust. Then they were safely through the manipulated flux of the city gates.

The firing stopped. The walls thrummed as full integrity was restored, and the shrieks of indignation from below continued unabated.

Andy was about to leave when he had a spur of the moment idea. Lifting his sniper rifle, he altered the scope's resolution and rechecked the slopes of Mount Boleni. As he suspected, the distortions were gone.

*

(Sengennon Strait-12 miles north of Rhomane City)

Sand, agitated by the wind, swirled along the bottom of the redundant riverbed.

"So, where's this captain of yours?" Searc Calhoun complained.

"I don't know," Lex replied. "This is definitely the right place, look." Using his sword, he pointed off across the Sengennon Strait.

Only five miles away, directly opposite their position, the Grisson Gap loomed like a large ugly scar cut into the south-western tip of the Erásan Mountains. The Gap was reported to be the source of the dried-up Issamun River. City archives recorded the fact that, although dry for centuries, the area still flooded during the stormy season at the end of each year. Those waters were responsible for the canyon of the same name—the one where they had disturbed the Horde ogres only two hours previously—and when flowing, eventually emptied out into the Great Asterlan Lake, thirty miles west of Rhomane.

Both men scanned the rocks and ridges lining the edge of the dusty watercourse. Then behind, at the shimmering distortions that were steadily closing on them. Although greatly reduced in number, the Horde seemed determined to keep coming until every last one of them was dead.

"Aye," Searc complained, "and there's the head of the old river on this side of the strait. So, where the bloody hell is Houston? I don't think my kindred will entertain this game for much longer. We've been running long enough."

The two hour flight had been emotionally exhausting, and both leaders could see the men would much rather settle the matter now than let it drag on any longer. "I think I'm inclined to agree," Lex said. "Let's form up and take them on. At least we can relax for a while before making a break for the city."

Searc spotted a nearby hillock. "I'll get one of the lads to take a peek with those fancy eyeglass things, and see how many we have to deal with. You get your men ready so we can take the best advantage."

While Lex issued instructions to his bugler, Searc whistled directions to a runner.

Once he'd finished, Lex asked, "What are you going to do?"

"Me? I'm going to support my man Duncan, up on the mound. He's got a bow, so we'll be quite safe." *And hopefully I'll get in a cut or two for good measure!*

Before Lex could object, Searc sprinted away to join his fellow clansman on the crown of the hill.

"Do you see anything through those binoculars, Duncan?"

"I do, Searc, but not where you'd think. Take a gander over there."

Searc stared in the direction his friend indicated and noticed an odd shimmer in the air. At first, Searc thought they had run into an ambush. Then he realized the distortion was huge, and missing the usual sparks of hot red lightning normally given off by Horde devils. Puzzled, he looked closer.

Then it struck him. "I think I've just found his royal asswipe. It seems the captain brought one of those invisible shield thingies with him. You know, they were talking about them back at the city? Pity he neglected to tell *us* about it. Let me go and give Lex the good news. Oh, and Duncan? Stay sharp for any surprises, and don't go getting yourself caught in the shite with no way out." Searc punched his man on the arm and ran back down the hillock.

As he closed on Lex, the soldier turned toward him with a puzzled look on his face. Searc grinned and beckoned furiously.

Lex stood in his stirrups and smiled. Then he shrugged, as if expressing his bewilderment at Searc's behavior.

Searc was about to call out when he noticed Lex was lifting higher than usual in his saddle. A loud report boomed forth, followed immediately by a multitude of other shots as the opening volley from the ambush blasted out. Corresponding explosions began to tear the advancing Horde apart.

Lex kept rising, a look of shock on his face. He fell out of his saddle, and many of his men stopped firing.

"Ware the enemy, you fools!" Searc screamed. "Your captain was hidden in the rocks all along. You finish off the monsters; I'll take care of the young officer."

Lex hit the deck and rolled onto his back, coughing blood.

Dropping to his knees beside him, Searc could see an expanding stain soaking through the dark blue of Lex's tunic, right above his heart. Unbelievably, Lex smiled, reached out, and fixed him with a gaze that gripped him to the core.

"Don't move, laddie," Searc said, "let me . . ."

It was too late. Lex's gaze shifted. Moving through Searc, it expanded on into infinity, and vanished.

Searc lowered his fellow warrior's head to the floor. Cold fury burned through him. *The bastard! Does he think us naïve?*

Picking up his axe, Searc Calhoun went in search of monsters . . . of the backstabbing variety.

Chapter Twelve

Eggshells

Mac concluded his report, met the gaze of everyone sitting along the high table, and walked back to his seat on the bottom tier, satisfied he had covered every point.

Saul opened the floor. "Questions?"

Professor Ephraim Miller launched straight in. "Lieutenant, you're absolutely positive the spliced components worked? You were completely invisible to the Horde until the moment you dropped the shields?"

"Yes, that's correct. The stealth technology already incorporated within our armor bends light around the wearer, masking us to plain sight. It also includes a thermal compensator to match that of the surrounding environment, thereby reducing our heat signatures. The addition of null-energy generates a field that masks our presence completely. We still need to test

exactly what our safety parameters are, but it will save us having to tiptoe around all the time."

"And you experienced no adverse affects?"

"As long as we stayed within one hundred yards of the emitter, none whatsoever. On the one or two occasions we strayed a
little further, we noticed the Horde were able to sense something.
They couldn't pinpoint us, but it did make them edgy. Overall?
I think we've got something to play with. Also, their reactions
gave me the idea about how our friends out there detect us."

Saul cut in. "What do you mean?"

"Well, they don't have eyes or ears . . . in the mundane
sense. So how do they actually perceive us?"

"We've known for some time they feed on the bio-elec-
trical energy we generate," Saul replied. "They must home in
on that somehow."

Mac nodded. "I appreciate what you're saying, but after
today, I'm wondering if there's more to it than that."

"In what way?"

"Well, after we dropped the shields, they recognized the
presence of humans instantly. But the first targets they attacked
were Diving Hawk's people. They were the only ones besides
us who were outside the skimmers. White Bear's party joined
in as the fighting began. My team seemed to rattle them. I got
the feeling our armor confused their ability to sense us in some
way. It wasn't until we began firing that they knew for certain
an enemy was close by. It's my strong opinion they reacted to
the concentrated presence of iron. It's an inert metal. How on
earth could an esoteric being do that?"

The governing body stared at each other, lost for words.

Ephraim rejoined the conversation. "Would you be willing to help me carry out a few experiments? I've got an idea
about that aspect I'd like to test."

"Certainly. What did you have in mind?"

"I'll tell you more once I've got the portable units up and running. I know Commander Cameron needs you for the spaceport mission, but this particular development may help refine our strategy."

"How long do you envisage that taking, Ephraim?" Saul asked. "I'd like to crack on with our plans as soon as possible."

"Only four or five days, Sir. A week at the most. In light of the intelligence Lieutenant McDonald collected, I'm loath to rush things."

"I agree," Mac added, "especially as we still have to consider the implications of what Andy Webb witnessed from his sniper position on the wall."

Saul looked across to his second-in-command. "What about it? You've had a chance to interview Specialist Webb in person and go through the data with him."

"I've got to admit, it has an alarming ring of truth to it," Mohammed replied. "The ANS-1X system digitally records everything its operator witnesses. I've been through the footage repeatedly, and had various facets explained to me in detail by Andy himself. Although we couldn't record exactly which Horde entities were congregated on the mountainside, they were definitely there. Watching us. Assessing us. Adopting alternatives to try and counter the new obstacles presented to them. If that's not evidence of a hierarchy, I don't know what is."

Mohammed noticed Mac was eager to speak. "Lieutenant? You want to add something?"

"Yes, thank you." Mac got to his feet. "Sorry to interrupt, but I feel it necessary to stress something here. Don't forget what my team and I do. Although we're very good at removing *problems*, we don't just kill. We're trained to keep our heads when the shit is flying around us thick and fast. We keep our focus. We observe. There is no doubt the Horde are petrified of iron. Look at the way they reacted the first time they encountered it. Two little bullets, you said. And they fled. Not only that, they then did something unheard of, and kept their heads down for two months. Until we turned up, that is.

"I don't think they responded so much to our arrival as to the presence of the iron we possessed. They know what it can do. What it means. And yet, look how they acted yesterday. It's anathema to them, but they still attempted to take us down. Yet not in the usual *let's just charge right in and swarm them* kind of way. Oh no. They did something else they've never done before. They laid in wait, muting their energy fields in an attempt to avoid detection. They set deliberate ambushes. They even tried to rush us from several different directions at once. Both missions encountered similar tactics. New tactics."

"They were being directed," Mohammed stated. "Told what to do, and when."

"Exactly. Which leads me back to my earlier suspicions. How do they see us? How do they see each other, for that matter? And communicate? Because you can bet the command post they positioned on Boleni Heights didn't use mobile phones to text each other the latest battle updates."

"Mobile what?" Ephraim asked, confused by the term.

"A rechargeable handheld communication device from the twenty-first century," Mohammed explained. "In use until twenty-one seventy-seven. That's when the first generation micro-com implants, powered by the body's own electrical field came out." He paused, directing his next question back to Mac. "What are you suggesting?"

"Simply this. The motto of the SBS is 'by strength and guile.' One of our basic combat tenets is 'be prepared.' Despite the apparent breakthroughs we've achieved, we can't afford to rest on our laurels. After the Ardenese ran into these monsters, they were surprised again and again by their tenacity. We know the Horde is strong. We mustn't forget how cunning they are, either. It's obvious *they're* prepared, and so must we be. Until we know for sure what they can do, we've got to walk on eggshells. So far, there's only one definite to emerge from all this. The iron works. Let's base any plans we make on that."

Mohammed nodded. "A sound premise. Ephraim? How are you progressing on that?"

"Very well, actually. While I've been working on the adaptation of the null-point energy, my deputy has achieved some remarkable results." He searched through the people seated below. "Brent? Would you care to elaborate what you've accomplished?"

Brent Wyatt, an engineer by trade from the year 2202, and a member of the eighth intake, got to his feet. Flicking through his notes on a handheld pad, he said, "Okay. First, something you already know. Iron works." He grinned and nodded at Mac. "It works so well we now know less than half a gram of the stuff will destroy your average ogre. A little bit less will still shred their essence enough to trigger self-immolation."

"And how do you know this?" Mohammed asked.

"Because yesterday several Native American braves assisted us with a little experiment. We issued them arrows without heads. Half of the shafts were dipped in molten metal with a fifty-fifty mix, the other in a smaller amount of pure iron. Doing so reduced range and penetration, but they weren't firing at solid objects. The only requirement was that they break the Horde's esoteric thresholds. They did that just fine."

"I see. For those of us who aren't so technical, what will this mean?"

"It means we have a head start. We've established two viable sites for iron ore extraction. The nearest deposits are thirty-five miles away in the Erásan Mountains. Records indicate its poor quality, but it'll do until we can get the flyers into commission. We'll need those other craft, because by far the richest veins are located a hundred and twenty miles out into the Abyssal Plain. That's going to take a little time, so we have to make the best use of what we already have. We've adapted the replicators to fashion replacement arrowheads and bullets out of Ardenese crystal. Once we've smelted down our existing supply of steel, we can coat the new tips in a strong enough solution to ensure they get the job done. A proper weight-to-balance ratio will be restored, so accuracy won't suffer."

Mohammed deferred the decision to Saul.

The commander ruminated for a moment. "I like it. But do we have enough to get by on?" He glanced across to Mac. "Won't that reduce your ability to operate?"

Mac shrugged. "Not necessarily. We're fortunate in that the vortex bringing us here scooped large portions of the rig through with us. Not only was the platform itself made of steel, but it was protected by several rings of .50 robot cannons. Fourteen, to be exact."

"And how many arrived here?"

"Five. Each of them has a double box of ten thousand rounds. I asked Shannon to deploy a system above the site of each gate. That leaves one spare. All those rounds and scrap metal will make a mighty fine source to supplement our existing stock until we can start manufacturing our own bullets. I've already spoken with Brent about your replication technology, and how you need a base template to work with. While that's great for solving our short-term deficit, we need to think long-term, and establish our ability to replenish supplies on a source entirely separate from the Architect."

"What do you envisage?"

"We manufacture our own bullets. It's fortunate that the vast majority of our weapons take nine millimeter rounds. The G40s, 420s, and the Sig Sauer p230s. Even if we create basic handheld casts and molds, we can produce in excess of three hundred units a day. More than enough for our needs. That leaves the heavy duty and specialized stuff—the shotgun cartridges, the .338 magnum sniper rounds, the 7.62s for the AK-48-GMR assault rifles—to the finesse of Ardenese technology. And the .50 cannon shells, of course. We'll need a massive amount of those to ensure we can maintain the devastating cover they provide."

Saul shifted his attention back to Brent. "How viable is all this?"

"Very, Sir. Mac and his team have kindly loaned us an example of each weapon and its corresponding bullet. The Architect is scanning their specifications into the matrix as we speak. Obviously, with power reserves as they are, we can't go into full-scale production. However, if we're willing to make some sacrifices, we can divert a limited supply of energy on a temporary basis, and ensure everyone gets a handgun and a few magazines of ammo. For personal protection, of course. Then we'll switch templates for the production of three basic forge-casts. Each will be capable of producing jacket casings and bullet heads. Once we've built up a reserve, we'll delete the program and do things the old fashioned way. By hand."

The mood within the chamber improved considerably.

Saul beamed. "This is good news, and will definitely help us out with our current problem." He craned his neck to get a better look at Marcus who was sitting quietly at the back of the auditorium, listening attentively. "Marcus, you and your men have been familiarizing yourselves with the wall. You told me yesterday you'd noticed something odd. Would you please share that with us?"

Marcus made his way down the steps to the speaking area. Once there, he addressed the table. "Although this talk of technology, replicators, and strange weaponry confuses me, I am still a soldier. It's the simple things we overlook that can often make the most difference. For example, you say the Horde has besieged this city for a number of years, and for the most part has concentrated its efforts on one particular point. A sound strategy. Yet when I saw the gates in action, I was stunned. That a solid edifice can be manipulated to allow objects to pass through it is . . . well . . . incredible. Magic, we would have called it in my day. And to a military man, an obvious weak point. Yet the Horde does not focus there, nor indeed on any of the other entrances. Why?"

An elderly woman sitting at the high table cleared her throat. Smiling, she inclined her head, first toward Marcus and then the rest of the room. "Hello. For those who don't know me yet, my name's Rosa Sophia, and I am responsible for the administration of this once great city. While this can be a burdensome chore, it has the benefit of allowing me to spend considerable time in the library. Marcus came to see me yesterday, and I was intrigued by his question. So I did some digging. I think I know exactly why the Horde ignores the gates. Here, let me share this with you."

She paused to pick up a handheld tablet. After tapping away for a moment, the air above the central dais began to shimmer. "I'm just loading a news report into the holo-display. It relates to an event that occurred in Rhomane some one hundred years before any of those monsters ever arrived. It's quite revealing."

An image clarified to show a small dart-shaped object impacting against a southeast quadrant of the wall. A blinding flash ensued, followed by a shockwave that encroached upon a suddenly visible shield. As the glare died down, a reporter's voice could be heard in the background:

> *"That was the awful moment when the Shivan-Estre
> met her end. For reasons as yet unknown, her naviga-
> tional beacon malfunctioned. Appearing from rip-space*

only seventy decans from the city wall, its pilots were helpless to prevent the inevitable catastrophe.

As with all such vessels, the Shivan-Estre was constructed of super-dense lydium. If not for the fact that Rhomane's own precincts are made of that same fermionic matter, the results would have been far worse than the death of the two crewmen on board and a bright light in the sky. We are going live now to. . ."

The scene paused, and Rosa replayed the moment of the crash several times. "What you are seeing might explain the reason for their interest in that spot. Remember, lydium is incredibly compact. The Horde cannot interpenetrate it. Nothing can. Unless, perhaps, it has already been weakened by something else made of the same material traveling at super-high velocity. As has been highlighted today, we're not exactly sure how they see or sense things. Do they perceive a minute weakness in an otherwise unblemished obstruction and view it as an opportunity?"

Saul was delighted. "But that's fantastic news. Not only does it fit with what we've been discussing today, but it gives us an opportunity to prepare for a possible breach." He turned to Marcus. "The southeast sector is comprised of disused utility buildings. In fact, the environs are totally uninhabited now, and have been turned over to farming. As a defender of our walls, how would you address this problem?"

Marcus thought for a moment. "Speaking plainly, Commander, I would need to view the area in question to give you a definitive answer. But as a soldier, I think the solution is quite straightforward. Ensure this chink in the armor is saturated in iron. Smelt it. Paint it all over the place if you have to. Use the wonders of the technology at your command to fabricate all manner of traps. Just make sure that if those beasts are successful in breaching the flaw, they cannot avoid walking face-first into the bane of their existence."

"Succinctly put, Marcus. Thank you. I like the way you think. I'll arrange for Mohammed or Shannon to give you a guided tour of the facility later today. Then you can give us your recommendations."

As Marcus made his way back to his seat, Saul drew the attention of each member of the top table. "Any other issues before we get onto the distasteful part of today's proceedings?"

Each high council member shook their head.

Saul then asked the same question of the department heads within the auditorium. Again, the answers came back negative.

The mood darkened, and Saul noted the looks of disgust among the Caledonian clan leaders who sat together in a tight knot, halfway down the steps.

Depressing a button on the console in front of him, he said, "You may bring Captain Houston and Lieutenant Smith in now."

A door opened in the opposite wall. The two men, covered in a multitude of bruises, walked inside, flanked by a pair of sentinels. Once they reached the circle, they halted.

As chilly as the atmosphere was, it got a whole lot colder as Saul made eye contact with the accused. He allowed them to stew in silence for a full minute before speaking.

"Captain Houston. Lieutenant Smith. You both know why you're here, so I won't labor the point. We had hoped the divide that existed between First and Second Platoons had been left behind on Earth. I know for a fact several of my officers went to great lengths to emphasize to you why the affiliations you had there do not exist here. I was hoping to see a superior level of maturity, as demonstrated by your fellow travelers from the legionnaire and highland contingents. Sadly, tragically, that doesn't appear to be the case.

"We have listened to the evidence of the officers and men of First Platoon, and have spoken for many hours with the warriors of Clans Buchan and Calhoun. While it cannot be established for certain who among your faction pulled the trigger, we have no doubt that Lexington Fox's death was not accidental. The joint maneuvers performed by him that day were textbook. He acquitted himself with a degree of professionalism and honor that is sorely lacking in the pair of you. Everyone should have made it home safely."

Saul stood and made his way to the speakers' circle.

Maintaining eye contact with the two disgraced cavalry officers, he growled, "We are no fools. Although we cannot prove conclusively his death was murder, we know it was. You know it was. This is Arden. We will not tolerate your petty mentality here. Do you understand?"

"Yes."

"Yes, what?"Saul bellowed so suddenly that the two men staggered back in surprise.

"Yes, Sir." they repeated in unison.

"I really hope you do, gentlemen." Saul came up and stood almost toe to toe with them. "Because we can't afford to waste a single life. That's the only reason you are still breathing on this occasion. Now listen very carefully, because I'm only going to say this once."

Saul took a step away, the better to hold their attention. "It has always been the case that an officer is responsible for the actions of those under his command. That tenet will apply to you in a very literal sense from now on. Your men had better learn to walk on eggshells, because if an 'accident' like this ever happens again, be in no doubt, *you* will be held directly responsible. There will be no debate, no trial, no appeal. We won't waste a bullet on you. You're either a part of our family, or you belong to the Horde. Have you heard what I said and understood its implications fully?"

"Yes, Sir," they snapped.

"Let it be recorded as such within the minutes of today's meeting." Saul's face grew darker. "Custodians? Please escort these men back to their rooms. They are to be stripped of their weapons and held in confinement until we determine what other restrictions to place on them. The same goes for every soldier within Second Platoon. No arguments."

"Certainly, Commander," chirped the nearest of the constructs. "We will facilitate your instructions immediately."

Before Houston or Smith had the opportunity to turn, Saul added, "While we'd never send you out on a mission unarmed, you'll have to earn the right to carry any form of firearm within these walls again. And don't worry, with what I've got planned for you, there'll be plenty of opportunity to show what you're really made of."

He turned his back and dismissed them.

*

"What do you make of that, lads?" Cathal MacNoimhin hissed. "A case of their hand being forced, or what?"

"Och, Cameron's no fool," Searc whispered. "He knows there wasn't enough to pin it on either of those skelpies, even though it must have been carried out under the ass-wipe's instructions. You saw the way he had it in for the lad ever since they arrived."

"Do you think he'd do it, though?" Cathal said. "Cameron? Would he actually feed them to the devils?"

"I've got no doubt the man has balls of steel," Kohrk Underwood replied. He watched the commander resume his seat at the high table. "Now he's involved his own honor, he has to show himself strong. And from what I've heard, he'd tip them over the bloody wall himself."

"Doesn't stop *us* from making a plan or two, though, does it?" Searc suggested.

Cathal ushered his men closer and lowered his voice even further. "What did you have in mind, Searc?"

Chapter Thirteen

Gelling Together

"If you could try to keep together," Mohammed called, "we've still got a way to go yet, and I wouldn't want you missing out on your evening meal."

He glanced back to see how the small party was faring. Marcus Brutus, together with two of his centurions, Decimus Martinas and Tiberius Tacitus, appeared as fresh as daisies. This didn't surprise Mohammed. From what he remembered, legionnaires were renowned for marching countless miles through all sorts of terrain. It wouldn't have surprised him if they viewed this excursion as nothing more than a brief stroll, something to be taken by all their members before the real day's work began. Cathal MacNoimhin and Stained-With-Blood also appeared relaxed. Mohammed listened in to snippets of their conversation as they whiled away the miles, chatting about their respective lives and tribes back home.

Behind them, ten yards further back, the two disgraced cavalry officers limped along beneath their own personal clouds of woe.

I suppose it must be painful, really. Searc's men did give them quite a hiding before they returned. Houston and Smith were fortunate Red and his clan were there to prevent things from getting too out of hand. Pity. It would have helped settle an ugly issue once and for all. Aloud, he urged, "C'mon, gentlemen, keep up. Not too far now before we come to the perimeter of the outer zone."

"Why are we walking anyway?" Smith complained. "This place is huge. Why couldn't we have just used the transporter device, or a skimmer? Or our horses, come to that?"

"Because you need to get an appreciation of what you'll be defending, young man," Mohammed replied, "and of the distances involved should you find yourself stuck out here on foot. And to be honest, we reserve our resources for more important use."

"So, it's about five miles from the central complex to the city wall?" Marcus asked.

"Yes, that's right. Who told you?"

"No one. We're used to counting off the distance as we march. Helps you keep track of things quite accurately. I'd say we've traveled well over four miles already. And, judging from the size of those cow-like beasts in the distance, there's roughly half a mile left."

"Very good!" Mohammed was impressed. "And you do that as a matter of course?"

"Usually. It's also handy if you have to direct archers or catapult captains. Understanding your ranges can give you the edge in a fight. As it will do here."

"You think so?"

"Most certainly." Casting ahead, Marcus explained, "We know that if the Horde breaches the wall, they will do so in *that* general area. At the moment, you can only spare one of the futuristic guns that Lieutenant McDonald was speaking about. A . . . cannon, yes?"

"The .50 millimeter? That's correct."

"So we will have to rely on a multitude of smaller weapons to prevent a flood of invaders. If we mark this area properly, and station ballistae, scorpios, archers, and so forth, at different distances from the breach, it will allow us to maintain a steady rate of fire without endangering our men."

"As in a tiered response?"

"Precisely. And if the wind is in our favor, you'll see something quite exceptional. When I was in Africa, we used to heat sand and fling it at our enemy. The damn stuff gets everywhere. In your hair, inside armor, on your clothes. And it burns like the seven hells. Of course, on this occasion, I'd want to mix a healthy dose of rust or other iron flecks in with the sand. From what I've seen, the results will be quite explosive. And we wouldn't have to resort to these bullets you're so concerned about. We could hold them in reserve should our efforts be in vain."

The party came to a full stop as the weight of Marcus's words sank in.

Eyes wide with excitement, Mohammed keyed a message into his tablet. Looking toward Houston, he explained, "I've just thought of an excellent project that will get your men out of confinement and keep them gainfully employed for a day or two. Sandbagging! Under Marcus's direction, they'll stockpile a combination of soil and rust to ensure the catapults have plenty of ammunition should the need ever arise."

Pleased with himself, Mohammed resumed their trek toward the utility buildings. A number of solar powered lights activated as they walked, casting a warm amber glow over the surrounding fields.

"What are those creatures anyway?" Cathal asked.

"Ardenese cattle and livestock, left here to help facilitate our infrastructure. Believe it or not, we've also got a number of sheep, goats, and a small herd of precious dairy cattle. Like your horses, they were brought through in respective intakes. They've adapted quite well, but have to be kept segregated. They have their own pastures to the north of the city."

"And these?"

"Over there are lolaths. The Ardenese equivalent of a cow. In the fields to the left are provats and yithans. They also give milk, although it's very thick and sweet and not to everyone's taste. As you can see, they look like a pairing between a lamb and an ibex. In the west quadrant, we have a rather large herd of rhobexi. Think of a cross between a deer and a bull, and you won't be far wrong.

"We were also left a number of staples. Porran, a wheat and barley combination, and rizet, a crop very similar to rice. All excellent for eating, and all very precious."

He made eye contact with Houston and Smith as they strolled. "And they're part of the reason we can't afford to be divided. These beasts and fields were left here for us. To sustain us, while we wage war against a relentless enemy. But they're dying out. Although we have a heavily mechanized and scientifically advanced system for crop rotation, artificial insemination, and food production, it's not enough. Simple soil depletion, stagnating diversity, and attrition are having an adverse affect. The crops are failing. The animals won't carry fetuses to term. The sheer grind of this siege is taking its toll, and unless we all pull together, we're not going to last. Only a closely bonded team can hope to survive the drastic measures we'll have to implement to survive. Things are going to get tough very soon. Guess what'll happen to those who don't fit in."

"We get the picture," Houston drawled, "so don't worry. My boys will toe the line, I assure you. No bother, no fuss." Much more quietly, almost to himself, he added, "No more *unfortunate* accidents."

A ringing back-hander from Cathal sent Houston sprawling to the floor with a cut lip. "See that's the case, laddie. Otherwise, you just might find a war axe *unfortunately* planted in your skull during the heat of battle. Understand?"

Houston scowled. Regaining his feet, he spat out a mouthful of blood.

Marcus stepped forward in an attempt to defuse the situation. "I would listen to what he says, Captain. Speaking from experience, you don't want to find yourself on the wrong side of the Iceni. Or any of the highland tribes, come to that. They have an uncanny knack for taking you by surprise."

Houston continued to glare. Marcus placed his hand on the cavalry officer's arm and leaned in close. "Leave it, you fool! If you keep acting in this manner, he will take it as a personal challenge and kill you on the spot. I don't imagine for one minute the threat of restricted duties or incarceration will act as a deterrent. Do you?"

Smith joined them. "Listen to him, cousin, for pity's sake. He'll murder us in our beds."

Marcus lowered his voice even further. "And don't think people will be sorry to see you go." He shrugged. "It's up to you."

Mohammed watched the incident silently, assessing each man's reactions.

Yes. I think we've got ourselves a good bunch here. Saul will be pleased to hear his gut feeling is paying off. They're already gelling into a team. Becoming part of the family. And if Houston continues to be difficult, they'll sort him out for us.

He coughed to attract everyone's attention. "If you've quite finished? We are here to discuss defenses, after all." Indicating the nearby buildings and warehouses, he continued, "Now, take a good look around. Work together. Anything you can think of that might assist in either preventing the Horde coming through in the first place, or delaying them if they do, will be most welcome. Remember, Arden's future depends on your efforts."

God help us!

*

The people gathered within the xenobiology laboratory were an unusual blend of characters. Warriors all, they represented a wide diversity of cultures and levels of scientific sophistication. All united by a keen desire to better understand the enemy they faced.

"What is it that the Horde does to us, specifically?" Mac asked. "I understand there's a degree of physical trauma involved from time to time, but I'm still trying to get my head around the element of psychic vampirism."

"It's best if I actually show you," Ayria Solram replied, "or at least share what we've been able to determine."

Ayria turned to activate a holo-emitter and brought up a three dimensional representation of a human brain. Enlarging it, she zoomed in on the synapses, which flared regularly with pulses of bright golden light. Ignoring Mac and his team, Ayria smiled at Snow Blizzard, Kohrk Underwood, and Flavius Velerianus. "In its simplest terms, what you are seeing here is a process that takes place inside your head, millions of times every second. Whether it's the automatic things like breathing and blinking, or the deliberate ones, such as choosing what piece of fruit to eat, it's all governed by what happens within the brain. Those flashes of light are electrical signals. They pass along special roadways, called synapses. It's the synapses that allow you to carry out the everyday actions required to live. To eat, drink, sleep and function, because they ensure the right message is sent to the right place."

Each of the three nodded, so Ayria added some embellishments to the scene. The simulation was joined by more holograms, those of a human being standing next to a monster. Ayria continued, "As you can see, the man is surrounded by an aura. That nimbus is generated by the processes taking place within the body. We think *this* is what attracts the Horde." Pointing to the fiend, she continued, "While it's difficult to show what our enemy looks like, we do know their matrix appears to be concentrated around a common core. That essence requires energy to maintain cohesion and stability. When their atoms become excited, they become visible, usually in the area of their jaws, talons, and eyes. Now look at this."

Ayria manipulated the controls once more, and the beast turned to grip its victim within its claws. The human tensed as if in great pain. Then he began twitching uncontrollably in the grunt's arms. Within seconds, the spasms stopped and the man slumped to the floor.

"This is an actual simulation of a number of real life attacks captured on surveillance," Ayria said. "It takes roughly five seconds for one of them to kill a person. But not in the way you might think. Look again, but this time, watch the image of the enlarged brain."

As the spook attacked once more, Ayria emphasized the electrical pathways within the cerebrum. The result was shocking. At first the signals flowed as they should, randomly and in a number too great to comprehend. Then the brain flared, and a massive wave of energy surged in one direction, toward the site where the ogre had gripped its victim. Seconds later, the network of glittering filaments darkened, before sparking into haphazard flashes of weakening cognitive function. Finally, after about four minutes, everything went black.

"What happened?" Mac gasped.

"You should ask yourself what *didn't* happen," Ayria countered. "Take a peek at the vital function readout."

She pressed a button, and certain areas within the man's body were clarified in 3D close-up. The heart was most noticeable. Thudding wildly, it attempted to maintain a steady rhythm, but in the absence of the correct stimulus, quickly seized and arrested. The lungs also fluttered madly, inflating and deflating out of sync before collapsing entirely. Had it not been for the enhanced optics, no one would have known what was taking place inside the human, because the face betrayed no hint of the agonizing death he was suffering.

"This person has been paralyzed," Snow Blizzard stated. "Robbed of life essence, this *electricity* that makes our brains work, he cannot endure. Although drained, his body still fights to live. It is a hopeless struggle."

Ayria was impressed. "You are exactly right. Even when the grunts resort to physical violence, they don't kill outright. It would deny their feast. The brain, although stripped of its ability to function, is still very much alive. Unfortunately, it is now unable to perform its job of sending the right signals to the correct places in our bodies. And that's why these beasts are such a nightmare. Imagine, if you can, the pain of a combined heart attack, stroke, and lung collapse. And then being unable to express that agony in any way. I'm telling you now, if you ever find yourself in a situation where one of your comrades has been taken, the best thing you could do for them is put a bullet between their eyes."

Everyone was shocked at the brutality of the doctor's statement.

"That's what almost happened to Commander Cameron, isn't it?" Kohrk said. "When his friend died several months ago. He felt himself falling prey to the devil's touch before the blood-metal did its work."

"Yes," Ayria whispered, lost in the moment, "we nearly lost him on the day the answer fell into our laps."

"Is there nothing we can do to counter the effect?"Mac asked. "I mean, do they require skin on skin contact to initiate their drain, or just close proximity? Is there something we could rig to cause feedback so they overdose?"

"The Horde only needs to be within inches of you to feed," Ayria replied. "Their outer corona seems to be the defining barrier. Not their tangible essence. If any part of your body becomes enmeshed by it, the feeding frenzy is automatically triggered and will not stop until you are screwed, or the brute is dead. As to overloading them? I doubt we could ever manage that."

"Why?"

"When I conducted the welcome tour in the Hall of Remembrance with Mohammed, do you remember me telling you how each of the successive groups to arrive had been decimated by these things? How there's so few of us left?"

"I do, yes."

"Well, that's not because we came through helpless and unarmed. Far from it. Over the years, we've been equipped with some of the most devastating armaments you could ever wish for. Phasic blasters, teleron disruptors, photon cannons, ion accelerators, even plain old plasma rifles. But none of them were truly effective. I'm afraid to say, each and every single form of advanced weaponry we could lay our hands on involved the discharge of highly excited, compressed beams of energy. You can only guess what happened when we used them on the Horde for the first time."

"They fed on it?"

"More than that . . ." Ayria's eyes got a faraway look as she relived the experience, ". . . they became evil incarnate. It was as if we'd injected them with stimulants. I'm sure you've heard stories of berserkers from time to time? In Norse and Germanic mythology, some men became so enraged, so uncontrollable during the heat of battle they went into a trancelike state of overwhelming fury. They didn't feel pain or show remorse. They wouldn't stop until their enemies were dead or dying, and even then they had problems stopping them wreaking contin-ued havoc on fellow soldiers. Now imagine all that savagery rolled up into a seething mass of ten-foot high monstrosities."

Mac was stunned to silence.

Sam Pell, 4 Troop's technical expert, was intrigued. "If you don't mind my asking, Ayria, what wattage are we talk-ing about?"

"Of the weapons? It varied. The plasma rifles discharged around fifty megajoules of energy. The big cannons, up to one hundred thousand."

"That's more than lightning," Sam gasped, horrified at the implications. "Hell! It's even hotter than the sun. Are you sure there was no degradation whatsoever in their thresholds?"

"Oh, I'm sorry. I'm not explaining this very clearly, am I?" Ayria seemed embarrassed by her efforts. "But then again, I am a doctor. No, the weapons *did* work. Many thousands of the Horde were destroyed outright. But the process of their de-struction sent highly energized shockwaves through the rest of the swarm, which invigorated the survivors and boosted them to even greater ferocity. If the heavy guns were used, it actu-ally triggered a feeding and spawning frenzy, where thousands upon thousands of fresh spooks were generated. More, in fact, than we wiped out. They'd swarm at us like a tsunami, a never-ending wave of shrieking pressure and hate that drove some of us to suicide. In the end, we daren't use any of the armaments unless the direst emergency arose."

"What about nukes?"

"We have such ordinance. But again, what would be the point? I don't think mutual destruction was on the Ardenese agenda. The planet would be ruined if we ever used such things. And we'd be just as dead."

Everyone fell quiet as they digested the implications of Ayria's revelation.

"Would a shower of iron not work?" Flavius asked, puzzled that no one had thought of a simpler approach.

"Shower of iron?" Ayria repeated, unfamiliar with the term.

"Yes. When the legions are deployed to hotter climates, we utilize a method of assault that is nigh on impossible to defend against. We cook sand and use catapults to fling it at opposing warriors. The heated particles saturate the air and not only smother the enemy, but cause great discomfort or even injury when inhaled. I've been reading something on the histories of the peoples brought here over the years. Can you not adapt some of your missiles or explosive devices to simply burst in the air?"

"Yes!" Kohrk bellowed. He slapped Flavius heartily on the back. "Seed the bastards in blood-metal and watch them burn. Now that's more like it."

"It's a good point," Ayria admitted, noting how well the former enemies were now relating to each other. "I'm not a soldier, so I don't know if anyone has thought of that before or even mentioned it to the commander. But I will."

Then she had a thought. "Kohrk, why do your people call it blood-metal?"

Kohrk shrugged. "It's always been called that. Furies are eldritch creatures of the deepest theurgy. Our shamans say you have to poison them at their basest level—within their heart's-blood—to stand any chance of driving them away. Only iron can accomplish that feat. We are encouraged to eat it during ritual cleansing ceremonies whenever clans are besieged by dark mischief. Such knowledge has been handed down for generations among my kin."

"As it has with ours," Snow Blizzard added. "To my people, fey spirits are known as otherworldly aberrations seeking to gain entrance into our realm by possessing the weak and vulnerable. They are unable to do so when tribal lands are positioned in areas where star-metal has fallen from the roof of the world. Our own witchdoctors engage in the dream-quest to better understand the patterns wheeling through Napioa's hunting grounds. Through them, they are led to the best sites for settlement. If we are ever troubled by demons, we wear sky-tooth necklaces for protection as we hunt them."

"Star-metal?" Ayria echoed. "Are you referring to meteor strikes? Rocks that leave a fiery trail across the sky as they fall from the heavens?"

"Yes. That is correct."

A million and one thoughts crowded through Ayria's mind at once. *Did their mystics know something all along? Were they attuned in some way? Has the Horde, or something like them, ever been to Earth? Surely we'd know.* Then a radical idea came to her. "Kohrk, you mentioned your people would eat iron? What did you mean by that?"

If I can devise a method to enrich iron levels in the blood whilst avoiding toxicity, we might be able to repulse the monsters at the basest level. Hell! This just might work.

*

The huge beast snorted and raised itself to full height. Mesmerized, Small Robes stood stock still, extended her hand and held her breath.

Slowly, warily, the massive creature edged toward her. Its huge wet nostrils quivered as it inhaled her scent. Small Robes cooed gently, and tufted, triangular ears swiveled toward her, rigid with attention and purpose.

"C'mon, beautiful," she murmured, "I won't hurt you."

The proud head dipped tentatively toward her tiny fingers. Loud sniffing ensued, followed by a warm lick from an impressively long tongue that steamed in the cooling night air.

"What is it?" she squeaked, finding it increasingly difficult to contain her excitement.

"The database names them rhobexi," Penny Frasier replied. "And as you can see, they look like a blending of a small bison and a stag. He's a beauty, isn't he? That's Atilla, the alpha male of the herd."

"What do you have them for?"

"For food. To enrich the soil. And of course, to study. I'm a xenobiologist, and find these creatures fascinating. The Ardenese left them here for us to utilize, and I've enjoyed discovering how familiar they are to animals back home. It reminds me that, despite the vast distances separating our worlds, life went on here in much the same way as it did on Earth. Yes, they were much more advanced than we were, but they still had the same dreams. The same goals and aspirations. People had families. They grew crops. Loved music and the arts, and the beautiful world they lived on . . . ."

"And it was all taken away from them," Small Robes sighed. "They were helpless to prevent it."

"That's why I'm so determined to make this work. They're relying on us to reseed their world and give them a fresh start. Us too, when you think about it. We'd already be dead if it wasn't for their intervention. Gone . . . into goodness knows what." Penny turned to look Small Robes in the eye. "I'm glad your people came through. You, the Caledonians, and the legionnaires. You led much simpler lives than we did, and you have a keener appreciation for the land. I'm sure that if we survive the

coming months and eventually get to initiate the re-genesis protocol, we'll all be looking to you to help us step into the future."

Small Robes stared off into the distance. The sun was dip-
ping behind the Garnet Mountains as Se'ochan, Arden's moon,
commenced her journey.

*Yes. It would be nice to end the underlying tension that's
soiled things so far. But if we're truly going to unite, it'll take
a lot more than hopes and dreams. Even among the nine tribes
of the Cree, clan disagreements led to the terrible division between Blackfoot, Lakota, Sioux and Apache that brought us
here. My own husband-to-be, rejected his family name to pro-
claim himself Chief of all Cree. And here? Our cultures are
vastly different . . .*

*I wonder what the catalyst might be that eventually sparks
the light of unity?*

Chapter Fourteen

A Moment of Clarity

Mac scanned the route ahead from his position within the skidder. The cargo carrier was three times as large as a normal skimmer and twice as slow. But for today's mission, it would suit their needs perfectly.

So far so good. We've passed several pods of dormant spooks and they haven't sniffed us out yet. Mohammed's suggestion to use the modified ammunition appears to be spot on.

They were coming up on two miles from target. As he had time, Mac decided to examine the special ammunition they'd be using today. While mundane manufacturing methods were forging ahead apace, Mohammed had urged the Special Forces team to use an alternate source until it could be ascertained how sensitive the Horde actually was to iron. This mission in particular depended on stealth, and so he had commissioned the production of over ten thousand rounds of crystal jackets. Fashioned by the Ardenese replicators, the batch had been produced in only half a day and were melded to glass tips, each of which had been dipped in iron.

Mac removed one of the new rounds from a spare magazine and rolled it back and forth between thumb and forefinger. Then he hefted it in his cupped hand. *Clever idea. The weight and feel of them is superb. If these perform as expected, I'll ask him to produce more. We can use them on ops where covert movement is essential.*

Content, Mac turned his attention to their 'present' from Ephraim Miller.

The head of the technical division had excelled himself. Miller had been working on a device to destroy large numbers of the Horde without having to resort to energetic release. He had devised a cunning weapon that employed the use of an unstable micro gravity-well, sheathed within a vacuum. Programmed with an effective life of only three seconds, it was designed to activate and create a quantum vortex. If all went well, it would be able to crush their adversaries out of existence before it expired. As it was still in the experimental stage, it was unknown just how far its active field would reach, so Mac had volunteered to take a prototype with him on a trial run.

To maximize results, the dinner plate-sized device had been housed within its own null-point shield, and strapped to a fuel cell. In that way, once Mac chose to reveal its presence, he could be assured of attracting as many monsters as possible. Mac intended to activate it once the mission was over so they could assess its effectiveness from a safe distance.

It's a heavy bugger. But then again, if it works, we won't have to lug them about everywhere. We can use a skimmer to drop them off at strategic locations and detonate them when the time is right.

A barely audible chime sounded in his ear.

Time for final checks. Sitting forward, he activated the intercom-relay and spoke quietly and calmly into the microphone. "All squads standby for verbal checks."

Pausing to allow everyone in the two craft to come fully alert, he continued. "Alpha, do you copy?" Stu Duggan, Sam Pell and Jumper Collins were traveling in the same vehicle as Mac; each gave him a thumbs-up.

Mac returned the gesture. "We are the fire-team. We will broach the perimeter, secure the hangar, and call in the skidder to help us recover the drones. Understood?"

Each man replied in the affirmative.

Mac turned to Stained-With-Blood and the rest of the Native Americans who sat opposite. "Stained-With-Blood? For the purpose of this mission, you will be Blood-one. Diving Hawk, you are Blood-two. White Eagle, Blood-three. Dancing Snake, Blood-four. You men will act in support. You will protect Ephraim's 'present' and the perimeter breach to ensure our exit point remains free and unobstructed of the enemy. If an emergency arises, leave the device in situ, and fight your way to the RV point. We will activate the bomb remotely to create a diversion. Is that clear?"

"It is, Lieutenant," Stained-With-Blood replied. The rest of his warriors looked on impassively.

Mac glanced across to the separate party traveling alongside in the other, smaller vehicle. He called, "Bravo, listen in. Mark, Sean, Fonzy, Andy. You are our cover-team. On the next marker, peel away as briefed and set up an observation and sniper post below the astrometrics observatory on Boleni Mount. Andy, Fonzy? You will partner up with the ANS-1X. Mark and Sean will move down from your position to provide midrange cover with the 420s. Roger so far?"

"Roger that," Mark replied.

"Deploy Ullas and his Damonii around you on the hillside. They are your eyes and ears to danger. Any sign of trouble, get back to your sprinter and rendezvous at the spaceport breach. Confirm?"

"That's a yes, Boss. All clear."

Another gentle tone pinged out.

"That's your signal, Mark," Mac directed, "good hunting. Stay dark unless you need to update me urgently."

The skimmer peeled away, accelerating up the mountainside. Mac watched them go before diverting his attention back to the technicians within the primary skidder. He addressed the civilians. "People. Your job is to assist us in the loading of the drones. As long as you stay within the null-field, you will be completely safe. Remember, you have been equipped with pistols and drilled in their use, so you won't be entirely defenseless. Does everyone know what they're doing?"

Half a dozen anxious faces indicated their determination not to mess up.

Good. Here we go. "Fire-team? Final weapons check. Activate HUDs and bring personal shields online. Go to internals. Sam? Ensure the covert link plays through to the spare console so blood-units can keep abreast of the state of play."

The craft decelerated as the outer perimeter loomed.

In bygone days, the steady ranks of brilliant white pylons arching off into the distance on either side would have been enhanced by a curtain of shimmering blue light. A necessary precaution, to protect the unwary from the energies being unleashed inside as star ships maneuvered to and fro prior to departure. Now, the force field lay dormant. All that remained was an inner, meshed fence.

Mac suppressed a giggle. All that advanced technology and they still find a use for good old chain-link. Please God, don't let it be made of some unheard-of metal we can't cut through.

The skidder glided to a halt. Like a well oiled machine, Mac and his men slid over the sidewall and dropped to the ground. Fanning out, they quickly ascertained the way was clear. Mac signaled to Stained-With-Blood and his warriors to join them.

Once everyone was ready, they edged forward and positioned themselves against the railing itself. Mac removed a small sachet from within one of his pockets and broke the seal on top of the spout. Selecting two areas spaced widely apart, he sprayed solvent from inside the pouch over the top links. A pungent aroma filled the air. It was closely followed by a faint sizzling sound. Acid ate through the resin-covered wire, its progress marked by faint whisps of smoke. Within moments, the entire section sagged forward, to be caught by the waiting teams.

Beckoning the skidder forward, Mac used hand signals to indicate that the mine should be lowered over the side. Taking possession of the device, he glanced about, selecting an area several yards outside the entry point to position it. The breach should siphon the bastards into a more concentrated knot before we blow it.

Mac stared toward the Garnet Mountains in the west. About an hour until sundown. Perfect. Time to get the ball rolling. Activating the internal system, he called, "All units, those with HUDs are to switch to rotating frequencies now. Primary pattern will be sonic motion diffusers. Infrared and ultraviolet will be set to secondary. Remember, until we retrieve the drones, stealth is of the utmost importance. Do not engage the enemy unless you have to. Once we have our consignment onboard, it'll be gloves off. You know what's expected. Good luck, everyone."

With that, he turned and ushered the fire-team forward.

Mac had decided to avoid the terminal altogether and had fashioned their entrance in an area adjacent to the main building and opposite a vehicular subway. The plans indicated the four hundred yard long tunnel would give direct access onto the facilities service road.

Adopting a diamond formation, Mac led the way as they crossed into an outer zone that looked as if it used to be used for parking. The huge glass windows of the reception wing caught the ruby-red shafts of the setting sun and enhanced them. Reflected, they bathed Mac and his men in warmth and glory. Despite the danger, Mac felt an ineffable moment of peace and tranquility that made him yearn to stay in that one spot forever. He checked his step.

"Boss?" Stu queried.

"Relax, boys," Mac replied, indicating the burnished image before them, "just enjoying the moment, and catching some rays on a beach somewhere."

"Damn! And I forgot my sun block, too." Jumper patted himself down in a mock effort to discover the elusive tube of cream.

Suppressed sniggers skittered back and forth over the airwaves. Dressed as they were from head to toe in protective armor, the quip wasn't wasted on anyone.

"Okay, quiet down," Mac said, "my bad. Stay sharp. We've got a job to do."

Discipline restored, they pressed onward without incident until the tarmac began to fall away into the underpass. From his position, Mac could see the central roadway within was lined on either side by raised, gantry-style walkways. The angle of the sun created sharp contrasts between light and dark, and the interior soon became lost in shadow. Mac shut his free eye to help it adjust to the muted conditions they would find inside.

"Dust devil formation," he instructed.

The team split into pairs. As they disappeared into the gloom, each soldier positioned himself back to back with his buddy. Advancing, they pirouetted around each other. Progress was slow but sure. High and low, left and right, every nook and cranny was scrutinized with professional objectivity.

Ebony stretched away before them, exacerbated by the glaring aperture presented by the other end of the tunnel. The rotational frequency displayed on their HUDs reduced the disparity considerably.

Something caught Mac's attention. He froze. "Stop, stop!"

Scanning the causeways ahead, he could see an undulating distortion in the air. It was faint, but definitely something that shouldn't be there. Horde?

"Take a knee," he whispered. "Eyes on. Ten and two o'clock high."

As he waited for the rest of his team to consider the anomalies ahead, Mac tried to define what he was seeing. He zoomed in. Yup, it's them all right. At rest and in an almost catatonic condition. Ayria said they adopted this kind of state when they went inactive, but this is the first time I've really had a chance to study them asleep.

The rippling curtains had no defined parameters, and seemed content to etch the darkness in shivers. A baffling amalgam of substance and texture, the proximity of each specimen couldn't be clearly defined. Yet every so often, one of them released a pulse of electric-blue desire which skittered off through their collective consciousness. As it did so, rumbles of protest and outbursts of lurid scarlet energy split the air, distinguishing an alarming array of horns, talons, and fangs, all packed tightly together.

There must be hundreds of them.

"No second-guesses required then?" Sam said as another plasma ribbon crackled through the right-hand mass. Arching across the subway, the discharge danced through the sleeping essences lining the opposite catwalk, almost rousing them from slumber.

Waiting patiently for the disturbance to subside, Sam offered his opinion. "Boss, they're obviously in some form of suspended animation or sleep-like condition. Most probably to conserve strength while there's nothing about to feast on. But look at them. From the way they're acting, it appears to me as if some of them are dreaming."

"What makes you say that?"

"Remember our last op, where some of the Horde tried to ambush us? They'd hidden themselves under the ground and reduced their auras so they were practically indistinguishable from their surroundings."

"Much like what we have here."

"Yes, but we didn't see any of these static flares. They were awake, they were lucid, and in control. They were making a deliberate attempt to increase the element of surprise. This is something different. They're not expecting any action whatsoever. In fact, they're so chilled, they've flaked out. And what happens when a cognitive mind falls asleep?"

Realization sent a thrill along Mac's spine. It dreams! What the hell would monsters fantasize about? Hang on! But that would mean these sneaky buggers are . . ."Jesus, we've got to make sure this intel gets back. Guys, take things nice and steady. There's more to these spooks than we think. Don't do anything that might wake them up. Once we exit the tunnel, I'm going to relay a message back to Commander Cameron. Some egghead ought to be able to make sense of all this."

Glancing ahead, Mac could see where some of the Horde had spilled over the railings on both sides of the subway, only to lie inert on the tarmac.

Fortunately for us the road is so wide.

Tightening formation, they crept forward again. Mac advised, "Use your cold lights to mark the edge of the mass. Err on the side of caution. Give the driver at least a yard's grace on either side."

One by one, each team member removed a number of small plastic tubes from a special pocket on the side of his belt. The sticks looked inconspicuous until they were bent into an inverted V shape and shaken roughly. That procedure broke a small chamber in the middle of the rod that allowed two inert chemicals to mix together. Once combined, the liquid glowed with a soft, red phosphorus radiance. Designed to last close to twenty minutes, they would provide a safe channel for the skidder to navigate without having to resort to lights.

Slowly, arduously, the team picked their way through the slumber party from hell. Leaving their beacons every five yards or so, it took them just over ten minutes to emerge into the cool dusk air.

Adopting a defensive arc, each soldier scanned the vicinity. The dwindling light cast a spectral shroud over the scene. To one side, for almost as far as the eye could see, the silhouettes of a multitude of spacecraft in all shapes and sizes haunted the launch and standby zones. Further along, closer to the terminus, mystery hulks peeped out from the ranks of pens and hangars edging the field, hinting at further mysteries within. Witnessing the number of liners now lying abandoned chilled Mac to the bone. He recalled Saul's words from the briefing of only a few weeks previously. "How about that," he murmured. "Marie Celeste doesn't do it justice. It's a ships' graveyard."

"Yeah, except that these skeletons will probably still work when you crank them up," Sam ventured. "If they're powered by aqua-cells as the commander hinted, we could have an alternate escape route off this rock, right there in front of us."

"Link your HUDs together," Mac directed, "capture everything you can. The guys back at base need as much live-time information as possible for an accurate review once we've wrapped things up here." That reminds me.

Mac's com-set was strapped to the inside of his left forearm. Using the keypad, he compressed the data into a condensed file, and prepared to send it back to Rhomane. Had he been on Earth, Mac would only have needed to enter the command 'send' and a satellite link would have completed the rest of the task. Here, he would have to transmit the information via the skidder parked out at the entrance.

He hailed the driver of that craft. "Nick? Can you hear me?"

"Yes, I'm here," an anxious voice replied. "Do you . . . do you want me to come on through now?"

"In a moment. I'm sending you an important document for the operations room. Relay it on to them immediately. Once they've confirmed its receipt, you can join us."

"Okay. You . . . you're sending it now, yes?"

"It's on the way," Mac replied, as he pressed the button.

"Got it." There was a slight pause as Nick transferred the information on as requested. "All done," he confirmed. "S . . . so I can drive the skidder through now?"

Mac could hear how nervous Nick was. They're not used to this kind of pressure. I'd better get them busy and take their minds off things. Aloud, he replied, "That's right Nick. If you would be so kind as to take charge of your crew? Make sure they have their weapons ready, just in case, but leave the safety catches on for now. Fingers are to remain alongside the guard unless you know you need to fire. That's not going to happen, though. The only Horde we've passed are all dormant within the confines of the subway, up on the gantries. A few have spilled out into the road, so travel slow, and keep between the flares."

"Will do. I'm on my way."

Mac had an idea. "I'm sending Jumper and Stu back down the tunnel to meet you. Their stealth armor will be active, but we'll get them to trigger a green-colored glow-rod to mark their positions. They'll walk you through the rest of the way."

"Thanks, Mac. Much appreciated."

Mac nodded toward his comrades, and they scuttled back into the underpass. Once they had disappeared from sight, Mac spoke quietly with Sam Pell. He indicated the second building along the eastern quarter. "That's our target. The way looks relatively clear, so I don't want to go snooping about in there until we have to. We've got a few minutes, how about we check out the nearest ship?"

"What, go off mission?"

"Not exactly. After all, we are here to gain intelligence as well." Mac set his sights on a small shuttled-sized vehicle parked only fifty yards away. The front side hatch was open and a short platform had been lowered to the ground, presumably by its previous occupants. Directing Sam's attention toward it, he continued, "It's close. It's open, and we only need take a look. If we can record the state of the interior and what controls it employs, someone back at base might know how to power it up and fly it. Just think of the tactical advantage it would give us. We'll be in and out before Nick and the rest rejoin us."

"What the hell," Sam replied, "let's do it."

Scampering forward, the two men quickly closed on the abandoned craft. When they were ten yards from it, Mac made a looping gesture with the index fingers of both hands. They split up. Advancing in opposite directions, they commenced a slow circle of the ship.

Spinning constantly, Mac surveyed the area about him. The silence was otherworldly, and he had to fight down the feeling that something was going to jump out on him at any moment. The sensation increased as he met up with Sam below the open door. So where the hell are they? "Anything?"

"Not a squeak, Boss. For a place that's supposed to be overrun with Horde, it's a bit of an anticlimax."

"Unless they're taking shelter? Like back in the tunnel?"

"There's only one way to find out for sure."

"I'll leave my camera on the rotating bandwidth," Mac cautioned. "You switch yours to lowlight. Take in everything you can."

Side by side, the specialists crept their way up the tiered ramp. Entering through the hatch, they emerged inside what appeared to be a reception area. A swift check determined the front compartment housed a spacious flight deck, while the first rearward section contained the crew's quarters. A heavily armored archway led through to the back hold.

After ensuring to record anything that might be of value, Mac decided it was time to check out the cargo area. "C'mon, let's get this finished and meet up with the others."

Stepping forward, they discovered the huge doors were automatic. As he passed through, Mac staggered, overcome by sudden vertigo. Next to him, Sam also stumbled. Urging his colleague into a kneeling position, Mac whispered, "Check your radiation monitor. Something's not right here."

Glancing at his own patch, Mac could see the indicator was still showing green. Strange? Peering forward, he noticed the interior of the storeroom was masked by a large container. Squeezing Sam by the shoulder, he said, "You go left, I'll go right. Complete a figure-of-eight sweep of what's on the other side and then we'll get out of here, just in case we're being dosed with something that doesn't show up on our monitors. Agreed?"

"Yes, yes."

With infinite care, the two men shuffled forward.

Mac skirted the edge of the barrier and felt a tingling sensation in the air. He flicked his weapon's safety to the off position. Discerning that nothing else was moving within the compartment, he lingered for a moment to take stock before pressing on. As Mac maneuvered past the crate, he was presented with a confusing spectacle.

A gray void hung in midair. An asperity, rent through the specifics of reality. Mac backtracked and hissed, "Sam, retreat now. Get out, get out."

He'd only managed to take a few steps when the gyre flared, and a wave of dizzying proportions radiated from the anomaly. A sudden vacuum sucked the air from his lungs, and he was crushed to the floor. Forced to crawl, Mac scrambled into a corner and raised his machine gun into a firing position.

What the fu . . . ?

He froze as a shadow cast by an alternate dimension canted his senses like a ship in a storm. A twelve foot high apparition appeared. Sheathed in purple-blue radiance, and with a dancing coronet of violet and crimson flames above its head, it took a moment to gain its bearings before stomping toward Mac like an auger of doom.

Chapter Fifteen

Lessons

Marcus Brutus strode through the entrance portico, marveling again at the handiwork of the artisans who had fashioned the building directly from the fabric of the wall. Although completely unadorned, the grace and finesse of the joints and seam work was unlike anything he had ever seen.

Since his arrival, Marcus had done his best to accustom both himself and his men to their new surroundings. Their responsibility now was the defense of this city, and as such, he had insisted everyone avail themselves of the vast storehouse of knowledge contained within Rhomane's Great Library. Especially where it appertained to lydium and its uses.

As he climbed the stairs, Marcus ran his fingers along the impossibly smooth texture of the edifice before him.

It's without blemish. Not one nick or scar mars its perfection.

Created from super-dense, super-cooled, fermionic bom-
bardment, lydium was impossible to manipulate once it was
fashioned into its preferred form, and warmed above absolute
zero. In the case of the Utility Archive he now found himself in,
the matrix had been encouraged to flow out from the bulk of the
wall to form the frame of the building itself. A procedure adopted at a number of important structures around the outer rim.

Arriving at the level he desired, Marcus paused and removed his sword from its scabbard. Adjusting his grip, he
slammed the pommel against the structure as hard as he could.
A dull, metallic peal chimed along the hallways, causing a few
men to pause in their work and look up. Ignoring them, Marcus
peered closely at the area he had just struck.

*Not a scratch. Fire doesn't warm it. Bullets don't shake a
single fleck loose. Even acid has no sting against such obstinacy.*

He stepped onto a raised gantry positioned between two
towers.

*The only exception is this one small area, here. The site
of the impact.*

Marcus placed his hand against the unyielding stone. Apart
from an almost indiscernible difference in temperature, the
wall looked and felt exactly the same as everywhere else. Both
overwhelming and oblique.

*I can't even begin to imagine the power that would be
needed to break something so solid. So permanent. But the
majesty of the Horde's focus is terrifying. Such strength and
savagery. I daren't leave anything to chance.*

His fingers came away wet, stained in ochre.

*Ah, the oxidized mix hasn't dried here yet. I wonder if that
has anything to do with the anomaly?*

Turning, Marcus was caught in the rays of the setting sun,
reflected from the citadel. Bathed in fire, he couldn't resist clos-

ing his eyes and reveling in memories of better times. Of Gaul and Rome, and family and friends, sorely missed.

A shout from outside intruded on his solitude. Gripping the rail, Marcus strained to listen in on the exchange. He recognized the bark of one of his centurions, Decimus Martinas. Decimus's voice was as deep as a bullfrog's in heat, and three times as loud. Whoever was arguing with him was fighting a losing battle.

That'll teach them.

Marcus grinned as he discerned the identity of the whiner.

Doesn't that man ever run out of things to complain about?

Hurrying down, Marcus went to see what Houston had done *this* time.

*

The two entities suspended within the confining lattice strained for release. Although dulled by a seeming eternity spent trapped in isolation, their senses ached in the presence of so much eldritch life force. One such concentration of sustenance was tantalizingly close. If only it had been possible for them to just reach out and touch that elusive *other*, they would have gained the vitality needed to break free of their restricted existence. They groaned in mutual longing and agony.

Their memories were fragmented, reluctant to respond to mundane thought. Neither could remember how they had come to be in such a position, or for how long they had been there. Their only certainty was a vague *knowing* that there had been a time before this void when they had existed elsewhere. Such a notion felt right. Solid. Factual. But any attempt to capture and clarify such comprehension resulted in a stagnant splintering of focus that centered on their immediate need to feed. Here. Now.

Puissant resonances chimed among the energy nodes. Exerting its sight, one of the entities noticed a flaring outburst of passion congealing among the lesser lights nearby. The beacon was like a neon-red invitation. The captive mind tried to reach out and mesh with that other essence, to blend with it and convey the import of a message it felt compelled to utter. Yet no sooner had it made the attempt than it forgot what it needed to say.

Coldly, dispassionately, it consigned itself to wait.

There were many other sources nearby. Perhaps an opportunity to express itself would arise if it waited a little longer.

*

Everything turned white as a glaring flash claimed his senses.

A moment of dislocation followed and the world tipped alarmingly. The floor rushed up to meet him and Houston hit the ground, hard. He shook his head in a vain attempt to reclaim the wits that had just been knocked into orbit.

The ringing in his ears eventually subsided, only to be replaced by the throbbing ache of his jaw. Confused, Houston opened his eyes. Outlined by the illumination of solar beacons, a darkened cliff loomed before him, wavering behind a constellation of spangled stars. The more Houston blinked, the worse they swarmed his vision with glittering pinpricks of light that refused to dissipate.

Spitting out blood, Houston rolled onto his knees and tried to stand up. Unknown hands helped him to his feet. He heard a voice at his side, close to his ear. "Can you hear me, James? Are you all right?"

"Wilson? What in the. . . ?" His vision refused to clear.

The wall of rock dancing within his field of view rumbled forward, clarifying into a bull-necked man of impressive physique.

"What did you have to hit him so hard for?" Wilson Smith complained. "He's a captain in the United St–"

"*Was* a captain," Decimus Martinas barked, cutting off the younger man's protestation, "just as I was a centurion. And while our hosts have extended us a degree of courtesy in line with our previous standing, those ranks don't mean a thing here." Glaring at Houston, he raised a great ham of a fist and snarled, "*Here* we earn our honor. Our names. And you'd better get that through your thick skull. Because if you don't, I'll be happy to educate you on the way things really are. You've upset enough people as it is. Don't make things any harder than they have to be."

Houston's face burned crimson. He pushed himself away from his cousin, and attempted to stand unaided. *Bastard! I won't forget this.* "Well, you've certainly shown everyone how a lack of education expresses itself," he drawled, his voice laced with sarcasm. "Is that the only way you know how to settle a difference of opinion where you come from? 'I can't think, but look, I can hit?'"

Several other legionnaires standing close by bristled at the jibe. Decimus took a threatening step closer, his gazed turned to ice. "You seek to provoke me. That would be unwise, little man, for while I come from a simpler era than you, we didn't lack for sophistication. You forget. Many of the great monuments of Rome were built by soldiers like me. And it would surprise you, the kind of things you have to learn to be able to complete such undertakings. The principles governing the use of alchemy and compounds, for example, are fraught with risk. Mixed in the correct sequence and right quantities, certain elements are quite safe to handle or imbibe. In the wrong measures, however, such substances may prove . . . troublesome."

The menace in Decimus's tone was evident. As was his meaning. He advanced on the hapless cavalry officer again, maintaining eye contact to add weight to his words.

Houston felt like a mouse caught in the gaze of a cobra. He stumbled backward. *Don't you dare, you swine. You've already shamed me in front of my men once.* He struggled to keep the fear from showing on his face.

Decimus continued, "And we haven't even considered the physical laws regarding inertia or fulcrums yet. My dear man, did you know that if you apply a minimal amount of pressure, in exactly the right place at the most opportune moment, seemingly immovable objects can be brought tumbling down?" His hand abruptly snaked out. Catching Houston squarely on the forehead with his index finger, Decimus caught his opponent off guard and dumped him onto his backside. The shock of the maneuver sent the wind whooshing from Houston's lungs.

Cruel laughter split the thickening gloom.

The centurion looked around his men, and then back to Houston. Biting off each word, he snapped, "So no, little man. This isn't the only way I know of to settle disputes. I can resort to any number of options, both physical and intellectual to put you in your place. Try my patience again, and I'll demonstrate a more . . . inventive method to you."

"Do what you want," Houston retorted, "I'm glad I'll never be like you. Lackey!"

The centurion shrugged, unconcerned by the riposte. "And so you should be, *murderer*. For under *our* law we would have gathered as a cohort to draw lots. Those chosen would have been given the responsibility of beating you to death. Only then would the reproach against our honor be cleansed. You might want to think on that before you resort to subterfuge in future."

Decimus turned on his heel and stalked away. He was quickly followed by a gaggle of his officers, many of whom congratulated him slapping him heartily on the back.

Houston was distraught.

Wilson Smith and a number of soldiers from Second Platoon rushed to their fallen commander's aid.

"That was uncalled for, Sir," Sergeant Adam Wainwright spluttered, "and cowardly. You did well to control yourself."

Control myself, my ass. That gorilla would have torn me apart. "Thank you, Sergeant. It would seem not all officers are gentlemen. There's a time and place to resort to violence. And that imbecile obviously doesn't know the difference." *But I do.*

Houston noticed someone watching them from back in the shadows, by the utilities building. *Marcus Brutus?*

Realizing he'd been spotted, Marcus strode confidently toward the tight knot of men until he stood before the disheveled captain. It looked to Houston as if the other man were on the verge of saying something, but then he obviously thought better of it. Sighing deeply, Marcus drummed the fingers of one hand against his thigh, and delivered a withering look that conveyed bitter disappointment.

Houston glanced down, noticing the action had left a smear of red and bronze paint on Marcus's skirt. Before Houston could think of anything to say, Marcus shook his head, waved dismissively, and stalked from the scene.

"What do you make of that?" Wilson gasped. "Rudeness seems to be a requirement among their lot." His sentiment was quickly echoed among the team.

Ignoring them, Houston glanced at the now empty building in front of him. *What were you doing in there?* A sudden impulse to check formed in his mind.

Acknowledging the crowd about him, Houston replied, "Well, what would you expect from rabble? Sergeant Wainwright? Corporal Mitchell? See the men safely back to their rooms, will you? Supper will be served soon, and I'd hate you to miss it just because I needed a bit of support." He glanced at the guards from the first cohort hovering nearby. "Do it quickly before our sentries come running over and start prodding us with spears. Wilson, you go with them."

Cocking a thumb toward the archive, he lowered his voice. "If anyone asks, tell them I need to cool down a little. So I'm tidying up in there and making sure everything's ready for work tomorrow."

"What are you doing really?" Wilson whispered.

"I want to check something out. Tell my escort I'll only be a few minutes, and I'll fill you in when I get back, okay?"

Chapter Sixteen

Murphy's Law

Despite the nauseating sense of dislocation threatening to make him vomit, Mac took his time. He wanted to ensure he captured as much detail regarding this discovery as possible. Having completed his third sweep, he stared across the hold toward his comrade. He could see Sam was stunned by what they'd both just witnessed.

Not trusting the sound of his own voice, Mac flashed a hand signal, and they dragged themselves away from the cargo area. Once on the far side of the container, the overwhelming dizziness subsided.

Mac risked a final glance behind to ensure there were no more surprises coming their way. *The guys back at base will piss themselves silly. If the Horde can actually create these things, what's to stop them opening a door within Rhomane itself?*

Trying not to think too hard about the reality of such a
nightmare, Mac struggled to his feet and checked his equipment. *Good. Everything appears to be in working order.* He
waited for Sam to complete his own tests, then gestured again
and lead the way toward the open hatch. They moved slowly,
warily, just in case the beast was still lurking somewhere nearby.
It wasn't until they had descended the gantry and were safely
outside that both soldiers heaved a huge sigh of relief.

"Jesus!" Sam gasped, "I thought my heart was going to
leap from my mouth."

"That's nothing. Mine was beating so hard, I'm sure it's
cracked some of my ribs."

"Was that one of their Bosses? A Horde Master?"

"It must have been. Crown and all."

"But where is it?" Sam spun around in a slow circle. "It's
gone."

Mac peered through his weapon's scope, and scanned the
hangars and pens for the elusive signs of Horde spore. Turning,
he checked back toward the subway.

Nothing. I didn't know they could move that fast. Unless . . .

"Sir? Are you there?" A suppressed but urgent query cut
across his thoughts. Mac recognized the tone immediately.

"Mac?" the voice repeated. "This is bravo support team
here, come in?"

"I hear you, Mark. Keeping tabs on us, were you?"

"That's a yes. Is everything okay? We lost comms for several minutes. Then that spook ambled out of the door and made
its way over to that disc-shaped craft behind you, the one at
your five o'clock. We thought it had taken you out."

Mac glanced behind him. The nanobots in his head helped
him recognize the ship as an executive liner, the *Seranette*,
once used to ferry Ardenese politicians to and fro between the
colonies. "Do me a favor, Mark. Tag it for me, will you? You

won't believe what we discovered inside the shuttle. I'll give you a sit-rep later. For now, your recording will form part of the intelligence package I'll be putting together."

"Will do," Mark replied. He added, "Heads up, Boss. The skidder's just emerging from the tunnel. Better haul ass before the civvies start getting twitchy."

"On my way."

*

"How goes it?"

Mohammed jumped. He'd been concentrating so diligently on the monitors before him that he hadn't noticed Saul enter the room. "So far, so good. We lost contact with Lieutenant McDonald for a few minutes as his team passed through the tunnel, but he's back on air now."

"Problems?"

"None reported so far. Mac's team is very thorough. Not only are they playing nursemaid, but they're managing to collect a great deal of on-site intelligence that we might be able to use to our advantage at a later date."

"Oh, really?" Saul asked, his interest piqued. "Such as?"

"Well, for start, we expected the place to be crawling with Horde, yes?"

"Go on."

"That doesn't appear to be the case. While the teams did encounter several dormant pockets on the way *to* the spaceport, once there, the facility was remarkably free of enemy activity."

"Was it now?" Saul leaned in to take a closer look at the display.

"The only on-site location showing any sign of Horde concentration is the service subway leading to the safety apron." Mohammed pointed to one of the video-link replays. "See there?

That's a record of what we've been sent so far. As the HUDs skip through their frequencies, watch how the presence of dreaming ogres is revealed."

"Did you say 'dreaming'?"

"Yes, I did. With no food source readily available, it appears our ever hungry friends have gone into fantasy-mode. In fact, Mac sent us a confidential communiqué on the matter. For some reason, he didn't want to discuss it over the air. It's on my console over there. I haven't had time to read it yet. Mac's checking out one of the ships left abandoned on the tarmac and I don't want to miss the fun."

"He's what?" Saul spluttered.

"Oh, don't worry. Mac and Sam are waiting for the skidder to join them, so they decided to take a quick look around inside that cargo vessel . . . there." Mohammed tapped the screen to indicate which craft he was talking about. "Its hatch was open, and they informed me it would be a great opportunity to see what the layout is like. It might give us a head start if we ever manage to secure one for use in future operations."

"Hmm. Good idea." As he studied the feed, Saul noted a two to three minute disparity between *live* and *mission time*. "Is the time delay causing any confusion?"

"Not really. We just have to wait a bit for each individual info-packet to arrive. The relay via the skidder was added as an additional security protocol. It collects chunks of data, condenses it, and then sends it through to us in random micro-bursts. We thought we might need it to avoid detection by the Horde. But it looks as if the chameleon, stealth, and null-point technologies are blending together rather well. It'll mean we'll be able to employ direct comms in future . . ."

"Hang on a second, Mohammed," Saul cut in. "I think someone's trying to contact me."

Saul turned away to receive the message.

To Mohammed's eyes, his friend appeared to tense and then hold his breath.

"And foul play isn't suspected?" Saul's voice betrayed his growing displeasure.

There was a further pause as Saul listened to whoever was on the other end of the link. Then he breathed out, the relief evident in his stance. "Thank you, Shannon, I'll be right there. Have Marcus and Decimus meet me in the reception area, okay? I want the facts of what happened clear in my mind before I speak with any of the rabble."

"Sounds like trouble?" Mohammed offered.

"Oh, it is. It seems the black sheep of our family had a little altercation with Decimus in front of a large crowd of onlookers. It ended, as you might expect, with Houston on his ass, and Decimus pointing out how unwise it would be to press their difference of opinion any further."

"And?"

"And that was it. They went their separate ways, as Marcus can evidently testify. But somehow, our *thorn in the flesh* wound up in intensive care with burns to his hands and face, and a fractured skull."

"Say again?" Mohammed's eyes popped wide.

"You heard me straight. I'm just on the way there now to see what other delights this mess is going to unravel."

"Rather you than me." Mohammed chuckled as his friend stormed from the room. Sighing, Mohammed turned his attention back to the screens and relaxed. The operation was running like clockwork, and he was confident they would soon be in possession of the drones that would make such a difference to their fight.

He started to play the latest message stream. When the twelve foot high apparition lumbered out from the hatch of the supply freighter, his eyes bulged even wider than before.

*

Mac scanned along the length of the service road, then worked his way out onto the apron. "How many are left now?" he called over his shoulder.

"Two more and that's your lot," Nick replied. Despite the muting effect of the inter-link, the relief in his voice was evident. "The roof collapse was a blessing in disguise. It reduced our time here considerably."

"What will we have altogether?"

"Thirty-one containers. With twenty-five drones in each, it'll give us a minimum of seven hundred and seventy-five flyers to play with. Not including those we can salvage, and the obvious multitude of parts we've been able to recover from among the debris."

Hmm. A good number, but suspicious nonetheless. "Thanks, Nick. Let me know when your guys are loading the last one and I'll call everyone in."

"Okay. We'll be about five or six minutes. Although the grav-discs take away the weight, they're a bitch to maneuver when loaded. The rocks aren't making it any easier either. They're scattered over quite a wide margin and are slowing us down. Sorry, but if we try to go any faster than two miles per hour, I'm afraid we might spill something."

"No problems. Nothing's happening, so don't rush."

Mac lifted his rifle scope, and studied the area between the cargo ship and liner again. After a few minutes of fruitless observation, he gave up. *Nothing! So where did that Horde Master come from? And what's it still doing inside the Seranette?*

He called to his colleagues. "Fire-team, this is Alpha. Guys? Any movement from your positions?"

"That's a negative, Boss," Sam shot back, "west side is clear."

"Nothing here," Stu Duggan replied, from farther along the line of abandoned warehouses.

"Quiet as the proverbial grave," Jumper Collins whispered, from his high atop the fire exit gantry.

Mac glanced up toward Jumper's place of concealment. *And how come the only roof to cave in was this one? Over the very spot the drones were stored?*

Something nagged at the back of his mind. Walking away from the hangar, Mac positioned himself out in the open and looked up toward the location he knew would be occupied by his cover-team. The fingernail of a crescent moon rode higher in the sky, its wan illumination insufficient to clarify any helpful details. "Mark, are you listening?"

"I'm here."

"Are you close enough for the 420s to scan the top of the target in high resolution?"

"That's a yes. My optics will intensify Se'ochan's radiance. Why, what do you need?"

"It might be nothing, but I want to see if you notice anything unusual on top of this building in particular."

"Unusual?"

"I'm trying to understand why this warehouse is the only structure to suffer damage. Everything else appears intact and functional. It doesn't feel right to me. Just check it out, please."

"Hang on a sec . . ." The line went quiet as Mark carried out his task.

Thirty seconds later, he was back online. "Boss? Now you mention it, there is something rather odd about our target. I didn't notice it before because it was right under our noses."

"What is it?"

"The roof is covered in boulders. I've just skimmed the other facilities, and while one or two have the odd rock here and there, the drone hangar is littered with whacking great chunks of granite. Some as big as a house, and all concentrated around the site of the collapse."

Mac was perplexed. "Could they have fallen from the mountain?"

"That's what I initially thought. Especially as the force field would have dropped after the Horde swarmed it. But no, while I was taking a look, Sean inspected the culvert bordering the perimeter. If there had been a rock fall, the place would be saturated in debris. It's clean. He checked it twice."

But . . . but that would mean someone deliberately tried to bring the structure down. Bloody hell! This job just gets better and better.

"Lieutenant? We're ready to go." Nick's warning cut across Mac's line of thought.

"Er, okay Nick, we're on our way," he replied.

Reacting to the change in status, Mac dismissed his suspicions and mobilized his men. "Mark? We're on the move. As we approach the subway, draw your own squads in and begin falling back to your vehicle. When we clear the other end, make for the RV. Understood?"

"Loud and clear."

"Fire-team, this is Alpha. Close on me at the transport. We'll be leading the shipment through the subway on foot. Sam, you're with me at the rear. Stu, Jumper, you two will take point, lead the way with cold-lights. Switch to full automatic. From now on, if anything gets in our way, take it out with maximum aggression."

As his colleagues raced to respond, Mac addressed the skidder. "Nick? Let Blood-one know we're starting the return leg. When they've acknowledged you, make sure your guys line the deck of the craft. They are to draw their weapons. The shields will protect you, but we can't take any chances." As an afterthought, he added, "We'll hitch a ride with you until the mouth of the tunnel. Feel free to put your foot down until we get there. Once inside, Stu and Jumper will dictate the speed. Just follow the path of the glow-sticks. Is that clear?"

"Okay. It'll be nice to get out of here."

Amen to that.

"All teams, all teams," Mac called, "go, go, go."

Everyone sprang to life. Less than sixty seconds later, the hovercraft bristled with men and weapons. A barely discernible hum thrummed through its bulk as the drive engines engaged. Nick made a beeline for the gaping maw of the exit. With a lurch, the heavily laden carrier sprang forward, and the sound of metal clattering across resin rang out. Someone in close proximity gasped, "My gun, watch–"

Bam! Zing!

The hopeless warning was interrupted by the loud report of a gun firing, followed by the distinctive whine of a ricochet.

Mac knew what had happened before anyone had a chance to confirm it.

Sure enough, when he peered forward, one of the civilian handlers was rushing to pick up the pistol he had just dropped.

Imbecile!

Stifling his anger, Mac was on the open radio in moments. "All units, this is Alpha. We have just suffered a negligent discharge aboard the skidder. Be prepared for a hostile response. The Horde might now be alerted to our presence. Cover-team? Divert immediately to Blood-one's position and offer support from that direction. We may have to fight our way through the tunnel. If we emerge safely, provide suppressing fire until we are clear. I will detonate the mine as we ride through. Standby. Alpha, out!"

They picked up speed.

Mac called ahead, "Nick, forget my last instructions to you. When we hit the underpass, activate every lamp you have.

I want the inside of that place lit up like Christmas. Tell your folks to shoot at anything and everything that comes close. My team and I will take care of the rest."

As they skimmed across the barren field, Mac couldn't resist another glance back at the Seranette. Almost immediately, something caught his attention. *Eh?* He looked again. *Yes, there it is. A cocooned distortion near the bottom steps.*

Raising his machine gun, he used the magnification of its sights to check once more. *Screw me!*

As if a veil had been lifted, a conflagration of condensed energy blazed forth. Its silver and purple penumbra bloomed bright, bathing the surrounds in spectral contrasts of light and shadow.

It's charging itself. Openly displaying its position as it reacts to a threat . . .

Mac watched the monster closely . . . *But it doesn't know where we are . . . I wonder?*

Catching his breath, he fought against the allure of simply watching and activated his targeting laser. Adjusting the setting, he altered its frequency into the visible spectrum. A ruby-red lance of coherence stabbed out. *Here I am.* "Contact!" he snapped, bringing everyone to attention. "Seven o'clock low, at the base of the star liner, Seranette."

As the brilliant dot danced across the rippling substance of the Horde Master, the beast reacted unexpectedly. Throwing its arms wide, it froze, and waited.

What? Fighting against the jostle of the moving craft, Mac walked the beam across the monster's body and let it come to rest between a pair of intensely glowing eyes. His finger closed on the trigger. The Controller remained motionless, hands held high.

He knows I have him. And yet . . .

The jaws of the tunnel entrance closed about them, and the skidder plunged into darkness.

Damn! What's wrong with me? Why didn't I just take it out?

A discordance of sound and lurid, flashing light yanked Mac back to the present. Everyone at the front had opened up with their weapons. Pulling himself together, he shuffled toward the driver. Because of his advanced optics, Mac could see Nick was on the verge of panic and decided to keep himself busy by giving the out-of-his-depth technician some much needed support.

Mac kept his voice level and calm. "That's it, Nick. You're doing well. Just stick to the middle of the road and let us take care of the jaywalkers. I'm right behind you, so nothing's going to sneak up and bite . . ." Mac paused to destroy three wraiths running alongside. "Your back's protected, and we'll be out of here in a few minutes with a clear run toward Rhomane and a celebratory drink."

"But they're all around us," Nick squeaked.

"And so are we. We've got guns and iron and so many rounds that we won't have enough targets to shoot them at." Mac dropped to one knee as he changed magazines. The skidder rocked under the influence of multiple detonations.

Resuming his position, Mac continued, "Don't worry about all the explosions. As you can feel, the shields are absorbing the worst of the energy. You concentrate on your screens. Keep us moving, keep us safe." He tapped Nick's console. "Look, the exit's already looming."

He stepped away to peer around the stacked crates toward the front of the craft. *Yes, there it is. Just over two hundred yards to go.*

Then Mac noticed something that warmed his heart. Now the civilian crew had something to concentrate on, they were venting their nerves admirably. The null-shield was enough of a protection anyway. But now and again, a more daring ogre would risk the pain of scrambled atoms to throw itself against the fabric of the ship. Those attempting to gain a foothold in such a manner were met with a volley of steel that cut them to shreds within seconds. *Well done,* he thought, *despite the monumental screw-up, this will temper them for future missions. We'll make soldiers out of them yet.*

Firing off a series of rapid bursts, Mac issued further instructions. "Mark? We'll be hitting the exit in approximately one minute. Prepare your arcs. Anything that follows us out is fair game. The device is already primed, so give us a healthy gap to maneuver in. Once we've got some breathing space, pick up everyone on foot and hightail it out of there. The extra bodies will slow you down a bit, but we'll pair up for the rest of the journey. Everybody's going home tonight."

"Roger that. We'll be ready in less than thirty seconds."

"Good to hear."

Satisfied, Mac returned to his business of dispensing death. Swiveling rapidly from side to side, he emptied magazine after magazine into the swarming host. Chrysanthemum bursts engulfed the party in an eternity of all-consuming conflagrations. Time appeared to slow down. Empty casings cascaded to the floor, their tinkling music providing a tympanic counterpoint to the deep resonance of repeated implosions occurring all around them. A pressure wave began to build that threatened to burst eardrums and sanity alike.

It was carnage. Yet the waking Horde kept coming.

To Mac's eyes, the grunts appeared lethargic. Like bears, freshly roused from hibernation and pushed unwillingly toward conflict. He felt an uncharacteristic moment of pity for them. *This isn't . . . right?*

"Ceasefire!" he yelled. The skidder hit the ramp and ascended toward freedom. "Conserve your ammunition in case we need it."

Breaking free of the tunnel confines, everyone seemed to exhale at the same moment, slumping forward as if the cords to autonomic function had been cut.

Mac looked back at the results of his handiwork.

Hundreds must have died inside the alley of death. And yet a continuing deluge poured forth, as if from the gates of hell, roused afresh to action and retribution. Roaring with undiluted anger and defiance, they surged forward like the wall of a glittering avalanche, helpless to stop under the weight of their own momentum.

Mark's team opened up, scourging the no-man's-land in between with a swathe of iron and repudiation. And still the nightmare apparitions pressed forward.

What are they doing? Surely they must understand there's no way they can win?

A haunting shriek pierced the night, its timbre as cryptic as it was soul-wrenching. All heads turned in response to its plea. Mac understood instantly who had issued the call.

Glaring and sparking within a sea of conflicting emotion, a multitude of advancing spooks ground to a halt. Guttural barks and snarls passed between them as the more responsive individuals were brought to heel. Some ignored the command entirely. Raging forward, they charged toward the fence, baying for blood.

Mesmerized by the wave of impending death, Mac yelled, "Nick? On my command, slow the skidder to a crawl. I want to lure our friends into the gap." He pointed forward. "Then, as we clear the fence, stop *there* for a moment. I need to make sure our package is ready for delivery."

"Just give me the word."

Mac recognized a growing confidence in the Tec-head's voice. *Yup, he's a soldier in the making, all right.* "Okay. On my signal, cut the engine."

The hum of decelerating forces throbbed out over the din of the howling mob. Mac glanced across to the skimmer. Mark had just picked up the last of Stained-With-Blood's team, and they were already pulling away.

Perfect timing. "Get ready, Nick," he warned, "full stop . . . Now!"

Leaning across the side of the skidder, Mac studied the digital readout on the mine. The word *primed* glared back within a pulsing amber light. Tapping the final code into his wrist com, Mac waited for the telltale confirmation to register on the display. *Armed–Cloak Online* blinked into view and the screen turned red. The device disappeared from mundane sight, and one of the buttons on Mac's keypad glowed white.

He sat up and turned back to Nick. "If you please, driver? I don't want to be near this baby when it throws a tantrum."

A surge thrummed through the decking as the skidder resumed its course. Mac adjusted the rotational frequency of his HUD to get a better overall view of their pursuers. His hand hovered above his other wrist as he counted down their charge toward the fence. *Twenty-five feet; twenty; fifteen; ten; five; showtime.* He jabbed the pad.

The cloak dropped from the mine, revealing its rich energy source to the Horde for the first time. The brutes closest to it leaped forward, slavering and snarling like a pack of rabid dogs. Those behind began fighting among themselves in the panic not to miss out on the feast. Like the condensing eye of a hurricane, a writhing wall of flaring horror surrounded the bomb, paused momentarily in victory, then pounced.

Mac's finger twitched again. The button turned blue.

The scene behind them appeared to bend, sagging inward as if an incredibly dense weight had suddenly been placed across the canvas of their vision. Those ogres closest to the device seemed to fall further than should be possible.

A black dot appeared at the exact center of the mass. Reality fractured, and everything—the spooks, the ground, the remains of the chain-link fence, even the very air—warped, as if smeared across a shattered lens.

It looked to Mac as if a door to somewhere else had been yanked open, and he felt himself pulled backward by an intense wind. Those about him staggered, and were forced to reach out to steady themselves. *Bloody hell! It's working.*

The strength of the gust increased, and Mac became aware of a growing nimbus of light blossoming to life in the middle of the mob. That concentration bloomed, and a shockwave announced the moment the unstable quantum vortex collapsed.

Everyone was swatted to the floor.

A deathly hush ensued.

Raising his head, Mac stared in wonder at the results of their experiment.

Each and every single member of the pursuing host had been crushed out of existence. The only evidence Mac could see of their passing were the residual static discharges now spitting randomly from point to point through the air.

Wow! That was just a prototype, and yet it had an effective killing radius of at least fifty feet. Talk about useful in a crisis. Nice one, Doc. I can't wait to see them in action around the wall.

Spontaneous cheering broke out among the crews of both craft.

"Jesus! We actually did it," Nick gasped, as he struggled to his feet.

"It looks like it," Mac replied, "a pretty successful test run. I wonder what our surviving friends think about it, though."

They had traveled too far to be able to see properly in the dark. Dropping to one knee, Mac steadied himself against the side of the skidder and employed his weapon sights once more.

Even with his advanced optics, Mac couldn't clearly distinguish what he was looking at. However, the stationary Horde members appeared to have congregated in a tight knot about the entrance to the subway. Although their usual screams and cries were absent, the abundance of red and scarlet streaks among the shimmering electrum betrayed their high state of arousal.

Oh, they're pissed all right. I bet they think twice before coming near us again.

The undulating mass parted abruptly to make way for a larger, solitary concentration of silver and purple malevolence. *Hello? Is that the same Boss?*

Their range was becoming too extreme for the magnification of Mac's scope to manage, but he was sure the figure was moving slowly toward the site of the detonation.

He's checking it out. Seeing what he can find. Just like I would.

Mac wasn't surprised. *The more I see, the more I'm positive the Horde has been keeping a few aces up its sleeve. I don't know if the iron is making them think twice about their previous tactics, but something is definitely causing them to switch on. The debrief is going to be a humdinger, that's for sure.*

He slumped back onto the deck and opened the comms channel wide. "Congratulations everyone, that was a job well done. We got what we came for. Gathered a whole load of useful intelligence. Test-fired a new weapon. And most important of all, everyone's going home safe. All in all, not a bad day's work, even if I do say so myself. There's still a way to Rhomane yet, so stay sharp. Soon, it'll be hot showers and dinner all round. My treat."

A louder bout of applause broke out, and a feeling of exuberance spread among the company. Those with nothing specific to do began walking among their teammates, congratulating them heartily and slapping them on the back.

Mac smiled to himself. *Ah, they deserve it.*

The party atmosphere was suddenly replaced by one of profound shock.

What's wrong? Mac surged to his feet, rifle in hand.

Several of the civilian crew members were shuffling toward him with concerned looks on their faces. Stu Duggan was with them.

"Stu?" Mac's voice was ice cold. A flash of intuition made him ask, "Where's Jumper?"

"Boss, you need to see this." The dull, blank glaze in Stu's eyes spoke volumes.

Mac's chest constricted. His heart thudded loudly in his chest. *Oh no. Not . . .*

The small crowd led him forward to the bow of the craft where Jumper had been positioned on the homerun. Jumper was slumped between two packing crates, and because of his armor, appeared to be relaxing. On closer inspection, Mac could see a dark stain congealing on the floor about his colleague's feet.

Moving forward to kneel at his friend's side, Mac whispered, "Jumper?" Then he checked for a pulse, and found none. His fingers came away wet.

"He's dead, Boss," Stu stated. "It looks like the ricochet earlier on caught him at the narrow point between the helmet and shoulder plating. A million-to-one fluke. Hit the carotid artery and dropped him immediately. He must have bled-out during the firefight that followed."

Someone sobbed quietly in the corner, rocking gently backward and forward on his knees. "It's all my fault. I killed him," he keened, over and over again.

"That's Bob," Stu explained, jutting his chin toward the other man, "he experienced the negligent discharge earlier on as the skidder accelerated."

"Yes, I know." Mac bit the words out and had to suck in air to prevent his anger from bursting to the surface. Random thoughts tumbled through his mind. *All those years we served together after I found him wasting his time in 40 Commando. Afghanistan. China. Korea. His marriage to Tara. The birth of Nadine. Then the twins. That time in India when a cobra bit him on the ass because he didn't look where he was taking a dump.* A sad smile fought its way across his face.

All those missions we completed. And how many times did we save each other's life? God knows . . . I lost count. The smile transformed into a blade of bitter regret.

He survives all that shit, and then cops it because some civvy trips over his two left feet? Strangling down his ire, Mac cast his eyes toward the heavens and spat, "Thank you very much, Murphy. Nice one!"

After delivering a look of sheer venom toward the unfortunate Bob, Mac spun on his heel and stomped his way to the back of the skidder.

Alone with his anger, he was struck by a poignant thought.

Jumper, you sneaky bastard! Well done. At least one of us is safe for real now, eh?

For the rest of the journey, Mac stared at the stars and thought of home.

Chapter Seventeen

New Developments

The muted atmosphere within the sterile environment of the intensive care unit was as relaxing as it was tranquil. Seldom used since the days of the city's ascendency, the equipment and facilities adorning the department appeared as fresh as the day they were installed, all those years ago.

An EMS version of the sentinel program—a medi-orb—hovered protectively over the sole patient within the ward. Its sensors constantly scanned the autonomous functions and vital signs of the man below it, lying wrapped within a nimbus of soothing green light.

Ayria Solram looked on. In all her years as a doctor, she had never seen a case as perplexing as the one before her now. *Epidermal damage from the burns has been reduced to next to nothing. And while his skull was cracked from the fall, that's*

already beginning to knit over nicely. Swelling from the ensu-
ing trauma has also been contained. So why am I getting such
conflicting results?

She studied the readouts for body and brain activity again.
It was now two days after the accident, and while Houston's
physical condition was clearly in remission, the EEG continued to fluctuate wildly, as if the signal were in the grip of a
thunderstorm.

This doesn't make sense. His vital signs reveal the pre-
dicted behavior of someone in deep sleep. His muscles are re-
laxed. His respiration is clear and even. And his pulse rate is
so low, you'd be forgiven for thinking he'd slipped into a coma.

She glanced at his twitching eyeballs, then back at the holographic display. Forked lightning discharges dominated the
vista within his cerebrum. *So why are these readings indicat-*
ing Captain Houston is in a highly aroused state of permanent
REM? That shouldn't be possible.

Sighing in frustration, Ayria sat back, drummed her nails
upon the cool resin worktop, and thought hard. *I'm missing*
something here. I know I am. But what?

She closed her eyes and attempted an old remedy for clearing the mind, taught to her when she was just a child by her
grandmother. *Nana always was a stickler for keeping the old*
traditions alive. I wish I'd paid more attention when I was
younger. It'll be embarrassing if I have to ask among our new-
est arrivals for help.

Ayria concentrated on her breathing and heart rate. Slowing them down, she lulled herself into a deeply restful state.
Satisfied, she turned to the empty place within, the esoteric
doorway that would take her on a journey of discovery. *If* the
ancestors were listening.

*

Mac looked down at the cold pale body and couldn't help but think how peaceful Jumper looked. *It's the first time in years I've actually seen him stay still.*

A sad smile crossed his face as he addressed the memory of his friend. *That's why we called you Jumper. Even when you were asleep, some part of you always twitched about. Hyped up and ready for action. The only man on earth who had amphetamines running through his veins instead of blood.*

Unexpected feelings threatened to worm their way to the surface, and Mac found himself struggling to control an overwhelming sense of frustration.

"Had you known him long?" Bob Neville stood at the entrance to the viewing room. When Mac had arrived at the morgue, Bob was already in attendance, having come to pay his respects to the man he had unwittingly killed. Mac could see the guy was wringing his heart out at having caused such an accident, but had nevertheless allowed an awkward silence to build.

"Dennis." Mac's voice was hoarse with emotion.

"I beg your pardon?"

"His name was Dennis. And yes, I'd known him for quite a few years."

A brooding hush ensued.

Eventually, Bob shuffled forward and came to stand on the opposite side of the bed. A large plastic tray sat on top of an adjacent table, containing Jumper's uniform and the few personal effects he'd had on him at the time of his death. A small photograph of a woman hugging three children was uppermost.

"I take it this is his family?" Bob murmured, indicating the picture.

"Was his family," Mac replied. "That was taken several years ago now, when the twins were only five. His ex-wife, Tara, doted on them. As did Jumper. Even after the split, they worked hard together to ensure the kids didn't suffer unnecessarily. Nadine, their eldest, took it the hardest as she used to love going everywhere with her dad. Little Joe and Sophie didn't really understand what was going on at the time. But they adapted, as kids do. Jumper and Tara did a marvelous job. Kept up with parent evening thing at school. Sports days. And all the other important stuff that ensured the kids never felt left out."

Mac watched as a sour look crossed Bob's face. The other man clenched his hands. "And I'm the sad bastard who took their father from them."

Something inside clicked, and Mac decided to extend an olive branch. "Oh, they lost him a long time ago, my friend. Especially after he joined Special Forces. *Married to the Corps* is the term we use. And I think it happens to all of us who serve."

"That doesn't make me feel any better." Bob's tone was bitter.

"It wasn't really meant to. Remember, we're all lost out here. The moment the gateway took us, we ceased to exist. We're just unique among the dead in that we didn't have the opportunity to die properly. Instead of lying six feet under somewhere, we have to face each new day knowing that we might make a difference. In his short time here, Jumper certainly did. Now it's up to you."

"Hey! I'm not a soldier. I'd never really handled a gun before the other night. And yet, because of me and some stupid, bloody accident, a good man is lying there and—"

"And nothing you say or do can change that. You now owe it to Dennis's memory to learn from what happened and use it to make a difference. For us. For his children back home. For the sacrifice he made."

Bob looked shipwrecked.

Mac had an idea. Digging into the meager contents of the property tray, he fished around and removed two small resin discs attached to a piece of black cord. Handing them to Bob, he said, "Here, these are Jumper's dog-tags. Keep them as a source of inspiration. See what you come up with."

Bob held the green and purple emblems aloft and studied them closely. Both were engraved with the same words. *PO988453K COLLINS D. – B POS – C of E.* After a moment, he glanced toward Mac, his eyes brimming with tears.

Good! I see I've struck a nerve. Something constructive might come of this mess after all.

Nodding once, Mac left the morgue and made his way toward the canteen. *I'd better get something to eat before the debriefing starts. There's nothing like being forced to relive an unpleasant experience on a full stomach. Still. At least here, I don't have to send one of those dreadful next-of-kin letters.*

*

A confusing maelstrom of conflicting concepts and sensations fought their way to the surface. The entity felt as if it were swimming from the depths of an abyss against the tide. A sense of confinement remained, but it wasn't as overpowering as before.

Perplexed, it tried to organize its fractured cognizance into a more coherent form, only to discover the effort overwhelmed it. Instinctively, it relaxed. *I am weak. Diminished. Comprehension must wait until I have gathered my strength.*

Alarmed, the consciousness recoiled from structured thought.

Wha t . . . was . . . that?

Curious, it edged forward once more. Cautiously, warily, it tested the water. An echo of familiarity soothed the doubts that jangled through discordant memories and experience.

I'm . . . thinking.

A startling sense of dislocation and metamorphosis ensued. Scrutinizing the transformation, the strange being became enraptured. Although terrified, a multitude of fresh pathways flared within it, each pulse alive with essence and possibilities. Conditioned to an eternity of helpless inactivity, these new sensations inundated its raw perceptions with delight *and* distaste. As if what was happening was both natural, and yet at the same time, utterly repulsive.

Realization caused a flare of golden resonance to surge along the construct before it. Intuition kicked it. *That's a . . . a synapse.*

Thrilled, a startling truth struck home.

This is similar to the time before.

How it knew that, the entity didn't know, but attempting to clarify such knowledge only heightened its uncertainty.

Patience . . . ? It groped for a name. An empty void throbbed before it. *So who am I? What am I?*

Despite its frustration, the consciousness was desperate to understand itself better.

No. This is . . . right. An impression of *normal* flashed through its mind. *So why do I feel it's somehow wrong?*

Flowing outward, it discerned greater stimuli within reach. Hungry for more, it allowed self imposed barriers to drop. A million different sources swarmed toward it at once; the rush as delicious as it was disagreeable.

What form is this that limits me so?

A soothing, repetitive, rhythm lifted itself from the chaos. *Beep . . . Beep . . . Beep . . . Beep.*

Cool fabric, soft to the touch, registered on skin. *But what is skin? And why is this . . . soft?*

The noise in the background gained in pitch and urgency. *Bip! Bip! Bip! Bip! Bip!* It was smothered by an altogether harsher and more demanding tone which aggravated him.

I have a gender? I am . . . male.

The being discovered he was breathing deeply. The blaring alarm seemed to tug his respiration along at a corresponding pace. A thudding sensation filled his chest cavity.

Something touched him. He flinched! Whatever it was gripped him tighter and was uttering a string of different sounds.

Make it stop.

"Are . . . all right? Can yo . . . ear me?

Eh? Dialect? Someone is attempting to communicate verbally.

"Captain Houston. James. Are you all right?"

It moved closer. Another, sweeter sensation began to dominate. Inhaling, he became aware of a pleasant fragrance and remembered, *perfume, feminine, woman.*

Eyes opened. Bright, blinding light, exacerbated by shadowed surrounds, assailed his nascent comprehension. Blinking furiously, the entity comprehended a liquid texture upon his cheeks. *Tears.*

Some ran into his mouth, and he subconsciously smacked his lips in response to the salty taste. *I am wholly . . . physical in nature.*

Struggling to focus, he discerned an *other* in front of him. Fighting to sit up, he was immediately seized by vertigo and fell back onto the bed, exhausted.

"Wait there," a female voice said, "I have something that will help the dizziness."

The *other* moved away. She radiated a sense of bustling urgency that intruded on the peace and tranquility of this pleasant refuge.

Just leave me alone, I need to . . .

The room spun as secondary thoughts filtered through from a separate consciousness, this one inhabiting the same body. Comprehension dawned.

Another distinct personality!

He examined it closely. *Aha! It's subordinate now, but is natural to this flesh.* He instinctively commandeered the weaker psyche, learning as he went.

Satisfied, he sent a pulse along a set of specific neural pathways. A hand appeared. Mesmerized, he triggered a fresh set of impulses and watched as appendages—*no, fingers*—waggled. They clenched and flexed at whim.

I am emerging. My previous virile state is counterbalanced by . . . by something much more fragile. Mortality?

A different kind of need made his throat ache. On reflex, he swallowed. *Thirsty.*

My existence is muted . . . Or is it?

He struggled to remember something vitally important. Something he felt compelled to express, only to be waylaid by a residual taste of another emotion altogether. *Revenge?*

Why does that concept taste so good?

Chapter Eighteen

Christmas

Bloody hell! Saul Cameron basked in wonderment as he tried to digest the implications of what he'd just heard. *They've been here a matter of weeks, and already they've turned our world upside down and the right way up.*

Mac McDonald and his team were the last ones to leave. Watching them go, Saul's heart went out to them. *What a tragic waste. You expect attrition to take its toll in a place like this. And especially for a Special Forces guy who ends up in the thick of the action. But an accident?*

He shook his head, trying to put another negative chapter of Ardenese life out of his mind. *It's such a shame because apart from Jumper's death, the operation was a huge success.* Saul skimmed through the notes he'd made during the debriefing. It's as if all my birthdays have been rolled into one. I'm tempted to break out the flags.

Snorting, he thought better of getting ahead of himself. Ah hell. That can wait for the outcome of the next phase. I suppose there's no time like the present to get the gears in motion.

Turning to the only people left in the room, all high council members, Saul cleared his throat to draw their attention. "Ladies and gentlemen? If I may?"

A feeling of excitement had gripped everyone during the meeting, so it was only natural they'd be eager to discuss the implications among themselves. Saul waited patiently as the background chatter died down.

Once all heads were turned in his direction, he said, "Okay, now the debrief is over, let's discuss how we're going to move forward. I suppose the first thing we need to concentrate on is the issue of the drones." He made eye contact with his resources and technology head. "Ephraim? Have you completed a preliminary report for us?"

"I certainly have." Ephraim Miller beamed. He thumbed through the list on his mag-tablet, and quickly found the desired page. "Of the seven hundred and seventy-five flyers recovered, we have managed to uncrate and test just one hundred and ten. All but three are operational. It's been a bit slow, but now we're aware of the start-up procedure things should move along at a steady pace. I envisage us having the whole consignment done by the weekend."

"Any problems?"

"Not really. Obviously, we're a bit disappointed three have fritted out on us so far, but that's to be expected with any technical device which has been inert over a protracted period. I'm not too worried because the parts will come in handy. And even if the current ratio plays out through the entire batch, the city will still be left with over seven hundred additional resources it didn't previously have."

"What about the prospective upgrades?"

"I still have Brent working on the specifics, but it's looking good. Retrograding them with chameleon emitters will add less than two pounds in weight. Quite a bit more if we want to add null-point shield too. Obviously, this will affect range, altitude, and mission time. To begin with, operators can simply carry the units within the vehicles and deploy them once they arrive on site for each respective mission. This will be an important factor to remember if we seek to weaponize the flyers, as has been suggested."

"What about Marcus's idea of instilling reciprocal fear in our enemy by simply scattering iron filings over a specific zone? It's an adaptation of a method the legions use with their catapults."

"Lovely thought, isn't it?" Ephraim smiled, "with simplicity being the key. The dusting approach can be achieved in less than a week, especially as we won't have to bother cloaking those specific drones. If the Horde really are as cognizant as we now suspect, it will become readily apparent as soon as we start using the modified units. They won't know whether they've got an attack or straightforward patrol model hovering over their heads."

"And where do we stand on the sentry drones?"

"A squadron of eight are circling the city right now on trial runs, and are providing a live-time relay back to control. Initial tests show they have a twelve hour operating cycle, with a two hour solar backup. Once replenished, they are ready to go again within the hour."

"How many can I have at the wall?" Shannon De Lacey asked, "and what variations will they be?"

"I was hoping Saul would approve of letting you have virtually the entire first batch," Ephraim replied, casting a quick glance toward the commander. "The rest are coming online apace now, and we only need a few to experiment with as we add the additional Tec."

"Shouldn't be a problem," Saul agreed. "Defense of the city is a priority. An eye-in-the-sky and intelligence comes first. The other stuff can slide in later . . ." He suddenly remembered an important point, ". . . But Ephraim? I would also like you to start work on the stealth-bomber concept Mac's team proposed."

"Good point," Ephraim replied. "The additional weight of the shields and the new micro-gravity mine will have quite an impact. I'll ensure my department gets right on it."

"How far away do you think we are from working models? Bearing in mind you are dealing with unstable singularities?"

"Now we know the prototype works, less than ten days. The casings can be produced en masse, and a completed run of twenty will take the auto-lines about seventeen hours to produce. If you're prepared to divert energy for a week, we can stockpile a healthy number of them in both standard and miniature formats, before reverting to slower methods. Just use them sparingly to begin with. I'm sure they'll make a point quite quickly."

Excellent! Saul turned back to his defense chief. "Does that meet your requirements, Shannon?"

"Hell yes," she replied. "Getting a heads-up as to where the enemy is intending to concentrate their efforts will allow us to respond a lot more succinctly, especially if they pull one of their stunts. And being able to fight back will be even better." She looked thoughtful for a moment. "May I make a suggestion?"

"Please do."

"I'd like permission to assign an attack squadron within the city, too. Just an idea, but if the other items we're going to discuss—namely this portal, or gateway, or whatever it is—turns out to be a security threat, I want to make sure we can not only react immediately, but with maximum aggression. I'll need those flyers to be equipped with some form of iron deterrent. They'll be the first line of defense until we can get an emergency team on site."

"Good thinking," Saul replied, "it'll be done." He addressed everyone again. "As Shannon touched on the disturbing news about the vortex our friends possess, I think it'd be a good time to address this intelligence now."

No one objected, so Saul activated a holo-projector and ran the simultaneous images captured by Mac and Sam a few nights previously. One set had been recorded in natural low-light, the other skipped through infrared, ultraviolet, and acoustic mediums.

Adjusting the settings, Saul froze the separate profiles of both the emerging apparition and of the portal itself. Once he was satisfied, he said, "Opinions, anyone?"

"Let's get the easy part out of the way with first," Ayria offered. "I've been over these pictures with Penny Frasier. That's definitely a Horde Master. Rarely seen and now captured in all its glory in multiple mediums. Concentrating on the purely physical aspects, there's not much we can add to the little we know. They appear larger and more intelligent than their smaller hive members. But now we've had a chance to study the coronet in more detail . . ." She paused to enlarge the area around the beast's face. We think we might be on to something. Can you see that, the distinctive shimmering radiance inside the halo, surrounding its head? Having scrutinized the footage over the past day, we feel those emanations might be separate to the personal essence of the Master. You don't see it among the pack individuals. So we wondered . . . what if it's linked to the crown itself?"

"As in a specific energy field?" Mohammed asked. "So you're suggesting it's a form of enhancement? A device they wear?"

"I'm not suggesting anything," Ayria countered. "It's just a point we noticed on closer examination. The first time we've ever been able to do so, I might add. And having discovered it, I think it might be a good idea to devote further resources to understanding this aspect of our enemy better. Whether it's there simply to signify rank because the Master is bigger and more powerful, or due to the fact that it's a form of augmentation or technology we've never seen before remains to be seen. But drawing your attention to it now will allow us to factor this anomaly into mission briefings should a suitable opportunity arise."

"There is a simple way we could check it out," Mohammed said.

"How?"

"From what I understand, Andy Webb is one of the finest shots the Royal Marines ever produced. Why don't we ask him to take a pop at it? Just because the flames of the coronet dance around the Controller's head shouldn't present a problem to someone like him. If circumstances develop whereby he can guarantee hitting the mark without rupturing the nimbus of the Boss itself, it'd be interesting to see what happens."

Shannon grinned. "Sound idea."

"That could work," Ayria agreed.

"And if it does," Mohammed added, "it'll answer another thought that just came to mind."

"What's that, Mohammed?" Saul asked.

"Well, if it is some kind of device they wear, what's to say it doesn't control this vortex thing we've discovered?"

"That's a good point." Saul opened the floor. "C'mon everyone, what do you think this void thing is?"

"The mere fact the Controller stepped through it from somewhere else is a clear indicator we're dealing with a doorway," Ryan Davies, the training head, began, "but where it leads from is another matter entirely."

"I concur," Ephraim added. "I had quite an interesting chat with Asa Montgomery, one of my staff, on this very subject. As you know, we showed clips of these latest discoveries around our various departments prior to this briefing so we could bring as many ideas to the table as possible. Asa is a stardrive engineer from 2347, and has a natural flair for all things innovative. When he saw the clips, his gut reaction was that we're looking at something very similar to Ardenese Rip-Space technology. Remember, such generators were still beyond even the most sophisticated of our respective governments before we were marooned here. And while Ardenese nano-educators have helped us catch up remarkably well, we're still a long way from their level of understanding. Asa is the scientist directly responsible for monitoring and maintaining Rhomane's Tear-Shield, a remarkable adaptation of the hyper-drive theorem that allowed them to create what is, effectively, an impervious barrier. That's why they housed the gateway, the Ark, and indeed the Architect Archive itself inside such a contrivance. It puts them beyond reach. Or it should do, unless Asa is right and—"

"The Horde can do the same thing!" Saul gazed at him. "Forgive me for raising a whole load of annoying questions, Ephraim, but how could a bunch of monsters end up possessing such Tec in the first place? How do they power it? Who maintains it? I mean, just look at the size of this particular portal. It's inside the hold of a ship for God's sake. It doesn't appear to be rupturing the integrity of the surrounding structure at all. I'm no egghead, but even I know the level of sophistication required to confine such constructs within small spaces is . . . is . . ."

"Impressive. And beyond our current level of understanding." Ephraim shrugged. "Even the Ardenese hadn't refined their own hyper-spatial fields into such a compacted medium as this. Just look at the outer corona of the asperity. Do you notice how smooth it is? It's not so much tearing a hole through spacetime as folding it open in an unerringly relaxed fashion."

"So does this mean they've been taking us for a ride all along? I find that hard to believe. If they really possessed such levels of sophistication, they'd have been inside the city years ago. Or at least tried to make contact. All they've ever tried to do is swarm the wall and destroy us."

"Ah, but here's the point," Ephraim said. "The rest of the footage reveals a side to the Horde we've failed to recognize, or even appreciate might exist."

Taking the hint, Saul activated the monitors again. He added the long-range view of the container ship, but from the sniper team's perspective up on Mount Boleni. The Horde Master could clearly be seen exiting the hold and casually making its way toward the star liner Seranette. The scene changed back to a later recording from Mac's HUD. In this picture, the same Boss had been targeted by a laser finder.

"It's putting its hands up," Ephraim explained,."It knows we possess something that can destroy it. It recognizes it's in danger, and is throwing itself on its potential killer's mercy. Now, when you remember this thing also issued instructions to a baying mob of usually uncontrollable beasts, and later took the initiative to examine the detonation site of our latest weapon, I don't think there's any doubt that we're dealing with a highly intelligent being. It also helps explain why the Special Forces team saw what they did in the tunnel. Saul, if you would be so kind?"

Saul adjusted the view to include the recordings made of the sleeping grunts within the underpass at the starport. Silence ensued for over ten minutes as everyone absorbed the implications of what they were watching.

"Ladies and gentlemen," Ephraim declared, "behold our enemy at rest. Those flares and static outbursts represent a whole new change in thinking." He gestured, inviting Ayria to explain why.

"What you are seeing here," she said, "is the emotive display of a huge group of individuals dreaming. Remember, a dream is basically a collection of images, ideas, and perceptions absorbed subconsciously during the day, expressed in an involuntary way when the mind is at rest. Now, although it sounds simple, to be able to dream you need a mind to exist in the first place. There has to be a cognitive intellect. A psyche. A sense of self, capable of perceptive, rational thinking. We never attributed such a distinction to the Horde, which is a remarkable oversight on our part because they are more switched on than they've led us to believe."

"So why the change?" Mohammed asked, aghast at the implications.

"That's simple." Ayria glanced at Ephraim. "We think it's due solely to the fact that we now possess and are ready to use iron. Before the arrival of the ninth intake, the Horde was in the enviable position of being able to strive for their objective—whatever that is—by intimidation. Now they can't."

"So they're suddenly going to get all friendly and politely knock on our front door?"

"They've astonished us before, Mohammed. I don't think we'll have to wait too long before another unexpected twist comes our way."

"I don't like surprises of that sort," Saul said as he rejoined the conversation. "I think it wise to plan ahead. The Horde's bane is iron. So we need more of it to maintain our new advantage. The flyers are going to assist us greatly in this regard with topographical and mineral surveys, and hopefully, the acquisition of a cruiser from the starport. Thanks to Mac's initiative, there's a high likelihood we might be able to commandeer one and fly it. That'll go a long way toward speeding up the process. While we can make do with the poorer deposits from the Erásan range in the short term, we need to refocus our efforts on the rich pickings archives indicate exist out at the Shilette Abyss."

Saul deactivated the holo-projectors and turned to the City Administrator. "Rosa, I understand Jagpal has compiled a full list of the specialist skills our latest arrivals possess, yes?"

"Yes, that's correct. We've been most fortunate. Their diversity is amazing. How the Architect knew to acquire such a spectrum of talents from one place is beyond me. Mac and his specialists aren't the only gems to come through from the twenty-first century. Did you know the Husker-Trent team includes geologists, drillers, and operations experts in field assessment analysis? Even the few members we now have from the former terrorist group include a biochemist, an ex-diamond miner from South Africa, and a mountaineering expert who enjoys dabbling in something called potholing, whatever that is?

"Additionally, we can't overlook the building and construction skills possessed by the legionnaires. Any teams going out to the abyssal will need a solid, fortified structure to operate from, with a sustainable infrastructure. It's bread and butter stuff to Marcus's men. If the flyers are as effective as we hope in adding an additional defensive layer to the city wall, I'm hoping you'll consider sparing at least a centuriae of them to help out and maintain a permanent garrison there."

The proposal was met by mumbles of approval and agreement.

"Now that is good news," Saul murmured, "and it's something I'd overlooked entirely. Well done. Please ensure a detailed précis is sent to my terminal as soon as this meeting is ended.

Mohammed and I will look into it tonight. We'll have a rough idea as to how we can proceed by tomorrow morning, okay?"

Rosa nodded. Her fingers danced across her screen as she started to compile the necessary particulars.

"Any other business?" Saul asked, excited that events had progressed so smoothly.

No one responded, and he was happy to conclude the debriefing.

"Thank you, ladies and gentlemen. That'll be all. Ephraim? Don't forget the updates regarding each phase of flyer development. Ayria? I want you and Penny to raid the archives and get me as much information on Horde Masters and their characteristics as possible. Liaise with Rosa. Look for anything we might have missed previously. Shannon? Please speak with Marcus to see who his natural choices would be for running a separate garrison and what it will require to set up. Oh, and Ryan? Once the drone program is operating smoothly, cooperate with Shannon in setting up a series of emergency drills. Not only do I want the response teams to be on their toes, but I also want to find out, ASAP, which areas within the city might prove difficult to defend. Does everyone know what they're doing?"

Multiple affirmations rebounded. An enthusiastic vibe filled the air.

They're feeling positive, and it's about time.

Dismissing them, Saul became lost in his private thoughts.

Even with the news about the portal, it's still been a good day. We've got the Horde on the back foot. We're beginning to gain the upper hand. And who knows, this might even be the dawning of a new era?

He struggled to rein in his optimism. And failed.

Hell, this isn't just a good day, it's all my birthdays and Christmases rolled into one.

Saul grinned at the thought of giving Marcus the good news.

I wonder how many of them will clamor to be included in the first expedition? Mind you, I must admit, a change of scenery will do me good too.

Chapter Nineteen

A New Day

Someone called out to her. In its extremity, the appeal was voiced in exactly the same manner as in previous nights. Plaintive. Demanding. Urgent. Troubled. But try as she might, Ayria couldn't understand its meaning.

What do you want? she called, to no avail. *Where are you? What are you trying to tell me?*

As always, there was no reply. Or if there was, she was too far removed to comprehend it. Troubled, Ayria stirred in her sleep. On other nights, the plea had faded into the distance, its meaning lost among the subtle nuances of her dreams. Tonight though, something within her didn't want that to happen. For the first time in an age, she bared her soul in earnest appeal.

Nana! I'm sorry I didn't listen when I was a child. I know my head was stuck in the clouds, yearning for the stars. But in

my heart I knew you were telling the truth. Help me to under-
stand what this all means.

She waited for a reply.

Emptiness surrounded her, and gradually, Ayria relaxed
and allowed her mind to drift.

A piercing shriek split the silence. Ayria jerked awake,
alarmed by the timbre of the call. She looked about in wide-
eyed panic, only to find she was alone. Gone were the austere
furnishings of her room, with the muted back-lighting she liked
to employ when resting. Instead, she found herself transposed
to a cliff top, the likes of which she had only ever imagined.

A fistula of granite hung in the star-spangled vastness of
space. Adorned in cedars and verdant grass, it was bathed in the
warm light of an unknown sun. A fast-running river of crystal
clear water flowed past her position, only to disappear over the
precipice into the cosmic cataract. Spume filled the void with
diamond spray and rainbow hues.

Ayria was filled with a sense of utter peace and contentment.

An eagle appeared from among the clouds. Tucking in its
wings, it plunged toward her. At the last second, it veered to
one side. Blazing past in a flash of golden glory, it plummeted
into the icy depths. Its call brought with it the familiarity of the
summons that had woken her from sleep.

Comprehension sent a thrill of realization coursing along
her spine. *I'm dream-walking! I'm actually dream-walking. I
did it. But where . . . ?*

Ayria realized she was no longer alone. An old man sat
cross-legged on the ground near to the precipice in front of her,
staring out at the stars around them. He seemed transfixed on
a huge red sun in the distance.

Although aged, she could tell by the way he held himself
that this man had seen many summers of activity. His back
was erect and proud, powerfully muscled. Trailing down to the

ground, his midnight mane had been tied into a combat braid, and was dignified by long streaks of gray.

To one side, a huge wolf warmed itself in sunlight, its thick shaggy coat glistening with moisture from the falls. Before Ayria could gain her wits, the eagle reappeared. Gliding out from the haze of interstellar space, it gripped a fat, wriggling salmon tightly in its talons. Dropping the fish into the warrior's lap, it landed and loped across to the wolf. Its task complete, the noble creature preened the shaggy beast for a few moments before nesting down within the depths of its fur.

Confused, Ayria strolled closer to get a better look.

The elder ignored her. Producing a sharp knife from within the folds of his belt, he gutted the offering before him. Dividing the carcass into equal measures, he placed two portions to one side for the wolf and the eagle to share. The rest, he kept for himself. But instead of consuming his meal, the brave began to sing.

His voice was deep and resonant, and seemed to call on the essence of the cosmos. A thrill tingled along Ayria's skin as intuition flared within her. *The Old Man! What did Nana say his name was? Napee . . . Napo . . . Napioa. Yes, that's it! Napioa.*

Ayria noticed he had taken great care to remove the egg-sack of the salmon unbroken. As he chanted, Napioa squeezed its contents onto the grass. Satisfied with his preparations, he separated those eggs, one from the other. Napioa reached up into the void and gathered strings of vitality from the endless well of creative forces thrumming all around.

Ayria watched in silence as the old man wove the elements together into a likeness of the first comers. Soon, ranks of miniature people lay sleeping among the blades of grass, blissfully unaware of their place in the great scheme of things.

Out of nowhere, a great bow and quiver full of arrows appeared. Ayria could see the shafts were flightless. Undaunted,

Napioa leaned across to the sleeping eagle and plucked a multitude of feathers from its wings. He repeated the process with
the wolf, taking long strands from its fur to fletch each quill in
place. Once completed, he adorned the flights with their own
distinct sigils.

Ayria had never been an avid student of her ancestry, so
most of the marks were a mystery to her. Nevertheless, she did
recognize half-a-dozen symbols of familiar tribes in amongst
them. Having completed his task, Napioa selected a handful
of his resting creations and tied them to a corresponding set
of arrows.

Standing, he studied the heavens before him. His gaze
came to rest upon the ancient star he had been scrutinizing
when Ayria had first seen him. Stringing the bow, he cocked
his arm and with a loud *thrum*, sent his missile speeding off
into the night toward its crimson objective. Moments later, a
small flare confirmed he had struck his target.

Uttering a grunt of satisfaction, Napioa repeated the process. Hours passed. Time and again, the Creator selected a set
number of slumbering images from off the ground. After con-
templating them closely, he studied the firmament to choose
a suitable sun. Humming a song of farewell, he sent each one
speeding on its way toward a new home.

The number remaining dwindled. Ayria recognized some
of the markings on the feathers that were left. Apache, Blackfoot, Sioux, Innu, Naskapi, Lakota.

Selecting those at last, the old warrior took his time to
search the vault above him. Something caught his eye. A small,
insignificant, wan yellow sun. It was so very far away that Ayria could hardly see it. Taking careful aim, Napioa let fly. Moments later the tiny star flared, and he smiled.

Resuming his place before the precipice, the Old Man
recited an ancient mantra. The heavens whirled above them,

and the ages paraded past in majesty and grandeur. The cycles gradually slowed, and came to a standstill once more. A translucent moon smiled down, its radiance bathing everyone in an aura of exaltation and shadows.

The call that had haunted Ayria's dreams echoed out of the darkness. The eagle raised its head and shrieked in reply. It was joined by the wolf, which threw back its head and howled.

Napioa stood and clicked his fingers. His creatures responded. Together, they walked toward the precipice, and stood upon the very edge of the yawning abyss. Watching. Waiting.

The air contorted before them. A swathe of glittering stars disappeared behind a veil of shimmering, opaque mist. From out of the vapor, another plea rang forth.

"Attend!" he commanded.

Both bird and beast reacted immediately. Grasping a tress of the Creator's mane in beak and jaw, they leaped out into the cosmic sea. The vortex folded in on itself and sped away toward the distant red star. The eagle followed in hot pursuit, leaving an ever lengthening silver-blue strand behind it. To Ayria's surprise, the wolf turned and raced off in the opposite direction, toward the remote yellow star that had been last on the Creator's list. It too, trailed an ever increasing lock of luxuriant hair in its wake. Soon, both creatures were lost from sight.

The Old Man raised his arms and gestured at his cascading hair. Staring directly at Ayria for the first time, he challenged, "Do you understand?"

Ayria could only look on, bemused, as she tried to make sense of what she now witnessed. *"Feel, don't think. Let your intuition take control,"* the voice of her grandmother chided in her mind.

Napioa continued, "All life is fashioned from the same stuff of creation." Pointing with his left hand, he indicated the huge ruby disc basking within a rich scarlet penumbra. "The care I lavished on those first awakened . . ." he repeated the gesture to his right, ". . . was also given to those who came last." The much smaller star behind Ayria glittered like pale citrine. The old warrior concluded, "My children are one. When they call for aid, I hear."

His children? Is he talking about seeding the universe with life?

The Father Creator smiled, as if sensing her thoughts.

There's a connection between them?

The penny dropped. *Oh my . . . Arden's sun is a K-class Red Giant. He's telling me the appeal is originating from Arden.* She spun on her heel. *So that must be—*

"At last. The clouds that blind your spirit-sight are departing," Napioa boomed, cutting in on her reasoning. "Behold the truth!"

The two strands of his hair that stretched off into the distance burst into incandescent light. So bright, so vital was their radiance that they inundated Ayria's senses with a brilliance that blotted out the heavens and sent her reeling back toward the river. Driven to her knees, Ayria blinked furiously until her vision reasserted itself. As Napioa came back into focus, she saw him heaving mightily on his flaming locks, one after the other, and entwining each length into thickening cords around his arms.

At first, nothing appeared to be happening. But gradually, little by little, bit by bit, she discerned both stars and their encircling planets being drawn closer together. As they neared each other, an unfamiliar melody skirled through the ether, carrying with it a promise of resolution and balance.

Solar winds converged from two points, swirling in concert to form a mutual maelstrom in which the peoples of both worlds were lifted into the heavens, merging into one form. An alien voice, laced with anticipation, cried out from the heart of the storm, "Help me to remember who I am."

"Do you understand?" Napioa asked once more.

Before Ayria could reply, his eyes blazed white, and she was sent staggering across the grass into the frigid flow of the cascade. The bitter chill of winter's kiss closed about her, and Ayria found herself struggling to keep her head above water. The current pulled her under, and she felt the irresistible pull of gravity as it flung her over the cataract and into the void.

The world dimmed, and Ayria was swimming along an invisible tunnel. The current powered her forward at a blistering pace. She noticed a light ahead of her, shining like a beacon, and she made toward it. Moments later, she burst to the surface and full wakefulness. Bathed in sweat, Ayria took in the familiar surroundings of her room and flopped back onto her bed in relief.

Just as she was about to relax, Napioa's words echoed through her mind. *Do you understand, Wind of the Sun?*

She caught her breath.

Do I understand? I'm not sure. Even though it's part of my heritage, I've never done this kind of thing before. But that reference at the end? That's too much of a coincidence. It'll be a little embarrassing having to admit my neglect, but perhaps I'd better get a clearer picture of what this all means from someone who will know.

Ayria rose. Throwing on an old set of clothes, she made her way toward Stained-With-Blood's quarters. As she padded along the quiet corridors, the soul-lifting rays of a brand new day crested the horizon in the far distance. She paused for a moment, eyes shut, and reminisced on what her grandmother had told her all those years ago about the meaning of her name.

"As has always been the case, little one, our names have great substance. When we were first made, Napioa thought to

give our lives meaning. Purpose. Sadly, as the centuries have turned slowly by, many have forgotten the importance of remembering who they are. But not us. We are different. We of the Blackfoot Cree bring honor to our creator, by revering the sense of our origins."

"So what does Ayria mean, Nana?"

"Ah! In the true language, Ayria denotes 'Heavenly Wind'. Of course, with your father's name, Solram—which means sunsage—added in, it gives you special significance. His family had dream-walkers among them from the beginning. That's why your full title is 'Wind of the Sun', for one day, if you don't neglect your studies, you will be able to flow through the stars at will, and venture to places where no others can . . ."

Ayria resumed her journey. Snorting softly to herself, she mumbled, "Ayria Solram. Little *Wind of the Sun*, in the true Cree language. Or, as modern day people would render it, *Solar Wind*."

She thought once more of the details of her first ever dream-walk, and couldn't prevent an unnerving shiver from gripping her in its icy talons.

Too much of a coincidence by far.

*

An excited buzz filled the room. News of the mining expedition had spread through the city like wildfire over the past few days, and most people wanted in. As mission leader, Marcus Brutus was here to ensure things went smoothly. Exuberance aside, the team would be traveling over a hundred miles from the city, deep into unknown territory. Many things could go wrong, especially where their enemy was concerned. And while it wasn't known if dormant pockets of Horde might be found that far out, Marcus wasn't going to take any chances.

He cast his gaze around the people assembled before him, judging the mood of those he would command. The two opposing groups from the twenty-first century appeared to have buried their animosity remarkably well, and were enthusiastically discussing the implications of the combined venture.

Marcus checked the list on his handheld computer and did his best to put names to faces. *So, let me see if I've got this right. That's the Husker-Trent operations controller, Selwyn King. Although he won't actually be joining us on the trip, he'll be maintaining an overview of our progress from back here, in Rhomane. His knowledge and experience of ore management will come in handy.* Marcus had an idea. *I must get my centurions to liaise with him and discuss any tips he might have regarding the transportation of large quantities of minerals. Although we'll have the use of the skimmers and skidders, anything that enhances our performance will be a welcome addition.*

Now, he's speaking to . . . Marcus flipped forward a few screens *. . . ah, that's him. Joshua Osborne. The ex-diamond miner. That makes sense. From what I hear, the Shilette Abyss is a place of severe temperature extremes. Blazing hot during the day, freezing at night. I'm sure we'll all value his insights once we get out on the ground.*

The commander paused to study the animated discussion both men were enjoying.

Strange, only a few months ago they were bitter enemies. One, an extremist willing to die for his cause, and the other a family man, desperate to stay alive and return home. Look at them now.

King and Osborne appeared to be having a good-natured difference of opinion. They had obviously reached a stalemate, for they turned to a pair of roughnecks opposite them to help settle a question.

Having chatted to the oil drillers earlier that morning, Marcus smiled and readily identified them. *Oliver Prince and Gerry Hunt. Two of the biggest pranksters I've ever met. Their sense of humor will provide an essential ingredient to the success of our venture under hardship. And of course, if anyone knows the hazards of cutting through temperamental layers of compressed rock, it will be them. While my own soldiers have some degree of knowledge of open cast mining methods, these experts will help speed the process considerably. Especially if they manage to fathom out how to use the Ardenese handheld devices . . .* he glanced at his tablet . . . *focusing lasers? If these instruments are as good as people are saying, I'll ensure a decarius of my own men is instructed in their use. It'll help share the load and increase production.*

Closer to him, Marcus could hear several more experienced settlers who had lived in Rhomane for a number of years discussing with a group of his officers the merits of learning to drive the skidders. Terri and Stefan Hollander in particular were well known to his men, having provided transport for them on a number of occasions. The couple was well liked and had been a natural inclusion for the mission demographic.

They have a point. While the legion's individual skills will assist in the short run, our long term success will inevitably result from our full integration into this more . . . scientific community. We've already adapted with scant regard to the tiny machines within us. And many of the other delights this city has to offer are becoming second nature. Yes, the quicker we immerse ourselves within this more advanced culture, the better it will be. I'll make a point of raising it with Saul after I've completed this briefing.

A raucous outburst of laughter from the back of the room, near to the coffee dispenser, caused Marcus to raise his eyebrows in disbelief. Sergeant Adam Wainwright and Corporal

Joseph Mitchell of the 2nd Company were sharing a joke with two of the former terrorists, Sebbi Farah and Sebastian Coule.

Well, that is a surprise! Even our more fractious cousins are making the effort to act amenably toward their fellow colonists. It would appear their punishment duties are having the desired effect. Marcus pinched himself, just to make sure. *I wonder though, would they be so eager to commit themselves to the spirit of this undertaking if their absent captain was well enough to join us? We shall see.*

Of his own men, Marcus had decided to leave the first cohort where they were, defending Rhomane. Not only were they the best and most seasoned fighters, but Marcus had decided it the course of wisdom to keep Decimus and his unit away from the cavalry platoon.

After all, there are only so many beatings they can take before someone gets killed.

Marcus caught the eye of the centurion he had decided to use as garrison commander out at the abyss, Tiberius Tacitus. As captain of the 2nd Cohort, he had enough experience to keep people in line and deal with any problems that may occur over the periods Marcus himself would need to be away. The men were all veterans and proficient, both in fighting and utilizing the skills that would be required to erect a serviceable fort, and assist in mining operations.

Time to test the waters.

Marcus nodded, and Tiberius called the room to order. Soon, a sea of keen and happy faces was concentrated on Marcus, each displaying a clear sense of anticipation.

Marcus was impressed. *Looks like a new day has dawned after all.*

*

The team had taken Jumper's absence as Mac knew they would. Professionally and with quiet resolve. It had only been two weeks since the funeral, and while the frustrations of such a waste would eat away at them for many years to come, Mac was also aware that the best thing for his men right now was action.

When Saul and Mohammed approached them earlier with details of one of their most daring and audacious schemes to date, everyone took to the idea with relish.

Mac leafed his way through the pages of the mission outline once more, this time in the comfort and privacy of his own room. He had been asked to orchestrate a time sensitive, three-pronged attack, and needed the peace and quiet of his suite to plan things out properly. What he read made him smile.

So, spurred on by our outrageously good results so far, the boys upstairs are getting ambitious. They basically want us to acquire not one, but two small to medium sized starships, preferably a cargo carrier and an executive class luxury liner similar to the Seranette. He flicked through the wish-list appendix at the end of the section. His eyes widened in shock. *And not only do they expect us to achieve this remarkable feat in tandem, but we also have to nursemaid the usual scientific entourage, along with an additional four VIPs. Pilots. All of whom will be very precious to future successes, I'm sure.*

Shaking his head in disbelief, Mac absorbed the specifics of the third phase of the operation.

At the same time, they expect us to seize the astrometrics facility at Boleni Heights and secure it against further incursions. He snorted. *Is that all?*

Mac skimmed the details again to ensure he hadn't misread anything.

The past several weeks have brought us along in leaps and bounds. Retro-fitted Tec and weapons. Iron, with a new source about to be opened up once Marcus and his expedition get underway. Hundreds of flyers, many now equipped with offensive as well as defensive capabilities. The mines. Oh! And not forgetting Brent's marvelous adaptation of blended null-point and chameleon shielding. The portable defensive walls will be a godsend at Boleni Heights. And the proposed fort at Shilette Abyss, come to that. But I can't help thinking they're pushing ahead a little too quickly. It might be the dawning of a new era, but we can't push our luck. We still don't know what the Horde is really capable of. I've got a nasty feeling we haven't seen the last of their surprises yet.

He sat back and tried to clear his mind.

Buuut, if command are so keen for us to get results, it'll mean I can make a wish-list of my own, and *be certain to get what I want. I know, I'll get the lads down and have them go over my proposals. It won't hurt to have everyone's perspective. They might spot something I've missed.*

Of course, that only brought the memories of Jumper crowding back.

Chapter Twenty

Walk With Me

Stained-With-Blood sat impassively on the end of his bed and studied his visitor closely. Only thirty minutes previously, Ayria Solram had arrived at his quarters and asked to speak to him about a private matter. Intrigued, he allowed her to enter, thinking she would seek his opinion on a cultural matter, or something similar. Instead, she frankly and without a hint of embarrassment revealed the truth of her own origins, and of her remarkable talent as a dream-walker.

Ayria was as equally forthright in explaining why she had squandered her heritage. From childhood, she had been determined to become a doctor and help people. Remaining focused on that goal had outweighed everything else. Until fate decided to intercede. And what an intervention it was.

Through it all, Stained-With-Blood kept his composure. A raised eyebrow here. A gentle snort there. Hardly any reaction at all really, but one that would speak volumes to a trained observer.

His visitor completed her account. "What do you think?"

He noted the mixed look of apprehension and hope on her face, and how that inner turmoil was betrayed by the way she crossed her arms tightly across her chest. Smiling, he beckoned for her to take a seat.

Wind of the Sun, he thought, Ayria Solram. How could I, a shaman of the nine tribes, miss such an obvious connection? Just because she comes from a time centuries after mine, am I so blind that I fail to see the obvious? Is my faith so weak I would think our blood would be weakened?

"Before I reply," he began, "I must tell you of a vision I was granted myself, after having arrived here. The similarities are remarkable."

Without waiting for a response, he continued. "This then, is my experience. I too, received a visitation from Napioa. He took me to a place where he reclined upon a crag. A cliff atop a mountain with a remarkable vista stretched out before it. A star fell from heaven, and with it the Creator fashioned a blade. Having done so, he allowed his hair to form a great windstorm, the strands of which cascaded freely into the night. At a suitable time, he cut his hair and allowed the tresses to be consumed by fire. Instead of turning to ash, they became glowing embers, like fireflies, which rose up from the hearth and danced about his head, singing.

"Napioa then used the knife to cut his palm. Ichor flowed, rich and red. Its vitality created a sacred birch which sprouted instantly to life on the lip of the precipice. Once fully grown, the tree toppled over the edge and exploded. The remains refused to die. Seeds joined with the cinders of Napioa's hair. Together, they were carried away into the starlit sky. Soon, filthy creatures, dressed as coyotes, were drawn to the scent of blood. Each wore the mark of rival factions. Napioa himself encouraged us to dine together upon succulent fish."

A faraway look glazed his eyes. Shaking his head, Stained-With-Blood admitted, "Our father asked me at the time if I understood what he was telling me. I did, but was too proud to acknowledge that I should consort with those *I* deemed unworthy."

"So what happened?" Ayria whispered, not wanting to break the tale's spell.

"Ah! Napioa refined my appreciation, for he caused a new day to dawn before my very eyes. A fresh, clean sun commenced its climb into the sky. Before it had the opportunity to clear the horizon, another, greater star rose up behind it. Red and glorious, it swelled in size, swallowing the earth-light below it and bathing everyone on the plateau in consoling warmth and unity.

"Like you, the Creator asked me again if I understood. Before I could reply, the brightness folded in on itself and I found myself falling back onto our plane with Napioa's words echoing strongly in my mind . . . *Do you understand?*"

Ayria gasped. "And did you?"

"I thought I did." Stained-With-Blood sighed. "But it would appear certain aspects were but preparation for yet another, unforeseen chapter to this story. You and your involvement."

"My involvement?" Ayria was surprised by the warrior's interpretation of the vision. "Really?"

"That the fate of Earth and Arden are intertwined is clear. Our two dreams confirm this fact. We are to answer a plea that has spanned the cosmos. Blood calls out to its distant kin across the vastness of space and time. How we will do this, I do not know. But from what you have told me, you yourself would appear to be the instrument by which bitter enemies will be brought together and forged in a union of mutual consolation."

"Me?" Ayria spluttered. "But . . . but how? I'm just a doctor and a—"

"That is for Napioa to make clear," Stained-With-Blood interjected. "In the meantime, I will instruct you in the refining of your most precious gift. Come, Wind of the Sun, let us walk together in the spirit-world and see if the Old Man will reveal the path you must take."

"Now?"

"Of course. The matter is urgent; otherwise Napioa would not have reached out toward the two of us, separated as we were by thousands of years. Worry not. When your ordeal is over, you can learn more of your heritage from Small Robes. The insights of a woman are both subtle and deep. And to be truthful, when she hears of your ancestry, it will be difficult to keep her away."

Ayria laughed, nervously.

"Seriously!" Stained-With-Blood stressed. "She will be keen to discover the story of our people as they endured through the centuries."

He ruminated on the matter for a few moments. "Yes indeed. It will do you *both* good to spend time together."

With that, they prepared for a journey neither of them would ever forget.

*

The entity now possessing James Houston's body ran his hands along the wall as he walked. To someone who had existed for so long without any form of tactile stimulation, the sensation was mesmerizing. But then again, during the few weeks it had taken for him to gain full control, he had discovered most things would capture his attention. The host was still here, of course, but was now consigned to a dark recess in the back of a cavernous mind.

Rubbing the seam between two huge blocks of granite with his fingertips, he found the texture fascinating. *There's hardly anything to distinguish where one slab ends and the other begins. Remarkable.*

He still didn't know who he was. Neither did he have the faintest idea how he had come to be trapped inside the very fabric of the super-dense structure of the city's defenses. All that remained was a gut feeling that he needed to be here. In fact, it was vital, as others needed to hear what he had to say.

If only I could . . . remember . . .

Wonder of the moment slipped away as he fought to make sense of the jumbled tangle of his memories. Although he had noticed a miniscule improvement in the long days since his awakening, it was still proving to be a most frustrating experience. At odd moments, he would catch himself in mid stride and suddenly hold his breath, as if an unknown horror was about to descend on him. A moment of blind panic would follow, before an overwhelming acceptance of an inescapable fate consumed him.

But acceptance of what? And why do I need to . . . to express . . . ah hell! It's gone.

Shocked, the entity came to a standstill as he recognized something about himself.

I'm picking up more and more of Houston's mannerisms with every passing day.

He thought about that for a moment. It felt right.

Hmm, perhaps it will prove helpful to think of myself as James Houston. After all, I possess his memories as well as his body, and from what I can determine, he was a most unpleasant individual. I wonder how his contemporaries would view a new and improved version?

Somewhere deep inside, a suppressed consciousness screamed.

Oh, be quiet! 'James' snapped, addressing the petulant voice within. Perhaps we can work together to turn this unholy mess to our mutual advantage. Wouldn't you like that?

An hour marker chimed softly in the distance. Realizing the time, James muttered, "I'd better potter back to the medical center. They're expecting me . . . *us* . . . for a psyche evaluation. Whatever else I've missed out on, I can't be late for that."

*

The cavalry officers stood quietly on the observation deck of the inner marshalling yard, and watched as two squads from the 9th Legion went through their paces.

Centurion Tiberius Tacitus and his 2nd Cohort were defending themselves from a sustained attack by the 4th company, led by Amelius Crispus. Whilst utilizing men in standard *box* formation, Tiberius drilled the rest in the deployment of the new, portable, dual-energy walls. Incorporating both null-point and chameleon shielding, it was hoped the latest defensive measures would provide a considerable tactical advantage to those units forced to operate within enemy territory.

Three sets of emitter rods had already been triggered, and formed an open U shape. As the withdrawing centuriaes slowly edged backward toward the dormant side, their teammates prepared to activate the final poles.

A flurry of blunted arrows with lead-ball tips flew out from the 2nd Cohort, providing a moment's grace for the retreating wall of shields to unlock from one another. Their bearers made a break for the gap. As the legionnaires ran between their waiting colleagues, the final emitter was slammed into place and the barrier activated. Within seconds, it appeared to onlookers as if mirrors had suddenly sprung into existence, as the entire defending squad disappeared from sight.

Men on both sides cheered.

Someone shouted an order, and the 4th Company responded by shooting a volley of arrows at the invisible barricade. The barrage met the negating energy field, and dropped harmlessly to the floor.

"That was impressive," Corporal Stuart Williams of the 1st Platoon muttered.

"It certainly was," Sergeant Jake Rixton, his senior officer, replied. "Did you know, the Roman Legions built an actual encampment at the end of every day's march? Not only did it have staked walls, but they also dug a dry moat filled with oil around the entire fortification. That way, their attackers would have to battle uphill just to reach them. If it ever looked to the defending soldiers like they might get overrun, they simply set fire to the oil."

"Painful."

"And bloody effective. Just imagine how much easier their job will be with these new shields. I was speaking to Marcus this morning. His men are still determined to erect a fort whenever they make camp. But from now on, they'll do so behind the protection of the null barriers and be able to take their time about it."

Stuart nodded and shrugged in appreciation. "But you didn't just invite me here today to watch legionnaires play, did you?"

"Ah, you got me." Jake grinned. "You're right. I asked to meet you as I've something to discuss. Commander Cameron called me into his office this morning. The hierarchy has decided it's not good for 1st Platoon to be without a lieutenant. They offered me the job. It's not common knowledge yet, so keep it to yourself. But I'm going to say yes."

"Is it a brevet or substantive promotion?"

"Well, seeing as we're not going home, I've been told it's permanent."

Stuart slapped his friend heartily on the back. "Congratulations, Jake."

"Thank you. I've got some big shoes to fill. Lieutenant Fox was a very competent young man. I just hope I can do his memory justice. But that's not what I really wanted to talk to you about."

"Why? What else is there?"

"Well, seeing as I'm moving up the ladder, it will leave my current position vacant. I want you to be my platoon sergeant."

Stuart's jaw dropped open.

"Obviously, you get to select your own corporal," Jake continued when he realized his companion was too shocked to speak, "but choose wisely. It's essential to pick a candidate who's competent, and someone the men can trust."

"I'll get right on it," Stuart mumbled, "and thanks."

"Don't thank me just yet. Your acceptance means you have to submit yourself to a full medical. Part of the procedure, evidently. When we've finished here, get yourself over to the health center. They're expecting you. Oh, and give my regards to Surgeon Major Clark and Surgeon Captain Anders. Tell them I'll be along later." Shrugging, he explained, "With the skills they possess, they're too valuable to risk on general duties. That's why we haven't seen much of them over the past weeks. It looks like they'll be working there permanently from now on."

"They're not the only ones we haven't seen for a while."

Jake caught the reference to their former captain. "Ah hell! I'd forgotten about that."

"Do you know what's happening with him? Or when he'll be back?"

"No. And I don't care. Although I must admit, I'd love to see his face when he finds out I've been promoted to full lieutenant without his consultation."

Chapter Twenty-One

Shilette Abyss

The gentle pace of the horses continued to weave its subtle spell over Marcus and the rest of his company. He was dozing in the saddle. Despite his many years of service, Marcus had developed a soldier's habit of snatching rest where he could. And if an opportunity arose while he was quietly trotting along, it was only natural that custom would take precedence. Apart from the picket patrol, it was a pattern that had been adopted by most of the experienced riders about him.

The highway had been a great boon in that regard.

It had surprised the legionnaires to discover the route toward the Shilette Abyss was graced by a road so straight it would have made even the most stubborn and fastidious Legate burst with pride. That the Ardenese were a highly advanced society was obvious. That they had also liked to drive for the

sheer enjoyment of the experience had been a delight to discover, for it made their current journey so much easier.

Traveling east past Boleni Heights, the expedition took
the first major junction heading south. Although time consuming, the added distance guaranteed the avoidance of roving Horde packs, which seemed to congregate around areas
saturated with sophisticated technology. The passing of those
extra leagues was also eased by the fact that only thirty miles
beyond the southern boundaries of the spaceport, a major spur
of the carriageway branched off through the Forest of Tar'e-
esh. On the maps, this vast area was shaded green. In actual-
ity, the mission found themselves immersed in a sprawling
expanse of verdure and crimson tranquility. So refreshing was
the change from their usual environment that the exhaustion
fraying everyone's nerves to shreds over the past weeks was
soon reduced to nothing more than a dull ache. A mood that
improved dramatically the deeper they journeyed into the heart
of the unexpected woodlands.

They had been on the road for six days. The absence of
Horde infestation was only starkly evident but had allowed
them to make good time. Birds sang incessantly as they skipped
from branch to branch. Unknown creatures chittered and chat-
tered from the protection of the undergrowth. Lush grasses and
all manner of flora bursting with vibrant life stretched off for
miles in every direction. And welcome shade infused the air
with soothing relief. Even the roadway, although carpeted by
windfall and overgrown along the edges, provided a cushioned
walkway for the foot soldiers to traverse with ease.

Lulled once again into a state of happy reverie, Marcus
found himself back in his favorite place. Gaul.

*If only I could lead one last trek through that countryside. I
wouldn't give a fig about guerilla raids. They'd seem like noth-*

ing in comparison to what's going on here. And *they wouldn't try to suck my soul from me, either.*

He catalogued the distinctions his actions had earned. *The summons to Rome to appear before the Senate. My personal visit with Caesar Hadrian himself. My promotion thereafter.*

Although he knew such honors were a thing of the past, the flickering kiss of dappled sunlight on his eyelids made him sigh. Then he smiled.

"Happy about something, Marcus?"

The intruding voice sent a tingle of déjà vu along his spine, tugging Marcus from his daydream. "I'm sorry, what was that?" He struggled to focus his gaze on the person riding next to him. *General Quintus?*

"I said, are you happy about something?" Wilson Smith repeated.

Marcus snapped back to reality. "Just reminiscing. Like you, I've spent many hours in the saddle as a matter of course. Some days—and places, come to that—stand out above the rest."

"These woodlands are exceptional, aren't they? Who would have thought we'd find such a thing here? If the leaves didn't have a coppery-lilac tinge to them, I'd think we were in New England."

"Yes, it's certainly an enthralling place." Marcus shared the younger man's enthusiasm. A hungry look entered his eyes. "And one I'd like to explore more fully. I can only imagine what the hunting might be like."

"Why do you think the Horde has left it alone? I mean, the region is absolutely teeming with life. The reports said places like this were stripped bare."

"Then the reports are obviously wrong," Marcus stated, "as many of the colonists' assumptions have been up to now." He leaned sideways in his saddle and lowered his voice. "From what I have been told, the initial ravaging of the planet's surface was quickly over. Following their victory the Horde simply massed together, first in the vicinity of the major cities, and finally, at Rhomane itself. Then the siege began."

"So, life had a chance to survive out here? And there could be other places like this, scattered all over the planet?"

"It's a strong possibility." Marcus inclined his head. "We will know more when the other phase of Commander Cameron's plan comes to fruition. Lieutenant McDonald and his men will be starting their own operation in only two or three weeks' time. It will be interesting to see how things develop."

The younger man looked disappointed.

"Is anything amiss?"

"Not really," Wilson replied, gazing along the slowly moving column. "I'm used to riding for protracted periods of time, and it seems your men are accustomed to marching a considerable distance every day as well." He shrugged. "It's just that I can't help wondering how much quicker this could have gone if they'd allowed us to use skidders and skimmers. I mean, look how tired the scientists and other specialist workers are. Even at this easy pace, they look so saddlesore they won't be able to walk right for a month."

"A good point," Marcus acknowledged. "But therein lies the wisdom of strategy. Our mission is of the utmost importance. It is vital we locate and secure the site in which the mineral deposits are thought to be located. But remember, because the city has been isolated for so long, we won't know until we get there how accurate the archives are. Also, the actual Abyss itself and this forest are totally alien to us. They have to be checked out first. We also need to carry the supplies and utensils necessary to quickly establish a base of operations if things turn out favorably. Commander Cameron faced a conundrum. How could he move so much equipment over such a long distance without the need for machines which are needed elsewhere and which might draw our enemy's attention?"

Gesturing between them, Marcus emphasized, "That's where *we* come in. Cavalry and legionnaires. Although we can't hope to match the speed and grace of a highly sophisticated hover craft, we are nevertheless skilled at transporting large consignments over long distances at a speed unmatched by our contemporaries. And we can do so secretly. Additionally, the defensive measures we now have at our command will protect us, and allow us to set up a considerable series of fortifications from the outset. Just wait until you see what my men can build in a matter of hours. By the time the shuttle runs *do* begin, they'll have the luxury of berthing overnight within a city of fabricated domiciles."

"I'm looking forward to that." Wilson smiled. "I watched your men drilling a few times back in Rhomane, and it was very impressive. The guys couldn't believe how quickly you worked. To see it for real will be—"

Both men were disturbed by an outrider galloping full tilt toward them. The rest of the dozing company became instantly alert and began scanning the shadows.

Throwing up a hasty salute, the soldier reined in and addressed Marcus. "Sir, the forest ends abruptly, about a mile ahead. It . . . It's . . ."

"Spit it out, man."

"Sir. It's awesome, come and see."

Signaling for the immediate group to follow, Marcus put his heels to Starblaze's flanks and spurred his horse forward. A few minutes later, he reached several other sentries who were waiting to one side of the road. The highway veered away sharply to the southwest, so Marcus was surprised to be led off the tarmac and into the gloom.

An eldritch veil thick with antiquity closed about them. Specimens that looked like a cross between beech and cedar, oak and elm, ash and spruce, each endowed with massive boles, filed off into the distance. Stately monarchs of a forest that seemed to suddenly hold its breath in anticipation. Threading his way between iron trunks and cable like roots, Marcus wondered what secrets this brooding edifice must contain, and if it would ever be possible to find your way out if a person became disoriented.

You don't realize how dense this place is until you leave the safety of the main thoroughfare. I'll have to order markers placed to ensure our more inexperienced travelers don't go getting themselves lost. And I'll restrict hunting too, at least until we're more familiar with the area. Goodness knows how much further it goes.

He needn't have worried. After five more minutes of painfully slow travel, the swathe drew back and shafts of rose-gold brilliance punctuated the canopy in one place after another.

Everyone relaxed as they sensed a change ahead.

Even so, when the party broke free from dappled shade and rode into the harsh glare of direct sunshine, everyone was taken completely by surprise.

Mars preserve us!

Shocked, Marcus could only stare. *I can see why my sentry was rendered speechless.*

A shattered plain rolled away on both sides, providing a severe counterpoint to the undulating barrier of the forest's perimeter. The compact, ruddy surface of the plateau shimmered in the heat of the midday sun. As the mounted group moved out onto the shelf, their movements caused swirls of scarlet dust to dance into the air.

Shading his eyes, Marcus tried to make sense of what he was seeing.

The ground was littered with pock marks, each of which contained a smattering of gold and red rocks. A foul-smelling steam issued from a number of fissures and scalloped clefts. Wherever the vapors concentrated together, the soil was stained by a copper-colored residue.

Marcus could make out the shimmering white line of a bridge, about five miles away, obviously accommodating the continued course of the main highway. Closer to him, a smoother, rectangular area stood out in stark contrast to their cratered surroundings.

Hmm. Obviously a parking area for vehicles.

As intriguing as these distractions were, however, they paled under the imposing presence of the leviathan before them.

A huge canyon, over seventeen miles across and eight deep, gouged its way across the plane of their sight. Marcus knew from his mission briefing that the company now stood at one of the narrowest points of the Shilette Abyss. The gulf itself stretched away for over a thousand leagues, east and west; and for most of its length, the other side was so far away it would be impossible to see.

He marveled as to how the Ardenese had contrived to construct anything to cross such a gaping chasm, for the cliffs of the valley were an unstable maze of razor-sharp edges and unforgiving rocks that could give way without warning.

There, not three hundred yards in front of them, sat the real surprise. The bluff plunged away to form a huge cleft, a monster fissure over seventy feet wide which appeared to have been hacked into the earth to form a *V*-shaped crevice.

Cantering forward, the excited explorers discovered a tiered series of shelves, corresponding to levels of strata, leading down the cliff wall.

"It forms a chimney!" gasped one of the Husker-Trent geologists selected for the mission. Marcus glanced across to see Matthew Keegan almost falling from his saddle with excitement. "What a stroke of luck. Just look at the weathering. And the banding. We've struck red gold." The scientist's eyes glittered as he surveyed the multiple hues contained within the various layers of sediment.

"Weathering? Banding?" said Marcus, who was also finding it difficult to tear his gaze away from the stunning panorama before them. "I take it, that's good, yes?"

"Better than *good*, Marcus. We've struck the mother lode."

As the rest of the expedition emerged from the timberline, those closest to the lead group crowded round to listen to the geologist's explanation.

"Iron can easily be found in areas where there's a steady flow of water, or mineral hot springs," Matthew began. Gesturing to the canyon, he stressed, "*That*, we have in abundance. It must have taken millennia for the river at the bottom of this baby to have achieved what we see here. All those ribbons of color are iron oxides. Hematite, magnetite, and so forth. As the years have gone by, erosion has done the rest, and exposed the seams to open air."

Pointing to the violet and black layers closest to them, he said, "The deposits nearest the surface possess the highest iron content. The further down you go, the poorer the quality. Don't you see? The stuff we want is right there, at the top. The presence of this cleft is a huge blessing." Punching the air, he concluded, "That's why the dust here is so red, and why we have so many gold and brown mineral deposits. This whole region for miles around is so saturated in oxides, we won't even have to drill."

It took a moment for the news to sink in, before everyone gave a loud cheer.

Wilson Smith, who had been listening intently, had to raise his voice to be heard. "Excuse me, but didn't the maps of Tar'eesh show the presence of a huge lake within its boundary?"

Matthew Keegan's face lit up in further delight. "Yes, you're right. It did. The Esteban. It's an inland sea about seventy, seventy-five miles northeast of where we are now. My God, I'd totally forgotten that."

"Why?" Marcus asked. "Is that important?"

"You bet your ass it is," Matthew replied. "If I remember correctly, the Esteban's headwaters issue somewhere up in the Caglioso Mountains. That's the next range south from the Erásan massif. The Esteban also has underwater mineral springs feeding its sediment. With the proliferation I'm seeing here, don't be surprised if we find a raging torrent spilling into the Abyss further along the plateau somewhere. All the perquisites of another rich site."

As an afterthought, he added, "It probably explains why life is so abundant throughout this zone. The propagation of iron oxides must act as anathema to the Horde, and a magnet to everything else. If the spaceport operation goes smoothly, we'll be able to expand our search to other areas of the planet. Just wait until Selwyn King finds out."

And Commander Cameron. Aloud, Marcus said, "Please gather your fellow scientists together, Matthew. If you can, I'd like you to complete a preliminary check of the geological features of the plateau by tonight. Include everything you feel Rhomane will want to know. Be sure to add any recommendations you think are necessary as well. I want to ensure our first report secures us the additional resources we'll need."

Turning to his camp commander, Marcus said, "Tiberius? Have your optio begin the construction of our defenses. Start with the null-shield emitters. I'd prefer them placed within yards of the timberline. Once they're erected, I want three separate trenched walls with staggered entrances encircling the encampment. The final one will be the fort. Each tier is to have a moat covered by a collapsible bridge. Remember to factor in the weights of the vehicles that will be involved. Oh, and get Lucius to liaise with Matthew regarding the location of both the foundry and forge within the camp. I suggest you also put the smithy nearby. That way, we can group similar resources together and make them easier to find.

"Once he has his orders, send your Tesserarius back through the forest to mark a route. Again, remind him of the size of the transporters we'll be using to move the iron. Tell him to choose a path that harmonizes with any natural clearings and so forth. The less felling we have to do the better, as the trees will act as natural cover."

Finally, Marcus turned to the leaders of the mining crew.

It had been decided that the best man to lead the team was petroleum engineer, Leonard Tam. Leonard possessed over thirty years experience in the business, and was also a qualified geologist, making him perfect for the job. His second was the ex-diamond miner, Joshua Osborne.

"Leonard, Joshua?" Marcus began, "Will you men also cooperate with Matthew and his party, and pick the best site to begin operations? If you don't mind my saying, as long as the ore is pure enough to do the job, don't be fussy. Volume and simplicity will be an overriding factor for us to consider. Make your lives as easy as possible. Understood?"

Both men grinned and nodded, before moving off to start work.

Looking around, Marcus discovered the only person left close by was Wilson Smith. Catching the young man's attention, he said, "Need an assignment?"

"If you don't mind, I'd like to divide my platoon into two sections," Wilson offered. "I'll send half out on a roving picket now, while the other half rests. We'll continue to rotate every hour until the outer walls have been erected. Once they're up and running, I'll devise a more suitable rota to ensure we have time to penetrate deeper, and keep a continued presence within the Tar'e-esh itself. Long range patrols are our business. It'll be nice to know what to expect out there if we have to turn to the forest for refuge."

"Make it so," Marcus replied, pleasantly surprised, "and please include the vicinity alongside the highway, too. About half a mile into the trees will do. Look for places that might prove useful as staging areas. Just in case."

Wilson saluted and trotted off to deploy his men.

What a change. Without Houston's influence corrupting him, we might make a mature officer out of him yet.

Left to his own devices for a while, Marcus dismounted and ambled across to a safe distance from the precipice. Contented, he stared out into the vast abyss before him. The crisp wind, crystal clear air, and vibrant scenery soon had him forgetting how harsh the glare here actually was.

Perhaps I'd better put those sunglass things on?

Resisting the urge, he shut his eyes, let the sun warm his face, and allowed his thoughts to drift. A poignant notion made him sigh.

Who knows? Perhaps I'll come to love this place as much as Gaul?

Chapter Twenty-Two

Command Decisions

"This is turning into a real pain in the ass . . . Sir," Stuart Williams of 1st Platoon drawled. "Six days in the saddle. And for what?"

Jake Rixton ignored the pregnant pause before the honorific. Both men were newly promoted, and it would take a while for the reality of that fact to sink in. "It certainly is, Sergeant, and while I'm used to lengthy periods in the saddle, I'd prefer them to have some meaning."

He looked about his men as they rode, and could see they were becoming more and more frustrated with the tedium of mindless patrolling.

All this plotting and scheming isn't good for those of us who are used to straightforward action.

The first shipment of iron ore from the Shilette Abyss was due to arrive in the city in just over a few weeks' time. Saul Cameron had expressed confidence in the fact that the mere presence of so much blood metal should act as a huge deterrent against any aggressive move by the Horde. However, he was a man known to hedge his bets. As such, the Commander had devised a strategy whereby a major operation would be put into effect, to coincide with the last stages of the convoy's journey. Full details of that undertaking weren't public knowledge yet, but everyone knew the mission involved the starport, had multiple objectives, and was time sensitive.

Jake was initially overjoyed to think he would get an opportunity to be in the thick of things during his first command. Then he'd received his assignment.

Their brief was to recon the major routes north of the city, between the Grisson Gap, Issamun Canyon, and Asterlan Lake, for areas that could be used as staging posts in the unlikely event of the caravan having to divert there in an emergency.

Although disappointed, Jake was well used to the chain of command. Taking the rough with the smooth was part of everyday life for a soldier, and he reminded his men that they would be playing their part by doing their job to the best of their ability.

But that was almost a week ago. They'd already completed one huge circuit of the area and marked the best sites for further scrutiny. The bile of knowing this was as exciting as it was going to get had soured everyone's mood.

"Sergeant? Will you task Corporal Spencer to take a squad of men and head out along the Issamun riverbed again? Check out that cave where those spooks tried to surprise us. You know, that day when Lieutenant Fox was still with us. The day he . . ."*Ah, darn it!*

"Yes, Sir."

Rixton grimaced as Williams trotted off to pass along his orders. *Idiot! The last thing I need is to shoot myself in the foot like that. As if we need reminding of what happened the last time we were here.*

He was still champing at the bit when the sergeant came cantering back. Sidling up close to his lieutenant, Williams murmured, "Don't eat yourself up over it, Sir. It wasn't your fault. We all knew who was responsible . . . Talking of which, how did that slimy, no good, two-bit rattlesnake take the news of your promotion? You never said."

Rixton snorted. "Ah, now there's the thing. He didn't give a damn. I couldn't believe it. I'd gotten quite nervous about having to face him and almost didn't bother. But how would it have looked if someone outside of the regiment had sneaked in to hospital to surprise him? So I did it myself, and . . . and . . ."

"*And?*"

"It was a complete anticlimax. I know he was heavily medicated. He is still recovering from a nasty injury after all, but . . ."

"Oh, for goodness sake . . . Sir. *But* what?"

"That's just it, Williams. You're going to think I'd been on the whiskey or something, but I got the damndest impression I was talking to someone else. It looked like Houston. It sounded like Houston. But it didn't act like him. Do you know, he actually congratulated me on my advancement and wished me well?"

"Seriously? The Captain said that?"

"It knocked me for six, I can tell you."

They stared at each other, perplexed by the weirdness of the conundrum. Then Williams raised a valid point. "Hey, Jake. Sorry . . . Sir. Do you realize what this means? With Smith and Houston out of the way, you are effectively *the* ranking officer of the 2nd Cavalry Regiment. Hell, you're easily the most experienced of us all, anyway. I bet if you put your foot down, the commanders would listen to you."

He's got a point. This is a terrible waste of energy and resources. If timing is going to be of the essence, my boys can serve better by acting as flying pickets or an emergency reserve on the day. "Williams? Send a runner after Corporal Spencer and his men. They can't have gotten far. Once they return, have them rendezvous with us here and gather the platoon together. We're marching for Rhomane."

In answer to his sergeant's bemused look, Rixton added, "If the hierarchy went to all that trouble to promote me, they've got to expect me to start making command decisions sometime soon. This is my first one, and I don't intend for it to be my last."

*

"Are you sure you want to do this?" Mac asked, for the third time. "Because if you do, there's no going back."

He skimmed through the details of the latest evaluation report on the man before him one more time. "You've attended twice the number of training sessions of any other civilian here. Managed to qualify in not one but *two* close quarter battle theaters, and have achieved an above average pass for pistols, medium range machine guns, and immediate action drills. What interests me is the fact that your long range marksmanship has been assessed as outstanding. That's impressive by any standards."

Bob Neville had the decency to look embarrassed. "I've been working hard," he mumbled, "and although I'll always be a scientist, first and foremost, I want to be enough of a man to make a difference."

He stepped forward and placed a set of dog tags on the table between them. Mac knew them well. The words *PO988453K*

COLLINS D. – B POS – C of E were etched into the hard resin of both discs.

Well, well, well. Looks like he's grown a pair. "So, you think you're too good to be a soldier, do you?"

"No, not at all," Bob replied defensively, "I'm just aware of my limitations. Both you and I know I'm no warrior. I never will be, but at least now I can make a valid contribution."

Mac studied the man before him. *Yes, I believe you can.* "They say a volunteer is worth ten pressed men. And when that volunteer is properly motivated, he's worth double. You may regret your decision in the future, especially with what we've got coming up. Nevertheless, congratulations. You're in."

"Eh? That's it?"

"Oh yes. Be they military or civilian, I have complete autonomy as to who gets to be on my team. And your ass, dear man, now belongs to me.".

Chapter Twenty-Three

Red Gold Rush

Entering his office, Marcus slapped the dust from his breast-plate and skirts before removing his cloak. Damned stuff gets everywhere. Still, I shouldn't complain. We're fortunate this is the only real problem we face.

The expedition had been on site for just over a week. All fortifications were complete, and the mining operations had begun the previous day. None of the patrols had reported any evidence of Horde activity, and the Ardenese laser cutters were making ore extraction an incredibly swift and easy affair.

It'll be nice to get the first shipment off. Then I can get back, and catch up with what Decimus has been up to. I can't wait to see how the Arc of Death looks now it's finished.

Having shaken out his cape, Marcus hung it up next to his sword belt and strode toward his desk. A handheld computer had been left beside his in-tray pile. A flashing cursor in the top left corner of the screen showed it was active.

Ah, the report Leonard said he'd help me with.

Although Marcus had made an effort to familiarize himself with the newer and more sophisticated tools of his trade, using tablets to write reports was not one of them. Thankfully, he had plenty of willing volunteers to help in that regard.

Retrieving the pad, he sat back in his chair and activated the message.

Let's see if a scientist can write anything near to what I recommended, in plain language.

To: Commander Saul Cameron
From: Praefectus Marcus Galerius Brutus
Initial Report: Shilette Abyss Mining Expedition

Saul,
I hope this opening summary finds you well.

You will be pleased to learn that events are proceeding apace. The fort and surrounding defenses are now complete. Patrols of the nearby forest and adjacent highway are undertaken at all times of the day and night by joint squads of Legion Equitata and U.S. Cavalry. At the time I write this testimony, we have been on site for eight days, and Horde sightings remain at zero.

Now that the shield wall is in place, our operations here will be masked from sight. We have remained undetected so far, and due to the stringent security protocols I have initiated, I am confident this will remain so.

Now to business.

Iron Ore Extraction
The deposits found within the Shilette Abyss canyon show unique characteristics. Iron is usually found at locations where there has been a steady aquatic flow over thousands of years,

or where there is a proliferation of mineral hot springs. Lower grade accretions can precipitate out of purer water sources, where they collect in layers at the bottom of lakes or streams.

However, the features of this entire region display advanced geological block modeling, with a blending of chemical variables. We have established the grade distribution of Fe, and SiO2 as bimodal, due to a consequence of both mineralization and extreme weathering. Distribution of suitable contaminants is low.

Because of this, we have made a remarkable discovery. Huge quantities of naturally occurring bedded ore, arranged in geological sequence, are available to us. The cliff face of the plateau has partially collapsed and opened the sedimentary layers to the elements. As such, we have incorporated an 'open shaft' approach to extract the banded magnetite and hematite found here. These particular examples alone have been assessed at 92% to 94% pure, and will be the first minerals extracted.

We are also blessed with an abundant smattering of both goethite and limonite. Although of a more inferior quality (60% – 65%), this will still provide a valuable and additional source of low grade material if stocks ever become depleted.

Patrols have established the presence of nearby outflows from the inland Esteban Sea. Although shallow, the creeks are saturated with chalk, clay, and peat deposits. From what we have ascertained so far, those locations will be an excellent source of granular 'bog-ore', which we may be able to exploit in future, should the need ever arise.

Personnel
So far, everyone has buckled down to the task at hand, and appears to be working well together.

My chosen centurion, Tiberius Tacitus of the 2nd Cohort, will make a reliable camp commander. His optio—or lieutenant as you would call him—Lucius Scipio, is a career officer with a sound tactical mind. Between them, this expedition is in safe hands.

Any disciplinary or security issues arising will likewise be handled decisively by the appointed tesserarius, Staff Sergeant Tiberius Cenus. Tiberius is a twenty year veteran of the legion and a man who exacts high standards from those he serves with.

I must confess, his job is being made all the easier by the efforts of the young cavalry officer, Second-Lieutenant Wilson Smith. Free of the influence of Captain Houston, he has proven an energetic, willing and exemplary soldier, who has taken the lead in providing long range patrols. Both he and his men are to be commended.

Once their disciplinary tenure is completed, I know Lucius would be happy for them to remain in post, as they have bonded to the rest of the family here remarkably well.

The combined mining operations and geological survey crews are a wonder to behold. Because of their professional standing, each department under Leonard Tam and Joshua Osborne take pride in achieving results. And results are exactly what they've been producing.

The drillers, led by Oliver Prince and Gerry Hunt, have adapted to the Ardenese equipment with amazing proficiency. Because of this, we cleared nearly half a ton of refined ore on our first day. Were it not for our security measures, this would have been a much higher figure, but I am determined to ensure our undertakings here remain undiscovered by the Horde.

(See my addendum—appendix A—at the end of this report regarding absence of enemy activity in the Tar'e-esh area—and proposed response).

Alexander Du'pre, the former terrorist and biochemist, has proven himself an absolute godsend to Matthew Keegan and his experts. It was Alexander's analysis of nearby streams *that established the existence of iron oxides within each of the outlets.*

Likewise, the former leader of their organization, Sebbi Farah, has devised a most ingenious splicing of Ardenese and remaining Earth technologies. Her knowledge of computers has not only improved the security coverage of our surrounding area, but has also boosted the range of our covert transmitters to fifty miles. She is currently working on several backup flyers. It is our hope that she will be able to incorporate a relay system through their software that will provide a live-time audiovisual link back to Rhomane within a week or two.

Transportation

We are on target to fulfill the first shipment fifteen days from now.

Because of this, I will be dispatching Lieutenant Smith and a section of his men back along the main Tar'e-esh to Rhomane freeway in just over a week's time. They will be dropping off a section of riders at three strategic points along the route, to establish covert staging posts. It is envisaged the advance party will liaise with the incoming supplies somewhere in the region south of Arden's main spaceport. Once they meet up, please advise the drivers to follow their guidelines exactly. Suitable concealed paths have been fashioned through the forest, to facilitate speedy ingress and maintain secrecy.

Facilities have been incorporated into our infrastructure to accommodate up to four skidders and six skimmers at a time. Thereafter, I propose we commence regular mechanized shuttle runs once per week, along with a new schedule of radio updates, every evening at sundown.

*

This concludes my first report as acting base commander.

Expectations are high, as is morale. This location is capable of providing a ready source of precious iron ore for the foreseeable future. Extraction and smelting methods are simple and straightforward. I sincerely hope our efforts instill a feeling of hope and renewed enthusiasm among our friends back home. Remember, this is but a first step into uncharted territory. It would appear many more options are opening up to us than was originally anticipated.

I have confidence that your latest endeavors are going well. If successful, they will prove a great boon to future production here and at other sites yet to be discovered.

Upon my return, I look forward to discussing recently gained tactical intelligence with you, in person.

Marcus.

"I like it," Marcus murmured, "and although I haven't got a clue what some of those scientific terms mean, it will provide a succinct, informative, and hopefully encouraging précis for the command staff back home."

He glanced toward his dusty cloak on its peg.

Although I must admit, I think I'll miss the place.

Chapter Twenty-Four

Once More into the Breach

The rolling countryside sped past. Leaning back, Mac lifted his head to the sky and savored the breeze sweeping across his face. Not only did it take the bite out of the midday heat, but it helped him relax before the coming storm.

Sitting down, he rested against the side of the skimmer and closed his eyes. *I don't suppose it will hurt to review things one last time.*

Because of the specifics of their last mission, they had thought it prudent to avoid the use of the subway to gain entry to the launch site. There was obviously more to the Horde than had previously been realized. Thus, it would be fair to assume their enemy would have taken precautions to prevent anyone using that avenue of approach a second time. At Mohammed's suggestion, the entire team encamped into three vehicles—two skidders and one skimmer—and simply utilized the excellent freeway running adjacent to the spaceport's environs. It was a far longer path, but one that circumvented an area of known danger.

Traveling just over twenty miles along the Rhomane to Floranz highway, they continued south until they were well past the facility's western precincts. Taking the first east running link road—one that would eventually branch onto the route to the Forest of Tar'e-esh—they cut back for several miles before diverting north, overland, toward the southern perimeter fence. One skidder, containing Mark, Sean, Andy, and the Boleni Heights crew, peeled away at that stage, intent on their own specific agenda.

The other two groups forged ahead in the remaining vehicles.

Soon, Stuart and Fonzy would lead the skidder team toward the cargo ship objective, while the rest would stay with Mac and Sam in the skimmer, and hopefully secure possession of the smaller vessel.

Mac checked his watch.

By my reckoning, we should arrive at the fence in just under five minutes. Totally unexpected and unobserved. If our intelligence is right, two craft suitable for our needs will be parked half a mile apart, not far from our point of entry along the southern apron. The Promulus, *a diplomatic executive shuttle used by the former First Magister of Rhomane, and an ex-military freighter, the* Tarion Star. *Records indicate they're equipped with some of the most sophisticated tear-space drives the Ardenese ever developed, so they're bound to be top-notch models.*

He ran through a few calculations in his head.

Hmm. By now, Mark should have arrived at the astrometrics lab. He'll be deploying his men and equipment from the skidder. It'll be interesting to see how Jake Rixton's boys handle themselves. Clever idea of the lieutenant's, to offer a section of his officers and their horse, and have them carried to the target site on the transporter. Now we'll have a flying cordon to harass uninvited guests and keep Andy safe while he's manning his sniper's position.

The shimmering outline of their destination grew larger by the second.

Mac turned to study the two pilots opposite him: Angela Brogan and Danny Ricci. Both were absorbed by the detailed schematics of the *Promulus*, displayed on a 3D projection in the air before them. Like the other pilots selected for this mission, they were from a time close to a thousand years into Mac's future. As such, they were well used to handling craft that were completely beyond his understanding.

Additionally, prior to the assignment, Saul had asked the Architect to construct a set of *mind-mesh* flight simulators of both target ships. All four candidates had been training intensively over the past weeks, and now felt confident of being able to nurse their respective charges home, using either manual or thought control software. The fact that they only needed to activate the aqua drives on this occasion had raised everyone's hopes considerably. Earth had, evidently, developed similar technology herself during the late twenty-third century; therefore, the concept was common knowledge to all those involved.

So, all I have to do is get the guys onto the flight deck without being detected, and while they're familiarizing themselves with the layout, the engineering boffins will power up the aqua-cells.

Mac glanced down at the pile of shield emitters stacked by his feet. *I'll have to make sure we get the timing of that phase spot on, just in case these new babies don't work as well as expected.*

"One minute," Nick's voice advised over the radio. The skimmer decelerated. "Prepare for deployment."

Someone's becoming more professional, Mac thought. *Let's hope it continues to spread among the rest of the civilians.*

As the two vehicles glided toward the fence, the smaller skimmer maneuvered in behind the skidder. Several crewmembers on board the larger craft ran forward and sprayed the chain links with solvent. Moments later, the familiar odor of burning metal filled the air, accompanied by a faint hissing sound. The acid ate through the wire in seconds, and Nick used the weight of the skidder to push through the hole.

Once inside, the two hovercrafts paused while the distance to their targets was assessed with passive rangefinders.

"Stu, do you see the *Tarion Star?*" Mac asked. "It's the vessel directly behind the *Promulus,* another seven hundred yards in from the apron."

"Yes, yes," Stu replied. "Give us a few minutes, and we'll be on site and ready to conduct preliminary sweeps."

"Wilco. I'll check with Mark up on the mount so we can synchronize our efforts."

Adjusting his position, Mac triggered the scope's rotating bandwidth. He was able to scan across the entire width of the facility and up onto the crown of the mountain with remarkable clarity. By means of the viewer, it appeared as if a small nest of ants had been stirred into frenzied activity. Tiny figures scurried about, here and there, setting out equipment and preparing for the next stage of their coordinated attack.

"Mark, this is Alpha, come in?"

"I'm here, Boss. You ready to go?"

"We will be shortly. Stu and his squad are on final approach to the *Tarion Star.* We're about to deploy at the *Promulus.* Once the shield walls are operational and the flyers are up at both locations, I'll give you the signal to enter the next phase."

"Understood. For your information, our cloaked sentry drones are already patrolling, and Bob Neville's about to activate the armed squadron. I've tasked two of them to skirt both the underpass and the Seranette for signs of enemy activity. That should give us plenty of warning if anything comes from that direction."

"Good thinking."

"The science team has given the control room and backup generators the once over. They are confident they can initialize the computer core in less than an hour. Once everything is ready, we'll hang fire for your word."

"Roger that." Mac couldn't help but feel he was missing something. "Mark? Remember, we don't have to rush. Seeing as the astrometrics facility has to be held fast, and you're ahead of schedule, ask Lieutenant Rixton if he wouldn't mind lending you a few of his men to scatter the gravity mines. Those boys are surprisingly switched on, and using the horses will leave your skidder free to concentrate on the null-shield. Just explain what you want, and get Andy to oversee the dispersal before he sets up his sniper post."

"Will do, Boss."

"Alpha, over and out." Mac ran the viewfinder across the deserted field once more. Pausing on the distinct profile of the *Seranette*, he wondered, *So where are you this time?*

He eventually turned back to assess the progress of his own small squad.

Sam gave him a thumbs-up. "Area's clear, Sir. Shall I dispatch the pylon team? Get the defensive generators in place prior to activation."

"Do it. And once it's done, escort Angela and Danny inside with the Tec-heads. We might as well enjoy the comfort of a few minutes' grace before the sweating really starts. I'll stay here and wait for the ready signal."

Sam nodded and began issuing directions.

Mac resumed his scrutiny of the wide open expanse.

You're here, somewhere. I know you are.

*

Decimus Martinas shook his head in disbelief. *Why do they persist in being so wasteful of their lives and resources?*

Baffled, he continued to watch as the Horde threw themselves against the wall. In many instances the brutes were able to swarm over one another like insects before the effects of the fermionic matter took hold and ruptured their energy matrixes. Flash after brilliant flash blazed forth, followed by the dull *thud* of yet another implosion.

Turning to his companions, Decimus noted the contrast written across their faces. The Native Americans looked on stoically, as if their senses were blunted to the savagery before them. The Caledonians, however, appeared deeply shocked at the wanton disregard of such peril.

"Why do you think they do it?" Cathal MacNoimhin hissed. "We know them to be intelligent creatures, both cunning and devious. So why the charade? Do they think we'll forget what we've learned about them?"

Other highlanders murmured agreement. None took their eyes from the scene below.

"I've given up trying to fathom these beasts," Decimus replied. "That they are crafty is beyond doubt. I have the standby cohort working in tandem with those new flying machines at other strategic points around the city, just in case this ploy is another of their ruses. So far, my concerns have proven invalid. As always, the demons appear focused upon this one spot. And we are ready for them should they prove successful."

Everyone turned to view the recently completed internal fortifications.

The inner lining of the wall had been painted in a tar, lydium, and iron mixture that had stained a whole section deep brown. Now the concoction had cooled and hardened, it was not only extremely resilient, but would prove fatal to the touch of any ogre that came into contact with it.

In the unlikely event of a Horde member being able to endure such a transition, they would find themselves within the confines of a sealed building complex, the walls, floors, ceilings, and doors of which had been daubed in a similar coating.

If by some miracle they were also lucky enough to survive that, the beasts would then encounter an area christened *the Arc of Death* by those who had constructed it.

The previously cultivated fields had been cleared of all crops and domestic beasts. Now, a semicircular feature extended out from the wall for a distance of a full mile. Inside it, a staggered series of manmade trenches and hillocks were clearly evident. Multiple layers of razor wire had been stretched out at the bottom of every ditch, while iron-tipped stakes had been positioned along each crest. Currently, a succession of collapsible bridges connected every mound to the one behind, enabling defenders to retreat in an orderly fashion as their ammunition depleted.

By far the biggest characteristic of the Arc was the moat. Positioned exactly half way out from the wall, it ran from one end of the construct to the other, dividing the killing field into two. At nearly one hundred yards wide and three yards deep, it bristled with solid steel rods which had been driven over five feet into the ground. So tightly packed were those spears that it was difficult for an armored man to thread his way between them. It should prove an impassible hurdle for the Horde.

At multiple points throughout the trap, white posts had been erected to act as distance markers for the ballista captains to aim at. The catapults formed the final stage of the mundane defenses and beside each one, sacks filled to the brim with a sand and iron-filing mixture stood ready.

Indicating the masterpiece before them, Decimus said, "It is a daunting array, and one *I* would not like the prospect of having to navigate during battle. For the demons to even contemplate such a hurdle, where the slightest touch will mean death, will indicate a resolve we should prepare for now. They do not fear the breach, my friends. If they do ever get through, I doubt that even this great edifice will dampen their ardor, and I must admit. *That* worries me."

The Iceni warriors murmured between themselves for a moment, before coming to a decision. Cathal spoke for them. "We hear what you say, Centurion. Me and the lads will take a little jaunt down to the Arc and mooch about for a wee bit. See if we can find any evidence of mischief. If the devils make the mistake of sticking their noses through while we're there, we'll give 'em a run for their money and make them bleed. And don't worry. We'll save some for you."

Laughing, they crowded forward onto one of the transporter pads, and disappeared from sight.

By the gods, they're a loud and boastful bunch. Decimus grinned. *But I'd have them at my back in a fight any day. At least they put their money where their mouths are . . . Unlike some idiots I could mention.*

He turned his attention to the Sioux braves, who were still studying the killing field.

"And what about you, my friends? Do you think our efforts are in vain?"

Diving Hawk continued to survey the huge construct for a few moments longer. "I do not doubt that the spirit demons will come," he replied impassively. "They have no other purpose in life. What they will do once they achieve their goal? Now *that* remains to be seen. We must be ready."

With that, the entire group walked away without another word.

Decimus studied them as they went. *Strange lot, those Indian warriors. They don't say much, but when they do, they strike the heart of the matter. And fight?* He snorted. *I have a feeling we'll be very glad they're here in the days ahead.*

Several contingents of his men began another patrol of the battlements, leaving Decimus alone for the few minutes it took to complete the sweep. With only his thoughts as company, he tried to imagine what he'd do if confronted with an ogre, face to face.

Patting his newly forged sword, he grimaced. *I'd take as many with me as I could. They'll never kill me without a fight, that's for certain.*

A roar from below caught his attention.

Rushing to the wall, Decimus leaned out and peered down. A bristling mass of conflicting energies had piled itself against the cold might of the barrier.

They've managed to reach up higher than they've ever done before.

He looked closer. *What in Mercury's name are they doing?*

Trying to improve his angle, Decimus held on tightly and edged a little further out onto the lip of the buttress.

Another burst of howling distracted him from the sound of rapid footsteps, approaching from behind. Some form of sixth sense warned him at the last second.

Who is—?

Too late.

Just as he was about to turn, rough hands shoved him hard in the back. Helpless to prevent himself from tipping over the side, Decimus didn't even have time to draw his sword before the ground swarmed up to meet him.

*

"Are you sure it's really necessary?" Ayria Solram complained. "We've been attempting this every day for over three weeks now, and I don't seem to be getting any closer to clearing my thoughts than I was at the beginning."

"And that is precisely your problem," Stained-With-Blood countered. "Your scientific mind is too cluttered. As I've stressed repeatedly, don't try. *Do.* Stop thinking. *React*, and let gut instinct guide you. There is no need to scrutinize every little idea and action. Simply allow the spirit of this world to embrace you, and carry you to where it needs you most. Napioa will be waiting. You'll see."

Strangling her frustration, Ayria forced herself to stop pacing, and took her position on the floor before Stained-With-Blood once again.

"Why do we have to sit like this anyway?" she whined. "It's uncomfortable. How you manage to relax when your muscles are this cramped is beyond me."

At last. Stained-With-Blood smiled. A gleam entered his eye. "Why? How would you like to position yourself?"

"Well. When I had my experience, I was in bed, lying down. I was warm and calm. Restful."

"And?"

Ayria didn't seem to get the gist of his question, so Stained-With-Blood emphasized, "And what *weren't* you doing?"

Her eyes widened in comprehension. "All those things you mentioned, because I was half asleep."

"So why don't you put yourself in a similar situation now?"

Ayria stared at him, mouth agape.

He continued, "For the past two weeks I have been encouraging you to sit before me. A matter of habit, for all Blackfoot spirit-walkers adopt such a position when engaging in dreamquests. To us, it is natural. You, however, are from a time far removed from ours. It's *your* skills we are trying to open, not mine. Yet not once did you think to take that first vital step. What posture do *you* feel will be most conducive for you to achieve a relaxed center?"

The penny dropped. Ayria's jaws snapped shut.

"It is often the first steps that are the most difficult, yes?" Stained-With-Blood murmured softly, chuckling, "and now you have learned an important lesson, you'll find things will proceed much more quickly."

"Oh, you've got to be kidding?"Ayria gasped, dumbfounded. "Why didn't you just tell me?"

"Because that's not the way it works. As I mentioned, you think far too much." Extending his hand, Stained-With-Blood invited, "Now, shall we begin again? Properly this time."

Grimacing, Ayria struggled to her knees, waddled across to the bed, and plopped herself down on the edge. Flopping back, she made herself comfy, and muttered, "Yes. Here we go again."

Chapter Twenty-Five

Royal Flush

Mac completed another patrol of the perimeter. The combined shield generators were working perfectly, masking both the team and their activities from sight. But Mac knew that wouldn't last once the engine startup sequence was initiated. The Horde would react, and fall upon them like a wave.

And they won't give a toss what barriers we've erected. So we'd better be ready for when they arrive.

He ran his thumb along the shimmering potency of the fence. A chilling tingle numbed his hand within moments and spread along his arm. Stepping back, Mac was forced to flex his fingers repeatedly to restore circulation. Once he could feel again, he checked the stability of the portable pylon.

Solid as a rock.

But in this case, appearances were deceiving.

When they had planned the execution of this mission, the command staff had thought things through as thoroughly as possible. Resources, especially the new Tec under development, were a precious commodity that couldn't be wasted. So while it was appreciated the Boleni Heights facility had to be held permanently, they knew that wouldn't be an option out on the airfield itself. Some of the equipment would need to be left behind at the expense of procuring the spacecraft.

Therefore, Brent Wyatt had designed a weaker form of emitter. They were lightweight, less resilient, and possessed a lower energy threshold than the permanent variety. Easier and quicker to manufacture than their bigger brothers, it was hoped they would be perfect for assignments where equipment had to be abandoned, or an orderly retreat made.

Let's hope these babies work as they should. But just in case . . . .

Mac stooped to check the couplings between the shield-rods and the claymore booby-trap he'd positioned a few yards out from the *Promulus.*

Oh yes. A three second delay on a sixty degree arc should work like a charm. Then our friends will discover what old-fashioned, directional fragmentation mines can do. Thousands of steel projectiles traveling at nearly four thousand feet per second will make our feelings perfectly clear.

The skimmer was parked below the aft section of the *Promulus* itself. Sam Pell had set up a mobile command post in the rear, and was overseeing each phase of the operation. It had been just over an hour since their arrival, and although the environs of the spaceport seemed tranquil, Mac knew they couldn't relax. Ambling over to his colleague, he said, "How's it going?"

"All quiet, Boss," Sam replied, waving his hand at the monitors in front of him, "and ahead of schedule."

The top left-hand corner of the display unit revealed multiple perspectives, each one showing a view of the spaceport and surrounding environs.

"What am I seeing here?" Mac asked.

"Those are the flyers. Both offensive and defensive versions. Most of them are patrolling Boleni Mount while the crew finishes the initial preparations. As you can see, the double-layered shield wall has been activated, and the earthwork surrounding the astrometrics facility has just this minute been completed. Courtesy of the ion cannon, I might add. At twenty feet by thirty, the moat is deeper and wider than individual Horde ogres have been known to leap, so they won't be prancing across unexpectedly to say hello. There are only two access points into the compound, both via retractable bridges. All Mark has to do now is lay out the barbed wire along the bottom of the trench, and then seed the mountainside in a mixture of mundane and gravity mines as per the agreed pattern."

"How many drones have they been allocated?"

"Fifty to begin with. Although Bob Neville said that'll double once everything's fired up. When they are, he's suggested we assign a squadron to shadow the iron convoy's route."

Hmm. Sound tactics. "Bob Neville? How's he holding up?"

"Sound as a pound," Sam replied, catching Mac's inference immediately. "A little slow sometimes, but Mark thinks that's because he's trying to be thorough, and basically determined not to screw up again."

Good to hear. Mac had a sudden thought. "Sam, how come they managed to use an ion cannon without attracting the Horde?"

"Simple physics, Boss. Remember, they've got the real deal when it comes to shielding. Ephraim manufactured a set of barriers with the type of capacity we hope to employ permanently in the future. When fully deployed, the curtain totally masks whatever's within the protective matrix. They can see out, operate, transmit and so forth. But nothing gets in without the corresponding code. Mark simply created a self enclosed bubble of seclusion while they finished the work."

"I see. So what's our situation here?"

"The *Tarion Star* pilots, Tara Becket and Hiroshi Taganaka, have signaled they're ready to go. Their team is on standby, ready to infuse the aqua drive generators. And Stu has just dispatched the skidder toward our location to pick up our skimmer."

"Hopefully Angela and Danny have made similar progress?"

"You could say that." Sam stifled a chuckle. "They've been ready for the last fifteen minutes and have instigated an ad hoc electronic poker school to while away their time. Everybody here's in on it. Good for the nerves, so they tell me."

Mac gasped. "Are you serious?"

"Oh yes. I'm doing quite well this hand."

"What?"

"Look at this." Sam tapped one of his screens. "See? I'm playing via the main console instead of my own info-pad. I need one more card for a straight flush. If I win, Angela has to take my place on kitchen assignment for the next three off-duty rotations."

"Sam! We're mid-mission, for pity's sake."

Despite his indignation, Mac found it difficult not to find the image of a highly qualified pilot up to her elbows in vegetable peelings or soapy suds mildly amusing. It was a chore each individual in Rhomane shared on a regular basis.

"Don't worry, Sir," Sam added, "all our defenses are online and ready to rock and roll. Having had a chance to familiarize themselves with the flight deck operating procedures, Tara, Hiroshi, Angela, and Danny all agree, once the drives are initialized, it'll only take four or five minutes for the cores to reach optimum temperature. We're just under two miles out from the main building. The Horde has been assessed as running at, what? About thirty miles per hour? Even if they start sprinting the second we fire up the engines, it would take an alert ogre four minutes to reach us. And the boys have laid out a few extra deterrents to slow them down."

"Such as?"

"We know our friends are wary of the new gravity mines, yes?"

"Yes, go on."

"Well, see the two passenger liners here?" Sam pointed to one monitor in particular. "That's the *Horatius* and the *Cybele.* They're only four hundred yards out from the *Tarion Star,* and because they're so large, we believe they'll form a natural funnel as the pack tries to charge us."

Mac assessed the positioning of the different craft abandoned in that vicinity. "I agree. So what have we got out there?"

"To tell the truth, Boss, not a lot. Stu didn't think it necessary. Following our last mission, the Horde knows what we can do to them. The emphasis is to make them twitch a bit. Think twice, perhaps, about blindly rushing in. So he got Fonzy to drop a claymore out on the tarmac, about twenty yards in front of the choke point. Of course, they'll recover from that almost instantly. But when they do, our screaming friends will run smack bang into the micro-gravity mines. There are only two, but they won't know that, especially as Fonzy's positioned them to collapse the ships in on each other."

"I like your thinking. That should buy us the time we need, eh?"

"Yes!" Sam shouted, clenching his fist in victory.

"Eh?" Mac was startled by his colleague's sudden enthusiasm.

"No more chores for three weeks, yeeeeha!" Sam pumped the air again.

"I take it you got your straight flush then?" Mac grinned as he realized what his colleague's outburst related to.

"Sorry, Sir, but that was an important—hang on a second . . ."

Mac automatically tensed, and turned to scan the vicinity.

"Yes, yes. Roger that," Sam replied, in response to an unknown message.

"Report?" Mac ordered.

"Mark's just updated me, Sir. They're ready to go and the science team is standing by to prime the computer core."

At last. "Right, let's see who we can *flush* out then. Pun intended. Sam, advise our pilots it's time to throw their cards in. All hands on deck, now. Once they've acknowledged you, lock your screens and prepare to embark."

Staring up toward Boleni Mount, Mac continued, "Mark, this is Alpha. Do you copy?"

"Mark here. Go ahead."

"You have about three minutes before things begin to hit the fan. The *Tarion Star* skidder's on the way across to pick up our skimmer and noncombatants now. When they're clear, we'll power up the engines. As soon as you observe any signs of Horde activity, get Andy back inside the compound. Remember, you've got to hold for at least a week until Rhomane sends the permanent contingent to relieve you."

"No problems, Boss. We're dug in, fully prepared, and the last mines are going down as we speak. I can't see us getting callers anywhere near this side of Christmas, so you don't have to worry about us."

"I won't. Alpha, out."

Mac could see the larger hovercraft closing from the direction of the cargo vessel. Nick was at the helm, along with one other civilian crewmate. Mac knew Stuart and Fonzy would already be inside the *Tarion Star* itself, ready to lay down covering firepower should anything go wrong during the preflight protocols.

"Sam. Are you ready?"

"Just coming." Sam's fingers flew across the keyboards. Powering down the terminals, he initiated a transfer of command overrides to Mac's wrist com. "All done."

Mac typed a code into his pad. The shimmering protective barrier surrounding the *Promulus* flared once, and folded into the floor. No sooner had Mac and Sam begun to ascend the gantry than the skimmer pilot maneuvered his craft toward the rear ramp of the skidder.

Mac shouted down, "Nick? You have one minute before I give the order for a world of pain to come calling. Deploy your shield and stay covert until you reach Rhomane's northern doors. Do not stop for anything. See you on the other side."

"Good hunting," Nick replied, flashing a thumbs-up.

Mac grinned. *Yup! More professional every day.*

Nick collected the skimmer and accelerated away. As Mac raised the protective curtain again, he initiated a blanket call. "All units, all units. Be advised. *Promulus* and *Tarion Star* will be initiating engine burn in T-minus sixty seconds from . . . now!

"Armed teams. You are to cover all exits and observe the enemy as they come to us. Activate enhanced optics on a rotating three band frequency, and then await further instructions regarding fire orders.

"Mark. Once you see the Horde begin their rush, leave it for thirty seconds and then get your guys to initialize the command reboot. Spook attention will be diverted, and you should be totally masked behind your screens. As the main display comes back online, you'll be able to watch everything in high definition close-up. Should be quite a show."

Reaching the main entryway, Mac paused to look out across the tarmac toward the *Seranette. And how many other ships contain a surprise like you?*

"Ready?" Mac called over his shoulder.

"Just give us the word," Angela Brogan yelled from the flight deck.

A few of the other crewmen murmured in response. A grim and determined atmosphere congealed in the air about them. People began to fidget.

Mac glanced at his watch. *Thirty seconds.* "Fire Teams, this is Alpha. In a few moments, our enemy will begin their charge. You don't have to do anything at this stage except watch and wait. Remain calm. Most of all, stay alert. While we expect them to rush us from the direction of the terminal and service tunnel, this is the Horde we're dealing with. They're sneaky bastards, so let the shields and booby traps do the work for us. Once a target becomes highlighted within the energy discharge, let them have it. Safetys off. Weapons hot.

"Pilots? It's time. Do your thing."

Everything went quiet and people held their breaths.

When nothing happened immediately, a sense of anticlimax set in.

Then an almost imperceptible vibration trickled through the bulkhead. Mac had to concentrate hard to realize it was there. Moments later, a faint whine intruded at the edge of his hearing. Deepening in resonance, it gained in pitch and the trembling increased. A glittering skein of power crackled into existence, coating the outer hull in a mesh of blue light.

One minute.

"Contact!" Mark's voice cut through the stillness.

"Where and away?" *Jesus, that was fast!*

"We have movement from the terminus and underpass. Several of the hangars along the western perimeter also show signs of grunt activity."

"Roger that. Wait. Out," Mac acknowledged. *"Tarion Star,* this is Alpha. Stu? Did you copy that? We may have incoming from your northwest quadrant, bypassing the chokepoint. They'll hit you first."

"Yes, yes, Boss. I'll have Fonzy lead the fire team in covering that arc. He's got a HK420, so they'll present little in the way of opposition. I'll take care of the rest with the Remington."

"Good to hear. All units, standby while—"

The background tone abruptly rose beyond hearing, cutting Mac off mid-sentence. As it did so, a continual reverberation settled into place. The *Promulus* flexed.

"Angela? Danny? What's happening?"

"Apologies, Lieutenant," Angela replied, "we're priming the takeoff thrusters. Too much juice, too quickly. Sorry, we're kinda learning as we go here."

"No problems. But please be careful. The smell of fear is quite repulsive in close quarters, and I doubt you've had time to familiarize yourselves with the air recirculation system yet."

The vibrations reduced, and a smattering of nervous laughter broke out among the crew.

Mac didn't have time to think about it. "Mark, update please?"

"We've just initiated the main core reboot. Barriers are holding, and the Horde doesn't even know we're here, which is good news for us, but bad for you. Boss, it looks like the gates to the abyss have been opened. Where the hell this lot is coming from, I don't know."

"Flushed them out, have we?"

"Royally flushed is the term I'd use. I've never seen so many, not even at the city walls. You'd better get ready. A tsunami of death is heading your way."

"Understood. Mark? Go radio silent. I don't want to risk the chance of you being discovered until we're prepared to reveal our presence there. See you on the other side."

"Enjoy the duck shoot."

Mac snorted, only to grow serious a moment later. A different, more urgent resonance was impinging on the background thrumming of the ship. The shuddering grew more exigent, more intrusive. A rumble echoed toward them from the horizon.

Mac lifted his rifle and used the scope to get a better view.

He caught his breath. *Okay, then. Let's see who's got the strongest hand this time.*

Chapter Twenty-Six

An Ace up the Sleeve

Saul rushed into the control center, desperate to catch up on the events he'd missed. "Sorry I'm late, Mohammed. Are they away yet?"

Mohammed didn't look round. "We're just about to find out."

A bank of widescreen monitors covered the main wall, each depicting a different scene. Before them, an array of key personnel sat at various consoles, each fulfilling a vital function in the events unfurling out at the main starport.

Tapping his com-set, Mohammed called across to the command operator. "Amelia, bring up the lead tracker drone, will you? Put it on screen three and transfer a feed to my terminal." Turning to face Saul, he added, "We've had this particular flyer stationed above the field at high altitude all morning.

307

It's cloaked and equipped with high resolution read and record optics. This is a live-time feed."

The picture wavered as the appropriate adjustments were made, before zooming in on a scene of shocking clarity. A seething mass of chaotic turbulence, shot through with lurid outbursts of strontium red and sizzling orange vehemence, streamed across the tarmac. Two main waves disgorged from the terminal building and underpass at a frightening rate, supported by a smaller surge issuing from the berthing pens to the northwest.

"Is that ... ?"

"I'm afraid so," Mohammed said bitterly. "I know we should be pleased, as it shows our gambit is working. After all, this will keep the main eastern highway clear for Marcus. But it would appear our friends have brought in reinforcements from somewhere."

"But where? I thought the entire spook host from around the planet was supposed to be here already?"

"I've got my suspicions, but we'll chat about that afterward. You've got enough to deal with at the moment."

"Tell me about it. Yet another distraction I could do without."

Mohammed sidled closer. Lowering his voice, he said, "Did you make any progress?"

"Not really," Saul admitted, letting out an exasperated sigh, "apart from confirming what we already knew. The Caledonians are beside themselves with anger. They had a lot of respect for Decimus, and are furious to think something like this could happen under their noses. Cathal is adamant that he and his warriors all left at the same time. He assures me they stayed together for at least an hour afterward as they checked out the arc of death. The same goes for Diving Hawk and his Sioux braves. Although they returned to their rooms, the time it took them to get to the other side of the city removes them from suspicion. As far as anyone is aware, Decimus was fine, in good health, and in the company of a detachment of his legionnaires when the others departed. So, apart from his own soldiers, no other person was in the vicinity at the time."

"And did *they* see anyone during the course of their patrols?"

"Not a bloody sausage. I'm back to square one."

"Sorry to play devil's advocate," Mohammed whispered, moving even closer, "but have you considered Houston? The two did have a very public falling out, after all."

"That's the thing, Mohammed. Because you were busy in here, the security detachment notified me of the death first. We went straight to Houston's room, thinking we'd catch him with his pants down. Case solved."

"And?"

"You've seen the change in him since his accident. We got there, charged in, and found him naked apart from his socks and slippers. He had his hands against the wall, was staring off into space at goodness knows what, and was mumbling about how good it was to be free of constraint. When I asked him what he was blithering on about, it only seemed to make him more confused and upset. He actually crawled under his bed and hid. I seriously doubt he even knows what day it is."

The two friends stared at each other as they tried to make sense of the latest conundrum to plague the city they had pledged to defend.

"Sirs?" Amelia called, breaking the silence. "I think you'll both want to see this."

Turning back to the main monitor, they couldn't help but gasp.

*

If not for the arcs of ruby-colored lightning stabbing their way through the seething mass of the mirage, Mac could have been forgiven for thinking he was looking at a huge distortion caused by the interaction of cool mountain air sweeping over heated tarmac. But he knew better, especially as the ululating cries betrayed exactly what the advancing apparition really was.

Mac kept the crosshairs of his telescopic sights fixed firmly on the area between the *Horatius* and *Cybele*.

Any second now . . .

The claymore triggered, and thousands of pieces of shrapnel found their targets. A rippling series of shockwaves tore a widening swathe through the front ranks of the Horde's charge. The devastation expanded as the trailing spooks simply ploughed into those in front who were desperately trying to scramble out of the way. The carnage intensified, creating a chain reaction of self immolation which defined the features of those creatures along the leading edge in horrific clarity.

Why are they so keen to risk themselves against the iron? They're obviously terrified. Surely they can't be that *hungry?*

At last, the combined echo of explosions and screams of outrage reached his ears, creating a grating contrast to the deepening hum of the *Promulus*'s engines.

And now . . . ?

He watched, transfixed, as the swarm continued to pulse forward. The scene within his scope appeared to warp, as if reality had somehow thickened. An area of darkness folded into existence, swelling into a swirling gray void shot through with coruscating bands of silver-blue energy. The grunts closest to the anomaly were yanked into the air and sucked backward into the maelstrom. Seeing their comrades snatched away so easily, the rest of the pack attempted to scatter. The gravity-well condensed, bending the air into a corkscrew vortex that dragged the slowest victims, clawing and screaming, into oblivion. A flare of white light and accompanying thunderclap announced the moment the device winked out of existence.

Mac blinked in surprise as the forward end of the *Horatius* crumpled and sagged.

That was a micro-mine? Damn, but someone's been working hard.

The charge had stalled, and the panicked ogres presented an even easier target to the second booby-trap. Detonating moments later, it consumed more than fifty of the Horde before they could react. Within seconds, the wreckage of the *Cybele* joined the *Horatius* on the tarmac.

Mac felt the vibrations running through the superstructure of the *Promulus* cease. Distracted, he glanced toward the flight deck. "What's happening? Is everything okay?"

"Yes, yes," Danny shot back. "We are now flight ready. We're just holding off so as to give the *Tarion Star* time to clear the runway."

"Why? Aren't they prepared for takeoff as well?"

"Almost. Hiroshi said they're having a little problem establishing the antigravity field. Something about a glitch between the software that micromeshes the aqua, and tear-space drives. The *Tarion Star* is fitted with the very latest generation of engines, so it's taking a little longer than anticipated for the union to initialize. They should be away within two to three minutes."

Two more minutes?

Mac had an idea. Looking back at their hapless enemy, he could see the main body was still milling around in confusion. The smaller band that had issued from the flight pens, however, had just reached the shield wall surrounding the cargo carrier. Each impact created a burst of neon blue brilliance that left a negative image across his vision.

"Angela, Danny," he called, "change of plan. Lift off now and take up a position twenty yards south of the *Tarion Star*. Keep us at the hover. We'll provide additional cover from the air until they're ready to go."

"Roger, will do."

In eerie silence, the *Promulus* peeled away from the ground. Mac felt no sensation of movement whatsoever, not even when the landing struts folded back into place. On a whim, he reached out toward the enclosing energy mesh.

A voice said, "It won't work."

Mac turned to find one of the Tec-heads, Jayden Cole, standing right behind him. He'd seen her at a distance on a number of occasions, but never this close. He thought her fiery hair and piercing green eyes were quite breathtaking. "Hmm?" he mumbled.

Jayden nodded toward the web enclosing the ship. "Trying to push your hand out. We're cocooned in an inertial dampening field. It allows us to cut through a number of mediums without feeling the effects of resistance, so obviously, an inbuilt safety feature ensures nothing can pierce the bubble."

Mac snatched his hand away. "So how am I going to fire out of the port?"

"That's why I'm here." Jayden flashed a winning smile. "Angela sent me down to cut the buffer around the hatchway. As long as we stay on maneuvering thrusters, certain portions of the net can be lowered. The Ardenese used to do it all the time, to exchange passengers and cargo in flight. We can't have you missing out on your fun now, can we?"

"Lucky me." Warming instantly to the confidence exuding from the woman next to him, Mac added, "But you might want to stand back. It'll get a bit noisy."

"Oh, I wouldn't miss it for the world." Jayden whipped out an AK-48-GMR assault rifle from behind her back, and prepared to fire. She appeared very familiar with her drills.

Hellooo?

Noticing Mac's appraising look, Jayden coolly raised an eyebrow and tapped him on the forehead. Pointing past his shoulder, she drawled, "Shouldn't you be concentrating on what's out there?"

Feeling suitably chastised, Mac turned to survey the scene. His focus immediately reverted to what was outside.

The *Promulus* had already reached the *Tarion Star*. Angela and Danny had maneuvered the liner so they were now hovering only seventy feet off the ground, directly above the teeming press of monsters impinging against the temporary shields. Although much smaller than the primary mob, Mac was nevertheless unable to count how many Horde were testing the barriers. Flash after flash blasted out as the brutes expended themselves in a hopeless gesture.

Yeah, but for how long? "Tara, Hiroshi, this is Alpha," he snapped. "Get the problem sorted. We don't know the full capability of the portable emitters yet, and now is not a good time to find out."

"We're going as fast as we can, Mac," Hiroshi called back. "We can't push it in case we cause an ignition stall."

"How long?"

"At least several minutes. Sorry, the schematics were slightly different to those we'd been given, and we choked the injectors on our initial attempt."

Jesus Christ! "Stu? Fonzy? Are you listening?"

"Yes, yes, Boss," Stu replied. "Don't worry about us. I've got two fire-teams in each starboard side hatchway. As soon as the curtain drops, the claymore will take out our nearest visitors, and we'll drill the rest. It'll be a high pucker-factor moment, but we should be okay."

"Copy that. Follow the plan. We'll thin their ranks from the air while the main body is still trying to get their shit together. Alpha, out."

Mac stopped to ensure he was secured to the hatchway with a safety line. Jayden did the same. The ship pivoted around to gain a better firing solution.

Right, here we go. "Sam? Are you ready at the rear doors?"

"Affirmative. Scott and I are clipped on and awaiting your orders."

"Okay, link your HUD to mine. This is your arc . . . ." Mac highlighted the field of fire to his colleague. "Jayden and I will take the rest."

"Wilco."

"*Promulus* fire-team. Stand-by, stand-by. You have your targets. Don't waste ammo. I want short, sharp bursts. Be clean and efficient, and wait for each chain reaction to subside before you shoot again. We'll start on those grunts about five yards out from the barrier. On my mark . . ." He brought his weapon to the shoulder. "Fire!"

A devastating first volley hammered down. Lurid bursts of flame-red and tangerine-orange intensity engulfed the roiling mass below them. As the concussions caught and spread among the crush, a narrow avenue appeared through the Horde ranks. A brief lull ensued as the crew paused to view the results of their opening gambit. Then the sound of gunfire resumed, becoming more sporadic as each individual took their time in selecting their next victim.

Empty casings tinkled to the floor. The glass ones smashed, but others chimed and bounced out of the doorway. Mac stared in wonder as the brutes directly below him imploded in agony.

Of course! Some of these empty shells are the old steel ones. They're a weapon in themselves, especially when they fall on our friends from above.

The *Tarion Star*'s engines steadily ramped up in power, sending a pressure wave radiating into the throng. A sense of urgency seemed to grip the ogres closest to the ship. Concentrating on two areas along the curtain, the Horde drove forward, again and again. The barrier at those locations flushed dull vermilion.

Mac accepted the inevitable. *It's going to give.* "Hiroshi, how long?"

"We still need a few minutes."

The shields bruised even darker, and a spattering of amber sparks flared along the length of the wall.

Too long. "Stu, Fonzy, prepare your teams. Any second now."

"Mac," Jayden said, "what's that over there?"

Mac didn't hear her as he yelled, "All gun teams revert to full automatic fire. Empty everything you've got into them. Keep the *Tarion Star* free of infestation."

"Mac!" Jayden yelled, over the deafening burst of gunfire. Slapping him hard on the back, she pointed. "I said there's something over there. What is it?"

Scanning the no-man's-land between their own vessels and those lying wrecked behind the larger congregation of monsters, Mac couldn't see what Jayden was getting at. The leading members of the greater host were jostling one another and preparing to charge. Individual essences became more and more defined as emotions ran high. Then a huge roar blasted out and the forward ranks broke free. Resuming their mad dash, they quickly covered the remaining distance.

"No!" Jayden screamed. Grabbing Mac's head between her hands, she twisted his neck. "Not there. *There!*"

A strange distortion halfway between the two groups caught his eye. Looking like a gray glass helix, it hung silently in the air, slowly rotating in on itself. A *twang* of déjà vu just had time to pluck at the back of his mind before a familiar flash of light peeled the vortex open. Two huge entities sheathed in crimson and sapphire radiance stepped out of the portal. The scarlet and golden flames dancing around their heads were sharply defined and radiated overwhelming amounts of energy.

As soon as their feet touched the ground, the Horde Masters separated. The smaller one made its way toward the approaching storm; the other Boss turned and flowed across the ground at surprising speed toward the *Promulus* and *Tarion Star.*

What now?

Mac jumped as a sizzling discharge vaporized the shield emitters. Tearing his gaze back to the scene before him, he watched the tail end of the explosion decimate the beasts closest to the barrier. Before the ogres had time to recover, the claymore detonated, punching a hole clean through their ranks.

An earsplitting volley of death rang out from the ships, only to be answered by an even more deafening reply from the surviving Horde members.

Mac's eyes danced back and forth as he tried to calculate the speed of the approaching mob. *There are too many of them. Even if this smaller crowd delays the* Tarion Star *by seconds, the deluge will be—*

A thunderous declaration interrupted his line of thought.

Stunned, Mac watched as the entire host responded to the command, and ground to an unwilling halt. Wails of protest broke out. Some individuals within the packs couldn't control themselves and stomped forward once more.

The Masters reacted instantly. Clapping their hands together, each created a concentrated nucleus of power. Molding these to suit their purpose, they clenched their fists and made a clawing motion in the air. Those fiends that had acted defiantly were shredded on the spot, their essences subsumed by their executioners.

All firing stopped.

An eerie hush ensued.

Guttural barks sounded throughout the Horde ranks. Slowly but surely the two groups merged together to surround the *Tarion Star.*

This is not good. "Hiroshi? What in God's name are you doing? Taking a nap?"

"We're just about to reboot the antigrav unit. Any second now."

We don't have a second.

The larger of the two Bosses walked toward the remains of the shield wall. Mac felt an overwhelming sense of familiarity. *Is this the same one?*

A report pealed forth, loud in the silence.

Almost instantly, an area not two feet in front of the Master sparked brightly as the bullet rebounded off an invisible barrier. The ogre reacted instinctively. Flowing to one side, it dropped its posture, raised its hands, and prepared to slap its talons together again.

Another flurry of shots rang out. A swarm of angry flecks danced in the ether as further ricochets skittered through the air.

Amazingly, the Controller interrupted its gesture at the last second, and just stood there waiting, a ball of condensed fury glowing between its palms.

As abruptly as it started, the fusillade ended.

Then, with infinite care, the Horde Master did something extraordinary. It extended its arms to both sides and allowed the potency of its counterstrike to drain away.

"Hold your fire!" Mac bellowed.

He watched, astonished, as the beast made a gesture. The obedient mob reacted immediately. As one, they raised their claws in what looked like a cautionary gesture and cried out. Their voices melded together with a plaintive quality that made the humans lower their guns and look about in confusion.

Mac glanced at his comrades. "Are you recording this, guys?"

"Er, that's a yes, Boss," Stu replied. "What the hell is going on?"

"Damned if I . . . hang on, something's happening."

Holding its hands out in a non-threatening manner, the lead Controller gradually manifested its entire essence and made itself clearly visible to the naked eye. Soon, twelve feet of barely restrained power flexed and glimmered in the sunlight before them.

Its bulk was overwhelming, matched only by the might radiating through every fiber of its being. Ruby-red eyes glowered out from massive overhanging brows. The surface texture of its substance appeared almost fluidic, as if its nature were in a constant state of flux between scintillating light and deep shadow.

Huge fangs scythed down from a cruel face, and massive paws stretched and clenched repeatedly, as if it were fighting to exert control over its burning ferocity.

Now the crown was fully revealed; a nimbus of silver light in evidence around each of the flames dancing around the ogre's head. The argent radiance overflowed the coronet and cascaded down through the remainder of the Master's aura, infusing the rest of its matrix with majestic overtones that conveyed a sense of regal authority.

This one wants us to know it's in charge.

The entity walked slowly forward until it could almost reach out and touch the side of the ship. Mesmerized, everyone stared.

"Mac, Mac!" Hiroshi's voice was frantic. "We're just about to take off. Cover us."

"Will do," he replied. "Take it nice and easy. Everyone stay calm."

The engine pitch faded to nothing as the hyper drives meshed at last.

The Controller seemed to sense the change. Throwing back its head, it added its own voice to the chorus, creating a deeper counterpoint among the resonant backdrop. Then it stepped up and placed its hand gently onto the sill of the *Tarion Star*'s forward hatch.

The energies skittering through the cargo vessel began to ground out. The Boss shook its head from side to side in warning.

Stu leveled his machine gun straight at the monster's face.

The two faced off. Seconds ticked by with agonizing slowness.

Then the Master moved away and raised its hands in submission. Spinning on its heel, it dismissed the threat behind it and turned to look up, directly at Mac. Hauntingly, it repeated its admonition, emphasizing its meaning by waving its arms and crisscrossing them over and over again.

Without knowing how or why, Mac found himself on the verge of understanding the beast's meaning.

It doesn't want us to take the ships.

Then the *Tarion Star* was airborne and floating gracefully away from danger. Mac let out a huge sigh of relief. The Horde Master somehow sensed Mac's indulgence. Pointing at him, it exaggerated its movements as if trying to stress some hidden peril.

What the hell is it trying to say?

The ogre's eyes gleamed brightly.

Without warning, the world spun, and Mac was struck by a feeling of intense nausea. Slumping to the ground, he gulped down air in an effort to prevent bile rising in his throat.

Jayden knelt beside him. "Mac? Are you okay? What's the matter? Are you all right?"

He struggled to reply, blinking furiously to quench the blaze of fireflies now intruding on his vision. Before he could form a sentence, a deluge of thoughts and emotions cascaded through his awareness.

Battling to regain his equilibrium, he felt a distinct impression manifesting within his psyche, along with a specific term.

Pandora.

Chapter Twenty-Seven

Star Metal

They stood within a dry riverbed running along the center of a huge canyon. On either side, miles in the distance, towering cliffs punctured the cloud-swathed firmament and disappeared into mystery. A cool breeze freshened the air. Despite the gloom, a gentle phosphorescence filtered down through the veil, illuminating the landscape in silver and shadows.

"We did it," Ayria gasped, staring about in wonder. "At last."

"No, *you* did it." Stained-With-Blood's tone conveyed a sense of deep satisfaction. "Despite the years of indolence, your gift resisted atrophy. It would appear our blood retained its potency, despite the advancement of society through the centuries."

"But what do we . . . *I* do now? It's taken me three weeks just to get this far."

They walked slowly around each other, taking in the majesty of the vista surrounding them. Stained-With-Blood shrugged and stooped to sit, cross-legged, on the floor. "Now we wait. Napioa will reveal himself in due course."

Ayria completed another circuit before deciding it would be useless to protest.

You can never seem to rush these things. Sighing, she took her place before her mentor, who had already relaxed and closed his eyes to meditate. She was about to try the same thing herself when she remembered a point made during their previous conversation.

No. I've got to do this my own way.

Ayria gazed about her once more. *So, how would I relax if I was actually here?*

The zephyr stiffened and the haze above them rolled back, revealing an argent disc of serenity and splendor. By its light, physical features of the watercourse, previously hidden, became defined in crystal clarity.

Her face creased with delight. *Of course. I'd explore.*

Jumping to her feet, she scampered across the sand and up the shallow embankment. A wind-worn pile of rocks sat close to the lip. Climbing on top of them, Ayria cupped her hands over her brow, pivoted in a circle, and stared off into the distance.

Unbroken plains stretched away all around her, accentuating the isolation of her position. Apart from Stained-With-Blood and herself, nothing else appeared to live within the vast expanse. No trees, shrubs, or cacti, and certainly no other form of animal life. Apart from the gentle lament of the stiffening breeze, not even the background hum of insects disturbed the night.

So where the hell are we? And what is this supposed to—

An aged warrior stood atop an adjacent cairn on the other side of the arroyo. His finely muscled arms were folded across a barrel chest, and Ayria could see he was studying her closely.

Napioa! She couldn't help but wave as she clambered back down the outcrop, a gesture that only earned her a raised eyebrow in response.

Despite his age, the Father Creator stood tall and proud. The luxuriant flow of his waist-length raven hair enveloped him in such a way that it appeared to form a cape about his torso. He came to meet her and as he skipped lightly across the stones, the swirl of his mane added an air of power and majesty to his gait.

Stained-With-Blood had sensed the Old Man's arrival too, and stood to meet him.

The three beings came silently together and waited.

Ayria was bursting with questions, but a warning glare from Stained-With-Blood helped curb the excitement building within her.

Napioa appeared to find her exuberance amusing. He grunted once, then turned and squatted on the ground, facing north. The wind intensified, but for some reason neglected to disturb the grit and dust saturating every nook and cranny of their environs.

More waiting? Ayria glanced at her tutor for guidance. When Stained-With-Blood took a position next to Napioa in the sand, she quickly followed suit.

Ignoring them completely, the Creator lifted his head high and allowed his hair to unfurl behind him. He stared intently at the moon, his eyes becoming orbs of milk-white obscurity. Napioa appeared to be studying every facet of the lunar surface, and was obviously ruminating over something as he did so. More time passed. He started to rock back and forth. His mumbling grew into a soft chant, its cadence carried into the farthest reaches of the gorge on the wings of a multitude of eddies.

Just when Ayria thought she might go mad with impatience, the singing stopped. Napioa lifted an arm and waved his hand in a wide arc through the air. The moon wheeled away through the heavens, leaving the vault of the night sky in total darkness.

Ayria stared in alarm. It was pitch black; she could see nothing but the glow of the Creator's eyes. A crystal tone chimed in the gloom above her. A star blinked into existence. Another note rang out, only to be answered by a different point of light. In moments, the sky became filled by music and a glittering array of diamonds.

The spell was as piercing as it was captivating. It wasn't until Ayria felt a pain in her chest that she realized she was holding her breath. "That's so beautiful," she gasped.

Napioa snorted softly at her outburst. Other than that, he paid her no heed. Instead, he raised both fists above his head and squeezed his fingers tightly together. Greater illumination was restored by two dominant stars; one yellow, the other red.

Satisfied with his preparations, the ancient warrior gestured toward the smaller, yellow sun on his left. Its nimbus flared, and within moments a coronal ejection was speeding their way. The discharge intensified, morphing into a citrine-colored fireball of impressive stripe. It entered the atmosphere. Roaring like an augur of doom, it spat sizzling reminders of its potency. Flickering shadows careened wildly about the gulf as it rushed toward them. Ayria could feel the approaching pressure wave, and glanced at Stained-With-Blood for reassurance.

She needn't have worried.

Napioa opened his left hand. A thrill of summoning rippled outward. Unable to resist, the meteoroid altered course and screamed into his grasp. It struck with the force of a hurricane and a mesh of thrumming power bloomed about them, encompassing the projectile and crushing it into a concentrated ball of coruscating urgency.

Neither Ayria nor Stained-With-Blood suffered from the encounter. In fact, they both leaned in to get a better view as Napioa brought his hands together. The muscles of the Creator's arms and shoulders bunched and rippled as he compressed the fiery mass into a more malleable form. The remains cooled swiftly in his grasp, continuing to shrink until he was kneading a gray-black colored lump of metal. Napioa beat the block with his fists, lengthening it into a long knife, complete with handle. Lifting the weapon before him, he pinched along the edge of the blade, fashioning it until it was razor sharp.

Iron? A kick of excitement shot through Ayria. *That looks like the real deal. In its unadulterated form, it's extremely rare because of oxidization.* She glanced back up at the shimmering firmament above them. *Unless it falls to earth as a meteorite.*

She noted the faraway look in Stained-With-Blood's eyes, as if he too had recognized something about the process that was giving him pause.

Of course! He's had this type of vision before. Didn't he say his last quest contained a dream image just like this, where Napioa formed a dagger out of blood metal and then . . . Oh my God!

"I see you're both beginning to understand," Napioa crooned, as he considered them at last. "That is just as well. Now, attend."

The Creator made a flourish in the air, and a muslin sack appeared from within a splinter of time. Taking the knife, he slashed a hole in the side of the bag. A multitude of seeds spilled out onto the parched ground. Sorting through them, he picked out two that seemed to satisfy him. Holding them carefully, he blew gently, and the kernels went spinning off to land on opposite sides of the riverbed.

The world reeled, and both suns moved closer, taking up new positions above the adjacent rocky outcrops. No sooner had the orbs settled into their respective places than Napioa took the blade and made repeated chopping motions, left and right. The distant cliffs split asunder, and a tumult of waters cascaded from the fresh clefts.

The Old Man took a deep breath. As he inhaled, the ground where they stood trembled, and then heaved upward. Within the space of a few heartbeats, they found themselves sitting upon a hillock in the middle of the gully.

The exhalation of a growing sigh drew near. A trickling advance wormed its way along the creek, like the diseased feelers of a disfigured jellyfish. The trickle turned into a rush and the rush swelled into a torrent. Soon, they were surrounded by the powerful current of a stately river.

Napioa jutted his chin toward both sides. "Observe," he cried.

Ayria was surprised by what she saw on each embankment. To her left, the yellow sun shone down on a fully-grown aspen. The tree swayed gently under the influence of an unknown breeze, its blue-green leaves glistening in the spray of the surging waters. To her right, a majestic pine stood tall in the light of a crimson star. Cone-filled, its bristly profile hinted at resilience and antiquity.

It wasn't until Ayria looked closer that she realized each specimen had cracked the earth beneath its boughs. Extensive root networks extended down into the watercourse, where the best of the life-sustaining nutrients could be found.

But what does it mean?

As if hearing her thoughts, Napioa turned, gazed deeply into her eyes, and lifted the dagger before him once more. A residual nugget of the asteroid, left over from the making, still lay between his knees.

Stabbing down, he shattered the rock. Taking the fragments, he scattered copious amounts of pure iron ore over both shorelines. An amazing transformation manifested.

While the aspen bloomed under its altered circumstance, putting forth an abundance of buds and fresh growth, the pine fared badly. A shower of cones and needles fell to the floor, carpeting the rocks in foul-smelling mucus, and leaving its spindly branches bare. Great chunks of bark split away from the trunk. In moments, a single, withered seed dropped to the ground, where it lay dying.

Napioa intervened. Scooping up the produce of both specimens in one hand, he took his blade and punctured the air right in front of him. A void was rent in the very fabric of spacetime, through which strands of arcane energy flowed. The helix had a distinctive matrix, the mere sight of it tugging at a memory in Ayria's mind.

Still intent on his work, the Creator cupped his palm within the matter stream and allowed the eldritch essence of the cosmos to transmute the kernels.

Napioa clenched his fist and drove hard into the soil, burying his new creation deep in the earth. Rainbow whorls of power thrummed through the hummock and radiated into the atmosphere. The yellow star receded, and as it did so, thick, luxuriant grass sprouted beneath their feet, covering the mound in a vibrant carpet of life. The red sun began to dominate, shaking the valley from end to end as its gravitational mastery took hold. Loose rocks, dislodged from their perches along the banks, shuddered into the fast-flowing current. A different rumbling sound gradually intruded.

In the exact place where the Old Man had punched his hand into the loam, a remarkable sapling thrust its way out of the ground.

Haloed in a silver nimbus, the young sprout stretched its way into the heavens, forcing everyone to stand back. Its monumental growth spurt continued unabated. Less than a minute passed before a mighty root system delved its way into the riverbed on both sides of the islet, and the extensive canopy of a fully mature birch tree spread its majesty over them.

Ayria was awestruck. She had never seen such a magnificent paradigm in all her life. Her gaze roved across the grandeur of its foliage, drank in the vitality of the thickness of its trunk. It appeared to her as if steel hawsers had been fashioned into the bough of a living entity, which would never wither and die. The entire edifice radiated strength and might on a scale that dwarfed her.

She glanced across at her companions, and could see Stained-With-Blood was similarly impressed. Napioa, however, stood proudly with his hands on his hips. He studied his new creation and nodded in satisfaction.

Turning to face them, he said, "Think deeply on what you have seen. Every facet of your quest carries import, vital to the success of what is to come. You have it within you to succeed." He gestured toward the tree behind him. "Take a leap of faith into the unknown. *Become* the birch."

Without warning, Napioa disappeared. Ayria just had time to take one last look at the fey leviathan before them before it too receded from sight.

No! Not now. Let me—

It was too late.

Then Ayria was flowing backward along a tunnel of light. Her senses diminished, and thickened in some way, as if her mind were wading through treacle. She began to solidify, became more corporeal with every passing moment. She finally felt her heart beating within her chest again. Opening her eyes, she tried to get her bearings.

What? Oh, I'm on the bed. Is . . . ?

Sure enough, Stained-With-Blood was there, wide awake but still in his cross-legged position on the floor. She perceived he was troubled, and was clearly battling to come to terms with something that displeased him.

"What's the matter?" Ayria asked, concerned that he might not have found the whole experience as exhilarating as she had. "Wasn't that the most awesome thing ever? Napioa actually spoke with us."

Stained-With-Blood didn't immediately reply. Engrossed as he was, the turmoil within him became more and more evident. Ayria noticed he kept glancing down to one side of his body. Eventually, he heaved a huge sigh of resignation.

"It would appear I have erred," he said, "become complacent in my abilities. By teaching you, I failed to remember that I too am a mere infant in the Creator's eyes, requiring further instruction and reminders as the years go by. That was the second time the Old Man has revealed the path forward to me, by using a blade fashioned from star metal. I failed to note the relevance of it on the first occasion."

"Star metal? Do you mean blood metal? Iron?"

"Yes. And Napioa wielded it to create something that confuses me."

"In what way?"

"That the peoples of Earth and Arden are to unite is obvious. It has been all along. And yet, now I see a facet of the coming transformation that disturbs me deeply. One that I fear will prove difficult for the majority to even contemplate."

"Disturbs you?" Ayria echoed. "How? He's the Creator. Doesn't he have our best interests in mind?"

"Oh, I have no doubt about that." He shrugged. "But I see now why he stressed we need to take a leap of faith."

"What do you mean?"

Stained-With-Blood stared long and hard at her. "That I was directed to search you out across space and time is clear. Having done so, I must now prepare you to bridge a gap that may prove . . . difficult."

Ayria frowned. "In what way?"

"Would you agree that Napioa used the star metal to create a great work?"

"Yes, I would. There's no doubt about it. I've never seen anything so . . . so wonderful in all my life."

"And yet, in what way did he manage to fashion such a marvel?"

"Do you mean by the blending of the two trees? The aspen was obviously representative of the people of Earth. The pine, Arden. Their race has withered and almost died, after all."

"But how, *exactly*, did he unite the two races? Think."

Ayria pondered on what she had witnessed. Then intuition kicked in. "He cut a void in the air using the knife. And he manipulated the energies that cascaded out of it to transform the seeds of the already existing trees."

"Precisely." Leaning forward, Stained-With-Blood lowered his voice. "And tell me, Wind of the Sun, where else have you seen such a doorway recently? One that emits a terrible and unfathomable power?"

A chill ran through Ayria's core as she made the connection. Her jaw worked, but no sound came out.

"Do you understand my reticence now?" Stained-With-Blood continued. "And why it will be necessary to thoroughly prepare ourselves for the next stage of our journey? Faith is not possessed by everyone. Yet faith is exactly what it will take to enact the salvation of both . . . or should I say *all*, our races."

"You can't be serious?"

"Napioa is. Therefore, so must we be. Or should I more accurately say, so should *you* be. After all, you were brought here for this very purpose."

"But how could I . . . How could they . . . the Horde, possibly be connected to the future of Arden?"

"That, we need to ponder deeply upon. For without a doubt, only the use of star metal will guarantee success."

Ayria whistled in relief. "Well there you go," she muttered, "at least we have some breathing space. Although astronomy and physics weren't my exact fields of science, even I'm aware that pure iron is extremely hard to come by. Believe me; I know exactly how Saul and Mohammed will react when I present them with *this* little bombshell. But at least I can soften the blow by stressing we'll have time to look into different options while we search for any impact sites of relevance."

Stained-With-Blood shook his head. "Ah, that's just it. We *don't* have time. Remember? The vision showed an approaching flood, one that will sweep away all life under the red sun. Unless we act swiftly, urgently, all will be lost. And really, we haven't any excuse to delay."

"Why? Do *you* know where we're going to find a weapon forged in the heat of a meteor strike? They're very rare."

"They certainly are, child. But I know *exactly* where such a device can be obtained."

In one fluid motion, Stained-With-Blood came to his feet. Reaching behind his back, he displayed the tomahawk he always carried. Gazing past the decorative ribbons and feathers adorning the axe, Ayria concentrated on the smoothness of its dull, gray-black surface. Her eyes widened in recognition.

"This is Heaven's-Claw," Stained-With-Blood announced. "I made her from the remains of a star fall when I had only recently come to manhood. With it, I made the many kills that earned me my clan name."

Bowing formally, he held the tomahawk out to her. "I doubt she will be used as such again. Please accept this boon, and learn how she may be used to forge the salvation Napioa has foreseen."

Numbly, Ayria held out her hands to receive the weapon. As her fingers curled around the smooth, cool metal, she could only think of one thing.

Nana! What the hell do I do now?

Chapter Twenty-Eight

Eggs in a Basket

Angule of the Unium Tier peeled back the superficies between mediums and stomped his way, flaring and spitting, onto the dais within the Hall of Eclectic Spheres.

The abruptness of his arrival jarred the senses of the entities lining both sides of the causeway. Waiting for the release of absolution, they had no choice but to endure the bitterness and frustration radiating from him in waves as he bristled past. The intensity of those emotions struck them like a physical blow, provoking a backlash of the basest, most primal energies imaginable.

Despite his agitation, Angule had no wish to see his lesser Kresh expend themselves in wasted expression. *Patience, your time will come*, he crooned. As gently as possible, he released the wash of a soothing balm across their umbilical membranes.

Pacified, the massed host of the third level withdrew into a vast ocean of barely restrained brooding malice before resuming their slumber.

Angule paused to survey the heaving mass surrounding him. *Too many remain in idyllic ignorance, unaware of the travesty that has befallen us. We must act soon, or be forever lost.*

Behind him, the vext shimmered again, and Raum of the Duarium Tier materialized upon the podium. Angule flashed a warning as she manifested. Forewarned, the younger entity managed to rein in her feelings before they could agitate the simmering nursery to violence.

He watched her approach. Raised from innocence only three cycles ago, Raum's aura betrayed the signs of one newly assigned to her position. The nimbus of her essence had a tendency to stray into the lighter spectrum whenever she became overly excited. The fledgling flames of her coronet still stuttered on the occasions she was forced to pierce the root of the quantum-matrix. But that would pass. She had already acquitted herself well under very trying circumstances. Angule had witnessed her acting without hesitation to preserve the interests of her race, although it had cost some of the infants their lives.

Yes. She'll mature into a Kresh of the first order. I wish we had more like her.

He waited for her to approach.

Her senses skittered across his receptors. *Lega'trix*, she whispered in greeting.

Tribunus. Opening his thoughts, he referred to their failure, and probed: *So, how do you feel that went?*

Frustrating. We were caught unawares and responded by instinct. That was most unfortunate.

Did you expect any other reaction?

Had we the chance to formulate a less aggressive approach? Possibly.

Interesting. Angule considered his companion closely. *Explain.*

One among their fighters appears to be sympathetic to your emotions. The intent behind your actions. That is an avenue to be exploited. Others of the higher Kresh have also experienced a similar state of unifex toward certain individuals they perceive within the city. Especially from among the new sources. We must find a way to bridge that gap.

Angule was impressed. Privately, he thought: *Yes indeed. She has great potential. Let's hope it hasn't blossomed too late.* Aloud, he admitted: *We might have an advantage there.*

How?

Haven't you heard? The lost children are no longer restrained by oblivion. The more cognitive of our brethren among the third rank can no longer sense their presence within confinement.

How reliable is that intelligence?

It's dependable enough. Mamone'sh and Orias are among the host assailing the barrier. They are rapidly approaching enlightenment. If they avoid unmaking, it is likely they will be advanced enough to leave the Trianium and join you among the ranks of the Duarium within the next cycle. By a cunning use of strategy, they were able to confirm neither presence remains within the fabricated density. They also uncovered a few other surprises as well.

Such as?

While the residual taste of a single immolation does taint the lattices, they can only detect that one. So, it is highly likely someone got through. We don't know who at this stage, as the wall creates too much interference. Nonetheless, it presents all sorts of possibilities.

But won't they be suffering from identity fracture? Raum's comment displayed a keen awareness of the disorientation emergence caused. *And won't they be dangerously unstable?*

For a while, yes. But that's unavoidable. However, some of us within the Uniam think the process will be muted in this case. Remember, they were the first to be afflicted and never underwent full transmutation. Somehow, the density of their prison arrested the change and held them in limbo. We're hoping sufficient residual memories remain intact for whoever survived to establish some form of détente.

That's a big risk to hang the future of everything on. Especially now the ruptures may start all over again.

There is that, Angule conceded bitterly. *And it concerns me, for not all of the Uniam are in agreement. Some promote a more . . . drastic course to reestablish equilibrium. It's so frustrating. You saw it. If I'd had just a little more time, or perhaps made the approach on my own, I might have been able to get the human to understand me. To warn him of the danger. I refuse to accept this is just wishful thinking. We have to work together. Or die.*

Lega'trix, it's our nature to crave the energy that restores a measure of lucidity. Without it, our infants in particular are driven mad. Crazed. Insensible. Savage. Even as we regain some semblance of control and advance toward illumination, the impulse to gorge is still there. I should know, for I emerged only recently. When faced by such instinctive rage, is it any wonder the humans respond with violence? Especially now they've discovered the anathema of our codex and seek to exploit it.

Nature or not, I don't like the prospect of what we face. If we are unable to establish peaceful contact, and soon, the others may decide the more direct solution is the only viable option. That won't be good for anyone. Angule's aura brightened in hope. *At least our failure brought some good news.*

In what way?

Well. Whatever happens, everything we need now lies within the city. As long as we remain patient, don't overreact, and exercise caution, we may at last achieve an outcome acceptable to all. In fact, I might even make an approach toward the new settlements the humans think they've established without our knowledge.

But will the others agree?

Gesturing his subordinate forward, Angule suggested: *If I act swiftly, they won't have much choice, will they? Care to join me?*

*

Mark Stevens gasped. "Well, that was unexpected!" He turned to the scientists clustered around the main view screen. "And you say this happened, what? Just under an hour ago?"

"Yes. We didn't want to disturb you at the time, as you were still directing the deployment of the final batch of mines," Bob Neville explained. "But do you understand now why we wanted you to see it? I've been here over ten years, and none of us has ever witnessed anything like it. For example . . ." Bob skimmed the feed backward. "Watch this."

The frame froze on the moment both Horde Masters materialized out of the portal, close to the *Promulus* and *Tarion Star*. Bob continued, "This is the first time we've ever had an opportunity to study two of them together. Tell me, do you notice anything?"

Mark leaned in, adjusting the focus and timeframe by twirling his finger backward and forward across the pad. *Okay, so we've got a couple of their . . . hang on! Is that . . . ?*

He tweaked the resolution until the pixels became ultra clear. "Do we have any more images from the other flyers to confirm this?"

"Certainly," Bob replied, "hang on a second."

A secondary screen next to the main monitor flared to life, revealing several pictures within picture. Each showed a similar shot, taken from different angles. Mark studied them closely before venturing a guess. "Are you referring to their obvious differences? Not just in size, but the intensity of their auras?"

"Perhaps. Look again. This time, concentrate on their diadems."

Mark did so.

The larger of the two ogres had a clearly defined coronet that blazed brightly about its head. Seven miniature conflagrations, like orbiting novas, revolved about a defined matrix. The micro-suns left a bright scarlet and gold smear across the screen as they danced serenely by. On this magnification, Mark could see a pearlescent halo surrounding each point of light.

He tapped the mouse to change view. His eyes widened. This Boss was graced with a garland of only four flames. Although bright, it was immediately apparent they were not as intense as those possessed by its companion, and they revolved about the monster's crown at an accelerated pace. Additionally, the entire corona of the beast flickered each time it displayed any overt signs of power.

Mark zoomed in on the wreath itself. *None of the lights possess additional nimbi. It's almost as if they're not strong enough to generate one yet.*

"What do you think?" Bob pressed. "We've got some ideas, but want to get your thoughts as a military man."

Mark was stunned. "If you're asking my opinion as a soldier, I'd say that's a form of rank designation. It seems to tie in with their auras, too. The paler one obviously isn't as powerful as the larger, more defined Master."

"That's what we assumed, too," Bob admitted. "Thank you for that, Mark. It confirms our latest theories that the Horde are far more intelligent than we believed. The very presence of a rank structure reveals an organization to their society that was previously overlooked. That's why *this* makes so much more sense now . . . ."

Bob manipulated the controls to show the moment the senior Controller placed its hand onto the decking of the *Tarion Star*. The crawling web of energies skittering across the surface of the ship dulled almost immediately, while the aura of the Master intensified.

Mark remembered the stark reality of this incident from the replay he'd watched a few minutes ago. *Seeing as they're showing me this again, it's clear I'm meant to ignore the obvious.* "Okay. What are we really looking at?"

As Bob repeated the process, the assembled scientists crowded round to get a better view. Bob said, "We initially thought the ogre was trying to feed. But in the past, whenever they've begun consuming an energy source, they're unable to stop until whatever it is they're draining is totally depleted. That's not the case here . . . ."

He allowed the feed to play on. As if the scales had dropped from his eyes, Mark watched as the scene ran its course. When it finished, all heads turned toward him.

Seriously? He snorted in disbelief. *The damned thing was shielded, so it probably wouldn't have made the slightest bit of difference had Stu opened up anyway. And it could have reached out and simply yanked him off the ship. But it didn't.*

On impulse, Mark reached out and played the moment over again. Then he allowed the feed to progress up until the moment the Horde Master retreated.

Look how slowly it reached out. It was emphasizing it wasn't there to attack him. And when Stu got twitchy, it simply let go and walked away as if the machine gun full of iron bullets behind it wasn't worth bothering about. Hang on . . .

Mark zoomed in, transfixed, as the *Tarion Star* lifted into the air. The Controller paused, and could clearly be seen staring upward. Its eyes suddenly blazed.

What was that? The only other thing in the air was the Promulus. *What was it doing?*

A thrill trickled its way along Mark's spine. He turned back to the people gathered about him.

"Do you see why we wanted you to take a look?" Bob asked.

"I do. Bob, get me Rhomane on the line. I'm sure they've already seen this, but we have to make sure they understand what they're looking at."

*

Saul Cameron was in seventh heaven. He knew he should try to keep his feet firmly on the ground, but a party mood had seized everyone in its clutches and he couldn't help but join in.

Not only had the operation to retrieve the starships gone well, but the first shipment from the Shilette Abyss had arrived exactly on time, just an hour ago. *This entire mission was planned around the convoy's progress, and while I knew the presence of so much iron ore would act as a huge deterrent, I couldn't take any chances. Talk about working like a dream. This heist was the ultimate distraction.*

As he wound his way through the crowd in the marshaling yard, Saul studied the latest report from the mining site.

I can't believe how well things are going lately. Just look at what Marcus has managed to achieve. Saul flicked down through the précis. *His base of operations seems nigh on im-*

pregnable. There are further deposits ready for exploitation. We have a prepared schedule for regular shuttle runs to implement. And a divided bunch of misfits have been molded together into a productive team. Jesus! Even Smith and his cronies are pulling their weight and making friends.

Saul stopped to scratch his head in wonderment. Several people following closely behind were taken by surprise, and walked into him.

"Huh? Oh, sorry," he mumbled. *Tiberius and Lucius will have a tough act to follow if they want to keep things running the way they are. And look at this. In a few days we'll have a live-time link into the encampment itself. Now that will prove to be a godsend . . .*

He paused again, peering through the press toward the icing on the cake. *Especially with the latest chicks we've gathered into the fold.*

The starliner *Promulus* and freighter *Tarion Star* took pride of place on the city's launch pad. Both ships looked as if they were brand-new and open for inspection, thanks to the energies of their recently activated exo-webs, which had burnt away all traces of years of accumulated detritus.

A huge mob of technicians and sightseers crowded around each craft, and the atmosphere had escalated into one of near jubilation.

Saul caught sight of Marcus himself, talking to several Caledonians.

*I've got to get him on the command team. His achievements are . . .*Then he realized who one of those clansmen was. *Cathal MacNoimhin. Oh shit!*

Marcus's expression suddenly hardened. Even at this distance, Saul could see the man's whole posture tense as his face flushed dark red.

"Marcus," Saul called across the heads of the throng, "Marcus Brutus!"

It was no use. The crowd was simply making too much noise.

Ah hell. I told Cathal I wanted to be the one to break the news.

Saul watched as a heated exchange took place between the two men. The outburst was brief. Within moments, the Legion commander had composed himself and appeared to be apologizing to the Iceni leader and his followers. His offer was readily accepted by the highlanders, who took it in turns to share handclasps with him.

One of them noticed Saul approaching through the crush. Nudges were exchanged, along with words of warning. Ignoring the concerned looks of those about him, Marcus immediately spun away, made eye contact with Saul, and drew himself up to his full height. Thunder congealed on his brow. Without a moment's hesitation, Marcus ploughed through the intervening press as if they didn't exist. His gaze never wavered from his target, and he didn't blink once.

Saul decided to wait and let the man come to him.

It didn't take long. More and more people looked toward them as they noticed a change in the ambient mood.

"Saul." Marcus extended his arm in greeting.

"Marcus," Saul replied, accepting the embrace. "We need to talk. Somewhere private would be best." It wasn't an invitation.

"That, I can appreciate."

Although Marcus didn't look away, Saul noticed the other man's eyes glaze over as he allowed his peripheral vision to take in details of their surroundings, and the reaction this confrontation was causing amongst onlookers.

"Please lead on," the legionnaire invited, "I am keen to discover the circumstances of my compatriot's death, and what progress you have made in determining the identity of his killer."

Turning on his heel, Saul surprised Marcus by heading toward the *Promulus* instead of the main building. The soldier fell in behind. As they worked their way through the crowd, both men exchanged pleasantries with passersby.

All about them, people relaxed again.

Saul was impressed. *Just look at the effect his example has on others. They can see he's upset. And who wouldn't be? He's just got back from an overwhelmingly successful mission to discover a close friend has died under the most suspicious circumstances. It's enough to sour the best of men. But instead of causing a scene, which he knows would be bad for morale, he's managed to strangle his personal feelings down, and keep his opinion to himself until we're away from flapping ears.*

Taking a crafty peek at the man next to him, Saul came to a decision. *Yes, I'll have a word with Mohammed and the others tonight. The sooner we get this man on the command team, the better.*

*

"No! You don't understand," a troubled voice yelled. "Keep away from the damned things. Stay away, I tell you. Don't you realize what . . . Don't you . . . Aaargh!"

Everyone started as a metallic tray and its contents bounced off the triple-layered, poly-resin screen. Several burly orderlies rushed into the room to restrain its highly emotional occupant.

"Do you see why I paged you?" Louise Smart, the duty nurse hissed. "One moment he was absolutely fine, asking all sorts of weird questions about life in our era and what it in-volved—of all things, how we prepared food in the twenty-third century and what it tasted like—and then we came in here to do his weekly blood work, as usual. He's used to the routine now, and collects the hypo-syringe and swab patch for us. Anyway, he sauntered over to the equipment locker, which as you see is over by the window. And when he glanced out, he totally freaked. I mean . . . look at him."

Ayria gawped through the observation port. A distraught James Houston was pressed against the external pane. Tears streamed down his face as he stared in wide-eyed horror at something outside. He tried to claw his way through the glass, frustration clearly mounting by the second.

He's working himself into a frenzy.

The porters closed on him. Houston saw them at the last moment and screamed in panic.

"Why won't you listen to me? Don't you . . . The danger. It's . . . *oof*!"

The charge-hands pounced and hustled him to the floor, knocking the wind from his sails. He kicked and thrashed wildly, as if the devil himself were tormenting him.

Ayria dithered, appalled. She had been on her way to Mohammed's office with Heaven's-Claw when she received the call to attend the medical wing. Responding immediately, Ayria had completely forgotten to return the tomahawk to her mentor. Glancing at the axe, she thought, *what the hell shall I do with this?*

"Wait!" she yelled. "Be as gentle as you can. Try not to hurt him."

Tossing the weapon to one side, Ayria rushed into the room and knelt beside her stricken patient. "James?" she crooned. "James? It's me, Ayria. Ayria Solram."

As she spoke, Ayria stroked his forehead with her fingers and brushed the hair from his eyes. *My God. He's sweating like the proverbial pig.* "James, I'm here. I'm listening. Tell me what's wrong. What's trying to hurt us?"

Houston didn't appear to hear. His gaze penetrated her and seemed to focus elsewhere, far off in the distance.

"Help me," she said softly, "how can I protect myself from something I don't know about? You've been making such good progress. Don't stop now."

Houston's disjointed comprehension appeared to gel. He wriggled an arm free and reached out to seize her by her wrist. "That's what I'm trying to . . . I'm trying . . ."

He's losing it again. Ayria came to an instant decision.

"Let him go!" she commanded the orderlies.

They complied reluctantly, and stood away.

Houston eyed them suspiciously, as if he was certain they'd cut his throat given half a chance. Ayria tried to recapture his attention. Holding his face between her hands, she shouted, "James!"

He jumped and glowered into her eyes.

Calmly, she added, "Thank you. Now, where's the danger?"

"Outside!" he gasped. His focus had clearly returned. "Can't you see? Can't you sense it?"

"No, I can't. Why don't you show me?"

Scrabbling to his hands and knees, Houston skittered across the floor to bunch himself into a ball beneath the exterior window. He glared back at her and gesticulated wildly. "Be careful, Ayria," he hissed. "Don't relax your guard for one moment. We can't . . . don't let them . . . It's awful. The isolation. The . . ."

Houston's voice trailed off as his concentration faltered yet again. His jaw flapped uselessly, and he appeared to forget what it was he wanted to say.

C'mon, James. Stay with me. For God's sake, don't make me have to recommit you. "Shall I take a look? I'll let you know what's out there, and you tell me if we have to be careful. Okay?"

Ayria stood and crept forward. As she neared the sill, Houston began rocking back and forth, mumbling to himself. Ignoring him, she braced herself against the frame and surveyed the scene below. *Okay, here goes nothing.*

"James? I'm looking down into the marshaling yard. A huge crowd has gathered to welcome Marcus and his team back from the Shilette Abyss. There are four skidders down there full of iron, so we're very well protected . . ."

Houston continued to sway, and started to giggle, as if at a private joke.

Okay, so it's not that, then. "A lot of people are helping them unload. Cathal MacNoimhin and his Caledonians. Some of the Sioux and Apache braves. Oh, Mac's there too, with the rest of his squad. They did a marvelous job, bringing back those ships intact. Just look at them. We'll—"

Screaming in terror, Houston leapt up from the floor. Taken by surprise, the porters froze, allowing him to shoulder his way past their position. Ayria felt as if time slowed about her.

He teetered through the door and collided with Louise, who had remained standing in the entrance. They tumbled heavily to the floor. Somehow, Houston managed to roll forward and his momentum propelled him, headfirst, into a trolley full of medical supplies.

The resultant *crash* brought everything back into perspective.

Louise screamed.

The charge-hands sprang into action.

Too late.

Clawing his way across the littered tiles, Houston fumbled about for support. Reaching up onto an examination bed, his fingers closed around something hard and smooth.

Ayria's hand leapt to her mouth. *Oh no!*

Houston surged to his feet. His scrutiny fell upon the object in his grasp. The discarded tomahawk.

The transformation was as shocking as it was immediate.

Whirling on the spot, Houston's face became a mask of adoration and awe. His chest heaved and for the first time in an age, he appeared to be in full control of his faculties.

Ayria remained stock still. "James? You're making everyone anxious. Please put the axe down."

The orderlies eyed each other nervously and continued edging forward.

Louise backed away and scrambled for the main door.

Ayria finally managed to get her feet moving.

"James," she called again, "don't do anything rash. We're here to help you."

Houston focused his gaze directly on her. Brandishing Heaven's-Claw, he raised it toward her and in a tone laced with relief and victory, shouted, "Yes!"

Everyone pounced at once.

Chapter Twenty-Nine

Online

"Initiate command override on my mark," Ephraim Miller directed, "three; two; one; mark."

An abrupt whine announced the moment the power reserves died. The lights went out. Every screen went dark. A pregnant pause followed. Someone coughed nervously and people began to fidget. Then the drone of rebooting computers and generators filled the air, heralding the restoration of services throughout the city. One after another, monitors and equipment around the control center burst back to life.

Ephraim's gaze remained fixed on Brent Wyatt and Asa Montgomery as they completed their analysis of the reformatted systems. Both men were hunched over their terminals, transfixed in the glare of new information now downloading from the restored astrometric facility, and a multitude of other sources around the planet. In the dulled illumination of the room, their features bore the wide-eyed stare of mad scientists, and Ephraim couldn't help but chuckle.

He couldn't restrain himself any longer. "Well? Did it work?"

Brent glanced at Asa. Asa nodded, pressed a few buttons and stood back from his console, a satisfied look on his face.

Brent surveyed the raw data, pursed his lips, and grinned. Straightening up, he flipped a switch. "All systems are now meshed. I'm transferring the information to your terminal. Get a load of this."

The command staff behind Ephraim crowded forward to take a look, forcing Ephraim to protest. "Ladies and gentlemen. Please. I know we've been waiting all week to implement these updates, but a little patience now will make all the difference. If I may?"

Shouldering his way through the press, Ephraim accessed his computer and listed the fruits of their labors. His eyes bulged. *My God! It's even better than I imagined.*

Reactivating the main wall screens, he directed everyone's attention forward. "Boys and girls, it would appear our efforts have been generously rewarded. If I could ask you to consider the center monitor first?"

Everyone shuffled about to get a better look. Ephraim brought up an overview of the countryside surrounding Rhomane City, encompassing a fifty mile radius. As the image solidified, a number of red dots appeared. After a few moments, some of them started blinking on and off.

"What are they?" Saul asked.

"Those are way stations, Commander. As you know, at its peak, Arden had these facilities scattered across the surface of the planet. They were governed by the sentinel AI program, and acted as signal-come-energy relay posts for day to day communications and power distribution. They also housed a squadron of flyers for maintenance, aerial surveys, and security. Obviously, a number of them were lost during the invasion. But not all."

"Are the flashing ones active?"

"Oh yes. Rhomane is surrounded by a fair number of such reserve centers, as are all the other major starports across Arden's four main continents. And really, it stands to reason. They were at the height of their culture, so we can only imagine the volume of traffic their controllers had to regulate. And not just here, through local airspace, but throughout the entire star system. It helps explain why so many redundant facilities ring each city. When they realized what the Horde was doing, some bright spark ordered the standby stations you see here to power down." Ephraim shrugged. "I can only imagine they hoped to use them again at a later date. In any event, their misfortune has provided us with an excellent tactical advantage."

"Why?" Mohammed asked. "Won't our enemy sense they are now online and simply drain them as they did before?"

Ephraim smiled. "Good point. Fortunately, one we no longer have to worry about, thanks to my team's ingenuity."

Ephraim tapped a sequence into his keyboard, and a separate segment appeared within the right-hand side of the screen. In it, a distinctive oscillating pattern could be seen, flowing in a never-ending wave from top to bottom.

"My friends," he announced proudly, "this is Trojan. A digitized, highly compressed signal employing a modulating temporal signature. Over the past month, Brent, Asa, and Penny worked together to create a means by which we could transfer our latest security protocols to whatever posts are still operational. This is what they devised."

"And what's it doing, exactly?" Mohammed pressed.

"Why, it's broadcasting the specific frequency of our combined null-point and chameleon shields. In effect, this carrier wave will cloak those facilities until we can get the flyers to drop an actual generator at each site."

Saul cut back in on the conversation. "So we'll be able to use these way stations?"

"We certainly will." Ephraim beamed. He paused to skim the accompanying schedule. "In this locality alone, we have the following centers at our disposal: Ho'lam Island, out on Asterlan Lake, forty miles west of here; Grisson Gap, which you all know; the northern sector of the Tar'e-esh Forest, twenty-three miles east; Tar'e-esh Plain, just south of the starport; and of course, Boleni Heights itself. Remember, these are the stations that weren't touched. As long as they remain under the protective umbrellas generated by the Trojan program, they'll remain invisible to the Horde. And because they're so close, we can get teams and flyers on site in a matter of hours. I tell you, they'll make a big difference. For example . . ." Ephraim's fingers flew across the controls once more, "tell me what you think of this little beauty."

The left-hand wall screen activated, showing an even larger image of the planet's surface. The scale along the top showed they were now viewing an area nearly five hundred miles in diameter. Within it, more than half a dozen zones were tinged olive.

A voice from the back shouted, "Ha! Iron."

"What makes you say that, Marcus?" Ephraim was intrigued that the legionnaire had made the connection before anyone else.

"Simple common sense. Although this is the first time I have seen such a view, several features are well known to me." Marcus strode forward and began explaining certain aspects everyone would be aware of. "That huge scar you see running across the surface of the planet is obviously the Shilette Abyss. A place very dear to my heart in recent weeks. The locale of our newest settlement governs a region known to possess one of the highest concentrations of iron ore on the planet."

Marcus drew their attention to the narrowest point of the canyon. "As you can see, the Rhomane to Genoas highway crosses the gorge at a point only five miles east of the encampment. That whole sector is green, corresponding to the mining site and surrounding ore beds we discovered throughout the Tar'e-esh itself, and the Esteban Sea. It doesn't take a genius to make the connection, especially when we also remember the lower grade deposits situated in the Erásan Mountains."

He pointed to another shaded patch not far from the Grisson Gap. "See? They match places we already know are iron rich. I can only assume the other areas also possess hematite, magnetite, goethite, and limonite in sufficient concentrations to be worth highlighting."

Ephraim was stunned. "Well done. You're exactly right." Addressing the rest of the command staff, he continued, "As Marcus correctly surmised, we are looking at a district that was once known as the Jurisdictional Prefecture of Rhomane. This entire province is littered with iron ore deposits of significant purity and abundance. One of the richest on the planet in fact, and that will—"

"How do you know that?" Saul asked. "Excuse me for butting in, but we've been using antiquated city archives to guide us for some time now. How can you say for certain these areas still contain what we need?"

"Because the satellites have confirmed it."

"What?" Saul was taken aback.

Several other commanders began muttering among themselves.

Then the meaning of Ephraim's actual words registered with Saul. "Are you saying these images aren't from patrolling drones?"

Ephraim smirked. "No, they're not. That was going to be one of my next surprises. People, may I present a little example of what Arden's Global Satcom-net can do."

Ephraim entered another cipher into the console before him. All three main wall screens skipped channels to present a series of starkly different vistas. A palpable shock ran through the entire gathering. Several people gasped out loud.

The first monitor showed the rim of a burnished orange-red sun emerging from behind the bulk of a majestic disc. The star's corona burned brightly, casting a warm scarlet glow through the upper reaches of the atmosphere of the world below it. The planet itself appeared etched in liquid flame around its edges, while the majority of its mass was cast in mystery and shadow.

The middle display revealed a similar scene but from a different perspective, this one being positioned above the terminator of sunrise and sunset. To the left of the picture, cotton-candy clouds swirled through a sea of sapphire-blue radiance. The crystal lens of the expanse was infused with vaporous trails of soul-wrenching tranquility. On the right, darkness dominated. Ebbing reluctantly under the relentless advance of dawn, it gradually surrendered its secrets. Noctilucent particles manifested themselves amongst the gloom, followed closely by the tallest mountain summits. Like beacons, they revealed tantalizing glimpses of the glory to come.

The final screen faced out into a Jovian sea of purple-blue grandeur. An ocean of midnight silk upon which the luminescence of a billion astral sprites had been cast in random abandon. Each pinprick blazed coldly with an unadulterated purity that struck the hearts and minds of the gathered assembly with the force of a sledgehammer.

Captivated, Ephraim became lost in the moment. *Somewhere out there, a lifetime away, our real home sails serenely through the heavens . . . How ignorant we were of the dangers that exist, just a cosmic stone's-throw away.*

"Are these satellites able to show us Arden in greater detail?" Marcus asked. "What is the term you use? Can they . . . zoom in and remain clear?"

"They can indeed, my friend. For example . . . ."

Ephraim presented them with a vision of remarkable scope. A solitary peak pierced the night. Protruding toward the sunlight like a symbol of hope, its alpine cap strained to free itself from the twilight mists congealing about its slopes in a miasma of serpentine possessiveness.

The image wavered, and a closer view of that same pinnacle resolved itself. Now, the cobalt-blue frown of a granite leviathan stood forth in pristine clarity, peeking out from hoarfrost-covered brows. A snowy crown adorned the apex, and where the rock face greeted the dawn, it glittered cruelly, burning as if the entire edifice were ablaze within a skein of ice and flames.

Above the slopes on one side, a huge bird of prey stretched its wings and soared amid the very epitome of serenity sublime made manifest.

Everyone leaned forward. Ephraim chose that moment to switch satellites.

A contrasting swathe of undulating greens and blues made everyone start. The picture flickered and intensified. The panorama scrolled across verdant forests, swaying grasslands, and undulating plains. The luxuriant fertility of the temperate zones faded as the scanners moved on, toward the equatorial region.

The gaping chasm of the Shilette Abyss hove into view. Once there, Ephraim manipulated the controls to skim east. Less than a minute later, he held position above a point where the two sides of the canyon seemed to bulge toward each other. Changing resolution, he smoothly zoomed in to present a live-time image of the mining site from less than two hundred feet up. People could clearly be seen, walking to and fro about their business.

Marcus suppressed a laugh.

Several others cheered.

Mohammed and Saul stared at each other, the implications of this latest development written clearly across their faces.

"These places you're showing us appear remarkably bounteous and free of infestation," Saul commented. "Do you think this confirms our latest suspicions? That something here in the city appears to be the Horde's target, and they've congregated in one location to get it?"

"Hazarding a guess? I'd say that was highly likely. But we can discuss that at tomorrow's briefing. By then, we'll have uploaded the specs of the rotational frequencies that Mac and his team use. Combining them to the already existing filters the satellites employ will give us an accurate assessment of exactly where on the planet our enemy is congregating. Be in no doub—the addition of the Satcom-net will provide us with a huge tactical advantage we never dreamed of."

"Such as?"

Ephraim scanned through the contents of his personal screen again. Then he glanced back at Brent and Asa. Each of them was privy to the information it contained, and both were grinning like maniacs.

"Tell them, Boss," Brent blurted.

"Tell us what?" Saul queried.

Ephraim grinned. "Remember how I told you a few minutes ago that having access to this global system was just one of the surprises in store for you tonight? Well, here's another."

A floating platform filled the main screen, appearing much larger than the other satellites nearby. "This is Veran 3," Ephraim said, "one of six space stations positioned in geosynchronous orbit around the planet's equator and poles. It would seem these particular ones were used as command and response posts for the upkeep of the planetary net. And get this. They're not only armed and equipped with transporter pads, but are linked into Se'ochan's lunar grid, too."

"Se'ochan has a defensive system as well? Why didn't we know?"

"Because certain records were compartmentalized. Need to know. Now we have access to the astrometrics database, we're discovering all sorts of new toys we can play with. Of course, preliminary diagnostics show they're powered down at the moment. So, if you don't mind, once they're safely protected behind the new shields, I'd like you to task a team to check out their systems and bring each one up to speed. Obviously, we'll prioritize the planetary web first, because . . . well, with what I'm going to show you next, I have a feeling you'll want a permanent contingent up there to keep an eye on things."

"You mean there's more?" Saul was clearly amazed there might be yet another shock waiting in the wings.

Ephraim didn't reply. Instead, he raised his eyebrows and pressed a button. The image that flashed onto the screen next caused everyone to fall silent.

"Ladies and gentlemen, may I present the Avenger Class deep space cruiser, *Arch of Winter*. And yes, before you ask, she *is* intact and initial scans show her to be the only ship left in high orbit to remain free of Horde infestation. The logs I have here indicate her captain had the foresight to abandon ship and open her to the vacuum of space rather than let her be taken. What's fascinating is the fact her sensors are active. But because she's surrounded by some form of dampening field, she has remained undetected. Clearly, we'll need to look into that and assess if the Tec is viable for hybrid application with those we're currently using."

Everyone stared in mute surprise.

Mohammed was the first to find his voice. "Ephraim, what passenger capacity does the *Arch of Winter* possess?"

"One moment . . ." Ephraim brought up the schematics of the ship. "From the guidelines here, I can see she's equipped with third generation rip-space drives, and was constructed specifically for long-range exploration and patrol. Five year missions, from the look of it. As such, she carried a combined military, scientific, and civilian specialist complement of . . . three hundred and ninety-eight officers and four and a half thousand crew. Families included."

"Is she capable of atmospheric entry?"

"Only for emergency landings, I'm afraid. Sorry, but she's wholly configured for the solar environment. On the plus side, that does mean she's equipped with a complement of shuttle-craft, side to side *and* orbital transport capabilities, and her hangar bay is huge."

Mohammed turned to Saul. Eyes wide with inspiration, he gasped, "Do you appreciate what an opportunity this gives us?"

He spun to face the room. "Do any of you realize what this means?"

"Why don't you explain your thinking?" Saul said quietly.

"If we can take possession of that cruiser, it means we have an option B. For the first time in an age, we're no longer stuck on this Godforsaken planet. Hell, if we plan things right, we could even make a run for Earth!"

Oh no! You can't be serious?

Mohammed's words created a strong surge of feeling throughout the control room. Ephraim felt it too, along with an initial surge of panic. "Whoa, hang on a second," he said forcefully. "Before we start getting everyone's hopes up, I really must insist we sit down and talk things through."

Mohammed frowned. "Why? What's there to think about? Even with the iron, we're still slowly starving to death. If we don't do something, and soon, we're done for."

Ephraim decided to cut to the heart of the matter. Ignoring everyone else, he addressed Saul. "I can think of a number of reasons why we shouldn't act rashly, all of which I will highlight in detail at our debriefing tomorrow. However, what everyone appears to have forgotten is the manner in which we were brought here. Remember, we weren't just plucked through space. We were selected from different time references. There's a temporal ingredient to our existence on this planet that could cause major waves if we went rushing back home."

Ephraim paused to let the weight of his words sink in. After a moment, he concluded, "Don't forget, theoretical physics is a specialty of mine, and a prerequisite of quite a number of my staff. Ask any one of us, and we'll be able to regale you all day on why we just can't risk the possibility of a paradox."

A hush fell over the room once more, and everyone waited while the commander chewed over the rationalization of his chief scientist.

Eventually, Saul came to a decision. "Of course you're right," he mumbled. Addressing the rest of his colleagues, he spoke louder. "He's right. This is something we simply can't rush. You all know me. I've valued your insight and your guidance for a number of years now. And I always will."

He turned to place a hand on Mohammed's shoulder. "And yours especially, my friend. But we all need to be involved in this. We can't do that until we've been able to scrutinize the information available to us. Weighed the options. Discussed the risks. We've been presented with a marvelous slice of luck, and I for one don't intend to squander it. Agreed?"

Saul gazed round the room, maintaining eye contact until everyone had nodded in reply. He worked his way around to Ephraim again.

"How long do you and your team need to interrogate the system and get us the facts we need?"

Thank goodness for that. "If we work through the night? I'd say we could make an informed opinion by this time tomorrow. But I'd want everyone on it."

"You have until the day after tomorrow, then. Be swift, but ensure your people are accurate. What takes place here in the next few days might determine not just our future, but that of Arden, too. I don't want mistakes."

Oh, great. No pressure then. "I'll get right on it."

Chapter Thirty

A Focusing of Purpose

Whenever the inadequacies of his kind threatened to disrupt equilibrium, Angule, Prime Catalyct of the Unium, could be found here, within the Plane of Eternal Prisms. There was something about the manner in which reality splintered and refracted off into a multitude of possibilities that helped soothe the seething cauldron of rage within him. Sublime expression, as always, simmered just below the surface, and preventing its emergence, now of all times, was crucial.

Brooding, Angule reviewed the travesty of their last Moot, and did his best to maintain a dispassionate veil across his receptors.

What are they thinking? It appeared to me that they deliberately chose not to comprehend the value of parley. To even contemplate unleashing the full might of the Host, unrestrained by dint or edict, smacks of a negligence deserving of ultimate immolation. Are the fools so blind as to think there won't be consequences? Such a course is a travesty waiting to happen. And even if their fool's errand succeeds and we seize our prize by force, there may be insufficient puissance left with which to elicit the regeneration.

The vext flared behind him. Angule hardened his shields and allowed his senses to wash across those who dared to intrude upon his solitude. *Raum?*

Lega'trix, Raum replied: *May we approach?*

Angule's scrutiny fell upon Raum's companions; the new Praefactors, Mamone'sh and Orias. Having ascended only two rotations previously, the latest members of the Duarium were unaccustomed to the restraint expected of those gracing the higher circles. Their auras continued to stutter and flare in an alarming breach of etiquette.

Outraged, Angule's indignation slapped against the efflux of their still evolving essences. Recoiling in alarm, both entities hastily erected their barriers.

My apologies, Great One, Raum added, covering for their gaffe: *But now they are managing to achieve a semblance of purer lucidity, both Kresh have information they wish to share as a matter of urgency.*

Information? Why do they feel it necessary to approach me with it now?

She paused to confer with her subordinates. The flames of their newly engendered coronets spluttered wanly under her interrogation. The exchange intensified, and a newfound focus and confidence allowed the fledglings to regain a measure of boldness. Their diadems solidified and blazed brighter.

Raum's own aura bloomed. Turning her attention back to Angule, she stated: *As you know, both Mamone'sh and Orias were excluded from the Moot while their status unified. How-*

ever, once blended to the Ix and apprised of the result, they were consumed by haste. They have intelligence regarding the fate of the lost child and feel you are the only one who can be trusted to react . . . accordingly.

Really? His gaze fell upon the newcomers once more. Thinking aloud, he voiced a blasphemous opinion: *How unfortunate then, that the conclave was not delayed until you were ready. I feel the vote may have swung in the favor of sanity.*

That is our consensus as well, Great One, Orias expressed with reserved dignity: *Our constant attendance at the forbidding meant we were able to witness the continued struggle of those who were lost. We shared in their conflict, and experienced firsthand their frustration and anguish. Felt the horror of being helplessly trapped and restrained. Tasted the confusing bile of insanity that threatened to strip them of substance. And yet they endured. And so, I speak on behalf of my Kresh brother when I say is it not a course of wisdom to ensure the survivor is given every opportunity to regain equilibrium? Especially when the source of his suffering now resides once more within the city? Will not his example inspire others, and lead all Kresh to salvation?*

Survivor, you say? For sure?

Yes, Lega'trix. We are able to verify that one of the children was lost in transition. The other subsumed the essence of its sibling, persevered, and survived transformation.

Remarkable . . . And providential.

Feeling motivated, Angule made a snap decision: *Raum. Convey my regards to our supporters within the Unium and Duarium. Ask them to meet us within the Gulf of Tears at the end of today's cycle. Whatever the cost, we must exploit this development with all haste.*

*

Ayria sat back down in one of the easy chairs opposite the commander's desk, and waited. She had just completed her part of what she obviously knew would sound like a fantastical tale of pure make-believe, and Saul could see the scientist within Ayria cringing in embarrassment.

He did his best to mask the disdain souring his expression.

"You can't be serious? You want us to risk our lives, our very future, on what? A message sent to you in a dream?"

"I know how it sounds, believe me, but . . . but . . . oh, for goodness' sake, Saul, this is *me* talking. I haven't survived here this long, witnessed so many friends struggle through adversity and watched them die in front of me to lose it now on a whim. C'mon. You must realize how difficult it was for me to even come here? Don't you trust me enough to at least consider what I'm saying might have some bearing on the weird events taking place around here lately?"

"You wouldn't be the first to succumb to traumatic stress, Ayria. Like you say, you've lasted here longer than most. I can only imagine the pressure you've had to endure over the year—"

"Cut the crap, Saul. I've been a doctor for far too long to listen to you trying to smooth talk me with psychobabble."

Fair point.

She turned to Stained-With-Blood, her expression pleading for help.

The seasoned warrior sat forward. He held the commander's gaze without flinching. "I have seen many summers, Saul Cameron, both as a brave and a shaman of my tribe. You people from the future tend to overlook the fact that life wasn't easy for those of us who lived centuries before mankind journeyed to the stars. In our lands, you either learned to adapt and survive, or you died. Fools perished even more swiftly. My very name should convey to you the kind of man I am, and why I have lived so long."

Stained-With-Blood paused to ensure Saul understood his point before continuing. "To put things in perspective, let me say this. I am a dream-walker, not a miracle worker or a crazed loon seeking attention. My talents lie in that I am granted insight regarding the road that lies before us. It is Napioa himself, not me, who reveals the course we should take. I am not here to mock your beliefs, or lack of them. All I do is interpret the Creator's guidance and allow it to influence my choices, and those faced by my tribe. So far—and I say this with all modesty—the Cree nation have been blessed. Past visions have proven unerringly accurate and by acknowledging them, not only have we, but many other tribes of the First People been well protected.

"It is a weakness of your era to see scientific development as progress. Sadly, in doing so, you have left behind the old ways that helped keep you in touch with the world and the greater cosmos about you. You forget. The universe would carry on regardless, whether you were here or no. Its cycles and rhythms are governed by forces that we will never truly understand. And sometimes, like it or not, it reveals paths to us in ways science cannot begin to comprehend. However, as you base so much of your belief on facts, shall we look at some now?"

Engrossed as he was by Stained-With-Blood's narrative, Saul took a moment to reply. Hunching forward, he murmured, "Okay. I'd like to see where you're going with this."

Stained-With-Blood gestured toward Ayria. "It is a simple fact that two people, divided through time by thousands of years, were brought together in one place. The odds of such a thing happening are astronomical. And yet, here we are. Not only that, but Ayria and I share an unusual bond. Our veins happen to flow with the same blood—separated by centuries, yes, but possessing an identical potency nonetheless. I am a tribal elder, in touch with the world in which I live. She is a scientist, a doctor who has denied her birthright for decades. And yet, we have both received visions from the Creator, separately and in tandem, which share an unusual commonality. The uniting of two peoples into one, and the astounding way this will be accomplished," he pointed to his tomahawk, which lay on the desk in front of Saul, "by the use of star metal.

"Now, I freely admit. Exactly how this will occur, I do not know. Neither can I comment on how these dreams tie in to the Ardenese plans for us. Is it all a coincidence, or part of a larger design instigated by a greater power? Therefore, I appreciate your turmoil. You, as leader, are responsible for our welfare, and much, much more, it would appear. The weight of two worlds hangs in the balance. You cannot allow personal preference to cloud your judgment, for your decision will have lasting repercussions. Therefore, I would ask you to respect this point.

"Just because you don't understand something, doesn't mean it isn't right. Recall certain factors of our last encounter with Napioa. He manipulated the energies that cascaded out of a void. One very similar to those we have recently witnessed. Wielding such power, he transformed the seeds of already existing trees into something new. That this relates to the peoples of Earth and Arden is clear. Yet we see an inference that it may also relate to more. Why this reference to the Horde? How is the star metal to be employed? And why is Wind of the Sun to play such a pivotal role?"

Saul frowned. "Wind of the Sun?"

"That's my tribal name," Ayria explained. "Remember, although parted by many generations, I am a bloodline descendent of the Blackfoot Cree nation."

"Ah, I see." Saul looked between them for a moment, searching for similarities in their features. "And you think you're both involved in this . . . these developments or insights in some way?"

Stained-With-Blood nodded. "From what Napioa has indicated, yes. The salvation of both, or should I say *all* races on Arden would appear to be bound together. That *we* were brought here for this very purpose is obvious. It is also clear that Wind of the Sun—Ayria—is a catalyst for the process by which unity will be achieved."

"But you don't know how that will occur?"

"I'm sorry, no. I am a dream-walker. Not a charlatan. When the way is unclear, I have seen the course of wisdom in waiting for the Creator to reveal the correct path. Never have I presumed to interpret his will wrongly."

Saul found Stained-With-Blood's admission comforting. And troubling.

"I appreciate your frankness on the matter," he responded. "I will return the courtesy. That you're both sincere is obvious. I've been Ayria's friend for quite a few years now, and she's always been a solid member of our community. Reliable, dependable, and possessed of a great deal of common sense. You, on the other hand, I've only known for a period of months. Nevertheless, I can honestly say I've never a met a man with such integrity. You tell it as it is, and are never afraid to speak the truth. Even when it hurts. I trust you both. So you've put me in quite a pickle. Against my better judgment, there's a part of me that can't ignore what you've said. But can you imagine the reaction I'll get when I put your proposals forward? The others will think I'm stealing meds from sickbay. So I need something . . . more, something concrete, to add weight to your request."

He shook his head in frustration. "Look, let me think on it awhile. I've got to try to get my head around it, because you've got to admit. It does come across as . . . well, a far-fetched fairytale."

Stained-With-Blood bowed formally. "Of course, we understand. But don't take too long, Commander, for time is not on our side. I would remind you of the fact that the vision showed an approaching flood, one that will sweep away all life under the red sun. Unless we act swiftly, urgently, all will be lost."

The respected warrior motioned for Ayria to follow him, and moved to take his leave. As they made their way to the door, he gestured toward the desk. "I will leave Heaven's-Claw in your care for today. Please ponder on the significance of the role this totem may play. Use it to guide you to your decision."

"As a matter of fact, you might be able to use the axe as a prop to help persuade the others," Ayria added. "Don't forget how Houston reacted to its presence after the arrival of the ships. He's . . . different since his accident. Changed in some way we haven't been able to fathom yet. Why do the Ardenese spacecraft freak him out so much? What is it about Heaven's-Claw that grounds him, and restores a measure of lucidity? I'm telling you, Saul. There's a connection here, and someone's got to try to fathom it all out."

The door closed, leaving Saul alone in the tranquility of his office once more. Too shocked to say anything, he allowed the details of the amazing meeting to spin around and around in his head until he felt he might spit in frustration. On impulse, he pinched himself. *Ouch! I'm definitely awake then . . .*

But where does this leave me? As fanciful as it sounds, I can't just dismiss their concerns. For goodness' sake, they're two of the most levelheaded people I know.

The tomahawk caught his attention, and the lines of its dull, gray-black surface seemed to make him look within himself. *Star metal. Pure iron. Fallen from the heavens. Sent to us from up above. A gift from . . . What am I thinking?*

A niggling worry wormed its way through the back of his mind. *Is there a pattern I'm missing? Did it all start after the ninth arrived?*

One particular thought echoed in his head. *What was it Stained-With-Blood said?* "*Don't take too long, Commander, for time is not on our side. I would remind you of the fact that the vision showed an approaching flood, one that will sweep away all life under the red sun. Unless we act swiftly, urgently, all will be lost.*"

Before he realized what he was doing, Saul reached for the intercom button.

I can't take the risk. "Mohammed? Will you ask Mac to join me in my office in thirty minutes? I want you in on the meeting, too. Make sure you bring a compilation of memory crystals covering every one of the lieutenant's missions from out at the starport. Combine them with the reports from the Boleni Heights crew, as well."

"Will do. What's up? Anything special?"

I'm going round the twist. That's what. "You'll see, my friend. If I were you, I'd bring coffee. Lots of it. I have a feeling we might be here some time."

*

Tiberius Tacitus raced through the compound toward the middle of the camp, doing his best to ignore the looks of concern from those who were, as yet, completely unaware of the emergency.

Following the custom of the Legion, the compound had been erected with security in mind. The most sensitive of the buildings, along with important personnel, were situated well away from the perimeter. That he was being called to the command center did not bode well.

Just another day in paradise, he kept telling himself, *just another day . . . please.*

Arriving outside the control room, Tiberius discovered his optio, Lucius Scipio, and an entire contubernium of ten men already in attendance. Their resident communications expert, Sebbi Farah, was also hovering nearby.

More worryingly, he noticed a crowd was gathering uncomfortably close to the danger.

Damnation! This can't be good. "Lucius, where's Staff Sergeant Cenus?"

"I've ordered him to double the guard, bring the entire camp to the ready, and to send a squad of Lieutenant Smith's men here on the double. You'll see why when Sebbi explains things to you."

Tiberius turned his attention to the former terrorist leader. While he had been talking, she had crept forward and was now peeking inside the command building at something just out of his sight.

What in Pluto's name is going on?

Realizing the centurion was waiting behind her, Sebbi backed carefully away from the entrance and ushered Tiberius to one side. Lowering her voice, she said, "It started about thirty minutes ago. We were all at work, and people started going down with severe nausea. Headaches, dizziness, feeling sick, and so forth. I thought it must be a bug someone picked up, or perhaps something they'd eaten. Then I started experiencing sudden bouts of vertigo myself. Every time it came and went, a tingling sensation crawled across my skin, as if I were covered in needles. Coincidentally, the equipment also began to fritz out. One second it was fine, the next we'd lose power and suffer signal degradation. At first I assumed it might be something to do with an atmospheric anomaly, or a solar flare. But the bursts kept coming in waves. That's when it hit me . . ."

"What did? What hit you?"

"A similar incident witnessed by the Special Forces guy, Lieutenant McDonald, and his team out at Rhomane's space-port a few months ago. I'd read the mission report regarding what happened to him aboard the executive cruiser, *Seranette*."

"You mean the magical doorway generated by the Horde demon?"

"That's right. Call me paranoid, but I think we've got something similar happening right here. Its coalescing much more slowly than the ones we're used to, but it's definitely forming."

Tiberius gasped. "How? I thought our shields and the proliferation of iron in this region would keep us safe and undetected."

"We all did. Whether that's the reason for the void's slow manifestation or not, we'll soon find out. But if I were you, I'd get one of those micro-gravity mines ready. Or a good half dozen, just in case."

A sound suggestion.

Tiberius was about to issue the order when an unnerving sense of dislocation washed across him, forcing him to stagger and brace himself against the doorway. He leaned too hard and found himself spilling through the entrance onto the decking just inside the control room.

"Tiberius!" Sebbi yelled.

Others rushed forward to assist, but they were too late.

Allowing his momentum to take him, Tiberius rolled for-ward and came up onto one knee in a battle-ready posture. He drew his gladius and fought to regain his equilibrium, which for some reason still seemed caught in a whirlwind of vertigo-inducing motion.

An asperity hung in the air before him. A rent in the very fabric of space that confounded the eye, set his teeth on edge, and made him want to spill the contents of his stomach onto the floor.

A portal! Inside our defenses. I must warn the others . . . and Rhomane. If they can do this here, they might—

The gyre flared and solidified into a more defined form. A pulse of light carrying the force of an earthquake radiated outward, bowling Tiberius over. He hit the ground hard, and his blade was knocked from his grasp. Clattering loudly across the floor, it came to rest against the legs of an adjacent computer station. He scrabbled forward, intent on recovering the only thing that might make a difference between life and death.

Breathlessness gripped him, and it felt to Tiberius as if one of the gods of Rome had reached into his chest and squeezed the air from his lungs.

Gagging for breath, he watched helplessly as a huge bulk manifested from out of the gateway. Wreathed in a scarlet and purple nimbus, its crown blazed brightly under the glory of the violet and blue flames that circled like dancing fangs about its head.

I'm done for. And there's nothing I can do about it except die like a man.

Struggling to his feet, Tiberius charged the monster. A stifled gasp alerted him to someone behind him. He didn't have time to wonder who had been foolish enough to follow him inside.

The Horde Master anticipated his move. Reacting faster than Tiberius thought possible, the Boss swatted him aside like a bothersome insect. A moment's agony, where every nerve seemed set ablaze in a sea of acid, ate its way into his soul. Tiberius collided with the opposite wall, bounced and fell, drained and exhausted at the ogre's feet.

Finish what you came to do! his mind screamed.

The monster did exactly that, only not in the way Tiberius expected. Dropping into a crouch, the Controller slammed its paws together. A shimmering curtain bloomed outward. Rippling like water, it expanded to encompass the entire office, effectively sealing it off from the outside world. Once done, the Master took its time to survey its surroundings.

Tiberius followed the ogre's gaze as it came to rest on his gladius. The beast made no attempt to avoid it. Instead, it lumbered swiftly toward the discarded weapon as if it were a trophy to be claimed and cherished.

A halo of concentrated power blossomed into view around the monster's wrist. It stooped to retrieve the sword, exercising great care to lift the prized possession by its ivory hilt.

Why is it not dying? How can it possibly survive the touch of . . . ?

The Boss strode toward him. It stood within touching distance, brandishing the sword above him. Tiberius fought his way to his feet and braced himself. *I'll not die on my knees.* "Get it over with," he snarled.

Instead of attacking him, the beast stabbed the tip of the blade into the floor. It carved a circle through the decking, around Tiberius. Once completed, it retreated a few steps before cutting another line, this one from left to right, in front of itself.

With infinite caution, the ogre placed the weapon on the ground between them. Stepping back toward the vortex, it paused and drew itself up to full height. After prodding the tip of one talon against its chest, the brute pointed toward the line. Then it swept its claws forward and reversed its hand, so the spurs were uppermost. Its form flared into terrifying clarity. As it did so, it made an aggressive clenching motion and slammed its fist into the open palm of its other hand.

Comprehension dawned in Tiberius. Noting his reaction, the Horde Master inclined its great head, reentered the portal, and vanished. As the asperity winked out of existence, so did the force field surrounding the command center.

A clamor broke out as legionnaires and cavalrymen, all armed to the teeth, came piling in through the doors. Fanning out, they filled the interior of the room with iron, and a barrage of questions.

Ignoring them all, Tiberius slumped to the floor and let the relief wash through him. Sebbi Farah lay huddled beneath one of the desks on the far side of the office. *So, you were my mystery observer.* He could see the horror and confusion etched across her features, and his heart went out to her for he felt exactly the same.

She scampered forward through the press of legs and repeated offers of assistance and made her way to his side. Flopping down next to him, she hissed, "What the hell is going on? Why go to the trouble of expending all that energy to breach our defenses just to draw some symbols on the floor?"

Tiberius laughed and shook his head. Not to be rude, but the simple release of tension was causing him to unwind in a time-honored fashion among soldiers.

In response to her look of outrage, he said, "You mentioned before that something here was similar to what happened to Lieutenant McDonald at the spaceport. Especially the second time. It was almost as if the beasts were trying to communicate instead of fight, yes?"

"Yes. Go on."

"Apart from the fact it didn't try to eat us today, I think you may be right." Cocking his thumb toward the signs, he added, "In fact, I'm sure of it."

"Why? Did you manage to fathom what they mean?"

"Oh, I understand only too well. About ten years before I was born, Gaius Popillius Laenas, a consul of Rome, was sent as an envoy to prevent a war between Antiochus IV Epiphanes of Syria and the citizens of Egypt. At the time, Egypt was a protectorate of our empire. For reasons unknown to me, the Macedonian didn't think the senate would respond all that vigorously to his incursion. He was wrong.

"Protected only by a small contingent of guards, Laenas met the pretender within the city of Alexandria, and told him in no uncertain terms to abort his attack and leave. Of course, Antiochus wasn't impressed to be met and ordered away from his hard-won prize by someone he saw as a mere lackey. So he tried to stall for time. Imagine his shock when Laenas used his staff of office to draw a circle in the sand around the king. Not only that, Laenus delivered an ultimatum. *"Before you step out of that circle, give me an answer to lay before the senate."* Of course, when faced with the prospect of conflict with Rome, Antiochus acceded. Only then did Laenas extend the hand of friendship and the possibility of peace."

Looking Sebbi directly in the eye, he concluded, "We've just been warned of an impending attack. And I've got the damndest feeling this visit was staged to make us aware that not all the Horde are happy about that. In fact, someone wants to extend an olive branch."

"From within their own ranks?"

"It certainly looks that way. Which raises all sorts of questions, doesn't it? Thankfully, much more agile minds than mine will get a chance to stew on it . . . ."

Scanning the room, Tiberius located his optio among the growing press of people. "Lucius? Get me Rhomane on the com-link."

Chapter Thirty-One

Weights and Measures

"Before we draw this extraordinary meeting to a close," Mohammed proclaimed formally, "would anyone else like to make a final statement?" He paused to survey the full complement of leaders and command staff the city had to offer. The debate had ground on for over three long hours, but he was impressed to find everyone still keenly alert and paying close attention.

Someone cleared their throat.

I thought he'd be the one to lead the way. "The chair recognizes Lieutenant Alan McDonald." Mohammed gestured to the speaker's circle. "If you please?"

The battle-hardened warrior stood, and with the eyes of the crowd upon him, made his way down the steps. Some spectators murmured words of encouragement as he passed. Most remained silent.

As Mac assumed his position, he was bathed in the ethereal glow of a gentle blue radiance. The metallic voice of the recording sentinel intoned, "You may speak."

"I'm not going to drag things out," he began, fixing both Mohammed and Saul with a cold, hard look. "We've split enough hairs, and been here long enough as it is. Nevertheless, there is something you need to consider when you deliberate your decision.

"It may surprise you to know that despite my gruff exterior, I was a student of the classics in university. I'd like to share an aspect of the tale of Pandora with you, because basically, although most people have heard of Pandora's Box, few actually know the history behind her story.

"The fable tells us that the first human woman, Pandora, was created by the deities Hephaestus and Athena, who acted on instructions from Zeus. However, Zeus, in retribution for the theft of the secret of fire by Prometheus, ordered Pandora to be fabricated from the mundane elements of the earth. He felt it only right that his punishment upon mankind should limit Pandora's power and influence over them. Hephaestus and Athena thought that cruel. Therefore, they saw to it that each of their fellow gods contributed a unique gift to Pandora's makeup, hoping she would be a more philanthropic example to her kin. As a sign of their confidence, the deities entrusted a sacred jar into her care, within which lay all the evils of mankind. Who better, they thought, to safeguard such a device than she who was created to bestow beautiful gifts on others wherever she went?

"You all know the story. Pandora became increasingly inquisitive as to the contents of the vessel in her charge. Although passing centuries and the retelling of this tale changed the identity of the jar into a box, the result is the same. Her curiosity got the better of her, and Pandora peeked inside. Thus were the woes of the world released, leaving only hope to battle against them. For as we now appreciate, once unleashed, they could not be bound or contained again."

"What's your point, Lieutenant?" Mohammed asked. "And why would this parable have any bearing on our eventual decision?"

"I don't think you can see the wood for the trees," Mac said. "Don't get me wrong, I'm not having a go. Things have been crazy around here lately, so it's no wonder certain details got missed. But sometimes you have to take a step back and look at your objective from a different angle."

"Would you be kind enough to clarify those remarks?"

"Certainly. Never forget, I'm a cold-hearted pragmatist. A specialist and a killer, who's walked the halls of a harsh and bloody reality for more years than I care to remember. I'm trained to spot loose threads and make connections. That's how I've stayed alive for so long in such a violent world. And that's why I'm positive you're missing the real issue, even though it appears too fantastic to be true. For example, it's a fact that two people, separated by what, fifteen, sixteen hundred years, were snatched from the jaws of certain death and brought to the other side of the galaxy at a time and place when their particular gifts were needed. It's also true they were privy to some pretty distinctive visions, or dreams. Hell, call them hallucinations if you want to. But try as you might, you can't deny their experiences were too similar in nature to be a coincidence. Especially when you take into account the details of the quest they actually shared together. You know these people. Their characters. Their reputations. They wouldn't come forward unless they were certain they were right. Why then, are you so ready to dismiss their conviction that the salvation of two different worlds depends on us following a course of action revealed to them by a higher power? Why on earth would they dream up a scenario like that? Why would they then make it even more unbelievable by adding a large dose of the Horde and their damned vortexes into the equation?"

Mohammed snorted to himself. *Nice one, Mac. Because, of course, they* wouldn't *dream of making up such hogwash.* "So, what threads do you think we've missed?"

"The ones that have been right under your noses all along. For years you've fought a losing battle against the Horde. Then we showed up. The ninth intake. Because of us, you got used to the idea of iron as a deterrent. Because of us, the Horde began making repeated attempts to communicate instead of tearing you apart on the spot. And for the first time, *because of us,* you gained an experienced shaman who could not only make sense of the smorgasbord of cryptic episodes we've been inundated with since, but who could also act as a mentor to a hidden diamond within your own ranks. Why the changes? Why now? Why the corresponding visions? Whatever your beliefs, there are just too many fluky events happening left, right, and center to ignore the obvious.

"I mean, c'mon. Do you seriously think yesterday's incident out at the mining site was a coincidence? For God's sake, just think of what our beastly friends had to go through to penetrate the null-point defenses. In an area saturated with iron? In a camp full of heavily armed people, where just one prick of the blood metal would mean instant death?"

Damn, but that's a good argument. Mohammed glanced at Saul, trying to gauge his reaction. As usual in situations like this, his closest friend wore the blankest poker face he had ever seen.

The lieutenant must have caught the brief exchange for he concluded, "If by any chance you're still undecided, don't worry. I've saved the best for last. I take it you all remember my little experience out at the spaceport? You know, when I led the teams to retrieve the *Promulus* and *Tarion Star*?" He waited while the command staff acknowledged his statement. "Have any of you, at any time, stopped to consider this little stunner? How would a mindless monster from another part of the galaxy know to warn us with the example of Pandora? How would it have heard of the name, much less understood the parable behind the story?"

A tangible shock radiated around the auditorium. Everything went still.

Stuff me! How did we miss that *little doozy?*

Pandemonium erupted, filling the chamber with shouts of support and calls for further debate.

Mac stood silently amid the chaos, staring directly into Saul's eyes. Then he turned his attention to Mohammed. Cocking his head to one side, the soldier raised an eyebrow as if mocking them both for their lack of insight. He spun on his heel, and strode away from the circle.

"Order!" Mohammed shouted, his amplified voice lifting above the din. "Please, ladies and gentlemen, remember where we are."

As Mac made his way back up the steps to reclaim his seat next to Jayden Cole, the ruckus subsided.

Mohammed didn't miss the repeated backslaps and handshakes Mac received along the way. *He's a popular man. And as sharp as a pin . . . .*

He then remembered to consider his friend's reaction.

Saul's blank expression had been replaced by a wide-eyed look of amazement. Trying to diffuse the awkwardness of the situation, Mohammed leaned in and whispered, "I know he's a hands-on kinda guy, but by God, he's on the ball. I wouldn't mind that insight being put to better use on the command staff. You've got to admit, he sees things differently than the rest of us."

Saul grunted. "You've got that right. He damned near took my balls off with that one. We'll discuss it as soon as this . . . circus is over. I don't know how many more slaps in the face I can take."

"Now don't get sulky," Mohammed chided, "you know it wasn't personal. Not with him. He's not afraid to speak his mind, and we need his kind of steel to keep us on our toes. Like it or not, that was one hell of a delivery . . . hang on a second."

Mohammed noticed a measure of calmness had been restored, so he addressed the room. "The chair thanks Lieutenant McDonald for his most insightful address." He surveyed the hall once more. "Anyone else? Perhaps someone who is willing to be a little . . . gentler?"

His attempt at humor worked. Bursts of barely suppressed laughter and a smattering of brief applause resounded around the chamber.

Three people stood up. Ayria Solram, Stained-With-Blood, and Cathal MacNoimhin. *Hello? This might drag on.*

"If the chair wouldn't mind," Ayria called out, "we've each prepared a very brief statement. Can't we just say a sentence or two from here?"

The command team regarded each other before shrugging in agreement. Mohammed replied, "The chair recognizes Ayria Solram, Stained-With-Blood, and Cathal MacNoimhin. If you could please wait a moment for the recorder sentinels to come over to you?"

An orb materialized over each of their heads. A familiar light radiated down over Ayria first, and the drone declared, "You may speak."

"Look," Ayria began, "I freely admit I haven't got a clue why I saw the things I did. I just know I experienced them as if they were as real and corporeal as the room we're in now. I'm a doctor, sworn to save life in any way I can. Perhaps that's why I'm so adamant we need to listen to what's been revealed. In fact, I'm utterly convinced we should. Please don't dismiss the visions just because they're beyond the realms of normal understanding."

She sat back down.

Eh? She wasn't kidding when she said they'd be brief.

The next sentinel introduced Stained-With-Blood. The distinguished old man took his time to survey the crowd before speaking. "Once again I stand before you as spokesman for the First Peoples of the Cree. Although you have little regard for our ways, we know the wisdom of following Napioa's guidance. If the choice were up to us, we would take the path he has revealed to enlightenment. However, as we now belong to a greater community, we will add our strength to whatever course you deem worthy."

Bowing formally, he reclaimed his seat among his fellow chieftains.

Then it was Cathal MacNoimhin's turn. After being invested, he said, "The five tribes are united under my lead. We don't pretend to understand much of the dark deeds and fey tidings that have taken place of late. The only thing we know for certain is the circle. We are born. We live. We fight, and we die. If we die well, our tales will endure through the generations. And we want our names to live forever. So whatever you decide, Alan McDonald, Saul Cameron, we trust you both. The pair of you carry the blood of our descendants in your veins. Your heritage is true. We will fight for you, either way."

As Cathal slumped down among his clan leaders, a background hubbub sprang up again. All heads turned toward the raised gallery.

Saul gestured, and the din petered out almost immediately.

"It would appear I have a great deal to think about," he murmured, "and it's not something I care to rush. But neither can I delay . . . for too long, anyway." His voice became stronger. "But I've always gone with my gut. It's got me this far, and it's helped us endure. I see no reason to start doubting it now. My dear friends, we will reconvene at twelve noon tomorrow, at which time I will give you my answer."

Saul rose from his seat, nodded briefly to the fellow officers on his command team, and made his way from the hall via a private doorway on the upper tier.

Mohammed felt unnerved. *He's clearly on edge. I'd better get after him and see if he needs help emptying his decanter.* "This meeting has now ended," he declared. "I'll see you all before lunch tomorrow. And please, let the commander be. He's got a lot to weigh up tonight, and the last thing he needs is a stream of constant distractions. If you have any gripes, bring them to me. Understood?"

Seeing that he had most people's agreement, Mohammed left by the same exit and rushed to catch up.

*

Lingering at the extremities of the Gulf of Tears, Angule cast his mind into the darkest depths of the void once more. Gossamer-light, his touch was refined to a superlative degree, giving no indication whatsoever that anyone was concealed within the overlapping layers of reality. The humans in their tiny settlement on the far side of the chasm went about their business with an urgency that reminded him of insects in a nest. But that was understandable. His last visit had frightened them badly.

Hopefully, it will motivate them to an appropriate course of action.

The vext rippled, indicating someone with the appropriate cipher was asking to be let through. Replying with the corresponding pulse, he unlocked the protective wards and watched as the portal solidified, before reforming into a make-shift transport helix.

A brief throb of energy accompanied the moment space-time was turned inside out, and Raum materialized before him. No sooner had she manifested than she slammed her shield into place and sealed the rift behind her.

Her emotions were laced with disgust and fear, an acid-ity that singed his receptors. *Must we meet in such a place, Lega'trix? The discordance of dynamic vitality threatens to desiccate my threshold.*

You know it is necessary, Tribunus, for how else could I have devised a means to penetrate their barriers? The more I learn of the correlation between our matrixes and the iron, the more refined I can make the process, and the swifter our objectives can be achieved.

But does the proximity of so much bane-metal not un-nerve you?

It disciplines me, young Kresh. Focuses my mind. And as I work to reduce the quantity I need to maintain optimum integrity, it reminds me of what is at stake. And really, who would suspect that rebellion would be fomented here; in the very place our codex could be unmade? Now tell me, did you succeed in your mission?

I did, Great One. As you suspected, Imperator Vetis and the fools who are swayed by his bravado reacted as you predicted. They are rousing the children of the Trianium as we speak. Soon, the rest of his cabal will arrive to invest the infants with power.

And who stands with our mighty liege?

Of the Unium? Lega'trexii Geryan, Jahi, Zuul, and Zagam. Of the Duarium, Tribuni Cayyem, Set, Urium, Desh, and Roth.

So, Lega'trexii Saffir, Buer, Foroon, Caym, and To'pesh are with us after all?

Almost, My Lord. To'pesh and Foroon are still undecided.

Angule bristled, agitated by the cowardice displayed by their newest High Circle members. Gripping Raum within a compulsive matrix, he commanded: *Dismiss them from our plans entirely. Unsure of themselves, they play politics at the expense of our future, and cannot be trusted. On no account can they be befriended by any who stand within our covenant. Understood?*

Of course, Lega'trix.

Suppressing his delight at the taste of conflict, Angule took a moment to reestablish serenity. *And what of the enlightened Duarium? Are any among our most recent arrivals infected by a similar reticence?*

Thankfully, no. Tribuni Limun, N'Omicron, and Vual, together with Praefactors Mamone'sh and Orias, are all with us . . . of that I have no doubt.

The Prime Catalyct of the Unium weighed his options carefully. He came to a decision: *Tell our faction to prepare and stand ready. For now, Vetis must think we are all in accord. We will force the issue, but at a time and place of my choosing. Now go, quickly. The hour of release approaches.*

As you command, Great One.

So relieved was she by the thought of leaving that Raum all but fled the Gulf. After she had gone, Angule returned to his musings.

Strange, that so great a fate should fall to ones so frail

Chapter Thirty-Two

Between a Rock and a Hard Place

As the sun began to set behind the Garnet Mountains, a squadron of brave solar beams persisted in navigating the buttress of intervening summits and valleys. The unblemished vista of endless blue liquidity became infused by a wispy gauze of milk-cream mist. A steady evolution of aquamarine to palest yellow, as if pure honey had been poured along the horizon to sweeten the bitterness of impending night.

Jayden Cole closed her eyes and inhaled deeply. Standing in the open window to her suite, situated in one of the tallest towers of the city, this was her favorite time of the day. She reveled in the sting of the westerly breeze in her nostrils, flowing as it did at this time of year from the distant massif. It always made her feel as if those far-off peaks were blowing her a kiss, and she savored the feather-light exhalation that transformed her exposed skin into a living tapestry of goose bumps.

She noticed the light caressing her eyelids grow dimmer. Drinking in the panoramic scene once more, she rested her hand against her stomach and studied the sky as it blushed through burnt umber, peach, and lilac contrasts. It appeared to her as if a child of the gods were at play with crayons in the heavens.

How often we take for granted the simple pleasures set before us each day . . . until it's too late.

Smiling, she glanced behind her at the source of her quandary. Mac lay spread-eagled across the width of her bed; his finely-formed butt and chiseled body a testament to hard living.

I didn't plan for this. I honestly didn't.

Although she'd only known him a short period of time, she felt sure he was the kind of man she could one day come to love and respect. He was kind, patient, considerate, gentle, and always willing to listen. A trait most men found difficult to even contemplate. He always made her feel as if her opinion counted, and that was a very special and rare gift.

But what to do? Should I allow myself to fall for him, knowing we might only have a few days left, or keep things as they are? He carries such a weight on his shoulders, I don't want to distract him . . . and yet, he deserves to know.

He stirred. Somewhere deep inside, he must have sensed he was alone on the bed, for he came awake with a start. Catching sight of her, partially silhouetted against the sunset, he smiled, relaxed, and extended his arms. "C'mon, beautiful, you can't just stand there in your birthday suit and expect me to do nothing."

Oh, Mac. I hope fate gives us a chance. All three of us.

*

The door at the rear of the raised gallery opened. Caught in the glare of the brightly lit chamber, Saul Cameron stalled, blinking away his discomfort while he allowed his eyes to adjust. He immediately became aware of a crisscross of chatter from the main floor below. It cut off almost instantly once he was spotted, and the already electric atmosphere ramped up to a whole new level.

Arrangements had been made to ensure those leaders and section heads that couldn't be here in person would be linked through by a real-time feed. He was glad to see that several large screens had been set up around the outer edge of the auditorium to facilitate this. They crackled to life as he took his seat, and more than a dozen sentinels assumed their stations at various points around the room.

Saul had also insisted that his discourse be broadcast live. He wanted to minimize the risk of disruptive rumors harming morale whilst ensuring every department had an appropriate heads-up of any imminent changes.

Out of habit, he glanced around the huge, U-shaped command tier, looking to exchange greetings with his closest friends and advisors. But, of course, they weren't up here today, and without his staff about him the area felt vast and lonely. The clock in the ceiling console blinked onto 12:00, and a soft chime announced it was midday.

Placing an activation crystal into its receptacle, he waited for his notes to load onto the holo-screen and prepared to deliver his verdict.

Here goes nothing.

"Thank you all for coming. I know many of you were unable to sleep last night, worrying about what would transpire today. I also understand how opinion has become divided over the past week, due to . . . unforeseen and unexpected interventions from the most remarkable of sources. One of my responsibilities as commander is to keep us all together, bonded into one big happy family. That's vital, now more than ever, and especially in this place. You know the saying, *"United we stand, divided we fall."* Well, I'm not going to let what we've worked so hard to achieve be discarded by the wayside. That's why I made a promise to deliver my decision today, and explain the reasoning behind it.

"None of us had any choice about being brought here. The specifics of the *why* and *how* were entirely beyond our control. But death's like that. It's entirely random, and doesn't extend the courtesy of asking permission before it comes knocking on your door. And the simple fact of the matter is—we're dead to the folks back home. Never forget that.

"The transference to Arden wasn't without conditions, either. The Architect was tasked to choose the best possible candidates to assume a sacred trust. A duty; to care for the dormant seeds of a ruined civilization in the hope of re-genesis at some time in the future. That's one hell of a responsibility. But we stood up to the challenge, didn't we?"

A multitude of heads nodded in agreement, for in this, Saul knew they were united.

He continued, "How we failed in the past, and how we're managing now—especially since the arrival of the Ninth—are some of the aspects I considered. Obviously, in recent months, new doors of opportunity have been opened to us, affording us all sorts of benefits we've never had the luxury of enjoying before. It's been no easy task, because along with the mundane, everyday strides forward we've made, there have been other elements I had to take into account. Strange, unexplainable things that stretch the bounds of reason. It put a lot of pressure on me, I can tell you, and the urge to drain my decanter was always there. But you'll be glad to know I managed to abstain."

A swell of laughter broke out, especially among those who knew Saul and his habits well.

"However, it saddens me to tell you I can't say the same for Mohammed." He smiled. "*He* is sleeping off a case of bath-mat tongue as I speak."

The outburst grew louder, and spread to the furthest corners of the hall.

Relieved his gamble at humor had paid off, Saul risked a smile in return and raised his hand for order.

Once peace was restored, he said, "Although I've lightened the mood a little by sharing a joke with you, I assure you, I didn't treat the issue before me with the same frivolity. Despite what some here might think, I listened to what everyone had to say. I've been up all night, running through mission reports with the sentinels and the Architect's avatars to obtain as full a picture as possible. We scrutinized the ancient histories, and pored over past clashes with the Horde from every conceivable angle. I also took into account some of the more . . . unusual encounters a number of you have experienced. I felt it only fair to be as accurate as possible in weighing the risks against the rewards, and the dangers against our long-term hopes for survival.

"In the end, I realized I didn't really have a choice at all. I never did. Because of my position, I have to err on the side of caution at all times. You could say, I'm not allowed to have a personal opinion. In the same regard, being popular is not my priority, either. Your welfare and safety is. And when it comes down to it, I've been forced into a no-win situation, because even though I'm trying to safeguard your future, I've had to make a choice that will upset a lot of people. For that, I'm sorry. But when it boils down to it, *we* come first. Arden, despite all she's done for us in extending an opportunity of life, comes second. And the Horde? Well, they don't even enter the equation. Again, I apologize if that sounds harsh, but we were granted a reprieve from death that I don't intend to squander on flights of fancy or what-might-have-been. So, to my answer . . ."

The mood within the room intensified. Without realizing it, most people held their breath, and Saul could see many of them hunch forward on their seats in anticipation.

Stay positive, Saul. Stay strong. "We have a huge range of weaponry and technology at our disposal. Until now, it's been mostly redundant because it's ineffective against the Horde. That would change if they were no longer a problem. Thankfully, due to the safe arrival of the first shipment from the Shilette Abyss, we are abundantly provisioned with iron. More than enough for what I have in mind. And what is that?

"Our settlements throughout the region of the Forest of Tar'e-esh will be abandoned immediately and selected stores and equipment will be relocated to Rhomane over the next month. Personnel will be assigned to new departments. Some here, others up at the astrometrics facility at Boleni Heights, which will be held a little longer to allow us to put the next stage of my proposal into action. You are now on notice, people. We're leaving!

"Don't worry, Ephraim," Saul added, flashing his scientific advisor a brief smile, "Earth is not an option. As you and others have correctly highlighted, we cannot take the chance of inducing a butterfly effect, or any form of paradox for that matter. Multiple universe theories aside, the mere fact we never met ourselves in the past doesn't guarantee we won't screw things up if we're not very careful. So, although we can't go home, we *can* use the *Promulus*, *Tarion Star*, and once we get our hands on her, the *Arch of Winter*.

"Don't forget, we also have access to the entire sum of the Architect's memory, too. That database will be downloaded and utilized to see us to a new home, wherever that may be. Now let me assure you. From what I've seen, the archive is extensive, and there are a lot of choices out there. Quite a few of the Ardenese outposts remained untouched during the Fall, because they were evacuated prior to Horde infestation. With the help of the Architect, I've selected a number of possible candidates, and will hold an appropriate meeting within the next few days to determine a prioritized wish-list. Obviously, it will mean we have to start all over again. But we've done that before. This time we will have the resources of the cruiser to assist us, and of course, whatever other Tec we can fit into the hangar. Then, once we arrive at our selected destination, we will utilize the full manifest of the planet's redundant infrastructure. It's not going to be easy. But at least we will be free of the constant threat of death, for it is my intention to destroy all remaining ships from orbit. Now, I know some of the Horde might survive that attack, but I don't really care. We'll be long gone. They'll be stuck here, forever."

Standing, Saul concluded, "That just about sums everything up. This verdict has been recorded and will be available for download within the next five minutes. As you appreciate, I won't be taking questions at this time, but you can pass on any queries or concerns you have via your appropriate command representative. Thank you."

As swiftly as he could, Saul made his way from the gallery and into the soothing gloom of the transitory corridor.

As he stalked toward his office, he promised himself, *Now it's my turn to put a dent in that decanter.*

*

Ayria Solram entered the counseling suite, nodded to the duty nurse, and made her way toward the private unit at the back of the ward. At her request, this was the only area in the entire city where the televised discourse by Saul Cameron hadn't been broadcast. James Houston's temperament was fragile at best, volatile at worst, and she hadn't wanted to take the risk of him flipping out over anything the commander might say.

Just as well, really. Since the arrival of the Promulus *and* Tarion Star, *he's become more and more unstable. It's such a shame I had to recommit him, but he detests the thought of anyone going near those darn ships. God only knows what would have happened if he'd been allowed to listen in to the announcement on his own.*

Grudgingly, she admitted, *Of course, I can guess how he's going to react now, when I inform him of the result. Still, the news will be better coming from me than anyone else.*

Rapping smartly on the door, Ayria fortified her resolve with a deep breath and entered the room. Houston was sitting on the bed, hugging his knees and rocking backward and forward. He appeared quite calm, and was obviously fixated upon a feature playing on a wall mounted TV. As she approached him, a snippet from the clip intruded on the threshold of her perception.

". . . Appearing from rip-space only seventy decans from the city wall, its pilots were helpless to prevent the inevitable catastrophe . . ."

"Hi there," she said. "It didn't go well, I'm afraid. But then again, I didn't expect it to. I know Commander Cameron has to balance the needs of . . . James, can you hear me?" *He hasn't even registered my presence.*

With infinite slowness, Houston reached to one side and picked up a remote control. Pressing a button, he allowed whatever he was watching to air again. Viewing it from the beginning, Ayria recognized the bulletin immediately.

"That was the awful moment when the Shivan-Estre met her end. For reasons as yet unknown, her navigational beacon malfunctioned. Appearing from

rip-space only seventy decans from the city wall, her pilots were helpless to prevent the inevitable catastrophe.

As with all such vessels, the Shivan-Estre was constructed of super-dense lydium. If not for the fact that Rhomane's own precincts are made of that same fermionic matter, the results would have been far worse than the death of the two crewmen on board and a bright light in the sky. We are going live now to . . ."

"James?" she repeated. "Why are you watching something so sad? You know it'll only upset you."

"Can you hear it?" he drawled, turning toward her at last. "There's something profoundly wrong with . . . the scale and pitch. They're not right. It . . ."

She noticed his pupils were unusually dilated, and he appeared to be dribbling uncontrollably from one corner of his mouth. *This can't be right?*

Annoyed, she snatched his chart from the counter and checked his medication.

"We're being warned, you know," Houston continued to mumble. "It . . . *This* is a portent of what will happen if we . . . if I don't . . ."

For goodness' sake! No wonder he's away with the fairies. That's double the amount of prozetapan I prescribed.

Sitting beside him on the bed, Ayria removed the control from his grasp and cupped his hand within her own. Speaking softly, she said, "Now don't you go getting yourself all worked up. It'll all be over soon. I've come to tell you that we're getting away from here. We'll be leaving the Horde and the city behind, and all our worries along with it."

Something she said hooked his attention. "Really?" He gasped in relief. "Good. Excellent. It's the only way we can be . . . safe."

"Yes, I know. Commander Cameron said that over the next month, we're going to pack our bags, and—"

"How?" The sudden tension in Houston's voice was a stark contrast to his relaxed nature only moments before.

"I'm sorry?" Ayria sat back in shock. Then she noticed the piercing lucidity blazing in his eyes.

"How *exactly* does the commander expect us to flee? Where on this planet does he think it's going to be safe?"

"We're not staying on the planet," she replied, edging further from him, "we've discovered a huge cruiser in orbit, the *Arch of Winter*. It's free of infestation and we're going to use her to travel to—"

"No! No! No!"

Aghast, Ayria backed away toward the door and scrabbled for the emergency button. The change in Houston was frightening. His eyes bulged. The veins on his temples protruded alarmingly. His entire face turned red and the cords on his neck stood out like they would snap at any moment.

Squeezing his temples, he groaned, "You can't. For the love of God, Ayria, you've got to stop them. I'd rather die than be trapped again."

Again? Baffled, she froze on the spot. "James? What are you talking about?"

"Please. You can't . . . aaargh!"

Gripped by a violent seizure, Houston doubled over and thrashed about on the bed. To Ayria, it appeared as if he were fighting off invisible assailants. After a few moments, the mad spasms stopped. Sitting bolt upright, he screamed, "Doctor! Help me. Quickly. It's got me . . . I'm trapped in my own . . . nnngh!"

Houston caught his breath and experienced another fit. This time, his entire body went rigid, arching up as if he were being electrocuted. Just as she thought his spine might snap, he let out a huge whoosh of air and slumped back down on the bed, exhausted.

"Do you need a hand here?"

Ayria jumped, startled by the unexpected voice behind her. Spinning, she discovered Lieutenant McDonald standing in the doorway.

"Mac," she gushed, "thank goodness."

"What's the problem?"

Ayria turned to assess Houston's condition. Although bathed in sweat, he now appeared completely relaxed again, and under the influence of his medication.

What on earth is going on inside his head? Aloud, she replied, "Just another day in the personal hell that is James Houston's sanity, it would appear." Shrugging, she went to physically check on her patient. "I didn't hear you come in. But thanks for backing me up. It got scary there for a moment."

"I'm sorry I surprised you. But I must confess, I didn't know you were here. I came for another reason. Now our proposals have been officially kicked into touch, I didn't think it would do any harm to take a look at Stained-With-Blood's tomahawk. Mohammed only mentioned it to me yesterday, and well, in view of the weird experiences I had with the Horde Master, I thought I'd check it out. Is it true it's made of meteor metal? Pure iron?"

"Yes. Evidently, it's supposed to play a vital role in our future here." She snorted. "As was I, until . . . ."

"I know how you feel. Even though it was a bit of a long shot, it was still a kick in the teeth to have our convictions so utterly squashed, eh? Still, we tried. That's all we could do. The thing is, I totally appreciate where Saul is coming from. He was caught on a knife's edge and had to err on the side of caution." He chuckled. "Doesn't make it any easier though, does it?"

Houston moaned forlornly. Looking toward him, they watched as he lethargically repositioned himself on the bed before turning the recording back on.

"Sorry, Mac," Ayria announced, "it's not here."

"Eh?"

"The tomahawk, Heaven's-Claw. I left it with Saul at the beginning of the week when Stained-With-Blood and I went to see him regarding the visions we'd been having. I'm glad you mentioned it though because I've been meaning to get it back." She gestured toward Houston. "Do you know, it's the only thing I can find that seems to bring him any relief. For some reason, as soon as he holds it, he becomes utterly docile."

"Pity it doesn't have that effect on the Horde," Mac replied, lightheartedly. "Mind you, whatever he's watching now appears to do the trick."

"Oh that. Hmm. Just another past tragedy that highlights why I won't miss this place when we leave." Guiding Mac by the elbow, she said, "C'mon. Let's go hassle Mohammed. If he gives us a hard time about seeing Saul, I'm sure I can pull the doctor's privilege card. After all, the welfare of my patients comes first, and that axe will serve a much better purpose here than just sitting on his desk as a paperweight."

Ayria closed the door quietly behind her. As they walked away, she could just make out a woman's voice as the clip played again.

"... *That was the awful moment when the Shi-van-Estre met her end. For reasons as yet unknown, her navigational beacon malfunctioned ...*"

Chapter Thirty-Three

An Accepted Gambit

Lieutenant Jake Rixton raised his arm into the air and reined 1st Platoon in behind him. He waited for the dust to clear before cupping his hand over his eyes to cut out the glare of the midday sun. He spent a full minute scanning the arrivals terminal of the starport before beckoning his officers forward.

"Sergeant Williams. Divide your section into squads and have them check out the vicinity of the underpass. Not too close, mind. Just enough to draw the attention of any spooks that might be hiding. Stagger your approach so the men can lay down overlapping fields of fire in the event you have to hightail it out of there."

"Will do, Sir. Do you want us to plug any of the bastards if our presence doesn't entice them to show their ugly faces?"

"Good idea. Only one or two, though. Get them riled enough to follow you. We won't be much of a diversion unless we actually make a nuisance of ourselves, eh?"

The men laughed. In the month Jake had worked with them as their lieutenant, he had felt himself grow in confidence and stature. He knew his sense of humor had always been a source of constant refreshment, and he was determined to keep it that way.

Jake turned to his new corporal. "Nick. Would you and your men please do the same along the western perimeter? Go as far as the rear of the hangar pens, then turn back. If you can't flush anybody out, rendezvous with me back here and we'll go for a little jaunt around the refueling stations. Remember. Be obvious, and make as much noise as possible. You know what to do if you're pursued. Holes have been burned into the fencing at regular intervals, so you can either cut across the airfield and regroup at Boleni Mount, or swing back toward Rhomane."

"No problem, Sir."

Both groups galloped off, leaving Jake alone to reflect on the objective of the day's mission. *So it's up to us to keep the Horde distracted, and occupied in this area. Should be simple enough.*

On a whim, he took out a pair of adapted binoculars. Activating the rotational frequency module fitted over the lenses, he studied the area again. *Damn, but it's quiet. Let's hope the boys can change that.*

*

Flavius Velerianus glanced at the modern timepiece on his wrist, then gazed off into the distance. The convoy from the Shilette Abyss was expected to meet up with his mounted equitata at any time, and he was keen to get into the last phase of the operation.

Life had been quite boring for him since his arrival on Arden. His promotion aside, the Ninth had been employed on defensive duties more often than not. As such, even when things got interesting, his squadron of horsemen always seemed reduced to a subsidiary role while others got to test their mettle. Finally, he'd received his first proper assignment, and he was sure it was due to his friend's recent promotion.

Thank you, Marcus.

Standing in his stirrups, Flavius tried to assess the route ahead. It was no use. The shimmering heat waves radiating up off the ground made it look as if the topaz-blue canopy of the sky had melted and spilled over onto the asphalt canvas below. The more he looked, the more frustrated he became as the line of the road streaked into rivulets of silver and gray contrasts. They confused the eye, confounding his ability to judge distance.

Why couldn't the forest have extended this far and saved us the trouble?

He checked behind. Mount Caglioso dominated the skyline, looking exactly as it had an hour ago. Huge, overwhelming, and of no use at all.

Bloody temperature extremes.

He turned to his optio, Claudius Vergilius. "Claudius. Assign archers to the roving pickets and dispatch a stick of riders along the highway until they make contact with Tiberius and his contingent. I know they're heavily laden with as much ore and equipment as they can carry, but this is getting ridiculous. We'll be sitting ducks out here if anything happens, and won't have the option of making a run for it."

"Right away, Sir."

As Claudius set about organizing the men, Flavius recapped the different phases of the day's exercise. Doing so made him appreciate how essential it was for everyone to play their part and be on time. Casting his eyes heavenward, he noted the milk-white disc of Se'ochan, Arden's moon, riding high in the sky.

That's so odd. I don't think I'll ever get used to seeing the moon during the day. But I keep forgetting, conditions are perfect here for that.

His reflection reminded him of another important phase currently underway. He glanced at the moon again. *I wonder if they're having more fun than I am?*

*

Ephraim Miller kept a careful eye on Asa Montgomery and Angela Brogan's vital signs. The AI mind-mesh interface they were hooked into was an extremely sophisticated piece of kit. Unlike the training simulators they had used, or the simplified models fitted aboard the *Promulus* or *Tarion Star*, these were designed to operate a five hundred thousand long ton deep space cruiser.

"How's it going, guys?" he asked.

"A little disorienting," Asa replied. "I have access to the inter-solar system, aqua and deep space rip-drives. It's as if I'm within the internal schematics of each respective engine chamber. I've managed to initiate a full diagnostic to see how we stand, and if there'll be any tinkering to do to bring this baby up to operational status."

"Excellent. Well done. Let me know when you've managed to initiate a full core override. Then we'll get the rest of our pilots up here for a little one-on-one with their new plaything."

"Roger that."

"And talking of pilots," Ephraim continued, "Angela? How are you enjoying your introduction to the *Arch of Winter*?"

"Bloody hell!" she squealed. "I always thought diamonds were a girl's best friend, but this? It's . . . it's orgasmic. Every present you can think of under the Christmas tree orgasmic."

Heads on the command deck turned in surprise. Beside her, Asa almost choked, then burst out laughing.

"Er . . . thank you for that. Not quite the explanation I was looking for, but succinct enough to convey the depth of your meaning."

Ephraim was perturbed to see almost everyone's shoulders shaking in poorly concealed mirth. *Children!* Pressing quickly on, he added, "Would you be so kind as to restrict your comments to those I can use to direct the technicians? You know. Those lesser mortals who will be preparing the *Arch of Winter*, and making her flight ready?"

"Of course. I apologize. But for a pilot, this is ambrosia. Like being able to fly yourself. The network meshes with you and connects on a level I've never dreamed of. Although it's on safety, I only have to think of a function or a command and that particular subroutine enlarges within the neural interface. The others are still there, but operating in the background. I've been practicing to see how many systems I can manage at once, and it's quite overwhelming and fatiguing, I can tell you."

"Will it be manageable in the timeframe we're looking at?"

"For basic maneuvers? Yes. Although I can see now why there are two main chairs. Essentially, the Ardenese operated a buddy system, like we did. Helmsman and navigator. The captain maintains an overview through his link, and is able to issue commands and basically keep tabs on what's occurring where in his ship. But the pilots have to manage some pretty complex mediums. So they split the workload. The sooner we get our guys familiarized, the better."

"And what about the onboard AI?"

"I can answer that," Asa interjected. "Sorry to butt in, but that was one of the programs I came across as I was working my way through the startup sequencers. It looks like the captain assigned her to maintain engine integrity when they abandoned ship. She's the one who manipulated the magnetic resonance chamber protecting the core to produce the dampening field surrounding us."

"She?"

"Yup. They gave her a gender . . . and a name. Serovai. It's based on the Ardenese word for security."

Amazing! "Well, I feel safer already. Please carry on, both of you."

Ephraim pottered about the deck for a few moments, and could plainly see everyone else was also hard at work. He checked his watch. *Amazing indeed. We're well ahead of schedule. I'll give it another half hour before I call for the* Tarion Star *to join us with the next contingent.*

*

Jake Rixton was growing increasingly anxious.

Twice now, his patrols had returned without having encountered a single grunt. On the first occasion, he hadn't been too concerned. It was a huge facility after all, and when the Horde slept, they liked to congregate in confined, well protected places. There were many such locations scattered about the spaceport and it would take all day to check them out. So while he didn't have time to examine every square inch of their target, he had been concentrating on areas of known infestation.

Radio reports had confirmed that, as usual, a whole mob of their enemy was assailing the wall back at Rhomane, a ritual they practiced on a daily basis from sunup to sundown.

So, they're about. But why not here?

He watched as both sections came back at virtually the same time, empty-handed again. They reined in and looked about, confusion on their faces.

That's just under three hours on site without contact.

"Sergeant Williams. Get on the radio to Boleni Heights, will you? Update them as to our situation and lack of Horde activity. Then ask to speak with Mark Stevens. Tell him I want a personal chat."

"On it now, Sir."

Jake addressed his platoon while contact was being established. "Men, I don't know about you, but I don't like coming this far with nothing to show for it. By all accounts, this is the quietest it's ever been out here, and while I would normally enjoy that . . . it doesn't sit right in my stomach."

"What are we gonna do, Sir?" Corporal Spencer chipped in. "Go hunting?"

"More like fishing. Why should we put ourselves out when they obviously don't want to play? There are three or four hours of good sunlight left. So I propose we take the long route home. South, through the starport itself, then we'll cut east around the lower slopes of Mount Boleni. You never know, we could get lucky."

"Mark Stevens on the line for you, Sir," Sergeant Williams advised.

"Thank you." Jake took the com-set from his colleague and trotted several yards to one side. Lowering his voice, he said, "Mark? Can you hear me?"

"Loud and clear, Jake. Go ahead."

"Look, I need your help. I know we're supposed to remain covert until the time comes for our own evacuation, but there's something not quite right out here. In a minute, I'll be leading 1st Platoon on a patrol through the facility itself. That'll take a couple of hours. Then we'll swing around the ass end of Boleni Heights and approach the lab from the opposite direction. In the meantime, I was wondering if you could use your influence to get us a squadron of flyers in the air?"

"Sounds interesting. Why do you need them?"

"Well, I was thinking . . ."

*

The wavy, disjointed blobs they had been studying for the last fifteen minutes gradually clarified into recognizable profiles.

At last! Turning to his optio, Flavius delivered such a hearty slap on the back it almost took the man out of his saddle.

"Excuse my exuberance," he said, "but things have dragged on for so long, I thought we'd never see the end of this damned road."

A voice from somewhere in front called, "Riders!"

Flavius looked back down the highway at the approaching knot of horsemen, and his face broke into a wide grin. "Ha! Look, Claudius. I'd recognize those flapping arms anywhere. Do you see how he looks like a chicken trying to escape the slaughterhouse?"

Laughter erupted about him. It was a welcome reprieve from the hours of creaking leather, jingling metal, and relentless clip-clopping that had grated on his nerves. *Good to see you, you old rogue.*

In less than a minute, Tiberius Tacitus, Lucius Scipio, and Wilson Smith pulled up beside them. The two centurions clasped arms.

"Well met, Tiberius," Flavius boomed.

"And you, my bowlegged friend. I noticed the reaction of the men around you as I rode in. Were you discussing the merits of my riding style again?"

"You call that a style? You have the grace of a lump of granite. Did they not have any oxen at your little fort you could have utilized?"

"That they did. But alas, I ate it in one sitting."

The two men hooted again, while the legionnaires in their company slapped their thighs. The appetite of Centurion Tiberius Tacitus was as well known as his lack of riding finesse.

The two soldiers addressed each other in mock anger.

"So why the delay?" Flavius barked. "It'll be nightfall before we make Rhomane now. Not a good time to be abroad with the likes of you. You'll frighten the men."

"I'm not sorry about that. I had no choice. Something called a sonic equalizer blew out on our main skidder. The one carrying all the ore. Without it, the blasted things don't float. It's like cutting the legs off your horse and expecting it to still be capable of trotting along."

"Big improvement in your case, then?"

"True. Damn hard to push, as well. It took Terri and Stefan Hollander nearly two hours to repair. I was going to send riders ahead, but Lieutenant Smith reminded me of the recent warning we received, delivered to me in person by a Horde Master no less. Thinking about it, I decided he was right and kept the convoy together until we could move as a single unit."

"Fair enough, I'd probably have done the same in your shoes . . . ."

An unspoken question hung in the air.

The two men stared at each other.

"And?" Tiberius growled.

"What was it like? Coming face to face with a devil in the flesh? And a bloody beast master, at that?"

Tiberius looked thoughtful. "Well, I can honestly say I'll never wear those particular undergarments again. The whole experience was—"

A dull *thud* came from the back of the column, cutting Tiberius dead.

Every head turned in that direction.

What on earth was that? "Tiberius? Is there anything you haven't told me?"

A plume of smoke ascended from the midst of the cavalcade.

"Oh, for Mercury's sake," Tiberius replied, "it's probably the skidder. The Hollanders are quite skilled as mechanics but they didn't have the right equipment to carry out a full re–"

Another, larger report throbbed about them.

Flavius stood in his stirrups. *Was that an explosion?*

The dual tones of a cavalry bugle and legion horn split the silence.

We're under attack? "Tiberius, rally your men. Claudius, alert the advance riders. Lieutenant Smith, spread your troops among the civilians. I understand some of them are equipped with modern weapons? Ensure they—"

Bang!

Flavius ducked reflexively as Wilson Smith fired at him.

Bang! Bang!

Screams erupted all around, filling the air with sudden pain and terror.

Why is he firing at me? "What the blazes are you—?"

An overwhelming concussion lifted Flavius from his saddle and sent him spinning through the air. Disoriented, he landed hard, the air knocked from his lungs. Gasping for breath, he became aware of an overpowering ringing noise in his ears. A sickening, burning smell issued from nearby. Automatically rolling to one side, he scrambled for his sword and pushed himself to his knees.

Flavius bumped into something. He saw the charred flesh of a severed arm. Lying next to it, face down, was his optio.

"Claudius," he croaked. Scampering forward, he rolled his comrade over. "What hit us? Claudius? Can you . . . ?"

It was only when he looked closely that Flavius realized his second-in-command was dead. Although open, his eye sockets were two empty wells, exuding a revolting, greasy black vapor that dissipated quickly in the breeze.

No! It can't be.

Blinking furiously, he looked up through a tangle of horses' legs and billowing dirt. Nightmare apparitions flared through a kaleidoscope of neon blue, and strontium red and black. Skipping in and out of view, they menaced anything they could get their claws on.

Many didn't get far.

Again and again, one troll or another would loom out of the press only to disappear in a conflagration of blinding light and heat as it was cut down by iron.

Wilson Smith sawed at the reins of his horse, maneuvering closer. He shouted something Flavius couldn't hear. The young officer called again, pointing repeatedly at a spot behind Flavius. "Behi . . . you . . . com . . . out!"

He drew his rifle from its scabbard.

Flavius felt as if a lead weight had been dropped on his neck. Groaning, he managed to turn, and caught his breath in alarm. There, not ten feet away, a huge scarlet and blue monstrosity loomed above him. Clothed in a violet nimbus, and crowned by four dancing flames, the Horde Master spotted him, bared its fangs and talons, and closed on his position.

Steadying himself with one hand, Flavius kicked for all he was worth, trying to scuttle backward. As he did so, he reached for his blade. Sound returned, and a discordance of screaming and yodeling wails assailed his senses from all sides.

Several shots rang out. The Boss didn't even blink. Protected as it was by an invisible barrier, the bullets ricocheted harmlessly away.

Seven feet.

Another fusillade rang out. That too was swatted aside as if it presented nothing more than a minor hindrance.

Get up, man, Flavius chided himself, *face this brute like a legionnaire.*

Five feet.

With a mighty heave, Flavius staggered erect. *I'll not back down.* Raising his sword high, he issued a defiant challenge. "Come then, demon, let's see who wins this day."

Three feet.

The apex of the monster's shield bloomed scarlet and yellow. A spitting sound snapped and crackled about it, as if flesh were being seared against red-hot metal. Simultaneously, a deafening volley of rapid fire disoriented both man and beast.

The Controller staggered backward, still alive, but with its defenses in obvious disarray. Flavius heard the sound of hooves and the whine of engines behind and above him.

He glanced up. *Flyers? Here? What . . . ?*

Then a heavier machine gun opened up, peppering the ground around him in fountains of dirt. Where the iron bit into the quintessence of an unprotected monster, its threshold sparked and erupted in angry bursts until its equilibrium was obliterated in a self-consuming implosion of flames and anguish.

Propelled backward, Flavius tumbled over and over before coming to rest on his knees once more. Hunching forward, he retched, the contents of his stomach spilling onto the soil. Sitting back on his ankles, he drew in a ragged breath of air, but couldn't prevent the scene from dissolved into a spinning vortex. The hardened soldier felt the world slipping away from him. Numbed, he was helpless to prevent his weapon from falling to the ground. Moments later, darkness descended, and his consciousness followed.

Chapter Thirty-Four

Second Thoughts

Mohammed began to relax. Although the battle was still underway, the tide had turned and the Horde attack appeared to be petering out.

Thank God Jake Rixton had the foresight to follow his gut feeling. If he hadn't suggested sending the drones out to check along the route, it could have been much worse.

Mohammed zoomed in on the exchange. From above, the scene appeared to be punctuated by angry sparks and violent blooms of light. Bodies and debris littered the ground, but now that Wilson Smith and Tiberius Tacitus had rallied the troops, the only casualties appeared to be those belonging to the enemy. Fresh craters scarred the site of each explosion; they increased by the second.

Whoever had the idea to coordinate their assault with assistance from the flyers is a bloody genius. The combined challenge appears to overwhelm Controller defenses.

He looked again. *But not on every occasion. Hmm. I wonder if that's anything to do with the intelligence Mark Stevens put in? He said there was a noticeable difference in the flames of their crowns. It seemed to correspond to their presence, or energy quotient. If that correlates to strength, then it tends to confirm his theory of a definite rank structure.*

As an analytical man with a keen mind, Mohammed could only nod his head in appreciation. *Brilliant tactics the Horde used. Protected by their shields, the Masters hit first, and targeted the convoy. They took out the lead and midway skidder and killed their crews. Then, having instilled panic and confusion, they unleashed their cannon fodder, and set about picking off any leaders they could find. Astounding.*

He scrutinized the console next to him. The live-time link was constantly updated as the names of casualties streamed in. It made unpleasant reading.

Glancing back at the tactical display, Mohammed saw that the next wave of flyers were still ten or eleven minutes out. Equipped with micro-gravity mines, they would make all the difference.

But they're still a long way off.

He had an idea. Standing, he caught the attention of the duty communications operator, Serena Taylor.

"Serena, patch me through to the *Arch of Winter*. Quick as you can."

His main monitor wavered, and the face of Ephraim Miller appeared. "Ephraim, how goes it up there? Enjoying the view?"

"I haven't really had time for it yet, Mohammed. We've been working round the clock, trying to establish an acceptable network between our systems and the onboard AI program, Serovai. Although she's recognized us as 'friends-not-foe,' her inbuilt safety protocols are preventing a full system power up. Brent and Asa are communicating with her now, via mind-mesh interface, but even with the Architect to back them up, it's slow going. I'll be glad when the Shilette Abyss crew finally returns. I'm going to ask you to send that computer expert up to assist us. What's her name? Sebbi Fary?"

"Sebbi Farah," Mohammed corrected, "and she's not here yet. The mining team ran into a hitch, which is why I'm contacting you. We need your help."

"That's unfortunate. In what way?"

"They were ambushed by a contingent of Horde Masters. And before you say it, I know. We hardly see sight nor sound of them for years, and now a whole bunch of them lead a surprise attack. Anyway, our lads and lasses have managed to hold their own, especially against the run-of-the-mill variety we're used to, but they could do with a hand to send the Controllers packing. A squadron of flyers equipped with micro-gravity mines is on the way there as we speak, but they're still ten minutes out. That's far too long. I was hoping you could use the *Arch of Winter*'s transporter system to lock onto the drones and push them along a bit. What do you think?"

"Good idea. I'll speak with Serovai and see what I can do."

Ephraim moved out of picture.

While he waited, Mohammed turned back to study the casualty list. The computer was dividing the inventory into three columns. Those who were dead, critically injured, or receiving treatment. Skimming through the growing number of fatalities, he recognized too many people he knew well, and was forced to bite back his anger.

Come on. Hurry up!

Ephraim's visage reappeared.

"Good news. Although temperamental, Serovai won't dither when she recognizes a true enemy. She has released targeting scanner locks and is awaiting the rough coordinates for transport."

"Hang on a second . . . ." Mohammed checked the tactical map once more. "The drones will be easily recognizable to her as they're equipped with Ardenese transponders. If she focuses her efforts on an area roughly twenty-five to thirty miles southeast of Rhomane's starport, she should pick them up. They are to be jumped to this location." Mohammed sent a twelve-digit grid reference. "Ask her to act quickly. Time is of the essence."

He turned from the monitor. "Serena? Link us in to the lead flyer of the backup pod. I want to see what's happening."

"On it, Boss."

The main wall-screen burst to life, showing a rapidly rolling vista of hills and valleys from a height of about two hundred feet. Before it, looming ever closer, a dark splotch signified the presence of distant forests. The signal abruptly broke off. The monitor went blank, and the sound of static filled the control room with a deafening hiss.

Moments later, the connection was reestablished. A picture resolved into the stark contrast of a wide asphalt road randomly dotted with people and vehicles, bordered by scrubland on both sides.

The alpha flyer came to an immediate halt while its onboard computer reassessed its new position. The edge of the screen turned red and a filter rolled into place across the camera. A series of cryptic commands scrolled down one side of the readout as the lead drone distinguished human friendlies from Horde targets. Within seconds, it started issuing orders for an attack. A multitude of dark shapes dropped from the sky and began bombing runs.

Within the control room, everything went quiet.

Sporadic gunfire continued to zing about at ground zero as the Masters reluctantly retreated. As yet, no one in the human cavalcade had realized a fresh wave of support was descending from above.

That abruptly changed.

From Mohammed's perspective, the panorama fractured inward at multiple points, as if a smattering of raindrops had been sprayed across the flyer's lens. Those Bosses closest to the deformities were seized by opposing tidal forces, and were mercilessly stretched and compressed in rapid succession.

Black voids bloomed into view at the exact center of every anomaly, quickly followed by a wash of spiraling vortexes.

Blazing flares marked the departure of a number of the more alert Masters. Several others were not so fortunate. Too late, they summoned their portals to escape. The conflicting gravities generated by the quantum mines prevented the gateways from stabilizing. Unable to find a proper anchor in space-time, the rifts shredded, adding their potential to an already volatile mix.

For a brief moment, the wildly contorting creatures were captured in photonegative agony, caught between reality and oblivion. Then their thresholds were ripped apart, and they exploded in a flash of blinding light.

A series of inverse shockwaves slammed together. Swelling, they intensified into a glowing maelstrom before refracting away in a secondary blast. Dirt, scrub, and a number of smaller objects could be seen billowing outward. Everyone within a quarter mile radius was swatted to the floor, as if felled by a massive sucker punch. Nearby trees swayed under the influence of hurricane-force winds, only to snap back moments later as air rushed in to fill the vacuum created by the explosion.

An eerie calm descended.

"Did you see that, Ephraim?" Mohammed asked.

"Yes! Yes, I did. And I really don't know how to respond."

"You don't have to. I'm the one who has to think of something appropriate to say. Although once we discover the full cost of today's opening gambit by our fiery friends, the commander's bound to want my head on a pike."

Mohammed sighed deeply before continuing. "But do express my thanks to Serovai. Her assistance was most timely, and gratefully received." He was drawn to the casualty list once more. "Actually, seeing as she's in a good mood, would you mind asking her if she's willing to transport a medical relief crew out on site? We've got people injured out there. Dead and dying. Time is of the essence."

"Of course I will. Anything to help . . . Oh!"

"What?"

"It would appear Serovai automatically linked in to our command system when she transferred the flyers. She's been listening in, and has already assessed the situation. This is her recommended response."

Ephraim transferred the AI's suggestions to Mohammed's desk. "When your teams are ready, she'll begin transporting them out to the highway."

"Thank you, Ephraim. That'll be all."

Stunned, Mohammed activated the report and perused its contents.

She's a lot more proactive than the Architect. I wonder why that is?

He yelled, "Serena. I'm sending you a list of protocols to be implemented immediately. Patch through to the *Arch of Winter*'s AI program and initiate the deployment, will you? Doctor Solram is to be beeped, and is to oversee the disposition of her emergency triage unit. Notify Sub Commander De Lacey she's in overall command of the recovery itself. Oh, and alert Lieutenant McDonald, too. His team is always good in a crisis and can provide cover until the area has been cleared. Apologize to everyone on my behalf for my absence. I'm stuck here, delivering bad news."

With that, Mohammed turned his attention to a growing list of pain.

Incident Command System — Mass Casualty Index — Report Form ARC-SeT-1

> *Citizens currently confirmed as deceased:*
> *Adam Wainwright (Mil-Sergeant)*
> *Amelius Tacitus (Mil-Decarus)*
> *Amrita Bahlrati (Civ-Medic)*
> *Andrew Palmer (Civ-Mech)*
> *Anthony Bragg (Civ-Sci)*
> *Claudius Vergilius (Mil-Optio)*
> *Cora Vasquez (Civ-Sci)*
> *Drusus Valerus (Mil-Leg)*
> *Edward Black (Civ-Mtc)*
> *Joseph Black (Mil-Trooper)*
> *Leonard Tam (Civ-Eng)*
> *Lucius Flavius (Mil-Leg)*
> *Matthew Keegan (Civ-Sci)*
> *Publius Martialis (Mil-Decarus)*
> *Quintus Fabius (Mil-Leg)*
> *Samuel Buchanan (Mil-Trooper)*
> *Shuji Tadako (Civ-Sci)*
> *Stefan Hollander (Civ-Driver)*
> *Terri Hollander (Civ-Driver)*
> *Thomas Grahame (Mil-Trooper)*
> *Tiberius Cenus (TessarariusTesserarius)*
> *Zebedee Jones (Mil-Trooper)*
> *Awaiting further command entry . . .*

Hold.
Incoming data . . .

*

Angule's essence flickered between deepest violet and midnight blue, a sure sign he teetered on the verge of cataclysmic expression. Exercising heroic self-control, he managed to strengthen his matrix and swallow down the boiling energies that seethed for release.

Why was I not kept abreast of this development? I am the Prime Catalyct of the Unium. Planning and strategy fall to me.

That, I cannot say, Battlemaster, Lega'trix Saffir replied: *But from what I surmised, it was not a deliberate slight. Circumstance itself may have conspired against us.*

Explain.

You know how Vetis has surrounded himself with lackeys. They plot. They counsel. Bolstering each other's spirits as they feast on their vanities. By all accounts, it was a chance encounter by Tribunus Desh that led to the confrontation. As everyone is aware, she is sensitive to the tones emitted by the bane-metal. She was simply engaged in an orbital of the vext network when she perceived a threat to our codex. Although distant, it tugged at the fringes of her capacity. She went to investigate. From the boasting Vetis and his cabal are currently spreading, Desh discovered a caravan of humans on the main road near to the borders of the green expanse. One of their traveling craft appeared disabled, and its shields had weakened while they undertook repairs. It was full of . . . what do the humans call it? Iron ore. Instead of attacking, she expressed supreme restraint and thought to notify Imperator Vetis. It was he who gathered all available Trianium from the spaceport, and together with those of his faction who were present, Vetis sped to intercept the convoy as it returned to the city. Obviously, because of the danger to our codex, he ensured his Lega'trexii and Tribuni led the assault before unleashing the children of the third tier.

Angule's ire began to cool. *So we are not suspected?*

No, Catalyct. We remain free of taint.

And yet, I sensed discordance among the vitality lattices. Has Lord Vetis tarnished his character by sufferance of loss?

I am afraid so. It has now been confirmed a costly tragedy befell us. Not only were Tribuni Desh and Cayyem lost to the eternal tranquility of night, but Lega'trix Jahi fell along with them. I fear the Cataract of Lost Hopes will resound to the song of mourning for many cycles.

Angule flared. *How is such a thing possible? A Kresh of his stature should have easily coped with the presence of bane-metal. It is an ability we acquire in ascendancy from ignorance. And* he *was Unium.*

Human ingenuity, I'm afraid. The quantum weapons they have devised were dropped in considerable quantities. Several landed on or near Jahi himself as he attempted to initialize the vext. The doorway became warped, and added its potency to the yield of the singularity vortexes manifesting about him. Zuul tells me Jahi's threshold was torn into several pieces before combustion took place. He caused quite a blast.

Realization struck Angule. *This could work to our advantage, brother. For does this not mean our numbers are more evenly matched?*

Alas, it does not. So outraged were Foroon and To'pesh by the affront to our honor that they have pledged their support to Vetis. Although new to our ranks, the addition of two Lega'trexii to his cause tips the balance in his favor.

Nevertheless, I must not allow such recklessness to continue, Angule retorted. *An age of strategy and patient nurture comes to fruition. It cannot be thwarted this close to the end by a lack of courage.*

A new plan of action began forming in Angule's mind. He said: *Saffir, I perceive a way this fiasco may be turned to our advantage. Am I not the Prime Catalyct of the Unium? Should I not be seen to support Vetis in promoting his vendetta?* Lowering the tone of his thoughts, he added slyly: *Of course, these latest developments require an embellishment or two of my own. After all, we don't want the final exhalation of fatal provenance consuming the wrong side now, do we?*

Enraptured, Saffir bristled in delight: *Your orders?*

It is obvious both Unium and Duarium require further training. The devices now employed by the humans are capable of disrupting our enhanced integrity with alarming ease. Therefore, I must devise a defense and share it with the entire cabal, for this will please our Imperator greatly. Of course, I appreciate our more aggressive brethren will be otherwise engaged for the next seven cycles as they mourn for our lost ones. And in this, Vetis must set an example. Therefore, it is essential we use this time wisely. An important aspect of what I have to share is for our faction's eyes only. You'll all see why.

Saffir's eyes glowered and steamed in approval.

Angule wasn't finished. *Then, I require the services of Lega'trix Caym, Tribunus Raum, and Praefactors Mamone'sh and Orias. Each has shown themselves sensitive to the quintessential nature of emerging Kresh. The children of the Trianium are being roused as we speak. I want to ensure we have our own people there as each innocent is invested with consciousness. If we can distinguish even the slightest potential among the emergent, we must ensure they are assigned to one of our pods.*

It will be done, Angule.

Excellent. We will convene at first matins tonight. As the brethren begin to moon-phase with the Cataract, we will disassociate our essences and begin our preparations.

*

Mark Stevens closed his eyes, bowed his head, and allowed the ambience of his surroundings to overtake him. In moments, he was floating in a sea of golden light, and reminiscing about better times.

During the months they had been here, Mark had begun to look on Boleni Heights as his new home. Although vastly smaller than Rhomane, the astrometrics facility had all the creature comforts you could wish for. This was because it was much bigger than appearances first suggested.

The array itself occupied the first three of six levels. Two were above ground, while the rest burrowed deep into the mountain. The parabolic dishes, telescopes, passive and reactive antenna clusters, imaging trains, and targeting scanners filled the top floor with an Aladdin's cave of hi-Tec material and equipment. Looking like a giant version of a mad scientist's crown, the edifice was linked to the multitude of computers and workstations on the ground floor below it by literally miles of cables, wires, and photonic relays.

Beneath them, on sub-level one, were the backup generators, scientific labs, and standby stations that allowed for continual research and development to be conducted on site.

Next came the habitat module. A self-contained environment of pastel shades, restful holograms, activity halls, relaxation rooms, and gymnasium that helped the days breeze past without boredom.

The fifth level was heavily armored, for it housed the main computer core, hospital, armory, flyer squadron, and vehicle bay. Hermetically sealed, the sterile environs were connected to the surface by an independent runway and localized transporter pad.

Finally, more than four hundred feet down, lurked the power room. A shielded cavern of titanic energies, kept in check by the arcane contrivance of super-advanced physics.

It had taken Mark considerable time to check out all the nooks and crannies, and every maintenance shaft and service-way the facility had to offer. But he was like that. Meticulous. Thorough. Patient. It came with the job. And where security was concerned, he never compromised. That had its perks, for being methodical had allowed him to discover the most amazing locations over the years.

He was in such a place now, on an overhead gantry near the junction of sub-levels three and four. The cave wall in this area was covered by a phosphorescent form of algae. Under normal circumstances it glowed brightly in the dark, and Mark found the blue-green iridescence enthralling. However, not two weeks ago he had been in the chamber as the sun came up outside. To his amazement, the lichen colony began smoldering with a rich amber radiance that filled the cave with light and warmth. Not only that, he was then astonished to hear the moss issuing an audible tone of such sweetness, it wrung his heart. The symbiotic association of the fragile life form blended so intimately with its environment that it appeared as if the algae were serenading the dawn of each new day. He was enchanted from the word go, and had been drawn here most mornings since.

Word had inevitably spread within the confines of such a small community, and now Mark found himself sharing the wonders of this phenomenon with a growing number of his colleagues.

The chorus ended. Mark breathed a huge sigh of contentment, blinked his eyes open, and thought, *God, I'm going to miss this place.*

The Horde attack of the previous week had spurred Commander Cameron into revising his schedule. Only yesterday, they had received fresh orders from Rhomane.

Ten days. Ten lousy days, and then we have to begin all over again. He snorted. *Still, I shouldn't complain. At least I get to make a fresh start.*

His mind was drawn back to the memorial service they had shared online. Saying goodbye was never easy. All the more so when it included friends and acquaintances that were gentle-natured and had just wanted to be left alone.

Thirty-seven lives wasted by those soul-sucking bastards. Thirty-seven! And it would have been far worse if not for Jake's hunch.

He was about to fill the air with curses when he noticed he wasn't alone. Bob Neville was among those who had come to listen to the 'sun-song,' as it had been dubbed, and he had declined to leave with the rest.

"Something I can help you with, Bob?"

"Er, there might be, if you don't mind?"

Although coming along in leaps and bounds, Bob was always subdued in Mark's company. And with the rest of the team, come to that. Mark realized it was probably due to the scientist's remorse over Jumper's death. While everyone else now appreciated it had been an unfortunate accident, Bob never seemed quite able to forgive himself.

Edging tentatively forward, Bob continued, "It's just that I've been mulling over one of the directives in the removal order . . . and . . . well, I had an idea."

"Which one?"

Bob produced his ever present computer pad and scrolled down to an active page. Highlighting a passage, he pointed. "This directive here. See, where it says:

> *. . . and all equipment and ancillary materials*
> *that prove too cumbersome or impractical for relo-*
> *cation are to be left in situ. While this may appear*
> *wasteful, the solution is nevertheless practical. Space*
> *will be limited onboard, and a selective approach*
> *will assist the community as a whole. While the Arch*
> *of Winter is . . .*

"Do you remember the specifics of the passage?"

"I most certainly do," Mark said, "I lived by it for years. In my line of work we tend to live out of a suitcase and never get the chance to call one place home for long. A few paragraphs on from that, it starts itemizing a list of *approved* and *inappropriate* items. Talk about insulting."

"Yes, well, I was wondering. Why don't we use the occasion for a bit of payback?"

"I'm sorry?"

"Commander Cameron has clearly directed that whatever we can't take has to be discarded and left here, correct?"

"That's right. Go on."

"Well, instead of simply dumping it, why don't we make a *gift* of it?"

"What do you mean by *gift*?"

"Think about it. Because of logistics, we're going to have to abandon the new power core and backup aqua-drives intact, along with a great deal of other equipment that took us weeks to set up. So, if we have to dispense with them anyway, why don't we do something useful, and arrange for a little housewarming party? You know as well as I do, as soon as we're gone, the Horde will inevitably check things out. They're always hungry. Let's make certain that what we leave is more . . . *appealing,* say, by moving three or four of the actuator cells into a more accessible position around the core. They won't be able to resist them. When the rest of the crowd sees their more inquisitive friends feasting away unharmed, it'll trigger a feeding frenzy. That will pull a whole mob of them in. Now, if we rig things properly so we can ensure they're nicely congregated around their meal . . ." Bob reversed his fist, and then flicked his fingers open, "Boom!"

Mark grinned. "I like your thinking, and goodness knows we all want payback for what they did to the mining crew, but won't that just prompt a whole new wave of spawning?"

"Good point," Bob acknowledged, "but I wasn't just thinking of using the core. I intend to pack the place out with quantum gravity mines."

"Oh, really? How many?"

"Once we're aboard the *Arch of Winter*, we'll never need them again. So I was thinking . . . *all* of them."

Mark spluttered. "What? Bob, we have over a hundred full-sized mines in the magazine. And more than four times that amount of the micro variety."

"Oh, I know. I believe the yield should be sufficient to completely crush this mountain and most of the starport out of existence. It will leave one hell of a crater and send quite a statement, don't you think?"

Mark tried to visualize the devastation such an implosion would cause.

"Of course, to get the command staff to sign off on this," Bob continued quietly, "I'd need your support. And that of anyone else someone of your influence could manage to get on side."

Bob, I'm beginning to look at you in a whole new way.

Placing his arm around the other man's shoulder, Mark steered him from the cave. "Let's discuss this in greater depth over coffee."

Chapter Thirty-Five

The Longest Wait

Mohammed's office looked as if a bomb had hit it. Stacked boxes were everywhere. Filing cabinet drawers hung half-open. Virtually all the seats and worktops were covered in an assortment of equipment and personal items, and a sense of frantic disarray infested every corner of the room.

Amid this clutter, the Vice Commander was in the middle of a meeting.

". . . and as you can see from the catalog, all relevant stores and administrative records are now in transit to the *Arch of Winter*." Dr. Rosa Sophia shrugged her shoulders. "I've had to be ruthless, but that doesn't really matter. The entire archive has been crystallized into pertinent categories and will be coming with us in storage."

Mohammed nodded to her. "Thank you for that, Rosa. It's great to see how on top of things you are." He took a huge gulp of coffee before pressing on. "Right. Now we come to city defenses. Marcus? As your men will be protecting the wall and the arc, we'll start with you."

Marcus had been listening from a position by the window. Turning, he paced toward the center of the room, and took a seat on a box. "We of the Ninth Legion are well versed in siege preparations, Commander. You need not fear. The bulwark is secure. You are aware our enemy was strangely quiet for a week. That period of grace is now over, and for the past three days they have assailed the city with renewed vigor. As usual, they concentrate their efforts around the site of the *Shivan-Estre* disaster. However, this morning my spotters detected a fresh area where they appear to be congregating in numbers. Thus far, our efforts to determine what they're up to have been frustrated."

"Why is that? Too far away?"

"Not at all. The Masters have erected a barrier of some sort. It shimmers like a mirage and defies scrutiny, even from the scopes of the sniper rifles."

"Hmm. We'll need to keep an eye on that."

"Already done. Cathal MacNoimhin departed an hour ago in a shielded skimmer with a contingent of his Iceni tribesmen. They will travel toward the Asterlan Lake for a distance of ten miles before looping round to the Sengennon Hills. The highlanders have sharp eyes, and will be using the filtered optic devices Lieutenant McDonald kindly made available." He nodded toward Mac, opposite him. "If they see anything of value, they'll radio in."

"How long do you expect them to have to remain on location?"

"As long as necessary, or until ordered to extract. They carry three days' worth of rations, but will be relieved every day. I will continue the rotation, using clansmen, until told otherwise."

Yet again, Mohammed was impressed by the tactical expertise the legionnaire brought to the table. *And some people thought them primitive when they first arrived.* Aloud, he asked, "What else?"

"In view of the latest development, I have asked Stained-With-Blood to provide us with teams of warrior braves. They too, have eyes like hawks and will form a walking security cordon. I've tasked them with patrolling the walls and isolated areas of the city to keep a look out for anything unusual. Additionally, I have revised the Legion's duty schedules. While the commanding centurion of each unit will devise his own watches, I intend to stagger their actual deployment. From now on, both the barrier itself and the Arc of Death will be manned by a full cohort, with one standing-by in reserve. A three day cycle will ensure the soldiers are fresh and ready to fight.

"And speaking of the arc. My men now patrol both halves of the killing field and the moat. The trenches have been deepened, the hillocks fortified, and we have doubled the quantity of stakes lining the fosse. All distance markers have been rechecked, and the ballistae and catapults recalibrated. They now stand ready. Rhomane is prepared. Of course, I cannot prevent our enemy from resorting to more exotic means of penetrating our defenses. Obviously, that is beyond my control."

Everyone understood his reference.

"That's in hand," Mac McDonald interjected. "Sorry to butt in, but as my Special Ops department doesn't really fit in to what's going on at the moment, I volunteered our services as makeshift hitmen."

"Really?" Mohammed chuckled. "Do explain."

"Simple tactics. With the redeployment of our resources, we need someone who can respond fast to an emergency, and hit hard. Sub Commander De Lacey over there was kind enough to loan me four of these nifty matter transponders . . ." Mac raised his arm so everybody could see the bracelet adorning his wrist. "From what I understand, the main transporters shut down when the city is under siege, leaving only the battle circuit active. A sound security protocol, but a pain in the ass if you need to get somewhere in a hurry. The wristbands allow us to activate any pad we want. Once we arrive, we have these . . ." Mac patted the heavy machine gun lying across his lap. "That's why I'm armed at the moment. All my team is on stand-by. If a call comes in, I have to go."

"But what if you run into a Controller? We've seen how resourceful they are against bullets."

"Aha! That's where my latest toy comes in."

Mac held his weapon up, so everyone could see the grenade-launcher attachment beneath the barrel. Smiling at Ephraim Miller on the other side of the room, he continued, "Ephraim and his boys have been busy. I now carry four racked, and four reserve mini micro-mines as part of my ammunition complement. While that's quite a mouthful to say, it's even more difficult to chew on, as I'm hoping the Horde will find out. The ambush out on the Shilette highway proved the Bosses don't display the same suicidal tendencies as their lesser minions. Now we have these, there's more than enough joy to share around."

I'm relieved to hear it. "And are there enough of them to go round?"

"Oh, yes. My specialists are the first to be equipped. Then a batch is going out to Mark at the astrometrics facility. After that, we'll kit out a small squad of trained civilians. I've got six or seven volunteers in mind, all of them pretty handy shots."

"Thank you for that, Mac," Mohammed replied. "I'll ensure you get your pick of candidates. But please make sure I have plenty of notice. If they're in an essential department, I'll need to find suitable replacements before they get released."

"No problems, I'll leave the list among the mess on your desk."

Everyone laughed at the jibe.

Mohammed glanced at the unsightly jumble that used to be his workstation. As a meticulously tidy person, he hated to sit in such an environment. *It looks like someone's used a bloody grenade in here already.* He sighed. *One more week, then it'll all be over.*

Turning to Sub Commander Ryan Davies, Mohammed said, "Something Mac just mentioned reminded me about Boleni Heights. You're overseeing that phase of the operation. How is everything out there?"

"Absolutely fine. Nothing to report, other than they'll be ready to move the day after tomorrow. In anticipation, I reassigned Wilson Smith and his unit to assist in the retreat."

"Wilson Smith? How have Jake Rixton and his men taken to that?"

"No problems whatsoever. Second platoon have been there for three days now, and the two squads appear to be getting on well. Without their former captain to sour the waters, the men have gelled back into one fighting unit."

"And who have they decided should lead them?"

"Now here's the rub." Ryan's face broke into a broad grin. "When Smith and his lot arrived, the young officer was good enough to defer to the older and more experienced soldier. That took humility. However, Jake reminded the other man that he himself had only held his commission for a short while. That took character. Stuff me if they didn't then get into an argument as to why the other should lead. It's the only time the two have almost come to blows. Quite comical really."

"And who won?"

"Young Smith, in a classic move, too. They were standing toe to toe, shouting and bellowing at each other, when Smith happened to glance at Rixton's shoulder patch. Smith let out a howl of delight, snapped to attention, and threw the older man a salute. When Rixton asked him what the hell he was doing, Smith gaily pointed out the fact that the former sergeant had been promoted to full lieutenant."

"And?"

"Don't you know? Smith hadn't served for all that long before he came here. He's still a second lieutenant."

Mohammed's jaw dropped. *I really must take another look at his personal file. I tend to forget their previous standing, as we issue our own commands.* "I'd totally missed that. And you've just jogged my memory about something important . . ." Turning to Ayria Solram, he continued, "How is James Houston? Is his treatment preventing the relocation of your department?"

"He's as fine as can be expected," Ayria replied, combing her fingers through her hair, "especially since the ships have been moved. Now he can't see them, he doesn't get as many panic attacks. The tomahawk helps, too. But do you know, I get the damnedest feeling about him sometimes. It's as if his mind has become wired in a different way since his accident. One moment he's with you in the room, and the next? He might as well be on a different planet. He gets the weirdest, faraway look in his eyes, as if he's viewing somewhere else. It's at those moments you can almost see another side to his soul. The confusion. The horror of being who he is. Where he is. Of not knowing . . ." Ayria's face screwed up in frustration. "Ah! I'm not a psychiatrist. If Helena were still alive, perhaps she could find the key to unlocking the mystery. As it is, I'm all he's got."

"Well, at least you make a difference," Mohammed counseled, "and a little help is better than none." Smiling, he added, "And what of the hospital?"

"We'll be finished by tomorrow. I've made sure some of the latest medi-beds were transferred up to the *Arch of Winter*, along with most of the pharmacy. The only section operating now is the sickbay module within the Archive. Oh, and the psyche ward. I didn't want to move James until the last moment."

Mohammed nodded in appreciation. Turning next to a woman perched on top of two large boxes, he asked, "How are the transfers and flight tests going?"

"Smoothly," Shannon De Lacey replied, "unlike me." Uncurling herself from her position, she stretched, manipulating her shoulder until it cracked. "Sorry, but it's not very comfortable up there."

Shannon began pacing up and down, and helped herself to more coffee as she spoke. "We've been keeping the shuttles down to a minimum. I thought the Horde might try to watch our every move, and Marcus has confirmed my suspicions. That new post is probably logging every run we make. Not that it matters. Most of the stuff we send up is transferred via teleport pads, so our friends won't know what's going on until it's too late. All they're seeing is what they expect. We've got our hands on new aircraft, and are training our pilots in their use. In reality, Angela Brogan has been up on the *Arch of Winter* for the past week introducing the more experienced hands to Serovai. She's handpicked a team of wing jockeys and navigators to form the nucleus of the flight crew for once we're in deep space. Although the majority of our voyage will be conducted remotely, we still need sufficient operators to handle everyday oversight and emergency maneuvers. On top of that, every department now has a running section onboard, and will be ready to go live in four, maybe five days' time."

"Excellent news. And what about the additional armaments I asked to be added to the manifest?"

"They're on schedule, too. Although the heavy cannons have been temporarily sited around the Archive."

"Oh, really?"

"Yes. Saul said he was going to have a word with you. He wants an extra bit of insurance down there, until he's ready to seal the rift."

And, as usual, he'll get around to telling me after *the event!*

"I see. Thank you, Shannon, I'll go and have a chat with him when we're finished here."

Finally, Mohammed turned to his scientific advisor.

"I've saved you for last, Ephraim. Now Serovai has lowered the security protocols, what can you tell us about our new girl?"

"Oooh, you'll love this." Swiveling round in his chair, Ephraim activated Mohammed's wall monitor, and brought up an overview of what would be their new home for the foreseeable future. Coughing once to clear his throat, he continued, "Ladies and gentlemen, may I introduce you to the Avenger Class Deep Space cruiser, *Arch of Winter.*"

He flipped the picture to show an exterior view, with dimensions.

"As you can see, she comes in at just over two miles in length, eight hundred yards wide, and three hundred yards high. Quite a lot bigger than any of the ships we were used to back on Earth."

Pressing a button, Ephraim highlighted the factors he felt would be of interest to his eager viewers.

"What you are looking at here are thirty, dual point, defensive and offensive photon batteries with laser backups." *Click.* "These are the subsidiary guns. And guess what—they're Menta accelerators."

"Menta accelerators?" Mac queried. "What's that? I don't think I've heard the term."

"Fragmentation. Hard ammo," Ephraim replied. "When you remember that the vacuum of space is an extremely hostile environment, these weapons make sense. No matter how advanced a society becomes, if you carry armaments that can pierce the hull of an opposing ship, or take asteroids out of the sky, it removes the need for high yield ordnance."

Very clever! Mohammed thought. *And, of course, so simple.*

Ephraim pressed on. "Now, these are the launch silos." *Click.* "As you can see, twelve are designed to launch nuclear payloads, while the rest are capable of delivering multipurpose warheads. Her current manifest shows a full stock of Excalibur torpedoes, Phoenix tactical strike missiles, and Sparrowhawk Darts. We will obviously be adapting some of them for wider use."

The image zoomed in, and the outer hull turned transparent to show the internal features of the main sections of the craft.

"Basically, she's divided into three compartments, each with its own sub-bridge." *Click.* "Fore, we have CIC, a fully equipped midi-hospital, crew quarters and habitat zone. Aft is engineering, subsidiary sick bay, science and astrometrics. Along the midsection we find the power core, backups, hangars and ancillary maintenance bays." *Click.* "There's only one main flight deck, I'm afraid. But it's vast." *Click.* "And here, on the opposite side of the hull, is a smaller, reserved launch-and-retrieval pen for a standalone EMT shuttle. A very clever idea. Sadly, the *Winter*'s complement of defensive and offensive craft are missing. The crew must have taken them during the exodus. But that doesn't really matter, as we can fill some of the available space with the ships we procured, and the full consignment of flyers."

Ephraim turned to face his audience. "That completes the overview, what else would you like to know?"

"What's her ready status?" Mohammed asked, getting straight to the point. "We're due to leave in seven days. Will she be ready?"

"Most definitely. With Serovai's assistance, we have now stabilized threshold integrity and full life support. Emergency, command, and medical scanners, both passive and active, are online, and our chameleon technology has been successfully spliced to the *Winter*'s current defensive matrix. The dampening field is a godsend, as it scatters any inadvertent energy signatures that may leak into the subspace medium. It means we'll remain invisible for as long as we want to. Fuel cells are at ninety-two percent. Because of her size, the cruiser replenishes at the rate of about two percent a day. Of course, once she's powered up, all weapons systems will automatically prime and be ready for use."

Mohammed beamed. "Now *that's* the news I wanted to hear, as it will allow us to execute our final act against the Horde before we leave for good."

"Do you mind sharing what that is with us?" Ryan asked. "Or is it classified?"

"No, I can tell you. Saul didn't want me saying anything until we could confirm weapons status, that's all. And why? We're going to make sure the Horde never comes after us. It was never clearly explained how they managed to secrete away on so many ships, or how they managed to infest so many systems, so quickly. We don't want to take the chance that they can somehow interface with the onboard flight computers and use the autopilot systems to pursue us, or escape. Therefore, before we pull away, we're going to complete a preliminary orbit of the planet, target the spaceports here, and at Cumale, Floranz, Locus, Genoas, Napal, and Elan, and obliterate them."

"Ding dong!" Mac spluttered. "Now *that* I want to see. But—and I'm just playing devil's advocate here—what happens if you miss a few ships? You know. The ones that weren't left in a nice big parking lot? Some private companies in my day had their own luxury liners and aircraft for business meetings. The Ardenese must have obviously done the same. If the Horde manage to find one, what's to stop them following?"

"Good of you to think of that. So did we." Mohammed turned to Ephraim. "Do you want to tell him, or shall I?"

Ephraim waved both hands in the air, declining the offer.

"Very well." Lowering his voice, Mohammed explained, "Gaining unlimited access to the Archive has allowed us to restore full satellite coverage around the planet. All orbiting assets are now online and under our control. The six Veran platforms in particular possess an impressive array of weaponry. With the assistance of the Architect and Serovai, we have prepared a command override of the entire system. We will initiate it as we leave orbit. Basically, anything attempting to exit the atmosphere after we're gone will be shot out of the sky with extreme prejudice."

Mac grinned. "I think we'd *all* like to see that!"

"I know. Whets the appetite, doesn't it? But for now, we have to endure the hardest part. To sit and wait for the last hours to drag by." *And I, for one, hate that.*

Mohammed stood. "Anyway, thank you all for coming. I'll take my leave. Duty calls, and I have to take the latest updates down to the commander in the Archive. Feel free to finish the coffee and see yourselves out when you're done."

As he left his office, Mohammed was struck by a poignant thought.

Ha! Saul and I arrived here from off a starship. Looks like we'll be leaving the same way. He smiled. *Now why does that have a certain eloquence that appeals to me?*

Chapter Thirty-Six

Telltale Signs

In detached silence, James Houston leaned against the window and allowed his eyes to become unfocused to the world around him. Inner calmness enfolded his mind. Like a veil, it shrouded him from unnecessary external stimuli. He grasped an anchor to reality tightly in his hands. He couldn't see or feel it directly, but he knew it was there because of the subtle vibrancy skittering from his extremities toward the deepest recesses of his soul. He found the sensation soothing, a relief against the friction that constantly raged within him lately, on every occasion he sought refuge.

Soon, James, he promised himself. *Soon.*

That's not your name, a weak presence protested. *It's mine!*

Nevertheless, it will suffice. Renewed corporeality brings with it a greater longing for stability and identity.

But not your own?

That will resurface. Eventually. For now, I have assumed yours.

It wasn't yours to take.

You are a tool. A vessel. Accept this fact, and once you have served your purpose, you will be free of concern once more.

So . . . so you'll give it back, then? A feeling of hope tinged the other's awareness.

Hopefully. But what this new awakening will reveal remains to be seen.

What do you mean?

I . . . I'm not sure. And yet—

No! Don't say that. You swore. You did, you . . .

Overwhelming panic boiled to the surface. The fragile grip on lucidity was broken, and reality reasserted itself once more. Uninvited, alternate perspectives crowded to the fore.

James felt the pressure of a cold, smooth surface against his forehead. Blinking, his sight clarified on the gloom of a bleak courtyard outside, empty save for security lights and patrolling soldiers. Tracking their course, he was momentarily confused by his surroundings.

Where . . . ?

Unnerved, he stepped back, and the harsh glare of sterile lights reflecting on glass distracted him. He winced and adjusted his focus. He was confronted by the ravaged image of a haggard and exhausted face. A stranger, with gaunt, hollow cheeks covered in two days' worth of stubble and caked, dried spittle.

A sense of dislocation tingled through his mind.

Don't I know you from somewhere?

His toe stubbed against something on the floor. He looked down.

Mine!

Recognizing it, James threw himself to the ground and crouched protectively across his token. It wasn't until he'd checked the ward once more that he allowed himself to relax a little. Spinning swiftly around, he retrieved the tomahawk and sat with his back to the wall. Dismissing the world, he pressed Heaven's-Claw reverentially to his heart and gave it his full attention. In moments, a feeling of deep and unending peace eased the agitation from his mind. James closed his eyes, let his head fall back, and began to doze.

A cool breeze added a fresh breath of consolation to his repose, bringing with it memories of another world where endless plains stretched off into the distance, and the smell of honeysuckle and wildflowers filled the air.

That's nice . . . eh?

Suddenly alert, he bolted upright. Clutching the axe to his chest, he allowed his scrutiny to rove back and forth across the room. Although he couldn't see anything, his attention was repeatedly drawn to a spot several feet in front of the entrance to his private bathroom. Intrigued, James leaned forward and felt the gentle caress of a hidden exhalation once more.

Where's that coming from?

Scuttling forward on his hands and knees, he skirted the area and extended the back of his hand toward the crack under the door.

Nothing. I didn't leave the window open, so where . . . ?

An unexpected chill descended about him, bringing with it a sense of euphoria that made him dizzy. His stomach knotted, and he had to back away to clear his head. For some reason he couldn't fathom, the phenomenon filled him with hope.

Mesmerized, he clutched Heaven's-Claw ever tighter, and sat back to await what would happen next.

*

It was a while since Mohammed had walked these halls. He always found the environs around the entrance to the Archive claustrophobic. The galleries and passages were exactly the same as everywhere else. But this far underground, the rarified air made it feel as if the walls might sprout pointed stakes and close in on him at any moment. He had also declined to use the only transporter pad servicing this area, as the abrupt change in air pressure always made him feel ill.

That's my own fault, though.

Descending yet another set of switchback stairs, he reached up to touch the side of his neck. Five years previously, he'd burst an eardrum during the closing stages of Operation Trident, the offensive that ended the Tyrian Colony Uprising of 2339. Because he had been so closely involved in the battle itself and the ceasefire that followed, he hadn't gotten round to having his injury checked out until after the armistice was sealed. By then, it was too late. And now, any sudden variance in temperature or atmospheric density brought on the most excruciating pain. That discomfort would invariably radiate into his shoulder and neck, and induce the blinding headaches he had grown to hate over the following years.

As he walked, Mohammed kept his mind from the burgeoning torture by running through the evacuation procedures, and looking for evidence of Saul's preparations. It wasn't difficult to find. At this depth, they were everywhere.

Joists, supports, and other load-bearing structures had all been rigged with explosives. Saul hoped that collapsing the tunnels would be enough of a deterrent to the Horde to prevent them from ever snooping around.

Mohammed supported the idea wholeheartedly. *Although not as formidable as lydium, millions of tons of intervening rock will make it extremely difficult to approach this place. Even for them. And, of course, if it doesn't work, there's always the tear-rift.*

He tried to recall what he remembered of that freakish anomaly, for in their ingenuity, the Ardenese had managed to contrive another fermionic edifice that was as equally impressive as the wall. This one, however, had been manipulated during its construction to bind to a fracture within the very structure of reality. How they had managed such an incredible feat was beyond current understanding, as the physics involved bordered on the realms of fantasy. Nevertheless, it had been their greatest and last defense against extinction.

Completing his descent, Mohammed turned a final corner and entered the solitary tunnel that led toward the true heart of the city.

He shivered and quickened his pace. *It's colder here than I remember, and more oppressive.* He automatically pressed one finger behind his ear and made a chewing motion with his jaw.

Then he noticed the machine gun posts.

Two of the missing .50 cannons had been bolted to the floor on tripods, in a staggered formation that crisscrossed the hallway and teleport pad itself.

So that's *what Saul has done with them! Good idea.*

The Ardenese had always been unsure as to whether the biophysical properties of the Horde prevented them from ever using the transport system. As such, they had never employed additional defensive measures on the approach to the Architect's nerve center. Recent events had changed that perspective.

No sooner had Mohammed registered the existence of the guns than they reacted to his presence. An urgent *buzz* grated forth, followed by the whine of hydraulics. The closer pod rotated until its barrel pointed directly at him. He glanced down. A bright red dot was centered in the middle of his body mass.

He froze. *Oh dear. What the bloody hell do I do now?*

He was just about to identify himself when an orange phosphorescence stabbed out from a corresponding monitoring array. Sweeping across him, it traveled from head to foot and left to right in a few seconds, and covered his entire form in a web of gridlines. The net turned green. Before he knew it, the laser marker winked out and the cannon returned to its stand-by mode.

Mohammed whistled in relief, and was struck by a moment of lightheadedness. He massaged his temples, and discovered he was sweating profusely. A bilious sensation caused his stomach to grumble, and he was forced to gulp down air to ease his nerves. *What the hell is going on? While I admit that was a little scary, I shouldn't be reacting like this. Just wait until I have a word with Saul. He could have warned me about the new security measures . . . making me all jumpy.*

Grumbling, Mohammed continued forward until he noticed an AI bio-detector spliced into each unit. Intrigued, he stopped to examine one. *Now that makes sense. Anything non-human gets both barrels.*

He grunted. *Here's hoping they don't fritz out . . .*

Then he discovered something else. *Is that a mini-launcher?*

Looking closer, he inspected the rack and feeder setup. *Oh, very clever. I see he wasn't slow in purloining a batch of the new mini micro-mines. He obviously doesn't want any unexpected visitors with glowing crowns until he's ready to seal this place off.*

As he nosed through the other equipment surrounding the defense pods, Mohammed was overcome by another case of the jitters. He felt his throat constrict, and thought for a moment he might vomit. His stomach clenched. *For goodness' sake, this is getting ridiculous.*

He decided it would probably be better to get inside the Archive as quickly as possible. The hermetically controlled environment would relieve the pressure on his ear, and hopefully help him clear his head.

Striding to the end of the passage, Mohammed paused before what appeared to be a dead-end. Hidden sensors had noted his approach, and no sooner had he come to a standstill than he was scanned again. This time, by a gentle blue radiance. A faint *hum* throbbed through the air, and a glowing arch blazed to life within the composition of the wall. The light dimmed, and a hidden set of doors manifested within it. They glided silently back into seamless recesses on either side.

A sentinel appeared in midair. "Welcome, Vice Commander Amine. Commander Cameron awaits you. You will find him with the avatars of Calen, Sariff, and Beren on the main platform."

"He's speaking with the—?" Mohammed caught his breath as he espied yet another machine gun post only fifty yards away.

"Worry not," chirped the construct, "the other defense positions have been notified of your arrival and will not activate on registering your presence for the rest of this visit. For your information, besides the sentry you can see, two more pods will be found within. One protects the entrance to the Ark, and the other is situated outside the gate room."

"That's good to know," Mohammed murmured, without taking his eyes from the lethal-looking barrel pointing directly at him. "It wouldn't be fitting to meet with this planet's former leaders with badly stained trousers, would it?"

"Will there be anything else, Vice Commander?"

Totally wasted. "No, that'll be all, custodian. Thank you."

The sentinel fizzled out, leaving Mohammed alone once more.

The unsettled feeling returned. Keen to be done with his errand and back in the familiar surrounds of his office, he hurried along. *I must be coming down with something. I'm an ex-fleet officer, for goodness' sake. I don't usually get this nauseous in pressurized environments.*

As he stretched his legs, Mohammed continued to flex his jaw and pull faces. *At least the pain is easing now. Perhaps I'd better get Ayria to check me over when I get back. I'd hate to take anything infectious on board the* Arch of Winter *on the day we set off. Talk about making myself popular with the crew.*

He was still grimacing as he swept in through the doors of the control room.

"Whoa! Are you demonstrating your war face for us, Mohammed?" Saul teased. Turning to the holographic simulacrums gathered about his computer terminal, he asked, "What do you think, guys? Impressed?"

Calen and Sariff exchanged bemused looks before resuming their studies. Sol Beren, however, a soldier born and bred, understood the jibe. "I think he needs to work some more if he intends to instill fear in his enemies. Perhaps a nice loud roar?"

"Ha ha, very funny," Mohammed replied. "The only thing you'll be hearing from me is the sound of my hastily retreating footsteps as I make my way back to civilization." He placed an info-crystal containing the details of the latest briefing on the desk beside Saul. Then he shivered. "This place gives me the creeps."

Calen's avatar looked up. "Come now, Vice Commander. This *place,* as you call it, is the last bastion of our race. Surely you can appreciate its mood was designed to reflect the solemnity and sanctity of its purpose?"

"Oh, don't mind me, Calen," Mohammed responded, "I didn't mean to be rude. I'm just not feeling too good, that's all."

Ushering the Ardenese scientist to one side, Mohammed steered him toward the observation pier, a projecting finger of highly polished wood and metal that stretched out above the void below. Reaching the circular balcony at the end, he placed his hands on the railing and looked down. He couldn't help feeling overwhelmed.

He stood at the very top of a huge shaft that had been cut down through the planet's crust for a distance of more than two leagues. Within that borehole, safely interred within a multitude of vacuum shells, were millions upon millions of genetic samples. Human. Plant. Animal. Insect. The entire spectrum of all the flora and fauna Arden had to offer. Safely locked away and lovingly preserved behind triple-layered polycarbonate resin, waiting for a time when they could at last be released, to reseed a ruined world.

Mohammed's gaze lingered on several chambers, as if each one contained a member of his own family. *And we're going to let them down.* Suddenly, he felt ashamed.

What he was thinking must have reflected on his face, for next to him, Calen gently sighed. In a soft voice laced with emotion, he said, "Worry not, Mohammed Amine. This battle was never really yours to fight. In our desperation, we clutched at straws and were willing to try anything to redeem ourselves."

"But you saved us, and—"

"Yes, we did. But we never expected you to commit suicide on our behalf. We trusted the Architect to select the best. Those who would have a fighting chance. And . . . well . . . if only the iron solution had been thought of sooner, things may have been different."

"How on earth the Architect went about selecting us, I'll never truly understand," Mohammed admitted, "but I've never looked on our community as the best. We've managed. But we also seem to have screwed things up."

"It has been my experience that our farsighted, artificially-enhanced super-friend has a different way of viewing things. What you may look on as insignificant, he may deem worthy of great honor." Calen paused to look around the chamber. "It would have been a dream come true to see the fruition of our labors, for our own DNA lies within. But—"

"Better the nightmare ends now and you quarantine this world forever."

Mohammed jumped, for he hadn't heard Sariff walk up behind. Staring into the former First Magister's eyes, he said, "So you support our decision to leave?"

"We couldn't refuse, not when your people have given their lives so valiantly."

They all strolled back toward the primary station.

"How long will you survive, do you think?" Mohammed asked.

"When the rest of the city is severed, the Architect will be able to divert all available resources into the Archive. Non-essential systems will be powered down. With nothing else to demand its attention, the Ark's preservation may be extended for nearly a thousand years, give or take a century. Who knows what may occur in that time?"

You'll still die. That's what. "How are you going to do it?"

Saul replied. "We're going to seal the Ark using a DNA cipher. That's what we were discussing when you came in." He directed everyone's attention to his monitor. "In the event that anyone ever returns here, be they human or stragglers from some distant Ardenese outpost, we've devised this."

He stepped back to show a 3D simulation of a stunningly complex vortex.

Beren took up the explanation. "Basically, we're going to remove the reactive element from the rip-space tear. You know? The point where we installed the entrance into the Archive itself? Once this has been achieved, the only way future access can be guaranteed is if the caller possesses the appropriate biological signature. Human or Ardenese."

"But there are no Ardenese," Mohammed protested. "So how . . . Oh!"

The penny dropped. He turned to the simulacrums. "One of *you* is going to volunteer."

"That's right," Beren replied, "our DNA also lies within the Ark. As the last protectors of our race, it is fitting that one of us has the honor of making the final sacrifice."

Mohammed didn't know what to say.

The awkwardness of the moment was thwarted by a vibration against his ear, alerting him to the fact that he had a growing list of queries backing up in his message buffer. He activated his com-set and listened in for a moment.

Damn. I'd better get back. "Sorry, gentlemen, I'll have to leave you to your deliberations. There's a city that needs relocating, and it looks like they can't do it without me."

Saul picked up the crystal Mohammed had brought. "I'll read this as soon as I'm finished, and hopefully catch up with you within the hour."

The avatars bade Mohammed goodbye, and he made his way back along the corridors. As he walked, he ruminated on the unfairness of the situation.

My God! As if they haven't been asked to sacrifice enough as it is. From what I remember of their history, they had to agree to lay down their lives to mesh the gateway and Ark together in the first place. Something about their dying essences providing the wormhole with a mortality key. And now, one of them is going to be asked to volunteer his mortal remains to the cause, effectively destroying any hope he'll have of further involvement with his race. Fantastic.

Stalking out of the Archive, Mohammed began the long trek back toward the stairs.

It's just so unfair. I mean . . . I know they're dead already. But to ask them to do such a thing? It's like fighting to bring a person back to life, just so you can kill him all over again.

Bile rose abruptly in Mohammed's throat. Staggering to one side, he braced himself against the wall and fought down the urge to vomit. *Bloody hell! I'm getting myself all worked up.* He looked around the passage and the nearby sentry guns. *Not a good idea, especially here.*

A chill gripped the air, and a fresh wave of nausea rolled toward him. His gaze fell on the teleport pad. *Hellfire! It'll be worth the pain just to get out of this place.*

Stomping forward before he had a chance to change his mind, Mohammed crossed the threshold and activated the transporter.

*

A choral resonance swelled in the ether about them, glorious in its vibrancy, and yet as tenuous as a wraith. The tonal characteristic of the base notes gradually changed. Ramping in amplitude and frequency, they went beyond the threshold of most living things' endurance.

And yet, the soloist's audience endured, enraptured by the precision with which the canticle was confined.

You have achieved congruence, Angule advised. *Regulate the cadence of the stream against the fermionic barrier. Sense its configuration. Taste the rhythm of the super-dense particles that pack its matrix so tightly. Do you see?*

Maintaining precision, Raum splintered her astral vision into different viewpoints so that part of her consciousness could step back and observe her efforts. Comprehension flared within the outer vestibule of her mind. *Yes, Great One. The molecules still dance, albeit grudgingly.*

Correct. It matters not how impeachable the structure is, all matter must obey the strictures of nucleic law. Do you sense the vast energy encapsulated within its form?

Yes. Yes, I do.

Excellent! Refine your observations, for you must find a way to exploit its capacity. Relax, and the tessellation you seek will manifest.

Rumbling closer to his charge, he softened the tone of his mood. *Now, focus your probe. Do not attempt to force your way through. Instead . . . ?*

Blend my way through, Raum recited, having listened attentively to the instruction given earlier to the assembled Lega'trexii: *Become the barricade and make it part of me.*

Angule radiated approval. Behind him, Saffir, Buer, and Caym exuded an air of barely restrained concern.

Do not be afraid of becoming trapped within the confinement, Angule continued. *Remember. The horror of isolation only snares that which tries to negate its nature. By seeing harmonic coherence and working in union with it, you will evade oblivion and emerge restored on the other side.*

A tinge of doubt dared to manifest within her cerebrum. Crushing it, Raum dismissed the very concept of distraction and intensified the eldritch concordance of her intent. To those listening in, it sounded as if the extract of her music now contained a promise of conflicts resolved and oaths fulfilled. Of unanimity and synchronicity.

That's it, Angule coaxed. *Explore those possibilities of unity. Embrace them. Augment your fabrication to the modulations now being revealed to your scrutiny.*

Raum concentrated, and in moments a singularity of thought and purpose hung suspended within the orchestrated ebb and flow of her construct. With the utmost care, she sent it tinkling and chiming toward the muted void of nothingness barring its way. The two mediums met. The pulse appeared to hesitate, as if studying the edifice before it, and then it began to darken. An unseen force closed in, compressing them in a growing nucleus of potency. Undeterred, Raum adapted the tempo of her refrain, attempting to keep pace with the fluctuating circumstances presented to her.

Slowly but surely, the tones emitted by the spark became more obscure. Longer. Deeper. Languorous.

The probe vanished, only to peal forth moments later from within an invisible core. The echoing resonance had been enriched, and now incorporated sonorous hints of a far superior quality. The eclectic sphere in which they had concealed themselves began to freeze, and an abrupt release of pressure through the quantum paradox seared their very souls.

Angule blended with Raum's thoughts. *What do you see, child?* As a courtesy, he opened his mind so that those gathered with them could witness the results of her first attempt to pierce the veil.

Eagerly, Raum extended her sight and phased toward the void.

Careful! Angule warned. *You do not wish to relocate. Yet!*

She tried again, more tentatively, and was shocked by what she saw.

As was Angule. Seizing his protégé in a coercive grip of stunning magnitude, he yanked her psyche back through the portal with such force that they were sent sprawling across the floor.

The enclave surged to its feet. Jolted into action, they manifested their surprise with bursts of arcane potency and barely suppressed rage that trembled on the verge of aggressive expression.

Releasing a wave of electrified pheromones, Angule quelled the backlash with a spectacular display of power that reestablished his dominance within an instant.

Hold! he bellowed.

His hands slammed together. The resultant shockwave not only threatened to rupture the matrix of their encompassing sphere, but also ensnared each Kresh within a skein of agonizing bliss.

They staggered.

Control your passions, Angule cried. *We are in no danger. On the contrary, Raum has discovered a wonder I never thought to actually see.*

A wonder? Saffir countered. Struggling to quench the flames of his own emotions, he spat: *Brother. If what you saw is no danger, why react as you did? We did not have sufficient time to focus on the object of Raum's consternation to be able to agree with your rectitude.*

The minds of the other Lega'trexii and Tribuni present prickled indignantly with similar sentiments.

Bathing the raw tincture of their nerves in a soothing cocoon of comfort, Angule lowered his shield and allowed them to observe what he and Raum had glimpsed.

The Cryptogen! Saffir exclaimed. *It . . . it actually exists? Here? Now?*

Of course, brother. How could you doubt me after all this time? With it, the re-genesis is assured. He gestured to Raum: *And now that our tribuni are acquiring the discipline and strength of will required to breach the barrier and undertake the transference, our plans can be accelerated. And just in time.*

That revelation brought them back to their senses.

Now gather round. Before I expand the lesson to include our Praefactors, I wish to demonstrate a technique that will hopefully reduce the thermal variance encountered every time we initiate the rift.

Chapter Thirty-Seven

Breach

Defying the chill wind that scoured the top of the battlements, Flavius Velerianus wrapped his cloak tightly about himself and peered down at the seething mass below. No matter how hard he studied his enemy, he couldn't define a purposeful strategy in their criminal waste of energy and resources. That they continued to send wave after wave of screaming ogres against a barrier that had defied them for decades was baffling. That they did so at exactly the same spot left him speechless.

We've all seen the recording. The Ardenese craft was utterly consumed in a holocaust that didn't even scratch the surface of the wall. And it was powered by an engine that would have destroyed half of Rome in the conflagration. So, if something that powerful was incapable of breaching this edifice, what hope do they think they have?

457

The rampart beneath his feet thrummed in response to the fury of endless detonations.

It's as if they want to shock us into defeat by their willingness to die like rabid dogs. Make us realize that even if it takes a thousand years and every life they have, they'll never give up until they succeed or are utterly consumed.

He covered his eyes from the glare of a particularly bright explosion.

Look at them. Climbing over themselves in their haste for a martyr's death. Unlike their accursed masters . . . Tricky, conniving bastards.

Still determined to pay the Horde back for the terrible losses inflicted upon his first command, he was struck by a sudden thought.

No! It couldn't be that simple? Spinning on his heel, he sought out his new optio among the press of men manning the fortifications.

"Antonius, to me."

Antonius Gaius Septimus, an eighteen year stalwart from Napoli who had worked his way up through the ranks, was soon at his side. "Sir?"

"How goes the relocation of our troops to the *Arch of Winter?*"

"On schedule. As directed, we are staggering the patrol rotations so the Horde is unaware of our true purpose."

"Who do we have remaining?"

"Tiberius Tacitus of the Second Cohort is yet to depart. Four centuriae of the First still man the walls. Besides them, only our brothers of the Fourth Cohort remain. They man the arc. Like us, they will be among the last to leave tomorrow."

"Good. Look, I have an idea. Get the horses. There's something I want to check out, and I need to move fast between transporter sites." In answer to the puzzled look his lieutenant gave him, he explained, "You're coming with me. We're taking a little trip to the western side of the city."

*

Climbing to the top of the observation podium, Marcus turned to the centurion commanding the Fourth Cohort, Amelius Crispus, and said, "I like what you've done with the place. Explain it to me."

Amelius surveyed the construct before him. "It's simple really. Apart from the men, every other resource here is expendable. It won't be coming with us. So I rigged the base of each catapult along the inner ring with explosives. The sandbags you see are lightly packed with a metal and shingle mix that should cause quite a stir if we ever have to use them on uninvited guests."

Marcus smiled to himself. *Outstanding.* "What fuses have you set?"

"For the one talent rigs, a full minute. It'll give the crews plenty of time to thread their way through the web of steel to the safety of a fresh position. Once you get this side of the moat, I've had it reduced to thirty seconds."

"Cut and run?"

"Exactly. Now that our foe has regained a measure of courage, and numbed themselves to the consequences of loss against the iron, I have little doubt casualties will cause them any delay. They'll come, and they'll come hard and fast. You've seen what happens when they sacrifice themselves . . ." He paused to indicate the sprawling maze before them. "All of this will be consumed. I don't want my people wasting themselves in futile gestures."

Good idea. "I agree with your thinking."

"Thank you. That's why I halved the ratio of teams out there, as well. Basically, I've ordered them to fire, and only reload if it appears safe enough to do so. If it is, fine. If not, they'll set their fuses, leapfrog the next post, and man the next available ballista. Once there, they'll resume firing until the support team in front of them has to abandon their position, whereupon the procedure will be repeated until they work their way back behind the new scorpio line."

Both officers turned to view two long rows of what appeared to be oversized crossbows embedded into the ground. Positioned in a *V* formation leading back toward the inner wall, they made it appear as if the Horde were being invited to storm an open set of jaws. The mouth was over a hundred yards wide, and protected by a smaller, secondary dyke that appeared to be filled with tar.

"What have you done there?" Marcus enquired.

"An iron and pitch mix. Once alight, it'll give us enough of a gap to get the cohort out and through to safety. Just in case . . ." he nodded to the emplacements atop the inner bulwark, "I'll have a detachment of volunteers manning that position. We'll storm them with arrows until the battlements have been drenched in another boiling-tar-and-ore recipe that will definitely give us enough of a breather to make it up to the Magister's level."

"Impressive. Do you mind if I make one tiny suggestion?"

"Please do, Commander. Anything that makes my life easier is most welcome."

"Listen for a moment, Amelius. Tell me, what do you hear?"

Both men paused to cock their ears.

"Try to ignore the men at work," Marcus added. "Phase them out and concentrate on what you can discern in the background."

Marcus watched as Amelius concentrated, and did as requested.

Amelius gasped. "I can hear our enemy outside the gates."

"Precisely!" Marcus slapped his fellow officer on the shoulder. "Now. If you can hear them from out there, imagine what they will sound like in here, confined within the arc and with walls on all sides."

"It'll be deafening." Amelius cast his gaze back across the killing field. "With all those men running about, I'll need to ensure they can hear and respond to orders."

"That's right. Although we are adapting to these new levels of technology remarkably well, the radios might not suffice. In the heat of battle, the legion will resort to what comes naturally. Tried and tested methods of communication that have seen us through many an ordeal."

"Thank you, Colonel. I'll intersperse the field with cornicen and signifiers. We'll use the horns and walkie-talkies until it gets too loud, and then revert to flags."

He's sharp and thinks on his feet. A man after my own heart.

*

As he materialized on the teleport pad, Mac immediately raised his hands and weapon high and identified himself. "Lieutenant Alan McDonald. Rhomane Command Team." Beside him, Sam Pell likewise froze, but remained silent.

Even while their molecules were still reconstituting, they were targeted by multiple sensors. Four beams stabbed out. One pair enmeshed them within a grid of glowing amber light, while the others illuminated their chests with crimson dots.

The web turned green, the target indicators blinked out, and the .50 cannons resumed their automatic scans of the entire gallery.

Phew! I nearly had to change my pants there. Now that's what first impressions are all about. If those monsters ever do

*manage to use the transporter system, they'll be in for a nasty
surprise.*

Without a word, both specialists brought their weapons to
the shoulder and swept the tunnel for signs of anything suspicious. Finding none, they relaxed and made their way toward
the entrance to the Archive.

Mac had only taken a few steps when he hesitated. *What
was that?*

Backtracking, he paused before walking forward once
more. *There it is again.*

He cocked an eyebrow and murmured, "Sam. Check out
this side of the corridor, will you? Tell me what you think."

Looking puzzled, Sam crossed the passageway and did
as he was asked.

Mac watched closely as his colleague strolled toward him.
Sam frowned, glanced at Mac, and then stopped. After retrac-
ing his steps, he started forward once more, waving his hand
in front of him.

"You can feel it, can't you?" Mac stated.

"There's a marked difference in temperature around this
one spot," Sam replied, "and I can't decide where it's coming
from."

"Me neither. There are no discernible drafts or other open-
ings nearby. So what . . . ?"

"Cold pooling, perhaps? We're a considerable distance
underground, and some places do act as a sponge to the chill.
I've encountered this before."

"So have I." Mac checked his wrist monitor. "But not by
this much. It's nearly ten degrees cooler."

"Fahrenheit?"

"No, that's just it. I'm talking Celsius." Mac thought for a
moment. "Switch to enhanced optics and scoot back along the
gallery for a hundred yards or so. Look for any other places

displaying such a discrepancy. Contact the guys, too. Ask them to check anywhere they think is vulnerable to surprise attack. I'm suspicious enough as it is. If we encounter this phenomenon again, it'll prove something's up."

"What about Andy and Bob Neville? They're on a static post above the First Magister's marshaling yard covering the ships."

"They can remain in situ. But get them to revert to thermal imaging. If their immediate area is clear, they can target further afield and get both Stu and Fonzy or Mark and Sean to take a closer look at anything out of the ordinary."

"I'm on it, Boss."

As Sam moved away, Mac stepped toward the hidden doors. Masked sensors activated. As the entrance revealed itself, a sentinel materialized in the air in front of him. "Good day, Lieutenant McDonald. How may I be of service?"

"Just completing my rounds, custodian. How's Commander Cameron?"

"He is busy within. The cipher is almost complete and will be initialized within the hour. Shall I announce you?"

"No. That won't be necessary. I don't want to disturb him. I was on security rounds and—" Mac was distracted by the secondary machine gun post within the interior corridor. "Why is that sentry post not activating?"

"Your presence has now been logged, Lieutenant. The system has been notified of your visit and will allow you unrestricted access."

"That's very kind, but I want full ultraviolet security protocols reestablished immediately. Command Identification: McDonald. Alpha. Three. Seven. Two. Tango. Confirm?"

"McDonald. Alpha. Three. Seven. Two. Tango, confirmed, Lieutenant. Ultraviolet response restored."

No sooner had the drone finished speaking than the lone emplacement came alive. Even though he stood on the threshold, Mac was forced to remain still while the familiar network of sensors completed their scans.

That's more like it.

"Thank you, sentinel. Better to be safe than sorry."

I do not want anything hitting the fan this close to the exodus.

*

Zuul, Grand Vizage and Vocalator of the Unium, stepped forward. *Who stands with Imperator Vetis?* he boomed.

Ahoo! roared the minds of the gathered host.

And who will fight with our mighty liege?

Ahooooo! The intensity of the reply thundered into the ether, setting the myriad prisms bordering the Hall of Eclectic Spheres ablaze in a paroxysm of light and glory. Primal hunger, strangled for an age, raged against enlightened restraint. Slowly but surely, each of the magnified entities occupying the raised dais allowed their self-control to crumble. Within moments, a deep-seated core of slavering rage dominated the Hall.

The hour of release is nigh, Zuul announced. *Revenge against those who caused our suffering is at hand. Soon, our victory will saturate this world in ruptured corpses.*

Caught in the wake, the massed ranks of the Trianium Tier responded. Flexing and surging with maniacal glee, they expressed their frustration with a surge of emotion so pure, so raw, that their umbilical membranes almost combusted with unrestrained fury.

Stand ready! The overwhelming presence of Angule cut into the thoughts of his faction, bringing them to heel.

Seeing he had refocused their attention, he continued: *Take your places in the line. Our first jump will take us to the staging post above the capital. Once there, close on me. Vetis thinks we will be transported en masse into the various insertion points about the city. I have ensured that will not happen. As soon as we phase, adopt* this *choral resonance.* His mind displayed an incredibly complex encryption. *Conjoined, our cabal will manifest within a structure that is seldom used. From there we will redeploy. Be alert, for as soon as we arrive I will attempt to mesh with the human who seems sensitive to my presence.*

He paused to ensure each of them was listening attentively to his instructions. *Saffir. You are with Limun. Buer, take N'Omicron. Caym? Vual will pair with you. Due to their inexperience, Mamone'sh and Orias will stay with Raum and myself as we attempt communication. Remember, shield yourselves heavily and stay hidden as much as you can. If and when you locate any children of the third tier who have shown themselves sensitive to our aspirations, draw them to you. But do not allow them to harm any human.*

They moved forward as the master portal was activated.

Most of all, do not worry. For them, battle will be joined instantly and we will not be missed until it's too late.

*

"Do you see what I mean?" Flavius Velerianus demanded. "There's not a single Horde Master among them. The tricky bastards ambushed my patrol and would have wiped us out if it weren't for divine providence. And now they've turned shy again? I don't think so. They're up to something."

Antonius gazed down into the confusing blaze of color below. "So where do you think they are? Because I must confess, I can't make head nor tale of what I'm looking at. It'd be hard to spot any form of crown amongst that lot."

"Oh, you'd know it if you saw one," Flavius spat, shivering at the memory. "It's like facing a wall of crimson and purple hatred wreathed in scarlet and blue flames."

A dull flash from out in the Sengennon Strait caught his eye. *Hello?*

Flavius studied the distant hillside. To himself, he murmured, "So *that's* where you've been hiding? But how many, I wonder?"

The apparition flared again, brighter this time, blurring his sight with a stark afterimage.

Whatever's taking place behind that glittering anomaly will not be good for the citizens left within this city. I'd stake my liver on it.

Over his shoulder, he called, "Antonius? You know how to use those radio things better than I do. Get on it and find Tiberius Tacitus for me. Tell him I'd like his counsel. If he has time before his shuttle leaves, ask him to come to this location."

As an afterthought, he added, "Oh, and get me Marcus and Vice Commander Amine, too. Better to share my suspicions now than not have the chance."

Using binoculars this time, he searched the irregularity for signs of any clues.

You'll not take me by surprise again.

*

"As long as you realize there's only one shuttle-run left," Mohammed stressed, "then it's up to you! I won't be here to hold your hand. We're about to transfer Command-and-Control to the *Arch of Winter*. Once there, I'm going to initiate the final withdrawal protocol and close the rest of the system down. If you miss those ships, you'll have to wait your turn at the emergency teleport pad along with the rest of the soldiers currently manning the defenses."

"That'll be okay," Saul replied. "Calen and I are ready to insert the cipher into the Architect's neural net, and then we want to run a final diagnostic to ensure it's taken."

"How long will that take?"

"About forty minutes."

Too long. "You are aware we're getting reports that the Horde is up to something? There are temperature fluctuations at various points all over the city. We don't need three guesses to know what that means. Whatever they're planning, it won't be good, so we need to be away from here before it starts. And Saul, once we begin the final phase, there won't be enough people to spare to come and get you if you run into trouble."

"Don't worry. I've arranged for appropriate chaperones. Mac and his team have offered to escort me to the surface, and then up to the staging area. I'm sure they're more than capable of seeing me to safety."

"Your choice. See you on the other side."

Mohammed cut the link and grunted in frustration. *If he gets caught with his pants down, he'll have to fight his way along a four hundred yard long corridor, and over fifty flights of stairs before he even gets to ground level.*

He was struck by a sudden idea. *I wonder if we could rig the Archive transporter buffers with enough juice for a one-way trip to the main pad? Of course, they'd have to activate it manually. But . . .*

He called across the room. "Serena? Patch me through to the *Arch of Winter.*"

After a few moments' delay, Angela Brogan's profile filled the view screen.

"Captain," Mohammed said in greeting. "Is everything prepared to get underway?"

"Yes, Vice Commander. All systems are five-by-five, and we're just waiting for all you stragglers down there to get your asses moving before beginning our bombing run."

"Excellent. Please advise Serovai we'll be transferring command codes to her matrix within the next thirty seconds."

"Roger that."

"I'll be up myself in a few minutes, via teleport pad. Could I ask that you notify Ephraim to meet me in the main transporter room on my arrival? I know he's busy, so apologize on my be-half, but there's something I'd like to get his opinion on. If he fusses too much, tell him it pertains to Commander Cameron's safety. That should shut him up."

Angela's face broke into a wide grin. "Will do. We look forward to seeing you soon."

The screen went blank.

Right, let's get this show on the road.

Mohammed addressed the room. "People. The time has come. Close down your workstations now, and immediately make your way to your disembarkation points. If for any reason you miss your scheduled departure, stay calm and get yourselves to the First Magister's courtyard. The emergency pad will remain active and protected by armed guards until every last one of us is out. Serena? Once you have control, transmit our protocols to Serovai and trigger the virus. I want every single system in this place fried beyond repair. Understood?"

"I'm on it, Sir."

Nodding, he mumbled, "See you all topside."

Making his way from the command center, Mohammed checked through the list of those combatants who would remain at their posts until the last minute.

Right . . . Marcus and his fourth cohort are manning the only real weak link. From what he tells me, a structured retreat has been prepared through the arc, and they should have no problem reaching the RV point. Flavius has the wall. He's already moving his men, and has kept the freshest soldiers back till last. Good strategy. We have roving patrols of Native American braves and Iceni clansmen lining the main escape routes. And Mac has some of his boys covering the actual departure yard itself.

Mohammed breathed a sigh of relief.

Joining the queue of personnel waiting to beam up to the ship, he savored the view from the quad and continued skipping through his directory, looking for anything that might present a loose end.

So, that only leaves Saul and Ayria. Saul's covered. If he isn't safe with Mac's guys, he won't be with anyone.

He checked Ayria's status. *The log shows her as leading a team to the EMS center to retrieve the last of the medical supplies. Fair one.*

His turn came to step onto the transporter pad.

Then she's taking a bunch of orderlies with her to collect Houston from the psych ward. Now that is a wise decision. He freaks out enough as it is when he just looks at the shuttles, so leaving him until last will cut the stress on everyone else.

Mohammed relaxed as the familiar tingle of the patter buffers began disassembling his molecules. He opened his eyes for one last look at the place that had been his home for the last three years.

A blinding flash from the direction of the southeastern perimeter caused him to throw up his arms and avert his eyes.

What the hell was that?

*

"And you say there isn't a single Controller among them?" Marcus queried. "Not a single one?"

"No, Sir," Tiberius Tacitus replied. "That's why he sought my advice and asked me to bring this to you. With so much happening, Flavius didn't want to go jumping to conclusions. The final straw was when his radio transmissions started being affected by the flashes from up on the Sengennon Hillside. He said—"

"Marcus? Tiberius?" Amelius Crispus interrupted. "My apologies for butting in, but something appe–"

A piercing white light cut him dead.

To the officers gathered on the command podium, it appeared as if a miniature sun had crested a false horizon that had somehow been placed within the city confines. Forced to avert their eyes, each of them spun away, dropped to one knee, and swept their cloaks across their faces.

"Claudius," Marcus barked to the cornicen, "we are under attack. Quickly, sound the alert!"

Turning to the signifier, he commanded, "Livius, signal the wall and inner—"

No sooner had the horn begun to blare than it was drowned out by a paroxysm of fury. Everyone was swatted from the dais like leaves in a gale.

The world spun. When it stopped, Marcus was on his back in the dirt. Winded, he lay where he fell, trying to regain his breath. A roar like an echo of the detonation continued building in the background. *That's not the sound of an explosion.* Instinct kicked in. Struggling to his feet, he staggered back to the platform, climbed the steps, and surveyed the scene before him.

The area where the utility buildings had once stood no longer existed. The structure had been replaced by twisted shells of smoking debris and rubble, through which arcs of scintillating light now coiled in expanding ribbons. A huge gray void hung at the exact center of the abnormality. Suspended in the air like the maw of some great beast, it was terrifying to behold. From that incongruity swept an overwhelming wave of ferocity.

A seasoned veteran of many campaigns, Marcus didn't let the horror of what he now witnessed rob him of the ability to act. "Amelius. Tiberius. To me!"

Marcus scanned the main body of the arc. *Excellent! Most of the inner and outer positions remain operational.* His gaze flicked to the series of mounds and trenches that had been incorporated into its design. *Fortunately for us, they were well built and properly positioned, and appear to have deflected much of the shockwave into the air.*

The only segment to suffer minor damage was the central avenue, upon which the command post had been erected. Disregarding the repeated outbursts now erupting along the edge of the defensive line, Marcus stooped to retrieve the signifier's flag. Lifting it high, he issued vital instructions.

Moments later, the arms of the first line of catapults began to swing. Next to them, their accompanying ballistae rocked slightly as they too unleashed their payloads.

The front of the moiling wave of heat and light flared. Scores of ogres were consumed by the opening fusillade, only to be replaced by hundreds more. Within seconds, thousands were throwing themselves against the cunningly arranged emplacements.

The soldiers held their ground. *Oh, well done. Well done indeed.* Marcus's chest swelled with pride.

Amelius and Tiberius came scampering up the stairs, with Claudius and Livius close behind.

Marcus took a final look around, and came to a decision. "Tiberius. A cohort without their leader is like a lion without its fangs. Stunted. Vulnerable. Your men have already left for the *Arch of Winter*. Please be so kind as to follow them." Raising his hand to cut off his fellow officer's protestations, he added, "I appreciate you want to stay. We all do. You are a centurion of the Ninth, after all. But you can serve us better by ensuring our people continue to have the best leadership they could possibly wish for . . . wherever they may be. Your final act here, then, is this. On the way to the transporter pad, notify the catapult captains to begin heating the sand and iron. I have a feeling we will need that fire shortly."

Tiberius struggled to contain himself. Discipline won the day. Without a further word, he threw Marcus a salute, nodded to his fellow legionnaires, and left the platform.

Turning to Amelius, Marcus continued, "As I mentioned, a cohort without their leader is like a lion without its fangs. Show me how the Fourth can roar. And bite!"

"What about you, Sir?" Amelius spluttered, stunned his Praefectus was allowing him to take command of the field. "Do you not wish to lead yourself?"

"Too many cooks spoil the broth, my friend," Marcus replied wryly, "and to be honest, your men prepared these defenses. You have an intimacy with them that I lack. I'm going to make a nuisance of myself up at the battlements." Over his shoulder, he called, "Make me proud."

Chapter Thirty-Eight

Transition

"Are you sure about that?" Mac gasped. "The wall has been breached?"

Jumping up from his seat, he clicked his fingers in the air to quieten the other people gathered around him in the mess hall.

"Yes, yes," Andy Webb replied, "Vice Commander Amine had just left when the whole southeast quadrant went up like a nova."

"Has there been a collapse? We didn't feel anything."

"Negative. But I'm looking at a king-sized void within the city environs."

"At the weak point?"

"You guessed right. Fortunately for us, the legion boys are already fighting back. Their response and the defensive arc they prepared are making mincemeat of the initial surge, but . . ."

"It's not going to hold, is it?"

"Right again. We're not just talking about a wave of spooks; it's a literal tsunami of them. And the more that flood through, the more explosive their deaths become. From what I can see from here, initial Horde casualties have already vaporized the entire supply of iron within the first fifty yards or so. It's like an expanding holocaust down there."

Mac juggled strategies in his head. He knew he had to make a decision. *Stop dithering and act.*

To the rest of the crews within the dining hall, he shouted, "Out. Leave your food and anything you can't carry. The Horde is within the city. Make your way to the evacuation point and follow the directions of the marshals you find there. Don't panic, we have soldiers lining the main routes. Now go!"

People erupted from their seats.

Resuming his conversation with the sniper team, Mac fired off a series of questions. "Is your area currently clear? Who else have you notified?"

"The courtyard is free of enemy activity. Bob's completed two resonance sweeps, and the only place we can spot grunt movement is down within the arc. And in answer to your second question, you are the only commander I've updated so far."

"Roger that. As soon as we finish speaking, link in to the main array and update Mohammed on the *Arch of Winter*. Tell him from me, "I told you so". He'll understand what that means. I want the fifty flyers I prepared for this eventuality deployed now. Sam and I will make our way down to the Archive to grab Saul. Finished or not, he's coming with us. Please let him know in advance, if he doesn't come willingly, it's going to get painful."

Still thinking on his feet, Mac continued, "Are Amelius and the boys holding? How much time will they give us?"

"Hard to say. They're sticking to plan, firing off a few salvos to slow the advance, and then retreating through the maze toward the more concentrated lines of defense, but . . . Jeez, Boss. I don't know. From what I'm looking at, it's as if a river full of demons has burst its banks. They just keep pouring through."

"In view of that, get on to Stu and Fonzy. They should be patrolling in the area of the second tier. If they haven't already, get them to scoot over to the inner wall. You know? The one Amelius and his men prepared as a chokepoint with the scorpios? Ask them to provide covering fire from that position until backup arrives."

"Backup?"

"They'll know it when they see it."

"Roger that. What about Mark and Sean?"

"Leave them free. I can't think of everything, and Mark will know what to do if he runs into trouble."

Just as he was about to sign off, Mac cursed himself for being so stupid. "Andy? Sorry, I can't believe I didn't verify this before. How many Horde Masters have shown their faces so far?"

"So far? None . . ."

*

Angule stepped warily down from the portal and swept the interior of their new environment with the lightest scan he could muster. *Nothing! We have been successful.* Turning back, he gestured toward the void and motioned for the others to follow him out.

The interior of the Hall of Remembrance was soon filled with the presence of ten extraordinary entities, each of whom was stunned to silence by the ambiance of their new and strange surroundings.

Angule took a moment longer to survey the location he had chosen for their incursion.

His cabal now occupied the center of a vast domed chamber. Before them, in front of an impressively proportioned window, stood a huge column of heavily veined rock. It glowed with a gentle blue radiance, and Angule could feel the subtle energies imbued within it. A sensation he found as relaxing as it was welcoming. Atop the structure sat a quadrilateral feature encompassed within a halo of power.

The perimeter of the gallery itself was adorned by a number of oversized bas-reliefs which appeared to have been cut directly from the fabric of the wall. Like the opening, they stretched from floor to ceiling, each giving the impression that the humans had left a gigantic written work on open display for visitors to read. Angule was unfamiliar with the characters etched into the surface of each relief, but the tone they emitted conveyed a sense of loss and deep sorrow.

We are the cause of such regret, he perceived.

A small podium had been erected before each edifice, upon which an artifact was positioned, highlighted from above in an unknown fashion by a soft humming radiance.

Treat this sanctuary with respect, Angule warned. *It is a place of commemoration to those lost to our savagery.*

His admonition was unnecessary, for each of his brethren was enamored by the quality of the room. Breaking the trance, he commanded: *Gather round, my family, for our work must continue apace, and urgently so.*

He displayed several different sets of coordinates to each pair. *These are locations you need to protect at all costs. Once on site, remain hidden for as long as you can and protect whatever stragglers you encounter. If you must expose yourselves, employ your heaviest shields, especially if soldiers are present with their quantum devices. Make it plain you are not there to cause harm. Remember, expression conveys purpose more clearly than posturing. I suggest you use the barbarity of the unrestrained Trianium to your advantage. Demonstrate your intent. The humans may surprise you.*

And what of you, Prime Catalyct? Caym asked. *Will you seek the Cryptogen immediately?*

Of course. And the lost child, for now we are within the sphere of restraint, I sense his presence . . . strange as it is.

*

"I know you wish to add our strength to the fight, brothers," Flavius stressed to his gathered commanders, "but as I found to my cost, our enemy is as cunning as they are brutal. We cannot abandon our post, for they may seek to exploit the advantage these battlements would give them."

"But we must do something, Sir," Centurion Quintus Aurelia complained. "While we stand here, our brothers are being overrun. The beasts are already halfway to the fosse."

Flavius surveyed the scene below. *And the cursed Masters still haven't shown their faces. Perhaps I can do something about that?*

He grinned.

"Galerius, Tiberius? You will both keep your centuriae at wall. However, I don't want it to appear that way. Galerius, your unit will continue to man the battlements. Spread them out and make them apparent. Tiberius, you will muster your troops and begin leading them away as if continuing the evacuation. As soon as you reach the curtain, reposition your squads along the inner corridors, ready for deployment back onto the main apron. Ensure you remain hidden from sight. Publius, Quintus? Your centuriae will stick to the plan and leave for the First Magister's courtyard now. However, take the scenic route." he nodded toward the inner bulwark. "Thataway. If you are still keen to lend your support, and assess the situation as needing your intervention, please feel free to do so. Understood?"

"Yes, Sir!" they chorused.

As his officers ran to carry out his orders, Flavius scrutinized the growing maelstrom below. *Now it's your turn.*

*

Mohammed ground his teeth in frustration. *We were so close to a clean getaway. Just one more hour and it would have been game over.*

"Sir? Vice Commander Amine?" Hanna O'Hara, one of the communication officers called. "I have a message for you from Lieutenant McDonald. Evidently, 'he told you so', and he wants the drones you prepared in advance."

"Yes, thank you, Hanna. I've been expecting his call. I'll get onto that right away."

"Drones?"

Mohammed turned to find Ephraim Miller standing right behind him. The scientist added, "I thought they were all supposed to be coming with us?"

"That's what we hoped. Now it looks like we'll be fifty down."

Addressing the ship's AI system, Mohammed raised his voice. "Serovai? Please would you be kind enough to initiate emergency program McDonald Omega Master One?"

"What's so special about these flyers?" Ephraim pressed.

"You'll see. Let's just say that half of them have been programmed to hunt for a very specific spectral signature. It's going to get hot down there, really soon."

*

Lathered with sweat, the horse wheezed with every stride, laboring terribly under the strain of their wild gallop. Ignoring his mount's protestations, James Houston hunkered down in the saddle and pushed it to even greater efforts.

C'mon. Just a little bit further.

The train was only fifty yards away. Chuffing loudly, it tooted twice and accelerated as it built up steam. His gaze remained fixed on the tail-end box cart. The door had been flung wide open, and an unknown woman leaned out into the wind, holding her bonnet in place with one hand, and calling his name.

An arrow zinged past his head.

James ducked and dug his heels into the animal's flanks as further missiles showered down around him. The yodeling cry of his pursuers drew ever nearer and he tensed, waiting for the inevitable impalement.

Twenty yards to go.

Arm outstretched, the woman called from the doorway, "Faster, James. You've got to ride faster. It'll be all over if you don't."

Ten yards.

He glanced back over his shoulder. The war party had fanned out on either side in preparation for the kill. Some had stowed their bows and drawn their tomahawks.

Two yards.

Drawing alongside, James furiously thrashed his reins from side to side.

I'm going to make it.

He leaned toward his mystery helper. Groping. Straining...

Their fingers brushed.

Thunk! A shaft sprouted from the doorframe, causing them both to flinch, and shy away from one another.

No. Not now. Gritting his teeth, he increased his labors. *I'm not going to die today.*

The whistle of another near miss hissed past his ear, and the cries of his pursuers grew more desperate.

He stood in his stirrups and reached out again. Their hands met, then clasped tightly together. With surprising strength, James found himself lifted from the saddle and yanked into the safety of the car's interior. The door slammed shut, just as a fusillade of arrows hammered against the exterior wall.

Adjusting to the sway of the train, James fought his way to his knees and allowed his eyes to adjust to the sudden gloom. "Who are you?" he asked, "and how do you know my name?"

"I'm Pandora," she replied, "and I've been waiting for you . . . forever."

She threw back her head and screamed.

Waking with a start, James discovered he was drenched in sweat and panting wildly. He sprang from his bed and stared wide-eyed around the room, searching for the cause of the woman's panic. It took him a moment to recognize the reality of his surroundings.

A dream. It was just a dream.

As his thudding heart regained a measure of stability, James leaned against a cabinet, shut his eyes, and inhaled deeply. His hand came to rest on the remote control. Flicking on the TV, he allowed the familiarity of his favorite recording to calm his nerves.

The gossamer kiss of a cool breeze added its welcome succor.

Aah, that's better.

Where . . . ?

Intuition brought lucidity and a heightened sense of alertness. His eyes snapped open, his attention drawn to the same spot that had mesmerized him repeatedly over the past week.

It's happening again.

James walked slowly toward the area in front of his bathroom. As he passed the bottom of his bed, he scooped Heaven's-Claw into his grasp and pressed it to his chest. The air appeared to flex. He froze, watching incredulously as the doorway bent inward, as if being sucked down a plughole. The entire entrance abruptly disappeared into a gray void.

James edged away, and then caught his breath as an icy backwash flowed into the room. The spectacle filled him with a thrilling sense of joy and expectation.

His grip on reason cartwheeled as something huge, something indescribable, stepped out of the tear. He was struck by an overwhelming sense of recognition.

Staggering, he gasped, "Are *you* Pandora?"

Chapter Thirty-Nine

The Ninth

Repeated concussions from all angles threatened to burst his eardrums. Ignoring the discomfort, Flavius swung his sword in long-practiced, measured strokes. His arm went numb as another detonation thundered against the iron studs of his shield. Leaping away, he allowed the sizzling discharge to ground out before bounding back into the fight.

It was at times like this when Flavius hated being right. His strategy to lure the Horde out of hiding had worked like a charm. Less than two minutes after Tiberius led his centuriae away, a rift opened above the southern gatehouse and a host of monsters issued forth. Once battle was joined, the swarm was bolstered by the arrival of four Horde Masters, who began directing their troops with alarming proficiency.

Flavius and his warriors had endured a frenzied ten minute assault that quickly drove them toward the edge of exhaustion.

"Hold!" he cried above the roar. "Hold the line. Tiberius and his centuriae will be with us any moment."

Men screamed in anguish as they succumbed to a horrific fate. Slashing out as they fell, several of the dying soldiers managed to take a number of devils with them. His heart swelled in admiration, and their example only served to make him all the more determined not to let the rest of the cohort down.

On the other side of the bulwark, Flavius could see his optio, Antonius Septimus, rallying three contubernium of hard-pressed legionnaires. The seasoned veteran's experience made a huge difference, for he had devised a tactic to avoid the crushing affect of being too close to the ogres when they expired. He had managed to attach his pugio to a length of chain-link metal capped by a leather thong. Whirling the dagger about him like a whip, Antonius was making such short work of those brutes nearest him that they were beginning to shy away from his wrath.

Then Tiberius and his centuriae appeared on the stairwells behind the fray. Dividing his force into two, he set half his men against the Bosses while the rest engaged the rear ranks of the enemy grunts.

Tiberius had used his head. Having the advantage of being able to see how the battle was evolving, he had positioned a squad of sagittaria within the front file. No sooner had the counterattack begun than his strategy paid dividends.

Flavius watched in amazement as a fusillade of arrows cut the shrieking banshees to shreds. Recoiling in panic, the spooks flung themselves headlong over the main battlements, or down into the arc below, to escape.

Pity the drop doesn't kill the bastards.

The Controllers found themselves alone atop the walkway. An eerie lull ensued as both sides weighed each other up.

An unseen signal passed between the ogres, and they advanced as one body. Calling for reinforcements from the vortex, they regrouped, but this time it was the Masters who led.

A volley of arrows arced out from the legion lines, only to bounce impotently off a glittering shield of violet and silver potency.

Flavius swore. *Pluto's beard. What are we going to do now?*

*

The longer Marcus looked, the more the rippling curtain of lava appeared to expand.

The effect reminded him of a time some years previously when he had attended a wedding party in Gaul. The groom, a newly-appointed tribune from Rome, loved to show off his family's wealth, and had employed over a dozen slaves to bring an oversized wineskin into the middle of the celebrations marquee. Unfortunately, the director of ceremonies had allowed the skin to be overfilled. The constant jostling, along with the simple act of trying to move such an awkwardly heavy object into the tent, caused the hide to split from the neck down. What started as a tiny rent quickly turned into a huge tear, and the entire contents gushed out onto the floor.

Marcus was staring at a similar sight now. Only it wasn't the product of the vine that cascaded through the gap. Instead, a molten sea of liquid fire flooded toward them. Curling and rolling in a deceptively languid way, sinuous tentacles of brimstone and sulfur surged out to fill all the trenches, crest every mound, and search out lone stragglers with surprising ease. Amid a cacophony of thunderous detonations, everything in its path was consumed.

The catapults fired again. A cloud of arrows rained down. Bursts of lurid flame shot upward as hundreds of ghouls died.

They just keep coming. How can anyone disregard such carnage with so little consequence?

He cast his gaze along the entire width of the arc. Judging. Assessing.

Although the defenses have done exactly what we wanted, they are being swept aside as if negligible. Anything not made of lydium is obliterated. They've already reached the moat. The speed—

"Look there!" Amelius shouted in his ear. "Can you see?" Pointing off to one side, he drew Marcus's attention to a glowing sphere of purple light hovering over the remains of the utility building. Within it, a small crowd of coroneted beasts huddled together. A brief flash announced the departure of almost half the figures inside.

At last! Shielding his eyes from the growing wash of heat, Marcus exclaimed, "I was wondering when our true enemies would reveal themselves. Amelius, direct the eastern batteries to concentrate their fire upon that location. I know the swine are protected, but at least we can distract them from . . ."

His voice trailed away. In front of them, the mad charge ground to a halt.

"What are they doing, Sir? Are they afraid of the dyke?"

"I wouldn't count on it."

Marcus paused to survey the slavering, snarling ranks of the Horde. In their highly excited state, the outlines of individual ogres were clearly visible, and the sight of thousands upon thousands of snapping jaws and flexing talons sent a shock of fear along his spine.

"The addition of the Controllers will make a huge difference," he murmured, "so for goodness' sake, make sure we seize the advantage while we can. Command all weapons to open fire."

Amelius conveyed the order, and within seconds the air was filled with iron.

The enemy's front ranks exploded skyward. Marcus nodded in grim satisfaction as a series of secondary detonations continued to ripple through the mob for nearly a minute.

"Again!" he hissed.

The throng pulsed. Monsters situated along the outer flanks shuffled inward to crowd in behind their compatriots. Those already to the front also adjusted their position. Thinning their numbers, they edged forward, toward the earthwork. Within the span of a few heartbeats, a distinct wedge formation had emerged.

They're going to attempt the moat.

In answer to Marcus's realization, a rippling skein of arcane theurgy bloomed outward from the knot of Horde Masters. Dancing across the heads of the gathered assembly, the web knitted to form a concentrated nucleus at the tip of the blockade. Once the leading file was enmeshed, the multitude reacted. Letting out a deafening roar, they marched forward.

Marcus held his breath.

As the first spook pressed into the iron stakes, the shield darkened to deep maroon. The ogre shuddered.

He's not combusting!

The strength of the seizure grew, and spread to the surrounding brutes. Their extremities seemed to inflate and undulate. Inevitably, after a few seconds, they succumbed to the anathema of their kind and disappeared in a blinding flash. The gap was immediately choked by willing volunteers.

"Did you see that?" Marcus gasped. "They lasted longer before dying."

"And look," Amelius cried, "a myriad still pour through the gateway."

Marcus made a decision.

"Sound the retreat. I want the wall and arc completely clear of our people. We'll fall back to the inner defenses and surround the teleport ring. Update the relevant commanders."

"How long do you think that will take?" Amelius queried.

"For everyone still in the city? That's about two thousand souls altogether. Maybe another thirty to forty minutes?"

"Marcus! The demons destroyed the first level in less than thirty minutes. And now they are protected by some eldritch contrivance of their masters."

The two men stared at each other. Their eyes said it all.

It was Amelius's turn to make a hard choice.

"We will stay," he stated. "The Fourth Cohort will hold them here, to ensure the safety of everyone else."

"You will die," Marcus murmured.

"Then we will die well."

Marcus could see his friend would not be swayed.

"Very well. Have your cornicen use the radio to get Flavius and his unit to fall back to the Magister's courtyard. Hold the Horde here as long as you can, but don't waste lives. Remember, the inner wall is well defended, and every second you delay them saves a life."

"Then we will save many." Amelius saluted crisply. "For the Ninth."

"For Rome and Rhomane," Marcus replied, returning the salute. Turning quickly, he made his way from the platform before his men could see the tears in his eyes.

*

Stained-With-Blood peeked in both directions along the corridor, listening. The way seemed clear, but he knew appearances could be deceiving. Stepping out, he moved to one side and pressed his ear and fingertips to the wall. Closing his eyes, he relaxed and extended his senses into the fabric of the stone-work. A minute or two passed before he repeated the process on the opposite side of the hall.

"This way," he murmured, indicating the route leading north. "We can loop back after the first stairwell and avoid the conflict now unfurling above us."

Small Robes came forward to stand by her uncle's side. She was followed by a band of Cree warriors led by Snow Blizzard and White Bear.

Snow Blizzard turned to the braves. "Protect the princess at all costs."

Bows at the ready, his men fanned out and moved silently along the passage. Vibrations radiated through the floor and walls, providing subtle hints of the fight raging overhead. Feeling them, Small Robes looked about anxiously.

Stained-With-Blood squeezed his niece's shoulder. "Try to relax, child. We are only several tiers beneath the evacuation point. Even if we encounter trouble, these hallways are well defended and aid will come quickly."

Reaching the intersection, the main party paused while several braves scouted ahead. One pair took up firing positions on the first landing below them, while two more scooted up to the next level. The sound of a cricket chirping signaled the way was clear.

As they ascended, the echoes of battle grew steadily louder. Someone could be heard shouting orders. A rapid volley of shots rang out, followed by the *crump* of muted explosions. The floor shook, and loose particles of dust were shaken from overhead ledges. The tramp of many feet resounded in the air.

Snow Blizzard signaled to his lead scouts, and they sprinted up the stairs to intercept whoever was there. Moments later, a command rang out, and the chime of armored boots approached. A face appeared at the banister, peering down.

"I am Centurion Quintus Scipio, and my centuriae are at your service. You are fortunate to have met us, for we are lending our strength to the defenses here while we await our turn at the transporter pad."

Stepping forward, Stained-With-Blood called up, "Well met, Quintus Scipio. You are known to me, as are your commanders, Flavius Velerianus and Marcus Brutus. How are your men?"

"They are well, if somewhat frustrated at having to leave at such a time. But orders are orders." Quintus glanced around the heavily armed war party, and then at Small Robes. "May I help you?"

"Yes, you can. The princess must be escorted to safety. Will you see her to the *Arch of Winter* on my behalf?"

"I will. But are you not leaving yourself?"

Small Robes turned to look at her uncle, puzzlement on her face.

"I will stay here," Stained-With-Blood replied. "Not only must I retrieve something precious to me, but our remaining warriors must be—"

"Uncle?" Small Robes interjected. "What are you doing? You can't leave. Not now. Why must you—"

"Hush, child. There is something I must do. Worry not, I will be completely safe and will rejoin you before you know it." He gestured to Snow Blizzard. "Your husband-to-be is a capable man. Both he and the centurion will guarantee your welfare until I can be with you again."

Snow Blizzard gazed long and hard at his former adversary. "You honor me," he whispered. Drawing his knife, the Cree chieftain pressed the blade to his hand and scored a line across his palm. "By my blood, I swear to protect her with my life."

Small Robes looked back and forth between the two men before lowering her eyes in resignation. A small sigh escaped her lips. "Be safe, my uncle."

The stairwell vibrated in response to a powerful, nearby explosion. Voices mingled above as updates were given and further commands issued.

"We must go," Quintus called down, "quickly. We dare not delay."

Making eye contact with his niece, Stained-With-Blood nodded once, then turned and ran back toward the bowels of the city.

*

Mac and Sam entered the Ark control room, only to find Saul Cameron still fussing over the controls of a large computer console.

"C'mon Commander," Mac advised. "It's time to leave."

Saul didn't appear to hear the request and continued working.

Okay. Have it your way. "Please don't make me angry," Mac warned, "you wouldn't like me when I'm angry."

Saul turned toward him. Maintaining eye contact, Mac unclipped his weapon and placed it on the table. Cocking his head to one side, he cracked the knuckle of each finger. "Because I tend to get rather aggressive."

Saul gasped. "You wouldn't dare!"

"That's the other lot," Mac retorted.

In response to the confused look on the commander's face, Mac added, "The SAS. *They* dare. And they win most of the time, too. Our lot gets things done by strength and guile. And just so we're clear, *Commander*. My job is to haul your ass upstairs and get you safely aboard the *Arch of Winter*. If you put your own safety in jeopardy, I'll get very . . . hands on. I'll give you one minute before I demonstrate what I mean."

Saul glanced at Sam Pell. Mac did too, and could see his partner was grinning from ear to ear. Nothing about the smile was friendly.

"Oh, very well," Saul conceded, "I suppose I was being overly cautious anyway. The seal is ready to go, and I can trigger the lockdown from orbit."

"Good to hear. Now let's get a move on. By all accounts, things are getting pretty volatile topside."

Mac retrieved his machine gun, and they headed for the exit. As the control room doors opened, they discovered a sentinel waiting outside, along with two of the .50 cannons.

"Greetings, Lieutenant McDonald. As requested, I have prepared the weapons for transport. Just enter the appropriate codes, and the localized translocators will activate and deposit them at the site of your choice."

"Excellent. Have the emplacements in the exterior corridor also been prepped?"

"Of course. The entire array has been linked into one circuit, as you requested."

"Thank you, custodian. That will be all."

"Why are you moving the sentry posts?" Saul queried. "I would have thought you'd want them to remain here as insurance."

"If I left them where they are, it would be a terrible waste of limited resources. Especially once the rip-space tear is sealed. We still have over a thousand people in the city awaiting evacuation, and these guns will make a huge difference once they're in the right place."

"So where are you sending them?"

"This pair is going to the chokepoint above the inner wall. They're fighting a losing battle up there, so ten thousand rounds and an entire rack of mini micro-mines will give them an edge they've been lacking."

Mac paused to activate the locator beacons, and typed a code into his wrist pad. "The ones outside will help form a last line of defense around the emergency pad itself. Fortunately, there are only two ways into the Magister's courtyard from the battlements, so we'll have things well covered."

A brief hum preceded the moment each of the cannons disappeared, and a strange prickling sensation crawled across Mac's skin. *Hmm. Must be a side effect of the transporter.*

Dismissing the sensation as of no consequence, he led the small group from the Archive. As they marched swiftly along, he eavesdropped on the continual chatter on the local network. It made painful listening.

Those blasted Masters have rallied their troops in a way we've never encountered. They'll be through the arc before the last of the stragglers makes it to the pad . . . Unless we do something about it.

Tapping his earpiece, he said, "Andy, are you there?"

There was a short interval before Andy Webb replied. "Sorry, Boss, I had to concentrate for a moment or two. Some of our soul-sucking friends were getting a bit too close for comfort. They're out of the picture now. How can I help?"

"Is the Horde advance still snowballing?"

"That's an unfortunate yes. They've organized themselves into one huge, diamond-tip formation. The Controllers are augmenting their minions' resistance to the iron in some way that slows the destructive process. They still explode, but it takes longer. When they do, it vaporizes everything in the blast radius, defenses included. As soon as the dust settles, their eager buddies slip in from behind to take their place. They'll be at the wall in five minutes. Six, tops."

"Where are the damned flyers?"

"On the way. ETA, three minutes. Talk about the cavalry, eh? Oh, and just to let you know, Stu, Fonzy, and Marcus said thank you for the guns."

"Are they making a difference?"

"Not yet, Boss. Sean's in the middle of adjusting the parameters on one of the cannons as we speak. The shields around the ogres are quite effective, so he's going to coordinate the firing sequence to activate following the detonation of a mine. We'll save some in reserve, just in case the Masters decide to get brave. In any event, it should spoil their parade quite nicely."

"Good thinking. Get Mark and Sean to liaise with Stu and Fonzy at the chokepoint. Once the flyers and cannons take over, have them orchestrate a structured withdrawal. We're on the way to the surface with the commander. Expect the second set of sentries at your location any minute now."

"Roger that. Safe journey."

Breaking the link, Mac saw they had reached the perimeter doors to the Archive. Activating the bio-scanner, he waited for the exit to manifest, and nodded to Sam to make ready.

The arch appeared, solidified, and glided silently apart. An icy chill washed over them from the corridor, and Mac was once again struck by the odd impression of insects on skin. As the robot sentries reacted to their presence, Mac felt his stomach turn, and was forced to take a few deep breaths to keep his queasiness at bay. *I've had this feeling before. Where . . . ?*

"Contact!" he snapped, bringing his weapon to the shoulder.

"What's happening?" Saul hissed.

"Wait!" Ignoring the distraction of the automatic sensors, Mac scanned the length of the passageway before them.

Nothing?

The nausea continued to build.

Reaching behind, Mac grabbed Saul by the arm. "Stay with me as I move. Sam? I'll check forward, you cover our asses. There's a Horde portal nearby. I can feel it. Remember?"

"Yes, I bloody well do. Nice one, Boss. Do you think it's our friend, or one of the other buggers?"

"We can only—"

Mac was overcome by a wave of dizziness. His vision swam, seeming to ripple like a corrugated roof. He staggered, and a translucent image loomed before his eyes. *Is that Stained-With-Blood's tomahawk?* His sight shifted, and the perspective of his surroundings appeared to zoom away from him, as if falling into a receding tunnel. A familiar mental voice echoed within his mind. *Cryptogen.*

The sensation faded, and Mac found himself on his knees, slumped against the wall.

Voices crowded him.

"Boss. Are you all right?"

"What's happening? Are we under attack?"

"Where's the danger?"

Shaking his head, Mac struggled to his feet. "It's okay, we're safe. I'm all right."

As his eyes came back into focus, Mac knew what he had to do.

"I'm sorry, guys, I can't go with you."

His announcement was met by stunned silence and looks of utter disbelief.

Turning to Saul, he said, "Follow Sam. He'll get you away from here."

Mac handed Sam two sets of locator beacons. "Place these on the guns and then enter this code." He paused to transmit the appropriate cipher. "You will find the sentinels ensured there's sufficient power available within those units to transport several people, as well as the emplacements themselves.

Activate them, and get the commander away from here. Once you've succeeded, join Andy and Bob in the First Magister's courtyard. It's going to get real busy there. Soon."

"What about you, Sir?"

"Me?" Mac snorted. "I think I'm finally going to discover the key to a longstanding puzzle."

*

Never in his life had Marcus felt so helpless.

For the last fifteen minutes, he'd been forced to watch a fellow officer and personal, long-term friend fight a losing battle that made his heart burn with pride and grief.

Amelius Crispus never stood a chance of winning. The intervention of the Controllers saw to that. Despite that fact, Amelius had clearly been determined to make the enemy pay dearly for every inch of ground the 4th Cohort was forced to concede, for he inspired his men to fight a rearguard action that answered the death of every legionnaire with at least two of their enemy's.

Adopting tactics similar to those employed by the Horde Masters, Amelius ordered his troops to form a double-layered, thirty-man wide defensive box. Once ready, he arranged the remaining soldiers into smaller bands of ten fighters each, and positioned them behind the protective line. Every time someone died, waiting archers peppered the Horde wedge with arrows while one of their comrades stepped forward to fill the breach. Even when a number of grunts were slain at once, sending stunned warriors sprawling to the floor, prepared snatch squads ran forward and dragged the survivors to safety, so other valiant brothers could take their place.

It was as glorious to watch as it was devastating, for attrition and sheer exhaustion eventually took its toll.

When the shield wall collapsed, the spooks surged forward, baying for blood. Yet still the legionnaires refused to run. Holding their ground, they grouped together, raised their swords high, and charged the advancing ogres.

The resultant explosion engulfed the area in a storm of anguish, and shook the inner wall to its foundations. Once the glare died down, less than forty men of the four hundred and fifty that began the fight remained.

They died as they lived. Fighting.

Marcus watched as the survivors limped and crawled toward the safety of the secondary moat. Artfully crafted, it served as another line of defense in front of the inner wall. *Now, only the scorpios and the guns stand in the way of our enemy.*

Eyeing the distance between the injured men and the howling ghouls, he assessed their chances of reaching the dyke safely. *Thirty, perhaps thirty-five feet? They'll never make it.*

"What are you doing?" he bellowed to the catapult captains. "Waiting for a bloody invitation? Fire!"

As the officers turned to reissue his command, they were staggered by a blast of immense proportions. A huge front segment of the Horde ranks abruptly disappeared amid a blinding inferno that forced most onlookers to duck down behind the buttress.

What in the name of Mars was that?

Ears ringing, Marcus looked around and noticed everyone had been frozen to the spot. He glanced up. *Flyers?* "Flyers!" he shouted, pointing into the air.

A cheer erupted from the gathered defenders as the squadron of drones dropped from the sky. Splitting into two formations, one flight continued to harry the monsters gathered before the inner gates, while the other divided into smaller groups and made a beeline for the Bosses scattered throughout the arc and along the battlements.

Further detonations rocked the city. Marcus felt the familiar tug of the pressure variance caused by the activation of the strange, futuristic weapons. Reality bent and warped in one place after another as hundreds of monsters were crushed out of existence.

He peered over the top of the battlements, using his binoculars to zoom in on the far wall. *And* still *they pour through the magic breach. Is there no end to this perversion?*

He jumped as the heavy cannons beside him went into action. The deep *thud-thud-thud-thud* of their cyclic pattern created a distinctive counterpoint to the higher tones of the lighter machine guns that quickly joined in.

Scanning further along the buttress, Marcus espied several familiar faces. *Ah, I see Lieutenant McDonald has spared a contingent of his men to come to our aid.*

He gazed back down into the horror of no-man's-land, relief flooding through him as he realized a number of flyers had taken up holding patterns above the heads of the fleeing survivors.

They're going to make it after all.

As if in answer to his prayer, a cluster of reverberating booms and flashes of lightning broke out at various points along the main parapet.

"The beast masters are thwarted!" someone shouted.

Sure enough, when Marcus surveyed the region of each outburst, he could see the widespread panic the drones had caused. A number of Controllers had obviously perished, and the aftermath of the gravity fluctuations were still wreaking havoc on Horde and environment alike.

The few Bosses still remaining began to flee.

As the last one disappeared into a portal, the glittering curtain protecting the front of their army frittered away. The massed ranks of the Horde stalled, as if robbed of their motivating force.

A moment's silence ensued. Then a *twang* from somewhere further along the barbican announced the release of an arrow. Burning with pitch, it arced through the air and fell squarely in the center of the secondary moat. The iron and tar mixture blazed into life, and the survivors making their way toward the gates shouted in jubilation. The sound of their voices jarred everyone back into action.

The ghouls moved first.

They hadn't taken more than a few steps before the robot guns adjusted their targeting trajectory and started decimating the center mass of their ranks.

Then the archers and ballistae operators opened fire.

The air was filled with a lethal mixture of spiteful-looking barbs, three-foot long steel bolts, and thousands of rounds.

Down below, a swarm of explosions ripped from one end of the Horde charge to the other, setting off a chain reaction of secondary detonations that forced Marcus to flinch. A multitude of ogres was consumed. Yet despite their catastrophic losses they continued to advance, pressed forward from behind by eager reinforcements and the mindless need to consume life force.

Cold reality clutched at his bowels. *At this rate, we cannot possibly survive.*

He tried to judge how many soldiers and other refugees still remained. *It would appear Amelius isn't the only one who may have to sacrifice his men this day.*

As Marcus calculated how many warriors would be required to hold the enemy at bay, he was approached by a legionnaire officer. The soldier was limping, badly bruised, and covered in burns. It took Marcus a moment to recognize Flavius's optio, Antonius Septimus.

"Antonius? How fares the upper wall?"

"It persists, Colonel. The flying machines have cleared it of all infestation, and remain to guard against further incursions." His face fell. "Pity they could not have arrived sooner."

Something in the way Antonius spoke conveyed a deeper meaning.

"What of Flavius?" Marcus asked. "Galerius? Tiberius?"

Antonius shook his head. His shoulders dropped.

"Survivors?"

"A mere twenty of us, Sir. I'm sorry we could not do more."

"You did enough, Antonius. More than enough. The Ninth Legion will be remembered with honor this day, for we did what others could not. Even though it cost us dearly, we protected those in our care from abominations such as this."

He gestured, and both men turned to look out into what remained of the arc of death.

Heedless of the bullets that shredded their essences, regardless of the iron fragments that rained mercilessly down on them, the monsters continued pressing relentlessly on.

Marcus added, "How could so few of us ever hope to stand against such numbers? Or their mindless willingness to expend themselves?"

Antonius didn't answer. A haunted look in his eyes, he stared mutely down into the carnage that had been their last, best hope against defeat.

He's in shock. And who can blame him?

"Get yourself and your men to the transporter," Marcus advised gently. "Your fight is over. Those of us who remain here will suffice."

Or die trying.

*

As Ayria Solram entered the counseling wing, she was struck by how large the ward looked without people to fill it.

James Houston's suite was at the other end of the module, and the *click* of her heels echoed around the room as she walked along the central aisle.

It's so quiet in here. But at least it's kept him out of the way until the last moment. I'd better call for an escort though, just in case he gets agitated when I take him out into the open. Although the ships aren't here, the fighting is bound to unsettle him.

She was about to activate her com-link when she discerned the drone of a TV report in the background. *He wouldn't be watching the same old thing again . . . would he?*

Pausing outside his door, she craned her neck to listen.

"That was the awful moment when the Shivan-Estre met her end. For reasons as yet unknown, her navigational beacon malfunctioned. Appearing from rip-space only . . ."

Oh, for goodness' sake. How does he not get bored by—

". . . you kidding? I'll never let that happen to me again. I'd rather die . . ."

Stunned, Ayria held her breath. She recognized Houston's voice right away. But something about the manner in which he spoke troubled her. *It's almost as if he's engaged in an actual conversation with someone.*

In an effort to gain greater clarity, she placed her ear against one of the panels and closed her eyes. For some reason, the gesture only made her feel lightheaded.

Houston was still speaking. ". . . that I hated the most was the isolation. The terrible loneliness of confinement. Being that close to someone and yet unable to utter a single coherent thought because of the mutating effect of the transition. Nobody should have to go through that. Or what you yourself have had to endure, come to that. You say you can help me prevent it? Then do something, quickly, for goodness' . . ."

Confinement? Mutation? Prevent what?

The feeling of dizziness persisted. Ayria was forced to brace herself against the doorframe to stop herself from falling. Even so, her curiosity prevented her from calling out for help, as it now sounded as if Houston were actually arguing with someone.

"... me to wait? Why? Who for? Don't you appreciate the risk? If we delay any longer, there's a danger I won't be able to shed this ..."

Ayria's stomach growled and she felt a lump rising in her throat.

I'd better get this over with. I feel like I might vomit if I don't get into the fresh air soon.

Grasping the handle, Ayria opened the door without knocking. She walked swiftly inside. "Come on, James, time to g–" *Oh my God!*

Frozen like a deer in headlights, Ayria willed herself to turn and run, but her legs refused to obey. She attempted to think of something that might delay the inevitable, but her mind congealed into a screaming nub of shock.

Struggling to breathe, she was only vaguely aware that James Houston existed, for her attention had been captured by his visitor. A twelve foot tall apparition of crimson and blue radiance, crowned with dancing flames.

Chapter Forty

Endgame

"Did you see that?" Bob Neville's voice hissed via the radio. "Over on the southern quadrant. Sector Six. Focus on the gatehouse parapet. Here, I'll light it up with the laser."

Andy Webb scuttled to one side, homing in on the scarlet hotspot. Concentrating, he soon understood what had caught his partner's eye.

"Got it," he murmured, "well spotted! It looks like the Bosses are back, though they seem to be happy to stay out of the spotlight."

Amending his resolution, Andy studied his target. He had an idea.

I wonder?

A swift check along the entire rim of the main battlements gave him his answer.

"It looks like they're popping up all over the place. I knew the retreat would leave us open to counterattack. They're pouring through that breach now, and there's nothing we can do to stop them spreading out. I think they're trying to circumvent the chokepoint by using the higher barbican." He scanned along the higher levels. "Damn! They can get within a few hundred yards of this quadrangle without exposing themselves to fire."

Kneeling up, Andy shuffled round from his position to survey the crowd of refugees surrounding the transporter pad below him. He caught sight of a familiar face. "Bob? Run down and have a word with Sam, would you? He's just sent Commander Cameron up to the *Arch of Winter*, so he's exactly where we need him. Take him to one side and update him personally regarding this latest development. Then ask him, from me, to adjust the parameter of the cannons to include those passages. If we have uninvited guests, I want them to get a large slice of *fuck-off cake* as soon as they show their faces."

Bob grinned, flashed a thumbs-up, and scampered off.

Right, let's see what else these assholes are up to.

Resuming his position, Andy continued analyzing the unfolding drama before him. He noticed a gradual change taking place within the sea of grunts down in the arc. Instead of simply pressing forward as they had been up until now, the latest arrivals were flooding toward the abandoned facilities lining the edge of the fields. He knew from experience that many of those buildings had contained direct access to other portions of the city. Although each section had been collapsed in on itself and filled with a lethal network of steel and other debris, he realized the Horde would make short work of those barricades without anything to distract them.

Hello? Looks like the Controllers are calling for backup.

He looked slowly from side to side, studying every tactical facet of the walls that came to his attention. *Now, where would* I *go?*

Selecting a quadrant along the western rampart, he allowed his eyes to relax, let his focus turn inward, phased out the sounds of battle, and settled to wait.

The minutes ticked slowly by.

A burst of light glared forth from within the confines of a nearby gallery.

There!

Smirking in satisfaction, Andy initiated an open com-link, and moved the sights of his weapon onto the relevant area. "All units, all units, stand-by," he calmly announced. "We have an incursion on the western perimeter of the Magister's courtyard. Repeat. We have an incursion by Horde Masters along the western perimeter of the Magister's courtyard. Level three. Sub corridor one. Enemy forces have just materialized two hundred yards along the main passageway . . . Wait!"

He paused to fire an armor-piercing round toward a Boss that had stuck its head out too far.

Zing!

An area not one yard in front of the monster's face blushed deep red as the bullet ricocheted harmlessly away from its barrier.

"I say again," he resumed, "enemy forces have materialized within the main passageway along from the square, and are hidden from the sight of the flyers. Mine details? Please respond to the threat. Sam? Get those bloody guns online, and send a message to orbital control to reassign some of the drones."

Andy was abruptly overcome by a feeling that someone had walked across his grave. He shivered, and an icy fingernail continued scratching its way down his spine.

What the hell?

He sensed danger approaching from behind.

Turning, Andy glimpsed two glowing masses lumbering toward him. Swathed in purple and neon-blue flames, each was adorned with a coronet that looked as if shooting stars had somehow been captured in midflight, and placed in orbit around their heads.

He had nowhere to go.

In desperation he lunged for his satchel, fumbling with the flap that concealed his personal supply of mini micro-grenades.

Too late. The beasts were upon him.

He tensed, and his skin prickled for the briefest heartbeat as the nimbus of their auras grazed his prone figure. Then the sensation passed.

What? Why didn't they . . . ?

Flipping onto his front, he watched, amazed, as both Masters ran past him and jumped down into the quadrangle below. As they landed next to the fountain, their compatriots in the adjacent hallway came spilling out, followed by a howling pack of ghouls.

People screamed and began to run, everywhichway at once.

Guttural snarls ripped back and forth between the two Horde parties.

Jesus! It'll be a bloodbath.

Overcoming his astonishment, Andy managed to grab a mine from his pack.

The growling intensified, and the larger group of brutes moved toward the isolated Bosses, sandwiching a group of civilians between them.

Perfect, how can I take them out now?

"Contact! Contact!" he yelled into his microphone. "Third tier, Magister's courtyard. I need emergency response teams here on the double. Be advised, noncombatants are caught in the crossfire; I say again, we have noncombatants in the arena. Exercise caution when firing."

Dropping his grenade, Andy snatched up a machine gun from an equipment bag and drew a bead on the closest grunts. *C'mon, you bastards. Get out from behind your Bosses and see how long you last.*

The two Controllers that had ignored him dropped into defensive crouches. Scintillating bands of power appeared between their talons. No sooner had the plasma fused into concentrated balls of light than they slammed their hands together, sending a vicious shockwave radiating toward their opposite numbers.

The shields of the rival Masters hissed and stuttered as they absorbed the potency of the attack. Washing over and around the extremities of those barriers, the energy ribbons continued on, coiling around the spooks taking cover behind them.

The vitality of every unprotected ogre on the landing was torn apart, and the victorious assailants fed greedily on their essences.

I don't believe it! Are they . . . ?

Stomping sideways, the largest of the nearer Bosses made a sweeping motion with the back of its paw, and most of the trapped human stragglers were swept unceremoniously aside and away from danger.

Most, but not all.

The smaller Controller surged forward, adopting a protective stance above the terrified woman still caught in the danger zone. Andy watched, incredulously, as a silver-blue curtain glittered to the floor around the unlikely pair.

He . . . Jeesus! That's Jayden. It's protecting her?

The lone Master attacked the other Controllers again. On this occasion, it hammered them with a coherent beam of arcane puissance so powerful it bruised the color of their shields black.

The paired Bosses responded with a dual counterstrike.

Bloody hell! I'd better let the others in on this.

"All units, all units, sit-rep," Andy said. "Be advised, along with noncombatants we have friendly Horde forces on the loose in the area of the Magister's courtyard. I repeat. Some of the Horde Masters you see are on our sid–"

Blazing bands of lightning arced through the air, scorching columns and spars alike. Andy was forced to duck and roll away from a bolt that fried his sniper post to molten slag. Peeking over the rim, he saw that the enemy Bosses had managed to erect fresh shields and were now coordinating their assault on the solitary Controller. Approaching from opposite sides, they kept it on the retreat until they were within touching distance.

Evidently, this was exactly what the lone Master had been waiting for. A scarlet nimbus bloomed into view around its talons. Punching outward, it perforated the defensive shells of its attackers and grasped them by their wrists. Flexing mightily, it yanked them even closer, and unleashed a stunning wave of theurgy that flowed outward from its matrix and into its fellow ogres'. The addition of all that extra power disrupted their thresholds and warped their ability to generate effective shields. Before Andy realized what had happened, their defenses had frittered away in a crackling discharge.

Battling to maintain its grip, the Boss looked back over its shoulder and stared directly into Andy's soul. Baleful red eyes flared, and a compulsion echoed in the ether between them.

Duty.

I understand, Andy replied.

Scrambling back across the parapet, Andy snatched up his discarded grenade, pressed the button, and threw it toward the struggling ogres.

The brave Master watched it coming. Opening its jaws, it swallowed the device whole, then heaved with all its strength to ensure its victims couldn't get away. Its aura abruptly darkened as it was subjected to an overwhelming constriction that distorted its essence like a crushed soda can. It gripped its struggling brethren all the tighter. In moments, they too succumbed to the effects of the micro-singularity.

A terrible keening split the air. Building in intensity, it rose in volume until it felt like the walls would crack. As the Masters ignited, they were snatched away into oblivion, and the noise cut off.

Chunks of debris and ruined trelliswork flew through the air in the rush to fill the vacuity left behind. Andy had to hold on tight to avoid being pulled from his perch.

I don't believe it! He sacrificed himself to eliminate the danger.

He glanced back to the remaining Controller, who was still crouched protectively over Jayden Cole.

So how the hell are we going to tell them apart?

*

The air still reverberated from receding static and quantum fluctuations. Because of this, the message from Vice Commander Amine came through in garbled, screeching spurts.

"Can you he . . . me? Marcus? Com . . . in, Marcus. We lost visu . . . and audible contact for a moment there. Wh . . . was that sound? What's happening?"

Marcus winced, holding the earpiece away from his head until he felt the charge drain away. "Fear not," he replied, "from what I can see, our foes were vanquished by the arrival of help from a most unexpected quarter."

"Are there really friendlies among the Horde?" Mohammed gasped. "I heard Andy Webb's update, and could scarcely believe my ears."

"Yes, it's true. Not only did one valiant Master destroy a considerable number of its brethren, but its ally then used its own body to shield a stricken woman from harm."

"How can you distinguish the good ones from the bad? Are there any more of them?"

"That, I cannot say, my friend. More demons arrive through the breach with every passing second. How many of them may be sympathetic to our cause remains to be seen. I just hope the flying sentries can tell which is which; otherwise we may lose the advantage."

"Good point. I'll get Ephraim and his lot onto it right away. How goes it down there?"

Marcus sighed. "We are struggling. Although the drones have made a difference, their benefit is limited as they will surely be depleted soon. We still have more than seven hundred of our people to evacuate. Without further sacrifice, I honestly don't know if everyone will make it out."

"Well, hang fire on that," Mohammed said. "Mac thought of an endgame strategy when he had the flyers prepared. Every one of them is fitted with a full-sized gravity mine. Once they run out of ammunition, they've been instructed to take up pre-programmed positions around the inner wall and courtyard. As you can appreciate, they'll form a very effective barrier. When we trigger them, half will simply drop out of the sky and destroy everything within their effective range."

"And the rest?"

"Ah! That's where the mind games come in." Lowering his voice, Mohammed continued, "The remaining drones will descend and slowly hover toward whatever remains of the spook front ranks. They'll do so slowly, giving our friends time to think about what's coming. As soon as their sensors confirm they are within five yards of any esoteric signature, they'll flip forward and detonate—"

"Allowing us more time to get our people away!"

"Exactly."

"Thank you, Mohammed. Anything that makes my job easier is much appreciated."

"Oh, I wouldn't thank me just yet," Mohammed replied with a chuckle. "Ephraim's telling me they can't think of a way to distinguish friend from foe when it comes to the Horde. You're going to have to ask for flag-carrying volunteers to stand as close to our new buddies as possible. We wouldn't want to start losing them to friendly fire now, would we?

"Marcus?

"Are you there?"

*

The sanctuary of the recessed colonnade provided the perfect cover. Constructed of fermionic matter, it also presented a formidable barrier to the plague of flying machines now swarming the sky. From a concealed point deep within its columns, Vetis scanned the smoking ruins of the open field before him.

The humans put up considerable resistance. Were it not for the abundance of the children of the third tier, our opening charge would have stalled from the outset.

He glanced back toward the breach.

And yet, Angule's strategy proved correct. The forbidding was indeed overcome. So why do some of his faction now oppose us?

Vetis felt a sympathetic twinge of frustration ignite the embers of his rage.

Beside him, Zuul tasted the bitterness of his ire. *Where are the rest of our brothers, Sire? And where is Angule? Do you imagine he succumbed to those accursed devices?*

I doubt it. He is the Prime Catalyct of our order. No, I feel both he and our scattered brethren are concealed, as we are, about different parts of the city . . .

Vetis looked again at the massed ranks of the Trianium below them, and reviewed the latest developments. To himself, he thought: *But what are you up to, Angule? What agenda do you now follow?*

Aloud, he continued: *Though I must admit. Now we are here, and I have witnessed the strength of the defenses, I think we ought to revise our strategy.*

He came to a decision. *The Kresh below us will suffice to act as a distraction. We of the enlightened canon must pursue a different path. Zuul? You are with me. I fear we must confront the root of our problem before we can progress this day. Along the way, we will gather Geryan, Set, and Foroon. Our combined strength will counter any hurdles we may have to face.*

Vetis expanded his consciousness to broadcast a subliminal message to his surviving cabal members.

Take courage, my brothers. The Cryptogen is close. My codex trembles in the proximity of Ix. I have selected a more suitable location from which we can plan the next phase of our operation. He paused to convey the coordinates. *We will convene there shortly. Do not delay, for our very existence depends on the choice we now make.*

*

Grimy, sweaty, and exhausted, Mark Stevens ambled up the last of many flights of stairs and emerged onto the eastern portico to the First Magister's courtyard.

Behind him, Sean, Stu, and Fonzy all crowded forward, eager to get a first look at the latest celebrity to join their ranks. As they walked through the final archway, however, they discovered they would have to join a queue, for a wary crowd had already gathered to witness the manifestation of all their nightmares come true.

"I don't believe it," Mark mumbled under his breath. *It's actually here.*

The crew was forced to wait while the automated sentry scanned them thoroughly. Once cleared, they joined the growing press of people milling about the fountain. Among them, Mark spotted Sam Pell and Marcus Brutus. Both men stood within touching distance of the Horde Master's towering hulk, and appeared to be coaxing the crowd to resume their places in the transporter line.

Making his way toward them through the throng, Mark espied Andy and Bob up on the main parapet. He was about to call up and ask why they'd moved their position when he discerned the charred ruins of their former sniper post, along with the crushed remains of several columns.

Hmm. I seem to have missed quite a show.

Pushing his way through to his colleagues, he embraced them both. "So it's true, then?" Eyeing the brute next to them, he murmured, "Are you sure it's safe?"

"Without a doubt," Sam replied. "This guy and his buddy prevented an absolute slaughter. I know Mac will be delighted for sure."

"Why's that?"

"Our newfound friend protected Jayden Cole from certain death."

"What?"

"Yup. When the other Bosses burst in from that corridor over there, she was caught in the middle. This one stood over her to ensure she wasn't eaten, by them or their grunts. His partner actually sacrificed himself to ensure the other Controllers were taken out of the picture."

Mark stared at the shimmering monstrosity with new-found respect.

"Not that it isn't nice to see you," Sam continued, "but why are you here?"

"Oh, the flyers have formed the final curtain." Mark gestured toward the arc. "That's why it's so quiet at the moment. Now the grunts don't have the protection of their Masters any more, they're obviously trying to decide who wants to die first. We're running low on ammo anyway, so I thought it best to withdraw back to this level, and let the automated responses get on with the job."

"And what machines do we have left to us?" Marcus asked.

"Well, once the spooks make their move, the first and second wave of drones will explode. Then the surviving Horde will storm the inner wall. We've booby-trapped all but three of the passages. Now they're not augmented, we're hoping the brutes choose the easier option and simply flood through the open doors and into the lower plaza. As they burst through, they'll run into the cannons. It'll be carnage. Of course, once the ammunition is depleted . . ."

"Have you devised a tactic for when it does?"

Mark grinned. "Ah. You're getting to know us quite well, aren't you? Yes. We've ringed the entire arcade with the last of our gravity mines. Not only will it wipe out every single scumbag in there, but it'll create one hell of a crater. By the time they manage to fathom a new way up here, we should all be long gone."

Mark had a thought. "By the way, how many are left now?"

"A mere four hundred," Marcus replied. "I may appear distracted, but I am keeping an accurate count."

"So, who's still here?"

"Along with the survivors from the First and Fourth Cohorts, it's mainly the last of the civilian and scientific personnel who were needed to close everything down. Besides them, I know of only two clans of highlanders who endure. Cathal MacNoimhin and his Iceni, along with Searc Calhoun and the Vacomagi."

"Only two? Have the others already left for the *Arch of Winter*?"

Marcus shook his head. The pained look in his eyes conveyed what his lips could not.

"Bloody hell! Where have you stationed them?"

"West and east, along the inner bailey. As you say, once the mines are depleted, the Horde will seek a different route to this concourse. If we still have people here, I want as much warning as possible to prepare."

"And what about you?"

"I will stay to the last. The care of this city was given into my hand. How could I leave when even a single soul remained?"

"What time factor are we looking at?"

"If all goes well? Twenty, maybe twenty-five minutes."

Sam cut in. "Guys? Come and get a load of this."

Sam held out his ever present Info-pad. Both Mark and Marcus shuffled round to take a closer look. A series of oscillating lines etched their way across the display, and a strange warbling sound blared from the speakers.

"Do you know what that is?" Mark demanded.

"I'm not quite sure. By the pattern, I can see it's a highly compressed electromagnetic signal of some sort. Judging from its amplitude and the way it keeps shifting through the spectrum, I'd hazard a guess that someone's trying to screw with our frequencies. But it's on a scale and strength I've never seen before."

"A jammer?" Mark glanced up, and then around the quadrangle. *The flyers? The pad itself, perhaps?*

The Controller sprang to life. Lumbering across to where they were standing, it dipped its massive shoulders and appeared to scrutinize the modulating wave-form on the screen. Mark had to fight the urge to shy away.

"Do *you* know what this is?" Sam asked. He held the computer up higher, so the ogre didn't have to bend so far to see.

The Boss obviously did.

Straightening, it pressed its huge claws against either side of its burning diadem, and squeezed tightly. A silver nimbus appeared about its head. Building in intensity, it throbbed once before fading into the ether.

"Now what do we—"

Sam was cut short by a corresponding flare right next to them. As it died, the air seemed to twist in on itself, and a portal folded into view. Before anyone could react, two colossal figures stepped out, wreathed in blistering electrums of purple and scarlet glory. One of them was larger than the other, and seemed to command the instant respect of its lesser brethren.

The friendly Controller bowed deeply to the grander figure before it, and everyone relaxed when they realized the newcomers presented no threat.

Mark seized the opportunity to study the lights dancing about each of the Masters' heads. Sure enough, the larger ogre had many more flames adorning the matrix of its crown. *That one's in charge,* he thought, *thank goodness for backup.*

The leader rumbled toward them. It assessed the signal, which had grown considerably in the short time everyone had been distracted, and issued a guttural snarl.

The hairs on the back of Mark's neck stood up.

The Boss then adopted a similar stance to the one displayed by its lesser compatriot only moments before. A familiar halo sprang into existence.

It must be passing a message of some sort.

The premier Master turned to look directly at him.

Can it hear my thoughts?

A grating sound like boulders being crushed in a press ground from its chest, and the great head nodded.

It's laughing at me.

Raising one huge paw, it lifted a single talon to its lips. A hissing sound, like steam venting from a fissure, blasted forth.

Bugger me! It's got a plan.

Mark looked about to see if anyone else had noticed.

Booooom!

The ground beneath his feet bucked, as the first of the gravity mines down at the secondary wall exploded.

Looks like the spooks have decided it's time to come pay us a visit. Here we go again.

Chapter Forty-One

Breakthrough

The hushed interior of the *Arch of Winter*'s CIC was a stark contrast to the absolute bedlam now unfolding on the planet's surface. Saul Cameron found the disparity highly aggravating. *This is taking far too long.*

"I need to know what's happening," he snapped, "give me sit-rep."

"The main body has started forward again," Mohammed replied. "Without anyone to direct them, I guess they're resorting to what they do best. Mindlessly charging to their deaths."

"How many did the first mine take out?"

"We can't tell for sure. Each blast releases severe electro-magnetic and gravity distortions which screw up the sensors for a few seconds . . ." Mohammed hesitated as another update was linked through to his monitor. "As I speak, the fourth drone has just detonated. However, I'm getting an intermittent live-time stream from Marcus, via the satellite relay, and he tells me at least a thousand grunts have gone up in flames so far."

"It's not slowing them though, is it?"

"What do *you* think? At least their reinforcements are just about dried up. Horde sign through the breach has slowed considerably over the last few minutes. Nice to know they don't have infinite numbers to call on, eh?"

"About time," Saul retorted bitterly. "I thought we'd never see the end of them."

He stepped closer to the tactical array and studied it closely. "Pity we can't do anything for fear of hurting our own people. How many are left?"

"Less than three hundred." Mohammed glanced at another screen. "From what I can see, most are now gathered in the vicinity of the teleport pad, but we still have a few patrols roving the corridors and watching out for likely problems."

"Three hundred? That's going to take us what, about twenty minutes to complete?"

"Thereabouts. We're cutting things fine, but at least the mines and robot sentries will slow the advance considerably now the spooks aren't shielded. Of course, we mustn't forget the Horde Masters."

"Can you see what they're up to?"

"Sorry, no. It's hard to spot them since they adapted their shields. Even then, we don't know what it is they're after."

Saul drummed his fingers in frustration. "When the energy fluctuations calm down, contact Mac and ask him to haul his ass along to the courtyard. He seems to have an affinity with these brutes. See if he can establish some form of communication with our new friends. The sooner we find out what's going on, the better."

*

The closer Mac got to the outer sections of the central spire, the more the evidence of the continuing struggle intruded. Bangs and crashes echoed along the empty corridors. Amplified by the acoustics of the city's layout, the reverberations resonated through the floors and walls, causing the doors and light fittings to rattle like chattering teeth.

Absorbed as he was by spectral thoughts and ghostly visions, Mac had been lulled into a state of uncharacteristic complacency. He turned a corner, and almost bowled into an unexpected stranger. His heart leapt into his mouth. The barrel of his weapon snapped forward, and his finger tightened on the trigger.

At the last moment, Mac jerked the muzzle of his machine gun toward the ceiling. He let out a loud whoosh of air. "Stained-With-Blood! Jesus, man, I almost shot you . . . and filled my pants in the process. People can't normally sneak up on me like that. What on earth are you doing here?"

"Lieutenant McDonald," Stained-With-Blood replied. "How unexpected. I am on my way to see James Houston. I was told his evacuation was delayed until now, to avoid any unnecessary complications during his relocation to the *Arch of Winter*. As he is currently housed within the psychiatric department, I find myself having to come all this way to achieve my goal."

"Why, are you going to help escort him to the transporter pad?"

"If Ayria requires my aid, certainly. However, my visit is of a more personal nature. As you are aware, Captain Houston's condition has been rather unstable since his accident. For reasons as yet unknown, the mere presence of my tomahawk soothes his agitation. Now we are entering the final stages of the withdrawal, I want Heaven's-Claw back. Not only has my

weapon served me well in battle, it is also an important totem
for my tribe. It is only fitting it be returned to its rightful owner."

"So Ayria is still here?"

"Yes. Houston is relaxed in her company, so she was deemed
the most suitable person to oversee his relocation."

At Mac's invitation, the two men jogged along the passage together.

"Actually, I'm glad I bumped into you," Mac admitted.
"I wasn't quite sure where I was going before. But I am now."

"What do you mean?"

"Well, a short while ago I was down in the Archive with
Saul Cameron. I was supposed to help escort him to the evacuation point. While I was there, I'm sure I was contacted by the
same Horde Master that has shadowed my footsteps throughout every mission I've been on. You know? The one who told
me, *Pandora*?"

"Contacted? How?"

"I had a waking dream. An honest-to-God vision. I saw
your tomahawk floating in the air before me. Without knowing why, I knew I had to get to it. It contains the answers to all
our questions. Like I said. Don't ask me *how* I know, I just do.
And what's even more fantastic is that along with the picture
of Heaven's-Claw, I heard a very clear and distinct word in my
mind. Cryptogen."

"And do you know what *that* means?"

"Haven't a clue. That's why I'm so pleased to have run into
you. I know exactly where Heaven's-Claw is now, and therefore, where I've got to go. You're the expert where visions or
dream-walks are concerned. Having you there will definitely
increase our chances of getting to the bottom of this."

The warriors entered the final corridor.

"Have you heard how our people fare?" Stained-With-Blood asked. "I've been traversing the bowels of this city on my own for quite a while, and have no radio."

Mac shook his head. "Sorry, can't help you. I don't know what the Horde is up to, but all I've been getting for the last ten or fifteen minutes is static. I guess we'll find out when we escort Ayria and Houston to the pad . . . ah, here we are."

Mac held the door open for the tribal elder, and followed him into the reception area of the psychiatric wing. A sense of excitement was building in the pit of his stomach.

As he crossed the threshold into the main ward, that sensation vanished as an icy chill swept across him. Stained-With-Blood felt it too, for he halted and glanced at Mac.

I know this feeling.

The muted sounds of a TV program droned on from the other end of the unit.

Mac brought his weapon up, and Stained-With-Blood drew a large hunting knife. They crept silently forward.

A piercing scream shocked them into action.

Ayria!

Sprinting hard, Mac made it to the private suite first. He put a boot to the lock and brought his machine gun to the shoulder. The door splintered and swung inward with a crash. Mac swept the room, instantly registering the situation.

Ayria lay on the floor just in front of him, on the nearside of the bed. Obviously in shock, she was transfixed by a monstrous apparition of purple and gold flames standing adjacent to her. The creature, however, had no interest in her. Its entire attention was focused upon the man kneeling in front of it. James Houston.

Houston appeared remarkably relaxed and totally unaware of the danger. With a beatific smile on his face, he extended his hands, inviting the Controller to take hold of Heaven's-Claw.

The glowing pits of the monster's eyes flared. With the utmost reverence, it reached for the tomahawk.

Mac racked a grenade into the launcher and took aim. Over his shoulder, he yelled, "Stained-With-Blood! Grab Ayria and drag her out of here. I'll deal with—"

"Stop!" Houston bellowed.

*

"Whatever they're doing, it's working," Mark yelled above the din of repeated concussions and warped pressure changes. "I've managed to restore signal lock. Tell the *Arch of Winter* to resume transporting."

Sam nodded. "I'm on it." He hurried across to the command post to relay the update.

The crowd of worried refugees was relieved to hear the good news. They shuffled back to their places in the line.

"Has the problem been solved?" Marcus asked, seeing the queue form up again.

"Yes. We finally sorted it," Mark replied, "or should I more correctly say, *they* sorted it." He gestured toward the group of Controllers standing in a tight knot by the fountain.

The subordinate ogres had taken up positions either side of their superior. Extending their arms, they grasped the primary Master by the shoulders and appeared to be channeling vast amounts of energy into him. In turn, the leader was generating a glittering column of power. At over a hundred yards wide, it encompassed most of the First Magister's courtyard, and extended upward as far as the eye could see.

"We think they've created an eye in the storm," Mark explained. "It's cutting through the interference. Because of that, not only have we been able to reestablish communications, but the transporter link along with it."

He paused to scrutinize his surroundings, a frown etched across his face.

"Problems?"

"Far from it. I've just realized we're not getting pelted by dirt and rock anymore. I think that curtain is preventing the smaller bits of debris from showering down on us. And I for one am glad about that. I was developing a nervous twitch."

Marcus chuckled.

The legionnaire was forced to catch his balance. A particularly vicious clutch of explosions boomed up from the arcade below, rocking their environs. People were thrown to the floor. An awful, grinding shriek pierced the roar of the blast. It grew in volume, the vibrations somehow managing to burrow their way into the ground beneath their feet.

A chunk of flagstone near the inner portico snapped upward. Fragments of stone split away, zinging through the air like shrapnel. Next to it, a huge chink appeared in the lintel of the ornamental arch. Enlarging, the fracture splintered downward until it met the pavement, whereupon the entire edifice crumbled onto the ruptured boulevard.

"Watch out!" Mark yelled. "The mines are weakening the integrity of the inner wall. The structures here are made from granite, not lydium, so stay away from the edges."

As if his warning had been heard by the gods, the quadrangle was gripped by an augmented shockwave from a cluster of further detonations. A resonating *crack* pealed through the ether, followed by a deeper rumbling.

Mark watched, aghast, as the balustrade along the outer apron started shaking. It wobbled madly from side to side, like a worm in the beak of a sparrow. A portion of cliff shrugged away from the courtyard and fell, taking the terrace with it. The cleft it left behind widened, working its way toward the teleport pad.

This is getting crazy.

"Marcus, how many now?"

"Two hundred."

Mark glanced back at the Masters. *I wonder if there's anything they could do to strengthen the foundations here?*

He shuffled toward them.

His leading foot moved down and sideways.

Someone behind him yelled.

Mark tried to right himself, only to discover there was nothing on which to purchase any form of traction. His legs sank deeper into the soil and he toppled. Bracing his knees, he waited for the shock of impact.

It never came.

Mark slithered amid a smothering cascade, tumbling over and over toward the plaza nearly two hundred feet below.

The seething mass of the Horde welcomed him with open arms.

*

"Stop!" Houston bellowed.

His demand was so laced with feeling and desperation that Mac froze, and eased the pressure on the trigger.

The huge beast before Mac seemed to stare into the core of his existence. Without breaking eye contact with it, he edged forward to put Ayria behind him while he spoke to Houston. "Why are you so keen to stop me blowing our friend away?"

"Because that's what she is." Rising from his knees, Houston added, "A friend. An ally. And this madness has to stop."

Bloody hell, he actually sounds lucid for a change. Hang on! She?

Yes, she is female. And yes, I'm quite rational at the moment.

Mac couldn't help but glance at Houston in surprise before catching himself and resuming his scrutiny of the Horde Master. "Did I just . . . ?"

Hear my thoughts? Houston smiled. "Of course. You appear to be sensitive to this form of communication. That's doubtless what attracted Angule to your presence."

"Angule?" Mac nodded toward the Controller. "Is that . . . ?"

No. A sense of wry amusement laced the alien impulse in his mind. *I am Raum.*

He gasped. "She spoke to me."

Houston moved to stand between them. "Perhaps I had better clarify what is happening." Placing his hand to his chest, he said, "Although I currently inhabit the body of the one you call Houston, I am not, in fact, him. Now before you start worrying, please relax. Your former captain still resides within, but he is currently . . . sleeping. Once I vacate this shell, his consciousness will resurface."

"Then who are you, and why are you here in the first place?"

In answer, Houston turned to pick up the TV remote control. Ramping up the volume, he explained, "It'll be easier if you watch this first."

A familiar report began to play.

> *"That was the awful moment when the Shivan-Estre met her end. For reasons as yet unknown, her navigational beacon malfunctioned. Appearing from rip-space only seventy decans from the city wall, its pilots were helpless to prevent the inevitable catastrophe.*
>
> *As with all such vessels, the Shivan-Estre was constructed of super-dense lydium. If not for the fact that Rhomane's own precincts are made of that same fermionic matter, the results would have been far worse than the death of the two crewmen on board*

and a bright light in the sky. We are going live now to . . . "

"That was my ship," Houston stated, so matter-of-factly Mac thought he hadn't heard him right. "The *Shivan-Estre*. The catalyst for the ensuing downfall of Arden. In our ignorance, we thought there was nothing we couldn't achieve. Rip-space technology was just one of many achievements that glorified our ingenuity and massaged our egos. The folding of the very fabric of spacetime. Had we thought to be more cautious of the consequences, we would have seen the hidden dangers."

"And you?"

"My name is Permian Hasanem, captain of the *Shivan-Estre*."

"How the hell did you wind up here? That report said everyone on board died."

"In a sense, we did. Unbeknown to us, continual use of the tear-drives creates a warp in the structure of reality." Houston glanced at Raum. "That distortion transmutes biological matter, twists it at a molecular level into something else. We were the first to undergo the change."

"We?"

"My co-pilot, Neran DeCoin, and I. As the stardrive exploded, we metamorphosed into . . ." His voice trailed away as he relived the horror in his mind.

Despite his better judgment, Mac was captivated. "What happened? Do you remember any of it?"

"Bits and pieces. The transition strips the mind of all cogency. You don't know who or what you are, and are reduced to a state where you are unable to express the simplest thought. Imagine, if you can, being incapable of grasping the fact that you even exist. That you are a valid, vital, living force. Time has no meaning. All you *can* comprehend is the fact that you suffer." Houston snorted and lowered his gaze. "Of course, we were driven to the edge of sanity. Beyond it . . ."

"But you're not like them." Mac gestured at Raum.

"The lydium walls froze the process. As you know, fermionic matter is incredibly dense. In a way, you could say we were lucky. Although our physical forms were stripped away, that's as far as it went. We became trapped in limbo."

Houston's eyes took on a faraway look again. "It was . . . horrific. We didn't know what had happened, only that there was something urgent, vital, we needed to say. But every time we tried to seize that thought, to evaluate just what it was we had to do, reality fractured off in a million different directions, and we soon lost the urge to even try."

"So you couldn't warn the others of the danger?"

"No. And sure enough, Arden continued to develop and test the technology." He smiled at Raum. "And this is what happened. The transmogrification began to convert us, at the molecular level, into something entirely different."

Mac frowned. "But there are differences, aren't there? I know I'm new here, but I've been up against the Horde on a number of occasions. For the most part, they're mindlessly savage. Raum, and this Angule you mentioned, are something else."

"Ah yes. I see what you mean." Houston took a seat on the end of his bed. "Like the others, the beings who eventually became Raum and Angule underwent the full transmutation. Reduced to insensible lust, they became oblivious, numb. Unthinking. Driven only to fulfill their most basic needs. To fight and ensure they lived to see another day. To answer the endless craving for sustenance. Round and round; an endless spiral of self loathing and greed.

"Unfortunately, the mutated condition requires vast amounts of energy to sustain it. Without such vitality, the Kresh remain at a lower level of consciousness, and begin to hibernate in an almost vegetative state."

"Kresh?"

"Those whom you call the Horde. All are Kresh individually, and part of the Kresh as a collective. Those few who feast sufficiently gain the strength of will to reclaim a measure of balance. They are able to fight their way free from the stagnation of endless id, and attain a measure of ego. As stability returns, so do echoes of their former selves, along with memories. Some, such as Raum, achieve sufficient equilibrium to establish a state of enlightened bliss. They realize what has befallen them, and what needs to be done."

"And what is that?"

"All vessels possessing rip-space drives must be destroyed, and every reference to the technology wiped from the archives. Those engines transmute biological matter. A Pandora's Box that should never have been opened. If you continue to operate the ships as they are, you will suffer the same fate, and the infection may spread among the stars.

"Of course . . . if you *do* manage to remove the threat, the more enlightened of the Kresh seek to attempt a re-genesis of our kind."

"A re-genesis?"

"That is correct. Ever since the Cryptogen came among us, some think it is now possible to reverse the effects of the mutation."

Remembering his vision, Mac made an intuitive connection. Pointing at Heaven's-Claw, he said, "The tomahawk? That's what you're referring to, isn't it?"

"Quite right. For it is only by employing the unique attributes of its matrix that this mockery of nature may be undone."

"But how? How can simple metal be used to undo such a monumental perversion?"

Houston shrugged. "That, we do not know. Only one who walks the Ix can show the way."

"Walk the Ix? What the hell does that mean?"

"Dream-walking!" a voice cut in.

All heads turned to Stained-With-Blood.

"Can't you see?" the elderly shaman said. "He's referring to the spirit realm." Stained-With-Blood looked at Ayria. "Napioa's vision becomes clear now. The star metal must be used by one guided by the Creator. Only then can his lost children be saved."

"Yes, but *how* do we do that?" Mac repeated. "Does anyone have the faintest idea as to how we actually go about the process?"

A familiar chill swept through the room.

"That remains to be seen," Houston announced, "and will no doubt require the insight of both races. In any event, it is fortuitous I am here, for I can act as intermediary between those factions seeking a more amicable resolution." He glanced about, as if suddenly unsure of his surroundings.

Mac caught the inference. "I take it not everyone among the Kresh is happy at the thought of returning to normal?" *We've got an incoming vortex.*

He made eye contact with Ayria and Stained-With-Blood. His gaze conveyed a sense of foreboding, for they quickly moved toward the interior of the suite and huddled together, next to Houston.

Raum reacted to Mac's warning. Reaching for her crown, she summoned her strength and intensified the halo about her head. The violet and topaz stars brightened into a gleaming argent nimbus. Gaining power, it flared once, then died away. Her task complete, she lumbered toward the door.

Mac went ahead of her, weapon at the ready, and scanned the interior of the ward.

He didn't have to wait long.

With majestic grace, a quintuple helix of gray and black foreboding bloomed into view. No sooner had it stabilized than five huge beasts stepped out. One in particular blazed brighter than the others. Wreathed in a corona of silver and purple, it carried what appeared to be a scepter of light in its claws.

Furniture and equipment burst into flames as the ogres spread out. They blocked the exit. Mac raised his gun. "I take it these are the ones who don't want an amicable solution?"

Raum moved forward and delivered a stinging, backhanded slap to Mac's shoulder. He was thrown to one side, and bounced off the wall. As he hit the deck, Mac rolled and came to his feet.

A blinding flare numbed him to everything else. When it cleared and he could see again, Mac was stunned to find the colossal bulk of a thirteen foot leviathan occupying the space where he had just been standing.

Screw me blind! There was absolutely no warning of his approach.

The Titan turned to address Mac and Raum: *Stand back and protect the Star Child. I will ensure the Cryptogen does not fall into the wrong hands.*

My God! I recognize that voice. He's the one . . . Angule?

Angule paused. *Fear not, human. I am Prime Catalyct of the Unium Tier. They will not find me an easy adversary to vanquish.* Angule flexed the width of his huge talons, and flaming golden swords appeared within each paw.

"I know they won't." Stepping forward, Mac fired a double burst of mini micro-mines at the nearest ogres. "Because you won't be fighting them alone."

*

Annoyed by the intervention, Angule was forced to wait while the quantum weapons did their work. Slamming his heaviest shield into place, he braced himself for the blast.

He called to Raum: *Protect the humans. The confines of this facility will exacerbate the backlash considerably.*

Reality warped in four distinct areas, bending inward as if dark matter had suddenly been dropped onto the mundane fabric of existence. Under the influence of immeasurable density, Geryan and Foroon lost purchase. Falling forward, their extremities elongated, stretching in multiple directions at once.

Behind them, Vetis and Zuul backed hurriedly away. Throwing up the strongest combined shield they could muster, they stabilized it by anchoring the defense in place with Vetis's mace.

Beyond their sphere of influence, Set bounded off to one side.

Loose furniture flew through the air, their flames quenched by the growing maelstrom. Careening into Geryan and Foroon, the substance of those items blended to that of each ogre. Panicking, they responded by spinning their own portals in a vain attempt to flee.

An unwise choice, Angule thought to himself, *and something I specifically warned them not to do in the presence of such intense fluctuation.*

He watched impassively as the integrity of the unfortunate Lega'trexii frayed. They howled, a terrible keening resounding through the room. Their essences continued to rupture. Sucked toward the constricting maws, they revolved like miniature plasma tornados. The screeching reached a terrifying crescendo.

The edges of each vortex stuttered and fluxed together into one larger asperity. Heavier items were torn free from their fittings. Submitting to increased gravity, they bounced and banged along the walls and ceiling until they too were swallowed.

The compression reached its peak. With a final shriek, Geryan and Foroon were crushed into nothing.

Everything condensed into a single point, then erupted outward in a blaze of incandescent light.

Angule lowered his shield and surveyed the scene.

Mac had squeezed behind the remains of a wall crenellation. The blood on the human's fingertips gave evidence of the efforts he had made to resist the gravity-well. Angule noticed Mac's weapons had been torn from his grasp.

Good. At least I won't be disturbed now.

He registered movement. Somehow, Set had avoided being consumed.

Raum! If you please? Teach this upstart the meaning of power and true equilibrium.

Gnashing her fangs and scraping her talons one against the other, Raum surged forward to engage her fellow Tribunus.

Ignoring the sounds of combat, Angule turned his attention toward Vetis and Zuul. They still cowered behind their protective barrier. *Come then, Imperator and Grand Vizage,* he teased. *Surely together you are more than enough? Or does your cowardice rob you of the capacity to express your rage?*

The bubble darkened. Angule could taste the fey energies cascading into its fashioning. The shell turned opaque.

Are they trying to escape? We shall see . . .

Raising both swords, Angule summoned the vast reservoir of his own legacy. He knew such a contrivance could not be easily breached, for his opponents were two of the most powerful Kresh to ever exist.

But then again, so am I.

He inhaled.

Arcane regency flooded his core with divine potency.

Exhaling, he unleashed a stream of venom that burst windows, incinerated doors, and gouged furrows through the granite walls and floors.

The room bucked, and the protective barrier distorted. It became encompassed within a sizzling skein of might that burned its way through layer after layer of vitality.

The shield abruptly burst.

Angule was shocked to discover the ruined shell contained only one occupant: Vetis.

Where . . . ? A momentary ripple in the vext gave him scant warning.

Zuul crashed down onto him.

Forced to drop one of his weapons, Angule turned and smashed his assailant away. Charging after him, he channeled a reserve of power into his left hand. Angule's talons glowed. As he reached Zuul, Angule struck first with his sword, then used his augmented fist to punch through the tarnished area of his opponent's shield.

Zuul slumped backward. As Angule closed the gap, he felt another aura bearing down on him from behind. *Vetis! As cowardly as ever, he seeks advantage from my distraction.*

An unexpected yell surprised him.

Angule glanced aside in time to see Mac flying toward them. Without a weapon, he had retrieved the first thing he could lay his hands on. The Cryptogen. Angule could see where the human warrior had used the remains of a cabinet to launch himself into the air in another vain attempt to come to his aid.

No!

Angule's warning was too late. Summoning his strength, Angule phased himself to the other side of the room.

Mac descended. The terrible blade flashed down.

If there was any doubt in Angule's mind that this was truly the device by which both races could be saved, it vanished.

The axe cut through Zuul's barrier as if it didn't exist. It pierced the Vocalator's threshold and ruptured the heart of his codex. A rabid wind rushed into the void, only to explode outward as the sum of Zuul's essence combusted.

So powerful was the resultant discharge that Mac became a blur, an insect, smeared across Angule's vision as he was swatted away. Smashing through the partition into the next room, his scorched body came to rest amid a jumble of broken equipment.

Instinctively, Angule fed on Zuul's remains. Beside him, Raum followed suit, employing the additional strength it provided to overcome and drain her opponent. Discarding Set's evaporating husk, she paused as if such things were an everyday occurrence, and looked to Angule for guidance.

Stay here. Prevent anyone else from interfering.

With no time to spare on unnecessary concerns, Angule dismissed Mac from his mind and turned toward Vetis.

There's nowhere left to run . . . my King. Will you face me as befits one of your station, or will you continue to demonstrate to my protégé and these humans how craven you really are?

Vetis stared back. Hatred darkened the vestiges of his flaming features.

Come then, Vetis retorted. *Let us see if you can withstand the might of your rightful sovereign.*

They advanced toward one another.

With every step, Angule could sense his opponent's tightening fury. He used those feelings to feed his own battle ardor. The building vibrated around them as the potential for ultimate expression blossomed.

Vetis burst into action. Raising his scepter high, he poured all his strength into the rod and delivered a double-handed, overhead blow that left a seething flash of light in its wake.

Shifting to one side, Angule raised his sword to block the challenge. The ether throbbed to the power of conflicting energies.

Both ogres sprang apart, circled, and smashed together again. A flurry of blows followed, etching the air in ribbons of plasma and concussive tremors.

Conscious of the fact that he couldn't allow his antagonist to establish a rhythm, Angule adjusted the speed and strength of his attack. The tempo of the conflict staggered, oscillating between blinding strikes and graceful ripostes. Back and forth they raged. Thrusting and smashing. Driving and slashing. As time passed, a maddening sense of ferocity and frustration congealed out of the whirlwind of chaos about them. So enraged did it become that eventually, neither bothered to defend anymore.

The conflict remained at stalemate until the unexpected moment when both Masters stepped in to deliver simultaneous blows designed to take the other's head clean off. They clashed together. Neither disengaged. Remaining corps-a-corps, they chose instead to pour ever increasing amounts of power into their weapons.

Bloated with energy, the atmosphere ionized, and a frenzied discord distorted their surroundings. Ramping exponentially, it could only end one way.

Booooom!

A thunderous report flung them apart, and a series of stunning aftershocks shook the building to its foundations. Struggling to clear his senses, Angule registered the fact that his sword had been destroyed.

Alarmed, he glanced toward Vetis, relieved to discover the Imperator's staff had likewise been obliterated.

The Titans stood. Maintaining eye contact, Angule seized the opportunity to refresh his matrix with raw essence from the ether.

Spotting the maneuver, Vetis made haste to do the same.

Let us end this, Angule rumbled. *Only one of us will leave this place alive.*

Flexing his will, Angule extended his claws and fangs to their full, impressive length. His entire form burst into lurid gold and purple flame. He advanced once more.

Time to die.

Both monsters phased, coming together again in a cyclone of violence that made their earlier efforts seem like child's play. Using tusks and talons, they bit and gouged, slashed and clubbed, tore and ravaged each other with such abandon they were soon covered in steaming rents and welts.

A sulfurous stench filled the room with an oozing malevolence of brimstone and shadows.

Disturbed by the volume of wounds he had received, Vetis panicked.

Encouraged, Angule changed tactics and pressed a purely physical attack. He stamped down with a massive, horned foot. A shockwave that split the floor in two radiated outward, right through to the next level. He stomped again, and the crack grew wider, splintering off into a myriad fissures that ran the length of the ward.

The Imperator was thrown to the floor.

Time to die, Angule repeated in triumph.

Leaping forward, he drove his talons into the center of Vetis's chest. Clenching his fist, he unleashed a knot of immeasurable cogency into his rival's codex.

Vetis jerked and went rigid. Forked lightning erupted from multiple points all over his body. The ground beneath his feet liquefied. Bricks, dust, and mortar rained down about them, only to vaporize with a sputtering hiss.

Glowing like a nova, Vetis appeared to inflate on the end of Angule's arm before blowing apart in an overwhelming release of energy.

Angule rocked in sublime ecstasy as he subsumed the full measure of his foe's vitality.

And so it ends.

A sea of conciliatory nuances bathed Angule in a rare moment of pleasure.

Savoring them, he contented himself by drifting among the myriad tones of eclectic possibilities that were now free to present themselves for his inspection.

He would have been content to stay there for a full cycle, but the sound of a human woman sobbing drew him back to the reality of what still lay ahead.

*

"Mac? Mac? Can you hear me?" Ayria cried. "I'm so sorry. There's nothing I can do for you. Not here, not without any equipment."

Her patient didn't appear to hear, or was unable to respond.

In desperation, she turned to the Horde Masters. "Can't you do anything? With all that power, are you telling me you can't somehow infuse his body with life? Heal his injuries?"

An alien presence filled her mind. The larger of the beasts moved slowly forward, and Ayria received the impression of a name. *Angule.*

Ayria Solram. While the more enlightened of the Kresh are able to counter our nature, and reverse the flow of energies that sustain us, I regret to say . . . it is impossible for us to regenerate wounds such as these. He hovers on the brink. Any infusion now would extinguish the wan flame that remains. The thought-stream became tinged with sorrow. *A tragic waste, for this man was incredibly brave to even attempt what he accomplished.*

Had Ayria not already been kneeling, she would have fallen to the floor.

But I'm going to lose him!

Numbed, she shuffled closer to the ruined shell. "Oh, Mac. I'm sorry. I wish you could hear me. I wish there was something I could do."

The charred and bloody mess on the ground before her made a strangled, gargling sound, as if trying to speak.

She bent closer and put her ear to the cracked and bleeding excuse for his lips. *Help me understand what you're trying to say,* she willed.

A weak gasp was the only reply she received.

Behind her, Houston snorted.

"Are you laughing?" Ayria rounded on him. "At a time like this, you dare to . . . to . . . "

"You misunderstand me," Houston retorted, "I meant no offence. But you forget. I can hear his mind. His reply to your concern was typically . . . stoic."

"What do you mean?"

"Allow me." Houston hunkered down on the floor between them. He placed one hand on Ayria's head, and with the other, tried to select a place where he wouldn't cause any further pain to the dying man. A difficult task, for Mac's body was a mass of burnt flesh, covered head to toe in evil blisters and welts that oozed foul-looking pus.

Houston eventually placed tender fingers against a gaping sore on the side of Mac's head. Turning to Ayria, he whispered, "Now speak to him. Quickly, for he is fading."

"Mac? Mac, can you hear me?"

Yes, I can hear you. I'm dying, not deaf. There's no need to shout.

Tears welled up in her eyes and blurred her sight. Such heroic reliance on humor to diffuse the awkwardness of the situation pierced her heart to the core.

"I'm sorry. I don't even have anything for the pain. I wish . . ."

Hey, enough of that. Stop fussing. It's my own fault. After all, only an idiot would ever dream of taking on a Horde Master with nothing but an axe, eh?

A cartoon sprang into her mind of a mouse, complete with mustache and beard, dressed in full Viking regalia, leaping through the air and swinging a double-edged battleaxe against the rear foot of an unsuspecting mastodon.

Talk about not thinking of the consequences.

In the vision, the mammoth, surprised by the suddenness of the attack, took an unexpected dump from a great height onto its unfortunate attacker.

Ayria burst out laughing, and the tears flowed.

Mac's chest heaved, as if he'd caught his breath. A strange rasping sound issued from his throat, along with a froth of bloody bubbles. *What's happening? Ayria? I can't feel . . . Are you there? It's . . .*

He twitched, and took a shuddering breath. His hand shot out to grasp her sleeve. *Tell Jayden . . . Tell Jayden I love her, will you? Tell he–*

As Mac exhaled, an all-enveloping blackness rushed toward Ayria. His arm went limp, and Houston severed the link.

"He's gone," Houston whispered hoarsely, his face a mask of grief.

They sat there in silence, not knowing what to do or say.

Stained-With-Blood cleared his throat. "The time for mourning must wait. We have no choice. Our city is still besieged, and we now have the means to end this conflict within our grasp."

Lifting Heaven's-Claw into the air, he faced Angule and Raum. "I am a shaman of the Cree. A spirit-walker. One who travels what you call the Ix." He gestured toward Ayria. "As is this woman. You called my star blade by a different name. Cryptogen. We must consult Napioa urgently, for we still need to learn how this . . . re-genesis is to be brought to fruition. What can you do to assist us?"

The Controllers communicated privately.

Angule's crown flared to life.

The remains of the outer ward became filled with astral light as every surviving Master answered his summons. A resonating mental voice, full of authority, boomed forth: *Buer, Caym, Raum. Take Limun, N'Omicron, and Vual and bring the children of the third tier to heel. Remove them from the city at once, and return them to the Hall of Eclectic Spheres. All of them. Curb their frustrations, and induce the hibernat. They are not to be woken until this is all over.*

Mamone'sh, Orias? You will remain with me as we attempt to parley with the human leaders.

Dismissing them, the Prime Catalyct turned to Ayria. *You are a prominent figure of this community. Do you think your kin will listen to our proposals?*

"I don't know," Ayria replied, uncomfortable with the attention. "Virtually everyone is on the *Arch of Winter* now, and focused on a new life elsewhere. Whether they go or stay will depend entirely on your true intentions."

True intentions? Woman, it's quite simple. Inform your commanders that if they lend us their aid, by this time tomorrow the conflict will be over. Forever!

Chapter Forty-Two

Re-Genesis

Saul Cameron counted off the faces of the people gathered around him at the table.

Mohammed Amine, Ayria Solram, Marcus Brutus, Shannon De Lacey, Ephraim Miller, Stained-With-Blood, James Houston—or at least, the entity inhabiting his body is here—a pilot by all accounts. And next to him, we have the avatars of Psi Calen and Gul Sariff.

Everyone stared at him expectantly.

That this extraordinary assembly should take place at all was a credit to the ambassadorial dexterity of Stained-With-Blood and James Houston, for they had skillfully overcome his initial reservations by highlighting the long-term benefits mutual cooperation would foment for everyone concerned.

That it should be held here, within the command center of the Ark, was a near miracle. Especially when Saul turned to consider the final members of the gathering.

I never thought I'd see the day when I'd let a living member of the Horde into this place. Let alone two of them.

Angule, the newly installed Imperator of the Kresh, stood off to one side with his assistant, Raum. Both were obviously fascinated by the sheer scale of the Ark, and acted as if they walked upon holy ground.

Saul had been apprised of their role in the ceasefire, and of their hopes for a permanent conciliation in the future. Although initially skeptical of their motives, witnessing the way they behaved around the historical remains of their race had only served to reinforce to him just how much was riding on his decision.

I suppose I'd better get this show on the road.

"Angule, Raum? Will you join us, please?"

As the two ogres walked across, Saul noted how relaxed everyone appeared in the presence of their former enemy. *They seem to have already made their minds up. Strange times indeed.*

Once everyone was ready, Saul said, "Before I make my final decision, I want to clear up a few issues. Just to be sure. I hope you can appreciate that?"

He turned to Calen and Ephraim. "Gentlemen, I understand we have to open the Gateway for a final time. Now, from what you told me, the wormhole operates by exploiting a side effect of the rip-space theorem, yes?"

Both nodded.

"Well, Angule made it pretty clear earlier on just how dangerous that kind of manipulation is, so I'm sure you can sympathize with my reservations over inviting further mutations. Are you absolutely sure our venture involves an acceptable risk?"

"If I may?" Calen offered. "My originator developed this technology; therefore I am the best one to answer. Simply put, there is very little hazard involved. Rip-space travel involves the generation of a paired set of doors in spacetime. One side of it opens *here*, while the other opens *there*. The gap in between is ripped out of place, or pulled together as it were, so it no longer exists, creating almost instantaneous travel through subspace. It is this splicing of two different astrophysical locations that appears to conceive the genomic warping effect. The Gate is different. Although it forms the same artificial entry and exit points, the medium between is left intact. It remains tangible. A conduit, along which matter can flow without being subjected to any transmuting effect. Of course, an added safety feature will be the fact that we're not going to actually send the Gate anywhere or anywhen. We're going to coil it back on itself to form a simplified Möbius strip, and generate the power needed to trigger the re-genesis matrix."

"Like a glorified particle accelerator or a self-sustaining dynamo. Yes?"

"Exactly right. That's what makes this scheme so elegant. Although the city doesn't have sufficient energy reserves to operate the system, this arrangement will literally sustain itself indefinitely. We're very fortunate."

"I see," Saul replied, "thank you for the clarification. However, you touched on another aspect I wanted to get straight in my mind. How are we going to ensure the tunnel loops back on itself? We don't want to risk any other poor souls being dragged here."

Ephraim took up the explanation. "That's easy. We'll focus the targeting nodes on the origination point. Once the initial asperity opens, Angule, carrying a portion of Stained-With-Blood's tomahawk, will position himself at the threshold of the singularity. As the secondary plane opens, the characteristics of the meteoric iron will blend to the unique features of Angule's codex, and fuse a permanent link between the two doorways, *here*, at this location, until we deactivate the cycle."

"And that won't kill him?"

No, Commander Cameron, Angule said. *That phase of the procedure will not harm me. Just the opposite, in fact. The puissance I will be subjecting my essence to will create an invigorating effect very similar to that of a spawning. Highly dangerous, were it not for how we propose to direct those energies.*

"Ah, yes. I remember your description of the formula involved. Most ingenious. I must admit, I'm going to find that particular stage a must-see event."

Saul took a few moments to review his notes.

"Ah, there it is. I made a point of highlighting this final query, as you didn't really go into that much detail about it. Would someone please tell me; onto what bio-frame are we going to bind the actual substance of the Ardenese race?"

Everyone looked decidedly uncomfortable.

Saul frowned. *Hello? Have I touched a raw nerve?*

Aloud, he said, "I'm no egghead, but I understand enough to follow the basic principles. The Ark contains the remains of the Ardenese people, as well as a comprehensive stockpile of all its flora and fauna. That material will be used to provide the biological template for us to build on. The Horde, who were once corporeal, will furnish the life force, the tincture if you will, to activate the genome. However, if what I jotted down is correct, we still need to endow that mix with a living genetic host."

The mood turned awkward. While most appeared ill at ease, Ephraim and Ayria in particular looked highly embarrassed.

"What aren't you telling me? Because even I can see we need to bind the essence we're going to create to the living DNA of a host."

"That's where I come in," Ayria admitted brusquely. "I didn't want to say anything as it will only cause arguments. I have to be the one to fill the final gap."

"Why does it have to be you and not a volunteer?"

"Because it would appear to be my destiny, Saul. Whoever steps into the matrix has to be able to walk the Ix, the spirit path chosen by the Creator."

In answer to Saul's look of incredulity, she said, "And before you start scoffing, just remember; Stained-With-Blood and I have been right all along. We *have* been receiving visions. Accurate, detailed revelations describing what must take place. The two races are linked across time and space. And yes, it would seem the Old Man—or whatever you want to call him—*has* had a hand in it all along. Humans were brought here to save the Ardenese. The specifics of *how*, exactly, can only be discovered by a person capable of dream-questing."

"And that's not Stained-With-Blood?"

"No."

"You're positive?"

"Yes. I was chosen for this. I'd stake my life on it."

"Won't you be doing that anyway?" Saul countered. "Throwing your life away over some noble gesture—"

"We're dead already, Saul, remember? We shouldn't be here now, discussing this. But we are. I've lived an additional eighteen years I wasn't entitled to. Eighteen years during which I've cared for a long list of new friends and acquaintances I would never have otherwise met. And for what? Because of the Horde, most of them are dead *again* now. Lost for all eternity. But I won't be. Accepting my fate means part of me will live on forever."

"Forever? Ayria! You won't exist."

"But my children will." Nodding toward the avatars, she explained, "I've already donated my ovaries into the care of

Calen, Sariff, and the Architect. They will ensure each egg is nurtured and fertilized when the time is right. It'll provide me with a whole host of descendents to help repopulate this barren world."

"An ingenious suggestion," Calen interjected, "and one made by Ayria herself. Future generations will look back on this moment in honor, and treasure her sacrifice for all time."

Saul was struck by a sudden realization.

"Hang on, does this mean the prospective population won't be truly human or Ardenese anymore?"

"Of course they will," Ayria replied. "No matter what we look like on the outside, we will always remain true to who we are. Take Angule and Raum, and all their friends as an example. It took a long time, but they fought their way back to themselves. This way, we'll have the best of both worlds."

Saul took the time to study each face around the table. *They've clearly made their minds up about this.*

After a seeming eternity of deliberation, he sighed deeply. "Then we'd better get on with it. For good or ill, the future awaits us."

*

It started with a barely perceptible vibration running through the walls and floor. A tingle in his toes that let him know the energies coalescing in the Gate room over two leagues below were reaching optimum levels.

Ephraim checked his monitors. Each one depicted a different scene, and at this moment he could see the focusing array had already established an outgoing wormhole. Angule walked toward the mirrored plane before him. After lingering at the threshold just long enough to encase a portion of Stained-With-Blood's tomahawk within an opaque barrier, he stepped in. The Imperator's codex was instantly stretched across the infinite expanse of null-space.

After waiting a moment, Ephraim entered a series of minute adjustments into the computer. The targeting emitters fired again, and a new quantum construct emerged.

He studied the emissions from the paired singularities closely.

"Gravitational constancy has been achieved," he announced, "event horizons are confirmed at three angstroms. Angule? If you can hear me, you have a *go* to introduce the meteoric material."

There was no audible reply. However, within moments of the request, a wrinkle appeared at the center of the glistening duality. Radiating outward as if a stone had been thrown onto the calm waters of a pond, the ripple gained the circumference, and the paradigm flared into a conjoined whole.

"Atomic fusing completed. Möbius accelerator established. Activating primary and subsidiary ion collectors." Ephraim flicked a switch, and the drone of countless capacitors charging throbbed in the air. Over his shoulder, he shouted, "Raum? You're up."

The Horde Master had been waiting patiently at the end of the observation pier. The circular balcony had been fashioned in such a way as to occupy a space equidistant from the surrounding Ark modules lining the chasm. It was perfect for their needs, as it also happened to be directly above the Gate, thousands of yards below.

Adopting a relaxed position, Raum reached up to her crown and initiated a pulse of astral brilliance. As it died, her entire form was encompassed within an argent halo of stunning purity.

My link to the Unium Tier is now active. Stand-by. We will deploy the safety filter on my mark . . .

Her construct ballooned outward, and concentric spheres of plasma appeared. Spinning in multiple directions at once, the speed of each orb increased until they became a confusing blur to the eye. Raum raised her own portion of Heaven's-Claw.

Mark!

The globes locked abruptly into place, forming a huge esoteric oculus. A sizzling skein, like a dancing web of lightning, skittered across the surface, enmeshing her body and suspending her in a nimbus of psychedelic light.

Raum disappeared, but her mental voice continued to give a running commentary via the speakers.

I am manipulating the vext. Prepare for conflicting tidal surges.

A tiny pucker formed within the kaleidoscopic maelstrom.

Opening the portal in three, two, one . . . now!

As the distortion swelled, the rainbow parade blinked out.

Ephraim felt the familiar tug of a void in close proximity. He peered toward the holo-projector on his console. The unit was broadcasting a live, 3D image of prevalent conditions between Ark control and the Gate room six miles below. He could see a vast reservoir of untapped potential building, which increased exponentially with every passing second.

Spellbound, he watched as each segment of cryptogenic material acted as a lodestone to the others. *Fascinating! It appears to be the mesons, not the baryons that are the energizing catalyst.*

Wraith-like streamers of fermionic matter connected, intertwining at an astonishing rate. As they meshed, the entire construct solidified and gained coherence. A choral tone of heartrending majesty reverberated around the chamber, and in the blink of an eye a titanic throb of energy knotted together and commenced its mad dash along the esoteric conduit.

The underlying tremor beneath his feet became much harsher.

"Watch out, Raum!" he warned. "The tsunami's on its way."

Adjusting his focus, he continued, "Ayria? If you could also get ready to go? I need you in position within the next ninety seconds."

He glanced at his left-hand screen, and his heart skipped a beat.

Ephraim had known Ayria for the last fifteen years, and counted her a rare treasure among the gems he had come to know during his time on Arden. Fiercely loyal to her friends, she was totally reliable, and could always be counted on to put the community ahead of her own needs. She'd lasted longer in this hostile environment than just about anyone else.

And here she is, putting her life on the line for her extended family once again.

An unexpected pain clutched at his chest.

Oh, Ayria. We'll miss you so much.

Strangling down the lump in his throat, he watched as Calen helped her remove the simple cotton gown she had chosen to wear to this, her last solemn duty. As naked as the day she was born, he didn't miss the anxious manner in which she repeatedly clutched at the remaining fragment of Heaven's-Claw. Despite her nerves, Ayria still found the time to smile, and accepted the avatar's assistance into the re-genesis chamber.

Christened the Pearl Bed, it resembled the two halves of an open clamshell. The amazingly sophisticated device was the pinnacle of Ardenese ingenuity, for it contained the final genomic catalyst that would trigger the re-genesis program and transmute a living body into the key for saving an entire world.

As Ayria took her place, Calen tenderly kissed the back of her hand, and solemnly lowered the cover. Once the seals had actuated, he turned and made his way swiftly over to his own computer console.

The background shudder intensified, and a warning buzzer sounded. Ephraim activated the umbilical, and as the Pearl Bed rose into the air, he checked his instruments again.

"Raum!" he shouted. "The plasma nucleus has almost reached us."

Thank you, Ephraim Miller. You need not concern yourself. I am prepared and waiting.

An escalating roar welled up from below. The gray helix above them expanded, and a glittering curtain descended across the outer vestiges of the balcony. Augmented by cyclonic pressure, the energy wave crested the bore and thundered into the gyre. Despite the protective barrier, the whole level juddered and rocked as if seized in the grip of an earthquake. The sound was deafening.

Transfixed, Ephraim stared as the fragile-looking vortex warped under the onslaught. It adjusted, then swallowed the entire potential of the opening blast.

Incredible! Who would have thought something so flimsy could do that?

The fluctuating surge stabilized into a solid, consistent beam.

It took Ephraim a few moments to realize that the strands of the portal were slowly twisting open. The outer folds budded into a flowerlike construct of glowing, blood-red petals. The stigma, however, remained separate and dark. Operating the miniature thrusters of the Pearl Bed, Ephraim gently nudged the casing forward until it was snugly encompassed within the safeguard of the central axis.

As the minutes ticked by, the blossom diffused into a tenuous cloud that flushed increasingly brighter. Crimson, ruby, cerise, rose, and eventually, pink.

The miasma pulsed and throbbed with eldritch possibilities. Crystal intonations of the purest clarity chimed forth amid a brilliant accompaniment of starburst detonations. Seconds later, the chamber was blanched in phototropic glory.

Raum chose that moment to speak.

Ephraim Miller. Brace yourself for the final phase. The experience is bound to be daunting. Take courage, for we will ensure to maintain resolution until the very last second.

Before Ephraim realized what was happening, the inner corolla of the node hovering high above him unraveled. A confusing network of stamenlike filaments folded outward and flowed toward the multitude of chambers lining the edge of the Ark. They bobbed and weaved within the dominion of the photonic flow, like new shoots basking in the warmth of sunlight. Almost immediately, they glowed white-hot. A haunting counterstroke cut through the all-enveloping cadence around them, and the ceramic shell of the Pearl Bed cracked open. The massed banks of indicator lights positioned on the exterior of every biogenic pod within the chasm blinked on.

Ephraim felt his nasal cavities throb as the pressure increased dramatically.

"Matter injectors charging," he yelled. "Calen? Stand-by for my signal."

His attention flicked across the readouts, coming to rest upon a final tier of energy-level gauges at the far end of his console. He watched closely as the display ramped its way up from red, through amber. As it hit green, Ephraim shouted, "Now, Calen!"

A prickling sensation washed across his skin, and his gaze snapped back to the main screen.

Down in the Gate room, Angule transmuted the sum of his remaining codex into a summons of irresistible force. A fresh rent in the fabric of spacetime opened. Through it, Ephraim was shocked to witness a terrifying glimpse of the Horde realm. Punching through the superficies, the Imperator issued his final command. And the Kresh obeyed.

The entire essence of his race was sucked through the portal and into the growing maelstrom beyond. The infusion of their genetic material with the augmented Möbius accelerator produced a staggering reaction. A blinding flash ensued, and the gateways were destroyed. Angule vaporized, and the cameras situated about him within the cavern went blank.

An overwhelming concussion rocked the foundations of the city. With nowhere else to go, the titanic energy now encompassed within the remains of the ionic stream stabbed upward.

Oh dear. I don't know how we're going to survive that . . .

As if in answer to his panicked thought, the iridescent curtain of protective power encompassing the control center expanded back down the shaft. The effect of the tremors subsided almost immediately, and Ephraim offered a quick, silent prayer to Raum's vigilance.

How the hell she's managing to retain their focus, I'll never know.

Like an erupting volcano, the surge advanced. Ephraim marked its ascent by the successive obliteration of each of the safety monitors along the shaft.

Jesus, that's fast. "Watch out, people, here it comes."

The chamber bucked as the beam thundered onto the command level. Raum reappeared within the threshold of the vext. For the blink of an eye, he could see her within the matter stream, arms thrown wide as if attempting to absorb the tincture directly into her matrix. Then she was gone.

The Pearl Bed was engulfed. Ephraim expected the device to burst into flame, but it didn't. With trembling hands, he reached out to his controls and changed viewpoints, so he could watch the unfolding process within.

The arcane energies flooding the shell had recognized Ayria's biological sequence. Instead of consuming her, they swirled around and through her, cocooning the entire construct in a web of astral fire.

The portion of meteor rock in her hands transmuted. Turning fluidic, it flowed along her skin until it covered her entire form. Then the mixture infused her epidermis and bonded to her molecules. Ayria began to sparkle, as if thousands of diamonds had been scattered across her body. Transformed, her atoms drifted apart, and prismatic reflections cut a glittering swathe through the air.

Instead of gliding away, the infant particles began revolving around a new, invisible center of gravity. Faster and faster they spun, performing complex, interwoven patterns that confused the eye.

Ephraim soon gave up trying to follow the path of individual ribbons, and pushed himself away from the unit. Only then did he realize what he was actually looking at.

Oh my goodness. That's a triple helix. A DNA strand!

The network of energy intensified, and Ephraim became aware of an expanded form of consciousness hovering in the ether about him.

"Ayria?"

The esoteric filaments throbbed, and the multitudes of capacitors were infused with energy. The magnificence of the spectacle was spellbinding.

"Ephraim?"

The voice made him jump.

"What? Oh, I'm sorry, Calen. I'm a little distracted by the grandeur of it all. How you ever devised a program like this is . . . well, it's simply breathtaking."

"Thank you, you're very kind. But can you congratulate me afterward? Sorry to be rude, but you need to fire the matter-builders. Until you do, the bio-spores won't be released into the atmosphere."

"Of course, of course," Ephraim spluttered.

Swiveling in his chair, he leaned across the desk and released a cap-lock. Flicking back the lid, he held his thumb above the button, and solemnly declared, "For Arden."

Depressing the pad, he looked up and held his breath.

A shattering clap of thunder blared out, knocking them both to the floor.

Picking himself up, Ephraim surveyed the command tier and glanced back into the air. The upper cavity was empty, spectacularly devoid of power. Puzzled, he tried switching to an exterior view, relayed from the astrometrics facility at Boleni Heights.

"Is this supposed to happen?"

"I can't answer that," Calen replied. "Remember, this was all theoretical. We never actually knew if it would work or not. I can ask Sariff and the Architect, but I doubt they'll be able to shed much light on it."

Now he tells me.

In silence, they stared the screen.

At first, nothing happened.

Then, with infinite grace, the cupolas crowning each of the spires atop the four main gates started to glow. A quartet of blistering plasma gobbets blazed furiously against the backdrop of the setting sun.

A choral resonance swelled in the ether about them, glorious in its vibrancy, yet as tenuous as a wraith. The tonal characteristic of the base notes gradually changed. Ramping in amplitude and frequency, they seemed to excite the domes into releasing their stored potency.

Four arcs of blue-white lightning stabbed into the sky. Converging at a point on the edge of the atmosphere, the bolts sizzled and intensified until a shimmering aureole had coalesced out of the efflux.

Time slowed, and the combined discharges continued unabated for several minutes.

A crucial factor must have been reached, for the curtain rippled. It expanded, and the wave front bloomed outward in every direction until it was lost from sight across the horizon.

Ephraim opened a channel. "*Arch of Winter. Arch of Winter*, this is Rhomane Command here. Can you tell me what you're seeing from up there?"

"Rhomane Command, this is *Arch of Winter*. Hi, Ephraim. Mohammed speaking. We've got a huge nimbus of power directly above the city. It's already five hundred miles across and is increasing in size and speed. At its current rate, it'll encompass the entire planet in less than sixty seconds. I take it this is all part of the plan?"

"We'll soon find out. I wouldn't worry too much. It's in the hands of the gods now, and at least *you'll* be in a good position to watch the show if everything goes pear-shaped!"

Chuckling, Ephraim cut the transmission and settled in to wait.

Although they were watching from the surface, Ephraim knew the exact moment when the exosphere was encompassed, for the sunset turned indigo and an ethereal phosphorescence washed the landscape in a spectral cast. At the same instant, he felt an abrupt release of pressure, and a strange, pins-and-needles sensation crawled along his skin.

Frowning, Ephraim looked at his monitors and zoomed in on the scene.

The newly formed lattice above them had shattered, and newborn seeds, looking very much like a blend of fireflies and glowing motes of ash, fluttered gently to the ground.

Soon, the entire globe was coated in a hoarfrost-like carpet of sapphire and violet snowflakes.

The flecks melted, and as they dissolved, the genetic codex locked within their templates meshed with the existing flora and fauna.

A wind as gentle as a sigh began blowing from the east.

Ephraim turned to Calen. "What do we do now?"

"Get everybody outside," the avatar replied, "and ensure you expose yourselves to the re-genesis matrix as much as possible over the next few days."

"And then what?"

"And then, my friend . . . Ah, something wonderful is going to happen."

Epilogue

The subdued atmosphere within the Hall of Remembrance created an environment fit for learning. Small groups clustered here and there about the auditorium, and the lively hubbub of animated discussion bubbled away in the background. Despite that fact, no one appeared disturbed, for the chamber was vast and the scale and grandeur of its furnishings muted any unwarranted distractions.

Designed to amplify sound, the Hall always made a huge impression on people; especially those visiting for the first time. Today's group was no exception. As the teacher led her pupils toward the center of the room, more than twenty little faces peered about in wide-eyed wonder.

Halting in front of a huge glowing obelisk that had been constructed directly beneath an oculus, Keera Solram clucked like a mother hen to ensure her chicks gathered round with a minimum of fuss.

Keera was only twenty-five and still some years off full maturity, but she already cut an imposing figure. Standing nearly seven feet tall, she matched the remarkable stature of the other adults around her. However, distinctive features of an ancient heritage shone through. Instead of the generic fair to auburn hair common to most of New Arden's population, hers was a thick and luxuriant raven black. Her smooth, softly tanned skin and dark sultry gaze were also a striking contrast to the paler complexions and piercing topaz eyes of the majority of her race.

Wherever she went, Keera drew attention, as evidenced by the number of admiring glances turned her way.

"Settle down now, children. C'mon, as quick as you can. Settle down," she urged as the class drew near. "Remember where we are, and why it's so necessary to be on our best behavior."

Indicating the monument behind her with a sweep of her arm, she said, "Now, this should be of particular interest to you. Can anyone recall its name?"

They all turned to study the twenty-foot-high monolith. Fashioned from a richly veined, solid slab of rock, it appeared to be seamless; springing up from the floor like a finger pointing to the open sky. Reverberating gently, all four sides thrummed under the influence of a hidden power source. The very top of the structure formed a trapezoid, around which a nimbus of pastel blue light glimmered softly.

A tentative hand toward the back of her brood inched into the air. Keera spotted it, but waited to see if anyone else would care to volunteer. When it was clear there would be no further takers, she said, "Marcus Amelius Brutus? Do you want to tell us what the obelisk is called?"

"That's the Reverence, Miss Solram. But people also call it the Chronicle."

"Quite right, Marcus." Pointing to it, Keera continued, "The light you see at the top isn't just for show, either. Not only does it serve as a power source, but . . . ?"

She paused as several children responded immediately and began jumping up and down on the spot. "Yes. Gabriella Houston. Do you know what it does?"

"Ma'am. It's a recorder. Built by the Founders over two hundred years before the Fall, it lists the unique life-sign of everyone living on New Arden. My mommy said it was originally made to catalog the names of the refugees brought here from Earth. But Daddy thinks Earth is just a fairytale."

How soon they forget. Keera smiled. "Well done. The Reverence certainly is a recorder. A library of information, in fact. The moment you are born, the Architect registers your unique bio-signature and allocates you a place in the Archive. Everything about you begins to get stored away. Who you are. What you do. Your achievements. So, as you grow up and become a productive member of our society, other people can come here and learn more about you and the great things you will go on to accomplish. For example, if you want to discover more about this machine's creator, Psi Calen, all you have to do is . . . ?"

A sea of wriggling fingers reached for the sky.

Good. They're warming up. "Lex Miller. What do we do?"

"We ask the Chronicle a question, and a sentinel, or an avatar of that person, will appear to instruct us."

"Exactly right." Keera addressed the rest of the class. "Isn't that exciting? To think that you can come here and request the presence of anyone who has ever lived over the past thousand years or so? *And* you get to speak to an accurate simulation of who they were. But, of course, that wasn't its original function, was it? As Gabriella correctly indicated, the Reverence was designed to register the details of all the exiles brought here from a place far, far away, called Earth. Now, look at this."

Gesturing around the outer edge of the hall, Keera high-lighted one of a number of huge carvings which had been cut directly into the fabric of the wall. Stretching from floor to ceiling, each was a similar size and gave the impression that the open leaves of a book had been superimposed into the rock. Every page was covered in writing. As she ushered them over to the final bas-relief, she drew the children's attention first to the frieze itself, and then to the dais in front of it.

"This one belongs to the Ninth," she said proudly, "a special group of people to whom all of New Arden owes a great deal." She nodded to an artifact mounted upon the podium; a large golden bird with open wings. Beneath it, strange letters depicted a phrase: *SPQR*. "Now, can anyone tell me what *this* is?"

Angule Whitehawk's hand was the first to shoot up.

"Yes, Angule?"

"That's the Eagle, Miss Solram. A bird of prey very much like a targén from the Erásan Mountains. It was a symbol of the Ninth Legion, from a place called Rome on Earth. My father tells me their soldiers used to march with it at the head of their armies, and that they would rather die than lose it in battle."

"Very well done, Angule. And well done to your father too, he obviously enjoys things of antiquity. Like the other relics within the auditorium, this eagle came all the way from Earth. In the end, the standard came to personify the strength and dedication of the entire ninth intake; for they were willing to give everything to ensure Arden had a chance of surviving. During the Battle of the Line, many brave men, women, and enlightened Kresh willingly sacrificed themselves instead of fleeing, and their names were recorded here, in a special section of the book so their memories could be preserved for all eternity."

Angule Whitehawk's countenance dropped.

"What's the matter?" Keera asked. "Has something upset you?"

"Some of the others tease me, just because I'm descended from a monster."

Keera stooped to hold his hand. "Honey! Don't let silly people ever upset you when they say things like that. We've already touched on this in class, remember? The Kresh were merely real Ardenese people who had been changed by the effects of the engines they used to use back then. History shows Angule of the Unium Tier was one of the heroes of the hour, and contributed his substance to the re-genesis matrix. Yes, your ancestors were bio-engineered from his regenerated DNA. But you should be proud of that. Without people like him, none of us would even be here."

"And those people are only jealous anyway!" a little voice interjected.

Alana McDonald had been listening in on the conversation, and came over to give Angule a hug. "My mommy and daddy tell me all the time what a good friend my great, great, great, etcetera granddaddy was to yours. *He* knew Angule was important. That's why he died trying to protect him. And *that's* why our families will always be close." She hugged him fiercely. "Angule was a king. Someone very, very special." She stood on tiptoe to kiss his nose. "And so are you."

Angule's face flushed deep red.

He was saved further embarrassment by the inquisitive nature of the rest of his classmates.

"So Earth is real then?"

"How did the engines make the Kresh into monsters?"

"Miss? What made them change their minds?"

"Why don't we have real eagles on New Arden? They look cooool."

"What do they eat?"

"Miss Solram? Has anyone ever been to Earth? Is it far?"

"Okay. Okay. Quiet down now," Keera urged. "Seeing as you have so many questions, I think it's time to divide you into groups and give you your first experience of the Reverence at work. Now, although the people you will meet are holographic, they have been programmed to assist in your education and are to be accorded the respect they deserve. I want you to take notes, because tomorrow you'll each be giving a two minute presentation based on your own family's early history in the years following the Rise. I'll be over here by the eagle if you need any help."

Given free rein, the brood scattered, and Keera was heartened to see them take to their task with gusto. Especially little Angule Whitehawk, who quickly conjured a simulacrum of his terrifying forefather, much to the envy of his classmates.

Left to herself, Keera seized the opportunity to open her mind and relax. *It's a shame the reality of our history fades so quickly. It's only been a thousand years, but even with the help of the Architect and the avatars, the truth about the exiles and the role they played in our salvation quickly fades into myth and legend.*

That's because most people don't share our legacy, dear, Ayria replied. *But isn't that the way of things? The richness of their heritage is something they soon squander. It falls to people like us to keep such memories alive. And look at the benefits it brings.* A sea of familiar faces threading back through time surrounded her, together with a sense of warmth, camaraderie, and history. *You're a very fortunate young lady, for you will never forget.*

No. I don't suppose I ever will.

Keera turned to the dais and read the full inscription beneath the eagle, for it was an axiom that had come to represent the ideals of her entire race.

SPQR
Serovak—Pluserak—Qen—Rhomanax
(For Security Prosperity and Rhomane)

Andrew P Weston

Andrew P Weston is a military and police veteran from the UK who now lives on the beautiful Greek island of Kos with his wife, Annette, and their growing family of rescue cats.

A criminal law and astronomy graduate, he is a member of the British Science Fiction Association and British Fantasy Society, and is a contracted writer of both fiction and poetry for several publishing houses and a growing number of well-established magazines. In his spare time, Andrew assists NASA on one of their research projects and, amazingly, still finds the time to submit regular educational articles for Amazing Stories and Astronaut.com.

When not writing, Andrew enjoys holding his breath, being told what to do by his wife, and drinking Earl Grey Tea whilst dressed as Captain Jean Luc Picard.

Make it so . . .

You can discover more about his work at:

Blog: http://andrewpweston.blogspot.gr/
Twitter: https://twitter.com/WestonAndrew
Amazon Author Page: http://www.amazon.com/Andrew-P-Weston/e/B00F3BL6GS/ref=ntt_dp_epwbk